WITCHES AT THE GATE

M GREENHILL

No one is born hating another person because of the color of his skin, or his background, or his religion. People must learn to hate, and if they can learn to hate, they can be taught to love, for love comes more naturally to the human heart than its opposite.

— Nelson Mandela

ONE

EINE KLEINE NACHTMUSIK

Salem, Massachusetts

Nothing but worms, cancer, and maggots. I told them to fix it.

Amos Solomon, Brother Superior within the Order of Chaos, frowned and glanced at the flickering overhead lights. The bulb's dull glow wasn't bright enough to let him study the old, weathered parchment carefully rolled flat against the makeshift architect-style easel.

He reached for the retracting desk lamp, switched it on, and returned his focus to the ancient manuscript. The sacrificial rituals needed to be performed in a precise manner. They would only have one opportunity to get it right, and he wasn't leaving anything to chance. As he poured over the pages to commit them to memory, his foot tapped in time to *Eine Kleine Nachtmusik,* Mozart's Serenade No. 13 in G major. A smile graced his lips, and he gave in to the serene calm enveloping him like a warm blanket.

Since childhood, music had calmed him. With each melodic note, he was swept away, imagining a future promised to the Order since the dawn of time. Music was the tool that allowed him to concentrate, and right now, he needed it more than ever. The incompetence of others weighed heavily on him to the point where he was ready to explode.

He'd spent the better part of his life devoted to fulfilling the prophecy of the Master's return. But every time they took a step closer, one of the Acolytes fucked it up.

He let out a sigh. He needed to stop killing the incompetents or there'd be no Order left. He cricked his neck and arched his back. Too many hours hunched over the ancient text had taken their toll.

Nothing the Master won't remedy.

He returned to reading the parchment, confident that a youthful body would be one of the first gifts bestowed. After all, he will have succeeded where all others have failed. He was humming the third movement when an Initiate scurried into the room and tripped over his own robes. The Initiate halted and bowed nervously.

Amos shook his head and narrowed his eyes. So much for peace and quiet.

"Yes?" he snapped. "What is it?"

The Initiate gulped, not once making eye contact. "I beg your forgiveness, Your Grace, but the Second Councilor is here. He's requesting an audience with you."

A surge of hope rushed through Amos. There was only one reason Noel would be here at this time of day.

Amos entered his plush study a short time later. "I trust you have good news."

Noel, the heavily pockmarked man staring out the window, turned and bowed. "Your Grace—"

Amos brushed off the remainder of the greeting. Formalities and tradition held a time and place. This wasn't it.

He waved his hands in a sweeping motion at Noel. "You took a risk coming here dressed like that. What if someone saw you?"

Noel glanced down at his attire. "Couldn't be helped. It was the first chance I've had, and I knew I couldn't trust anyone else to deliver the information."

The councilor's words had his attention. "Well?"

Noel let out a sly smile. "I have seven new names. And we now have four confirmed with the correct blood type."

Amos rocked back and forth on his heels. Perhaps this day wasn't a complete disaster after all?

"When did you want them?" Noel asked.

Amos' pulse beat faster, and anticipation surged through his veins. This was their chance. The astrological charts and scriptures gave them until the next full moon, or his plan wouldn't be possible for another hundred years. Finally, their Master would rise again.

"Tonight. They die tonight."

TWO

HARBINGER OF DEATH

Berkeley, California

The last time she looked, only one head rested on her shoulders. But from the way her students were staring at her, you'd think she suddenly sprouted another one.

Dr. Keira Wynter scanned the full auditorium, a frown on her face as she raised an eyebrow. "No one? No one can tell me the name of the law that laid the foundation for the mass Witch trials in Europe?"

An awkward shuffle echoed across the theater as students flipped through their textbooks with expressions of confusion mixed with something akin to panic. Marcus, her teaching assistant, rolled his eyes in their direction, and she suppressed a smile. She didn't need to use magic to pick out the rattled thoughts running through the crowded room of grad students. Their expressions were priceless. She had sprung a topic on her anthropology class that wasn't scheduled for three weeks.

She was about to put them out of their misery when the back of her neck prickled, and an icy chill raced across her arms. She shivered involuntarily. This was the second time today a strange sensation had come out of nowhere. A few minutes before her lecture began, the temperature plummeted, and a sense of foreboding rippled through the air. She had ignored it. Now it was back. And it seemed to be back with a vengeance.

Not wanting the class to know anything was amiss, she forced a smile onto her lips. "If it's any help, the law was agreed on in 1530 at the Diet of Augsburg under the Holy Roman Emperor Charles V."

The sensation pulsated in her chest and increased in intensity until it became too distracting to ignore. She tapped into her magic and branched out her senses to feel for what caused the disturbance. Careful to keep her expression neutral, she made it appear as though she were scanning her students, waiting for an answer.

To the rest of the world, she was a regular, run-of-the-mill anthropology professor at Berkeley. Only a select number of people knew there was much more to Dr. Keira Wynter than what she let the world see. Keira, and her sister, Dayna, were the last of the Ragnhild line of witches. A line that could be traced back to the Viking age.

Unable to detect anything magical that could've caused the feeling of doom, she double-tapped her clicker, and a new image appeared on the screen. "The *Constitutio Criminalis Carolina*, sometimes shortened to Carolina, is recognized as the first body of German criminal law. It specified that those found guilty of causing harm through witchcraft would be executed with fire. A—"

Without warning, the ground beneath her feet shook. Wild vibrations shot up the length of her body in spurts of energy. She became dizzy and reached out to hold onto the lectern in case she fell. Her pulse skyrocketed, and a bead of sweat erupted across her forehead. A high-pitched buzzing vibrated in her ears, and she flinched. Just as quickly, the chaos evaporated, and she was left disoriented.

What the hell was going on?

She blinked rapidly and looked over the sea of students, expecting panic and disarray. The auditorium was intact, and the students were silently waiting for her to continue. As with the students, Marcus' expression was one of confusion.

Her chest tightened. Had she just imagined the world shaking? Was she losing her mind? Puzzled she glanced to Marcus. One of the skills that marked him as Gifted was empathy. Why was he confused? Surely he detected her fear?

She ripped her gaze from Marcus and scanned the room once more. There was no magic she'd encountered that could cause this disturbance.

Whatever it was, it had affected her physically, and that scared her. But she wasn't in a position to do anything about it. Her classroom full of students would think she was certifiable if she declared she was a Witch and needed to cast a few spells because some invisible force unnerved her. It may be the twenty-first century, but coming out as a Witch probably wasn't the smartest thing to do. Things could get messy as it would invariably lead to outing Vampires, Gifted and other Supernaturals as well as the existence of Witches. Supernaturals walked a fine line living alongside Naturals, careful to never risk exposure. Mainly because history had shown Naturals didn't react well to the unknown.

Keira shrugged off her misgivings. She'd deal with the disturbance after class.

Her equilibrium fully recovered, she turned back to the students, stepped away from her lectern, and moved to the edge of the dais. Every student followed her path, their gazes riveted on her. With any luck they were assuming she had paused for affect, rather than was becoming as mad as a March hare.

"So…." She cleared her throat. "So, we have a Church that is losing its power base, the Protestants have just pulled away, and we have an entire class of citizens the Church can't control. A class who openly practices rituals against Church doctrine. Healing, midwifery, potions, animal husbandry, the list goes on."

She paused, looked into the nosebleed section of the room, and nodded to one of the few students she knew by name. "Mr. Collins, over fifty thousand people were put to death between 1450 and 1650. If you lived back then, what do you think your chances of *not* being charged with Witchcraft would be?"

The student she put on the spot slumped in his chair, clearly not expecting to be called on. He fidgeted with his pen. "Um … I'd say pretty high … I guess."

"And why would that be Mr. Collins?"

From the repeated clearing of his throat, she didn't hold out much hope for a correct answer.

He winced. "Because my family is Protestant?"

A small chuckle escaped her lips. "I'm afraid even the Protestants couldn't escape the laws set out in the *Constitutio Criminalis Carolina*."

She studied the sea of faces and opened her Witches sight.

An almost indiscernible shimmer radiated from a single student in the back of the class. A telltale sign of a Gifted. A Witch's shimmer would have manifested itself as a soft pale white, while red indicated a Vampire. "Can anyone tell us why Mr. Collins would have a more than reasonable chance of not being charged with Witchcraft during that period?"

Hands shot up around the room. She pointed to a young woman in the second row.

"Because he's a he," the student said.

Keira nodded and made her way to the far end of the dais. "That is correct. Over eighty percent of those tortured and burnt at the stake as a Witch were women."

She tapped her clicker, and the image changed to a macabre medieval drawing of three women with elongated chins and noses gathered around a demonic figure. "One of the major inventions around this time was the printing press. The Church used this medium extremely well to depict and scare the uneducated masses. We are looking at a woodcut from one of the Witch trial pamphlets that explained who these iniquitous Witches were and how to identify them. In our stereotypical example, we have three Witches supplicating the Devil. The key thing to notice is that they're all women."

As she continued her lecture, her rapt audience remained silent. Her classes in anthropology and folklore at Berkeley University were at capacity. And today's class was no different. As much as it pained her, the packed lecture wasn't because she was an inspirational teacher. She'd recently worked with the FBI on a high-profile abduction case related to a satanic cult. Her students were more than eager to see if she would give them any more information than had already been played over the news channels.

Mid-speech, she faltered. The burning sensation returned and was building to a crescendo. She tried to ignore it, choosing to get through the lecture rather than show weakness. "Early modern Germany was one of the most active hotbeds of Witch persecu—"

The air rushed out of her lungs, and she clutched her stomach. A wave of terror washed over her as a thousand voices screamed in pain. Each one more tortured than the next. Her body shook, and the ground jolted in violent spasms. Then it stopped just as abruptly as it began.

Her gaze darted around the room to find the source, only to realize that, as with the earlier incident, nothing had changed. Disaster hadn't struck. No one was running for their lives, and the earth wasn't moving. She touched a hand to her face. Had her glamor spell held? How the hell would she explain to the class how their middle-aged professor suddenly appeared twenty years younger?

She opened her mouth to speak, and the chaos erupted in full force. This time, its magnitude was one hundredfold. Voices shrieked in her head and overloaded her senses until she was blinded. A cold hand clenched her throat and restricted her ability to breathe.

The next moment the chaos stilled and was replaced by an overwhelming sense of loss. Grief ripped through her body and spread in a fiery inferno that threatened to burn her in its wake. In her confusion, she spun toward Marcus. Her eyesight hadn't returned, but she took a step forward and held out her hand in his direction.

Her throat was parched and raw, as if a million shards of glass had cut it. She managed to rip out a single tortured word before the darkness overtook her.

"Death."

THREE

10-54

Mystery Hill, New Hampshire

"Adam twelve, code four."

Ryker slipped the police radio off its cradle and pressed the call button. "Twelve, go ahead."

"Hey, sheriff, is Deputy Kolby with you? Another fight's broken out at the Rusty Chain, and I can't raise him."

"Copy that, base. Flying solo, just chasing up a reported disturbance at Mystery Hill. Keep trying. His radio is probably on the fritz again."

Ryker shook his head. For a bright kid, Kolby sure was stupid. How many times had he told Kolby to get his radio checked out?

"Copy that, Adam twelve. Will see if I can reroute Lima seven."

A muscle twitched down the side of his neck. Jonie would be livid if her bar was destroyed by a bunch of drunk, rowdy tourists. *Again.*

His fingers tightened on the steering wheel, itching to turn the car around and head back into town. He was on a wild goose chase anyway. The hiker who'd reported the scream was probably on a Molly trip and had mistaken the shriek of a barn owl for a woman. He'd been called out to Mystery Hill more than once by some paranoid delusional who didn't know the difference between a bird call and a woman's screech. Instead of taking a breather to let some common sense sink in, the hiker bolted from the woods and dialed 911.

Policy meant someone had to investigate, despite knowing the scream was a hiker's overactive imagination. He cursed. This was his night off. But Kamal had called in sick, and he was two deputies down, so he had to take the extra shift.

Ryker let rip a few more choice curses. He had several things he'd rather be doing. His lips curved. Brenda, Reba, or even better, the Tracey twins. The things they could do with their ...

Driving out to Mystery Hill to look at a bunch of old rocks and trees didn't compare. He sighed. This evening should've been spent in more pleasurable pursuits.

Ryker turned onto a side road and stopped in front of a closed chain link gate that led to one of the many tourist attractions around Salem. "Adam twelve to base. Have arrived. About to check out the report."

"Copy that, Adam twelve."

He exited the car, jumped the chain link fence, and strode toward the trees. If he checked the altar stones first, then the museum, he could be back on the road again in five.

As he walked down the well-worn dirt path, he scanned the area. Despite the limited light, this close to the main road, someone might note his unnatural speed as he raced the half mile to the Mystery Hill altar stones in less than thirty seconds. He cocked his head and listened to see if the hiker had grown a pair and returned.

No one was around. He sped up, dust billowing at his heels. The sooner he confirmed nothing was going on, the sooner he'd get to the Rusty Chain and sort out a real problem.

A grin spread across his face. The Tracey twins hung out at the Rusty Chain. Maybe he still had time to recover what was left of the night.

Four hundred yards up the hill, the hairs on the back of his neck prickled. His boot struck a small rock, which zipped across the dirt as his steps faltered. Something wasn't right. He stopped dead. The faint metallic scent of blood nudged his nostrils. Murky shadows lurked in the woods. The lack of light would have been an issue if he was still Human. Not so much for a Vampire who'd seen more than he cared to admit in his two hundred and fifty years. He scanned the trees using his enhanced vision and hearing.

Nothing.

Apart from insects' nocturnal scratching as they scurried under fallen leaves, and occasional hoots and warbles from birds in the canopy, everything was as it should be. So why was his gut knotted? He inhaled, his chest tightening. Death had stalked these woods.

He raced along the path and broke through the tree line into the clearing that contained the Mystery Hill stone formations. Any thoughts the hiker had been hearing things evaporated.

"Fuck."

Three bodies lay across the neolithic stone slabs around the center altar. In an instant, he was at the body nearest him. He crouched to take a closer look. The woman's arm hung limp, her fingertips almost touching the ground. His brow furrowed. The smooth, exposed skin of her limbs was far paler than it should be. Disheveled blonde hair covered her face, which was turned away from him.

Careful not to disturb the crime scene, he moved around to the other side of the raised stone slab to get a better view of her. His breath caught in his throat. It was Sarah, the eldest of the Tracey twins. The unusual tattoos down her limp left arm gave her away.

The long jagged open wound across her neck caught his attention. "Christ."

Her throat had been slit from ear to ear. The cut deep enough to sever the jugular veins and carotid artery but not severe enough to damage the larynx and trachea. His head jerked back. There should be more blood. And a lot more of it. He leaned closer to the wound and sniffed. Apart from the congealed blood around the cut, very little was left in her body. That explained her ashen skin tone and why the scent of blood was so faint.

He inspected the corpse. Sarah's feet were tied together with thick cable ties. Bloody red marks were etched into the skin around her ankles where she'd struggled to free herself, and when he pulled her hair away from her face, he discovered a massive bruise and cut on her forehead.

After checking the rest of her body for clues, and finding none, he made his way to the second body. A man, mid-forties, wearing a worn Def Leopard t-shirt, had met the same fate as Sarah. While his face was familiar, the man's name eluded him. As with Sarah, his feet were also tied, and his forehead sported the same cut. Ryker's eyes caught on the man's face again.

Damn.

"Zac Cole, Haverhill High's football coach."

Zac had come into the station to dispute a parking ticket a few months back. Mitos, one of Ryker's deputies and the one who gave him the most headaches, had issued a ticket because he didn't like the man's Prius.

"The lack of blood tells me you weren't killed here." His gaze scanned the clearing. "So how did someone kill three people and cart them to this neck of the woods without being seen?"

And by someone, he meant more than one someone.

He took his sheriff's cap off and ran a hand through his short hair. This nightmare was the last thing he needed. He cursed under his breath, straightened his shoulders, and headed to the third body. The Rusty Chain would have to fend for itself tonight. It was going to take all his deputies to keep the crazies away from this crime scene. Considering its mythical history, the moment news leaked about three dead bodies on the altar at Mystery Hill, they'd be swamped by all manner of press, kooks, and conspiracy theorists.

He drew closer to the third corpse, a teenage girl. His heart seized, and all the air left his lungs. A crushing weight pushed him down to his knees.

The only noise capable of escaping his lips was a tortured "*No.*"

He was unable to look away from her broken body. Like the other two, her throat had been viciously slit. The deep laceration churned his stomach. Familiar brown eyes stared up at him. He struggled to raise his hand, his arm leaden.

How was this possible? He had just seen her yesterday. Laughing. Full of life, full of endless possibilities. He gulped and forced his hand to cup her face. Holding back an anguished cry, he gently closed her eyelids. Even in death, she had the uncanny ability to make him feel Human.

"Annie," he said in a broken whisper. "What did they do to you?"

A tsunami of grief crashed over him, paralyzing him in its wake. She was the bright light that gave him passage to a world he'd shied away from for two hundred years. A world he now embraced, along with the bonds he had given himself permission to forge. How could she be gone? She was supposed to be old and gray before her life was over. Not be slaughtered just as her life was beginning.

After an eternity, he clenched his jaw and stood, careful not to disturb the scene. A flurry of wind raced across the clearing, throwing up a spray of dirt in its wake. He took a series of long breaths. White-hot rage swelled from the pit of his stomach, and he struggled to hold it back. Someone, or something, had taken the lives of three innocent people. People he'd vowed to protect.

Annie was only eighteen. How was he going to break this news to Zayne and Maize? Her parents were his closest friends. Would they still feel the same way about him after he ripped out their hearts?

He reached for his police two-way radio and took another couple of breaths before pressing the button. "Adam twelve to base. I have multiple ten fifty-fours out at Mystery Hill."

What he didn't report spoke volumes. Even had he not recognized them, he would still have known what they were by their scent. All three victims were Witches.

He scoured the area, but found nothing, so he sat next to Annie's body while he waited for his deputies and the coroner to arrive. It nearly killed him to not reach out and tidy her hair. Maize and Zayne didn't need to see her like this. But disturbing anything would compromise the evidence, and he wasn't about to let the killers get away on a technicality.

He snorted. Who was he kidding? If he had his way, whoever did this to her wouldn't live to see the trial.

Forty-five minutes inched by like hours. Helpless and unable to will her back to life—not for lack of trying—he kept asking the same questions over and over.

Why?

Why her? Why them? Why leave their bodies here?

Ryker was relieved when the cavalry arrived. At least now he could start searching for answers.

Just as the team finished setting up mobile lighting, Deacon Hunter, Salem's mayor, and the Vampire Ryker considered his father, strode through the chaos and systematically took in the scene. They stood a short distance away from the team sorting out the logistics of the investigation about to commence.

"I came as soon as I heard," Deacon said. "Any idea who did this?"

"Not a clue. I haven't got the heart to tell the crime scene investigators they're wasting their time. I've looked. The killers didn't leave a trace." Ryker stared at a pile of dead leaves on the ground and his voice broke. "How am I going to tell Zayne and Maize?"

Deacon rested a hand on Ryker's shoulder. "Do you want me to?"

Ryker shook his head. "No. It's my responsibility."

Deacon's hand dropped away. "This is going to be hard on you. That carefree, reprobate persona you hide behind like a mask doesn't work on me. Your fierce need to protect everyone is admirable. Noble, even. But this one will be hurting more than you'll let on. Don't blame yourself. This is not on you."

Pain shredded Ryker's chest. Of course, it was on him. It was his job to protect everyone. How had he missed a group of killers on the prowl?

"We Vampires can do many things. Reading minds is not one of them," Deacon said.

Ryker cast a sideways glance at his mentor. What'd given away his thoughts? He was sure his expression hadn't changed.

"What do you think happened?" Deacon asked.

If only Ryker had a crystal ball. For now, his instincts and experience would have to do. "Whatever it was, there are no signs of a struggle at the scene. No scuffed footprints on the ground. No pools of blood. I can't even tell from which direction they brought the bodies into the clearing or which way they left."

Deacon nodded at the victims. "But from the marks on the bodies, all three put up a good fight."

Ryker winced. Annie must have been terrified. "This is a nightmare. I already have my hands full with a missing Witch. Now I've got three dead Witches." He rubbed his forehead. "And what's with the missing blood? If someone were trying to blame Vampires, they screwed up royally. Slitting throats is a waste of good blood."

Deacon let out a deep breath. "Four."

Ryker raised a brow. "What?"

"Four dead Witches. A body was found at Proctor's Ledge two days ago. It was Oggie Truscott. I didn't think anything of it at the time and just assumed his heart had finally given out. But considering the significance of the location and who he was, I'm not so sure now."

Ryker rubbed the back of his neck. "There's going to be a panic the moment this gets out. Not only are we going to have a grand exodus of tourists, but the publicity from a ritual killing at a historic site will have the FBI sniffing at our door."

No matter which way he looked at it, the deaths fell into the hate crime bucket. The FBI would demand to spearhead the investigation. His muscles twitched. He couldn't let that happen.

To the outside world, they were a normal town in a normal county. Tourists spent a pretty penny to be scared out of their skin by Vampires, Witches, and anything else that went bump in the night. But Salem was a town of Supernaturals who pretended to be Humans pretending to be Supernaturals. They didn't need anyone poking their noses around to discover the truth.

He turned back to Deacon. "We can do without a repeat performance of the Roswell two incident of ninety-four."

Deacon grunted. "Don't remind me. Mass hysteria in a town of Supernaturals isn't a pretty sight. Especially when they think aliens are about to invade."

"We need to keep a lid on this," Ryker said "The local Supernatural population can't get caught up in conspiracy theories again. They already live on a razor's edge. They'll go into panic mode. Not only will we have people getting hurt again, but now, with the internet and social media, we won't survive the fallout. We need to keep everyone calm and keep outsiders from digging into our business."

Deacon's phone buzzed. He pulled his cell from his inside jacket pocket. "The governor, I can deal with, but we need to find a way to keep the Feds off our backs."

Ryker nodded toward the small crowd of reporters who had gotten wind of the crime. The deputies had erected cordons and were stopping the press from taking photos.

"That's not going to be easy, considering it's probably gone viral already."

"Then we have to find someone we can trust," Deacon said.

Ryker stared at Annie's body, silhouetted in the forensic team's lights. He'd failed to protect her in life, but he would certainly make sure he did so in death. His pulse quickened as a dormant memory hit him.

"There might be someone we can trust." Ryker reached for his phone. "A couple of seasons back, I spent some time with a Witch from California. She was out here from UCLA Berkeley for spring break. If I recall correctly, she couldn't stop talking about one of her professors who was some sort of hotshot with the FBI."

Deacon's brows drew together. "How is that going to help us?"

"The professor's a Witch."

FOUR

STAR 69

Berkeley, California

The apartment door slammed shut with an almighty thud. Keira winced as she leaned against it. Maybe she shouldn't have put so much energy into closing it. Pain radiated from the lump on the back of her head the size of an egg, courtesy of hitting her head on the way to the floor during her very public collapse on the dais. She whispered a familiar incantation and the glamour fell away. Gone was the fine-lines, crow's feet and wrinkles that marked time. The grey streaks in her hair melted away, revealing her natural vibrant auburn red. In less than a heartbeat she had gone from a woman in her mid-fifties, to her natural face that reflected a woman in her early thirties. Thankfully the spell held while she was unconscious. Using her pendant as talisman to channel power to the spell if she was unable to had been a wise decision.

She took a few deep breaths before turning on the lights. Felix, her ornery tabby cat, raised his head from his position on the couch and meowed at her. "Not so loud, I have a splitting headache."

A shrill beep from her phone startled her. As expected, it was Marcus making sure she'd arrived home in one piece. Since her undignified and very public blackout episode, Marcus had been as irritating as a mother hen. After picking herself up from the floor, she cut the lecture short to give herself time to recover. But much to Marcus' horror, she taught her evening class rather than cancel it. There was no choice. She'd needed to know if the source of the disruptive magic was still there. But the only thing she'd gotten from her lecture was more of a headache and less of an answer.

She gave Felix a quick scratch under his chin. "In hindsight, that probably wasn't one of my wisest decisions." Her vision blurred, and she put her hand to her forehead. "Mother Earth, stop making everything spin."

Felix stretched out a paw, then proceeded to clean it, eyeing her the entire time.

"Something's wrong, Felix. I don't know what. But whatever it is, it's left a small hole in the earth's power."

After checking the time, she chewed on her bottom lip and stared at her phone while her head throbbed to an erratic beat. It was 5:00a.m. in London. This couldn't wait. She needed to speak to her sister.

Felix chose that moment to venture off the couch and rub his body against her leg. A high-pitched meow she recognized as "food now" only resulted in another stab of pain.

"I'll feed you soon, but I have to know if the same thing happened to Dayna."

The only response was a snooty meow as Felix stared at her for a moment, then sauntered toward the kitchen in a huff.

She scrolled through her contacts list. "Much more of that attitude, and I'll be swapping your Temptations for a no-name brand. Let's see how demanding you are then."

Her sister answered before the phone had a chance to ring.

"I've been waiting for you to call," Dayna said. "Did you feel it?"

Keira let out a long breath. She wasn't going insane. "Yes, but I don't know what it was."

"Neither do I, but it scared the pants off me, not that I wear pants when I'm in bed."

Loud music played in the background. "Where are you?"

"Ibiza," Dayna said.

"I thought you were in London?"

"I was, but then I met this sexy DJ who's famous for more than just his music, if you know what I mean, and I decided to tag along. The place is fun, and the sex is great. I'm telling you, it's the sixties all over again."

Keira groaned aloud. "Do I really need to hear about your extracurricular activities?"

"You need to lighten up, Sis. I'm sure you haven't gotten any since women were given the vote. I sometimes wonder if you still know what to do." Dayna chuckled. "If you've got it, flaunt it, I say."

Keira flicked her eyes upward. Her sister, the free spirit, had inherited their mother's sense of adventure. But after three hundred or so years, she should've grown up, even a little bit. Well, if nothing else, Dayna certainly made life interesting.

"How's life in the boring lane?" Dayna asked. "You still playing teacher?"

Her sister was forever trying to push her buttons. Much to Dayna's consternation, Keira had learned long ago not to take the bait. "If you mean, professor, then yes."

"Look, Sis, DJ Hunk has some cute friends who would be just the medicine the doctor ordered to get you to loosen up. How about you ditch that mundane gig and catch the next flight to Ibiza?"

Keira let out a tired exhale. As far as Dayna was concerned, life was one giant party. "We've discussed this before. You know I can't just drop everything. I have responsibilities."

"Pfft. Always with the excuses. You've been making them since Susan B. Anthony was arrested, I'm starting to think you don't know how to live anymore. Which is why you need to get yourself over here right now. I'm sure we can find you a man who will—"

"Dayna. Focus. Something's wrong. I don't have a good feeling about this."

"Neither do I, but I checked for anything obvious. Apart from the usual twenty or so volcanoes that erupt per day and fifty-five earthquakes, nothing stands out."

Of course, Dayna wouldn't have thought to do the obvious. "Dayna, tap into your power."

"What?"

"Just do it. Try a tethering spell, but on something large."

She held her breath while she waited for Dayna to try the spell.

"Keira …" Dayna's voice was now more subdued. "Why does it feel like there's something missing?"

Relief flooded through Keira's veins, and she exhaled. "You feel it too? I thought it might have been my injury making me feel that way."

"Injury? What injury? Are you okay?"

"It's nothing to worry about. Now try it again. This time, reach out to Yggdrasil and draw power from there."

The line went quiet. When Dayna's sudden intake of breath shattered the silence, Keira knew she wasn't imagining things.

"How is that possible?" Dayna asked in a whisper. "There's a gap in Yggdrasil's power."

"I have no idea. But something has happened to the Tree of Life."

"You don't think—"

"No, I don't. Only a fraction of Yggdrasil's power is missing, so there's nothing to worry about. We're still safe."

Dayna let out a nervous laugh. "You're right. I'm just seeing ghosts when there are none."

Keira's hand traveled to her neck and gave it a rub. "But, still, I'd like to know what happened to the missing power. It's not much, but I'm still feeling the aftereffects from it being ripped from Yggdrasil."

By the time she finished her call with Dayna, she was still none the wiser. They'd explored all the possible reasons for the missing power, but each time they came up against a dead end. Her head was now throbbing. Probably more from her conversation with Dayna than the lump from her fall. Before she could hang up, Dayna tried to convince her, yet again, to hop a flight to Europe. No matter how much she argued the point, her sister didn't understand she had a responsibility to her students.

She was about to retrieve her crystals to work on a spell to get rid of her headache when her phone rang.

Dayna, don't you ever give up?

Her sister could wait a few rings. Maybe she'd get the hint.

Meow. Felix chose that moment to remind her he was still waiting for his dinner.

She gave him a quick rub behind his ears. "It's not going to kill you to wait five more minutes. I'm sure you've already begged for food from Mrs. Walsh today. She's the reason you're overweight."

The ringing phone was exacerbating her headache.

Without looking at the display, Keira answered with a curt, "I said no."

"But you haven't heard our request yet."

Her eyes widened at the deep baritone. Definitely not her sister—or anyone else she knew, for that matter.

"I'm sorry …" She held out her phone and checked the caller ID. An East Coast number. She cleared her throat and put the phone back to her ear. "How about we start again? Hi, how can I help you?"

"Well, for starters, is this Dr. Wynter?"

Her eyebrows drew together. This time, the voice was not as deep. Instead, it was gravelly. How she imagined fine whiskey might sound if it had a voice. No matter how nice the man sounded, she was distracted by a more pressing need to sort out her headache. She put the phone on speaker and headed for her room to retrieve her crystals. "Yes, I'm Dr. Keira Wynter."

"We're sorry to be disturbing you so late in the evening, Dr. Wynter. I'm a sheriff in New England, and I have our local mayor, Deacon Hunter, with me. You're on speaker. We understand you consult with law enforcement. There's a situation we're hoping you can assist us with."

Deacon Hunter? The name rang a bell, but she couldn't place it. She opened a drawer and pulled out a small black velvet pouch, only half listening to the sheriff. She tipped the contents onto her bed. "Oh? What sort of situation?"

The sheriff cleared his throat. "Several of our citizens were found dead a few hours ago."

Keira cocked her head and frowned. There was no way she wanted to take up another case right now. Not so close on the heels of the last one.

"Sheriff, I don't believe I caught your name."

"Kincaid. Sheriff Ryker Kincaid."

She positioned her crystals in a circle. "Sheriff Kincaid, I'm not sure why you would need my services. Dead citizens are your domain, being the local law and all."

Once happy with the arrangement, she reached for the large alexandrite crystal and placed it in the palm of her right hand. She curled her fingers around the red gem, closed her eyes, and mouthed an ancient healing spell.

"Doc, believe me, I am more than capable of dealing with law and order in my domain. But we aren't dealing with your everyday crime in this situation. The deaths were ritualistic in nature. We need to avoid the FBI coming in and taking over. It wouldn't be good for business or for many of the people who live here." Sheriff Kincaid let out a breath. "We'd like to deal with it ourselves and in our own way."

Keira squeezed her eyes tighter. The odd conversation made it difficult to focus on the spell. Her patience was running thin. "I don't know what you think I can do, Sheriff Kincaid. The FBI's division that deals with cult and hate crimes is reasonably competent to assist you in this matter."

Sheriff Kincaid cleared his throat. "Doc, if I can be blunt, we're trying to keep the FBI out of this, and we're in desperate need of the unique skills you possess. We need someone who understands the …" He paused, as if struggling to find the words.

"Delicate nature of our situation, which is anything *but natural*," a second voice finished the sheriff's sentence. Deacon Hunter, she presumed.

Her eyes flew open. Something in their voices stopped her from ending the call. "What aren't you telling me?"

She could now literally hear her head throbbing in the uncomfortable, drawn-out silence.

"All three victims shared something in common with yourself," Sherriff Ryker said.

"I'm not following you."

"They were Witches."

She stood up so quickly, her vertebra popped. If there was a mic, Sheriff Kincaid had certainly dropped it. He now had her full attention. Who the hell was she speaking with? One word in that sentence was never used by the FBI or any law enforcement agency for that matter. She had to assume both the sheriff and the mayor were Supernatural's. Kincaid mentioned the victims were Witches like her. Which implied not like them. Her mind raced a mile a minute. That could only mean they were Gifted, Vampire or Were.

And if a Gifted, Vampire or Were approached a Witch they didn't know for help, something was very, very wrong. As a general rule, the Supernatural races didn't mix.

"Where did you say you were from again?"

Deacon's deep baritone broke the silence, "Salem."

Fear ripped through her body. Unable to hold her weight at the single word, her legs gave out, and she sank to the floor. The pain of the alexandrite gem cut into her palm as her fingers clenched tighter. The agony of her hand competed with the thumping ache in her head. The missing power from Yggdrasil, along with the memory of the screaming from earlier, returned. A sense of dread washed over her and held firm, forcing all the air from her lungs.

Mother Earth, no. It couldn't be. Not again.

WHO SAYS YOU CAN'T GO HOME?

Salem, Massachusetts

Marcus jumped out of the cab before it came to a complete stop. He danced in a circle as he looked at the hotel and then cast his gaze up and down the street.

"This is, like, epic." He pulled out his iPhone, snapped it onto a selfie stick, and grinned like a Cheshire cat as he pressed record. "Dudes, you won't believe where VarcitySneakerHead is coming from this week. Me and my freshly-mint Air Jordan six retros are in historic Salem, Massachusetts. We are here to see waz up with all the crazy Witches, Warlocks, and Vampires. Stay watching to find out more. Don't forget to subscribe to my channel."

Keira paid the driver and waited for Marcus to finish. She had long ago given up trying to stop him from suddenly filming a segment for his weekly YouTube channel. She would never understand the logic of social media influencers, but his weekly ramblings on sneakers were paying for his tuition. Considering the debt that most students left college with, she'd learned to give him a little leeway. Provided she was never filmed or mentioned.

Marcus pushed pause. An expression of concern fell across his face "You sure it's okay for you to keep your old lady mask off? It's kinda freaky seeing you out in public without it."

Keira chuckled. "It's perfectly safe. Besides, we are highly unlikely to bump into anyone we know."

Marcus shrugged his shoulders. "Your call, but that doesn't stop it from being weird."

He shook his head and resumed filming. "Dudes, you is about to be jam packed with a lot o' cool stuff we're going to cool places as well. And I'll reveal that in a little bit later in the video, so let's see—"

Keira tuned out. Despite Marcus excelling in English studies, he tended to butcher the English language on his show. While she waited, Keira took in her surroundings. The street, filled with tourists, was similar to its sister—Bourbon Street, New Orleans—only louder and with a lot more variety of crazy.

"We aren't here on holiday or for your side hustle," she said as a reminder once he finished. A shiver snaked up and down her spine. The uneasy feeling that began the previous day increased the closer they got to their destination. "And the only reason you are here is because I'm doing your grandmother a favor."

Queenie Boudreaux, a New Orleans earth Witch and an old friend, made her promise to give Marcus as much exposure to the Supernatural world as possible while he was studying under her. Unfortunately for her, Keira never broke a promise. Salem and the surrounding counties were the mecca for all things Supernatural, and Marcus wouldn't have stopped hounding her until she agreed to let him come along for the ride.

"I know," he said. "But this was just too good to miss out on. I'm so going viral with my next video."

She reached for her luggage. "Just be careful. You know the rules."

Marcus scrunched his nose. "Take a chill pill. You spent the majority of the six-hour flight reading me the riot act. When did I ever—" His attention was distracted when two costumed Puritans passed them. "Man. Sandals and socks, seriously? Not a good start, Salem."

She snapped her fingers in front of his face. "Marcus. Earth to Marcus."

"Hmmm?" he murmured, still videoing the costumed men as they walked up the street, unaware they were being judged. And harshly.

She wheeled her bag toward the main entrance. "Marcus, focus."

Keira was going to regret bringing him. She could just feel it.

He raced to catch up with her. "You don't need me this afternoon, do you? I'd like to suss out where the local hotspots are so I can get some footage."

"Remind me again, why I bothered to bring you along?"

Marcus followed her through the doors to the hotel. "Because sneakers are not my only superpower. I'm the only one who'll tell you those Chanel pumps were a boring choice to match with your Bottega Veneta suit."

"You do realize that superpower was by osmosis. Your mother is an editor for Vogue, and your father is a buyer for Saks Fifth Avenue."

Marcus snorted. "Details, details."

She resisted rolling her eyes. Marcus' mother Edmée, was never as stroppy as a child. In fact, all the Boudreaux children were delightful. Marcus was the second Boudreaux grandchild Keira had taught. Olympia, Marcus's older cousin, had graduated UCLA the previous year with a PhD in Biological Chemistry. Like her mother and grandmother before her,

Olympia was an earth Witch. However, as with so many Witches of her generation, she neglected her power and potential for other pursuits.

To be fair, it wasn't just the current generation of Witches that abandoned their magic. Keira had seen the same story repeated across the years. With the world becoming smaller, magic was finding it hard to survive.

Once they checked in, she left Marcus to scout locations and headed out to meet with Sheriff Ryker Kincaid and Mayor Deacon Hunter. The mayor she had heard of. The Supernatural community had the ability to spread information faster than social media.

Deacon Hunter, Vampire and current mayor of Salem, had been the driving force behind turning Salem into a tourist attraction. He'd spent the better part of the last thirty years behind the scenes, turning a sleepy town into a multibillion-dollar enterprise. She was a little curious as to why he finally stepped forward in the previous election and took up such a public position.

The sheriff was another matter entirely. Apart from the scant information on the Essex County Sheriff Department's website, which was only two lines and no photo, she had no idea of what or who he was. More importantly, no amount of research on the two men she was about to meet gave her insight into the only question that mattered: how much did they know?

Late afternoon, and the streets teemed with families, college students, young couples, old couples, and the inevitable tourists. She swerved more than once to avoid oncoming pedestrian traffic. Many of the tourists donned elaborate costumes, and more than once, she found it hard to distinguish between the locals and the tourists.

The town she remembered had grown into something no longer recognizable. Her feelings, however, hadn't altered. This was the last place she wanted to be. Too many memories. Too much pain. Too much loss. But no matter how she rebelled against it, she had no choice. The terror she'd experienced during her lecture and the deaths of the Witches was connected. She needed to know why.

After a couple of wrong turns, she stood outside a narrow, colonial-brick building and looked up at the giant billboard plastered across most of the frontage. She groaned. The ground floor of the structure housed a blood bank. Based on the number of people queuing inside, it wasn't short on customers. How could Naturals be that gullible? Didn't they realize they were donating blood to Vampires? She looked for a second door, or a sign to indicate where the mayor's office was and frowned.

"This can't be the place." She took a step back. The number above the door read 3657. The correct address, according to her phone. "Why is the mayor's office in a blood bank?"

She entered the building to discover it looked very much like a typical doctor's office, except the female nurses were dressed as the brides of Count Dracula. Not seeing any signs that would direct her to the mayor's office, she took her place in the queue and waited her turn to speak to someone behind the counter. There were cozy chairs and couches positioned throughout the modest foyer. Navigating through them were overly made-up, pale-faced men in smart suits who checked on those who had newly donated blood. It took all her will not to laugh out loud at the stereotypical Vampires as they mingled with their prey.

A flash caught her eye, and she spun her head around to watch a family having a photo taken with another overdone Vampire whom she recognized from the billboard. She had to admit, this one was gorgeous and reminded her of a suave James Bond. If he was the typical bait to attract tourist dollars, it was no wonder people were more than happy to fork out twenty dollars a pop for an action shot with a Vampire who was about to bite them.

The family had barely cleared the exit when high-pitched squeals pierced her eardrums. She cringed as two college-aged women rushed from the back room and made a beeline toward the Vampire posing as a Human, dressed up as a Vampire.

The taller of the two gushed at the Vampire. "We're next."

Barbie Girl Number One wasn't shy. When Barbie One sauntered up to him, she pulled down her already low-cut top and batted her fake eyelashes at Mr. Bond, the Vampire.

Barbie One pointed to the top of her breasts, which were in danger of falling out of her one-size-too-small bra. "I want you to bite me right there."

Keira winced involuntarily at the girl's squeaky voice.

Not to be undone, her friend said, "And then you can do me."

Bond smiled; his eyes way too low to be looking at their faces. "Happy to oblige, ladies." His grin widened. "After all, you've kindly supplied me with my next meal."

At this, the Barbie twins giggled.

Keira wasn't sure who to be more scared for, the girls or the costumed Vampire. She pushed back the snort that almost escaped her mouth.

Mr. Dracula Bond, licensed to thrill, bent his head, opened his mouth, and grinned at the camera as his extended canines came into light contact with Barbie One's skin. A flash, and it was all over.

"So, what time do you get off work?" Barbie One asked as she twirled a lock of hair around a finger on her right hand and trailed the fingers of her left hand across where the Vampire's teeth had grazed.

"Sorry, babe, but a Vampire's work is never done. I'll be in the parade later this evening. But maybe if you swing by the Devil's Tavern after that, you can buy me a drink."

Keira was thankful when she reached the front of the line. "I have an appointment to see Deacon Hunter, but I'm not sure I'm in the right place."

The woman behind the counter chuckled. "He does it every time."

Keira frowned. "I'm sorry, I'm not following you."

The woman gestured to her right. "You're after the next door down, 3257A. Mayor Hunter always forgets the 'A'. Take the stairs. His offices are on the next floor up."

Keira quickly exited the building and raced through the correct door and up the stairs. As she reached the landing, a voice called out, "I'll be with you momentarily."

Not sure what to do, she looked up and down the small hallway. The floor held offices. The question was, for what? This wasn't the official city council's office, where the mayor usually resides, and the floor had no signage to give further clues.

"Sorry to keep you waiting." The deep baritone she recognized from the phone call gave him away as Deacon Hunter.

She swung around.

"Dr. Wyn—"

He stopped midstride and visibly swallowed. A shocked expression quickly replaced the welcoming smile that had initially greeted her.

"Annabeth?" he said in a whisper.

She physically recoiled and took a step back. A sense of panic fought to escape her carefully constructed exterior. Annabeth had been her mother's name.

Deacon cleared his throat and shook his head. "No. It can't be." His gaze dropped to the ever-present amulet around her neck. "You're one of her daughters." His eyes met hers. "So, the legends are true." He regarded her silently, and an unreadable mask descended over his features. "No one's heard from you or your sister in over a century."

How the hell does he know who I am?

Her fists tightened, and she raised her chin. "I don't know what you're talking about."

Her mind sifted through the clutter of nearly three hundred years of memories. She had never met the Vampire, nor had her mother ever mentioned knowing a Vampire. Witches and Vampires rarely mixed. But she wasn't prepared for the chuckle that burst from him as his face relaxed.

"You look so much like your mother." Deacon shook his head from side to side as he tapped a finger against his lips. He smiled, and his eyebrows rose at her staunch posture. "I can see you inherited her fiery temper, along with the matching hair. *Morsus Mihi*. Have no fear. Your secret is safe with me."

Keira recoiled again, stunned at his words and unsure how to react. The phrase was the one her mother had used to distinguish friend from foe. *How could he know that phrase?* More importantly, the Vampire knew about her and her sister. How? There were only a handful of Witches who knew their secret. She was certain not one of them knew or associated with Vampires. So how did he know who she really was? Her brain was ready to implode.

Deacon took a step closer and held out his hand. "Look, I think we got off on the wrong foot. Dr. Wynter, Keira, words can't express how much I appreciate you coming out on such short notice, and now, considering your connection to the place, I am not sure I know how to repay you. This cannot be easy for you."

She regarded the tall, distinguished man who looked like he just stepped off the cover of GQ, and debated whether to leave before things got any worse. The fact that he knew the one phrase that identified him as an ally gave her cause to hesitate. She had never met him, but there was no doubt he knew her mother. More questions than answers bombarded her as she wavered between standing her ground and fleeing.

She came to a decision and gathered herself. She was here now, she might as well finish what she started. "Don't mention it. And I mean, don't mention it."

His expression turned solemn. "Your identity is safe with me. You have my word on that."

She declined to comment on his promise. She would wait and see how much he knew before judging possible ramifications.

"I'd like to get started on the case if you don't mind," she said, changing the subject. "Where is Sheriff Kincaid?"

She was supposed to be meeting with both the men she spoke to on the phone.

"Ryker's been detained. He'll be here shortly." Deacon held out his hand. "How about we go into my office while we wait."

The office, which overlooked Main Street, was larger than expected. She made her way to the window while Deacon poured her a glass of water.

He came to stand beside her and held out the glass. "You'll find Salem has changed somewhat since you were last here."

She accepted the offered drink and turned to gaze at the street below. "It was a village when I left. Quite frankly, I'm not sure what to think. I've never seen anything like it."

A woman in a 1700s peasant dress sold trinkets to tourists out of one of the outdoor stalls. A gothic punk-style Vampire was selling Vampire, Witch, and Demon makeup kits in the stall next to her. Farther away, Keira couldn't help but balk at the spitting image of the Wicked Witch of the West from the original Wizard of Oz movie as she meandered up and down the main street, scaring the tourists.

He chuckled. "Well, we decided to capitalize on people's fascination with the macabre and things that go bump in the night. Since the city has such a rich history, it seemed logical to set up shop. It's a win-win. Tourists get to rub shoulders with Witches, Vampires, Demons, and all manner of beings. They don't need to know that it's not an act. We give them a thrill, a bit of a scare, and a holiday to remember, and they keep the dollars flowing in."

She recalled the blood bank on the ground floor. "Not to mention the blood."

He chuckled. "To be fair, fifty percent of the blood donated does go to the Red Cross. We're not that greedy."

"But why the elaborate costumes and the overdone makeup?"

The corners of his mouth quirked upward. "Unfortunately, since the era of silent films, we have become stereotypes. Vampires have been written as albino creatures of the night who can't set foot in the sun. Our Vampires play the part expected of them. It makes the tourists happy and deflects from reality. A reality that would set the Natural's world into a panic."

She had to agree, Naturals were better off not knowing they shared this world with others. But it was hard to believe Vampires and Witches roamed around the city pretending to be Naturals, who were pretending to be paranormal creatures of the night.

It made her head spin. "What about the new sparkly look that's all the rage from the Twilight books?"

Deacon's gaze fixed on his drink, and he swirled his glass absently. The ice brushed against the crystal and created a melodic sound.

He shook his head and exhaled through his teeth. "That's a situation I'd rather forget. The local Vampires refused, point blank, to scatter glitter over their bodies. They threatened to form an actual union."

A small laugh escaped her lips. "So how come no one's ever worked out the locals aren't fake? In all this time, not one tourist has stumbled on something they shouldn't have."

He held up his hands. "Don't get me wrong. We've had more than our fair share of close calls. But Naturals only see what they want to see."

"What about the local Supernaturals? How do you get the races to work with each other?"

"It wasn't easy at first. The deep seeded distrust between the Supernatural races caused more than one disaster in the first few years. But after a while things settled down. I suspect it was due to the forced proximity. They had no choice. They had to learn to live together-and so they did. Don't get me wrong, the races don't sit around a campfire together and sing Kumbaya. Witches still keep to Witches and Vampires to Vampires, but they do work and live in harmony. Salem and the surrounding areas give our Supernatural residents a place to be themselves without fear of persecution for who they are-provided they don't go beyond the boundaries we set for the good of the community."

Keira pointed to a small group of school children in two-by-two formation followed by an adult that could only be their teacher. The students were a mix of Human, Witch & Gifted. "I hadn't appreciated just how many Supernatural lived here until I arrived."

"If things go on as they have been, we will outnumber the humans in less than ten years. That would have been a problem a hundred or so years ago, but with the dimming of magic across the board, both Witches and Gifted blend in with the Humans so it's often difficult to tell them apart."

Keira frowned. "I'm not following you.'

"Vampires use their sense of smell to identify race. A small number of us can also detect how much power a Witch or Gifted commands. Your magic, for instance, shines brighter than a thousand suns. Annabeth's was the same. Alas, it has been an age since I've laid eyes on a Witch as powerful as you. It is a sad fact that Witches no longer command the magic they once possessed. Over time, with the proximity to Humans and inability to hone their skills, we rarely see magic performed to his fullest extent."

Keira was slightly taken aback. Vampires could gauge how much magic a Witch possessed. How was this possible? And what did he mean by some Vampires?

Deacon cocked his head, then nodded at the door, effectively stopping Keira from asking any questions. "He's here."

"Who?"

The gruff whiskey voice from the phone conversation earlier in the week called out, "Hey, Pops, did you move the phone charger?"

From the muffled way it came out, she assumed the sheriff was in one of the offices along the corridor.

Her breath caught when a uniformed man strode through the door holding a phone in one hand and a charger in the other. "Never mind, I found it."

Mother Earth.

His whiskey voice wasn't the only attractive thing about him. The blue of his eyes was as striking as a mountain stream in spring.

"Well, hello there! You must be the doc." He dropped the phone and charger on a table, quickly closed the gap, and held out his hand. "Sheriff Kincaid, but folks around here call me Ryker. I hope Pops has been behaving himself."

Vampire.

There was no doubt that, like Deacon, the sheriff was a Vampire. The distinct red shimmer that radiated from him was a dead giveaway.

She cleared her throat and shook his offered hand. "Keira Wynter."

When their skin touched, a sliver of energy skipped down her spine to her tailbone. She hadn't expected his hand to be warm. In fact, nothing about this situation was as expected.

Despite his impeccable speech that screamed gentleman and scholar, Deacon Hunter had not originated from England. If she had to guess, with his dark olive complexion, vivid green eyes, and sinfully dark hair, he hailed from somewhere in the Middle East.

Ryker, on the other hand, with his blue eyes and thick, dirty-blond hair, could pass for an All-American. Was the whisper of stubble by design or simply the result of one or two missed shaves? Whatever the reason, the overall effect was hypnotic. Since when did backwater sheriffs look like this?

Mother Earth, what the hell was wrong with her?

She yanked her hand away before her temperature rose any further. The man was a player, and she didn't need him getting the wrong idea.

Ryker's reference to Deacon suddenly caught up with her and she drew in a deep breath. *Pops*? That could only mean Deacon was Ryker's sire and had turned him into a Vampire. She gulped and turned back to Deacon. There was only one type of Vampire that could turn a human into a Vampire. "You're Ryker's sire. That makes you a Primordial?"

Ryker chuckled, gave her a wink and said, "I think she's overwhelmed at the family resemblance."

Deacon straightened a cufflink. "Yes I am. But for the record, I am not Ryker's sire. I stumbled upon him after he had been turned and left to fend for himself."

Ryker made his way to the wet bar. "Yep, he kind of adopted me."

"Worst mistake I ever made."

"You keep saying that, old man. One day you just might believe it," Ryker said with a chuckle.

She raised a brow. He was evidently referring to their actual ages since Deacon only looked a handful of years older than Ryker. No one quite knew how old Primordial Vampires were. If the Legends were true they were at least five thousand years old.

Ryker poured himself a drink and made his way over to them. His expression was nothing like the cheerful one from a moment before. His boyish charm was now on simmer, replaced with the hardened expression of FBI agents who had seen one too many deaths.

He stared at the liquid intently before speaking. "It's been a nightmare couple of days, I don't mind telling you. We appreciate you helping out like this. The state couldn't cope with having the Feds coming in and poking around. There's only so much we can hide under that sort of magnifying glass." He took a long gulp and headed for the small meeting table in the center of the room. "I suppose you're wondering how we knew to call you?"

Deacon indicated for her to follow, and she took a seat. "The thought did cross my mind."

"We heard rumors of a Witch working with the FBI," Ryker said. "We didn't know who it was exactly until two years ago, when a student from Berkeley spent spring break here." The corner of his mouth lifted in a half smile. "In addition to her spectacular flexibility and that amazing thing she did with her—"

Deacon cut him off. "This is hardly the time or the place to discuss a student's proclivities."

Ryker grinned. "I bet you're dying to know what she could do, though?" He shrugged his shoulders and turned to Keira. "In addition to her ability to speed up plant growth, she was a font of information about her professor."

Keira immediately knew to whom he was referring. It could only be Olympia, Marcus' older cousin.

So that explained how they knew she was a Witch. "Okay, so we know each other's secrets." She needed to move the conversation to the reason she was there. "Can you walk me through the case?"

Back in sheriff mode, Ryker slid a folder across the table toward her. "We have two problems. The first is who did it. We don't have the experience to know if it's a Natural that's gone on a random killing spree or if a Supernatural deliberately targeted them."

She reached for the folder but held back from opening it. "Why would you think it might be a Natural?"

While she hoped it was as simple as that, her sense of dread told her otherwise.

Deacon placed his elbows on the table and clasped his hands together, forming a steeple. "It's a sad state of affairs that while we are a major tourist attraction, we get a lot of threats from the general public. We're accused of everything from destroying society with our heathen ways to global warming. You name it, we've been tainted by it."

Ryker nodded. "In addition to the three bodies discovered at Mystery Hill, we have another unexplained death of a Witch in the Salem PD's jurisdiction, and we have a missing one as well. They're all linked. We just don't know how. The governor is putting pressure on us to call in the FBI. He doesn't want to lose tourist dollars, and if the public gets wind a killer is on the loose, they'll leave in droves."

"I spent the better part of the last two days trying to stop that from happening." Deacon nodded to the folder in her hand. "They've agreed to wait for your assessment."

She needed to tread carefully. How much did Deacon and Ryker know?

"What about the covens?" Keira asked. "How have they reacted to this?"

Ryker ran a hand through his short hair, and a frown creased his forehead. "Understandably, they are in shock. But that won't last. They'll want answers, and that's when the finger pointing will start."

"Did they all belong to the same coven?" she asked.

"Three were Fairlight, one Le Fay …." Deacon hesitated before directly making eye contact. "And one was Crossroads."

Her breath hitched.

He knows.

"And before you ask, I do not know whether the remainder of the coven has sufficient strength. Their numbers are as elusive as the wind."

Deacon's expression softened for a moment, and pity coupled with fear was reflected in his eyes. He knew. She was sure of it. But how could he be aware of the Crossroads' purpose? It had been a guarded secret for a millennium.

Ryker's eyebrows drew together. "Strength for what?"

Her forehead creased as she looked back at Deacon.

"I'm a Primordial Vampire of my word," Deacon said. "I made an oath to your mother to keep the knowledge to myself."

The air left the room, and the weight of her past pushed down on her shoulders. *Primordial?* Well, at least he understood what was on the other side of the gate. But how had he known her mother well enough to know the location of the coven and, by extension, the gate? A secret that many went to their grave to keep.

Ryker leaned forward and glanced between her and Deacon. "What am I missing here?"

Deacon pinched the bridge of his nose. "It turns out that I knew Keira's mother, but that's a conversation for another day. We have more pressing matters right now."

Keira's fingers brushed across the folder, its smooth surface belying the possible ugly truth contained within it. She hesitated as her stomach quivered. What was wrong with her? She needed to get a grip and stop focusing on worst-case scenarios. The death of one Crossroads couldn't possibly tip the balance. Could it?

Unable to put it off any longer, she opened the folder. When her eyes scanned the top crime scene photo, her throat constricted, making it hard to breathe. She studied the rest of the images, and dread raced through her body as invisible walls closed in and removed all traces of air. She reached for her amulet and fought to remain upright. No matter how much she tried, she couldn't tear her eyes away from the photo. Her worst nightmare revisited a hundredfold. Her breath came out in shallow pants, each one more painful than the one before.

A hand covered hers and violently ripped her back to the present. She followed the arm up and looked into Ryker's deep blue gaze.

"Are you okay?" he asked. "I probably should have warned you they were a little graphic."

The room plummeted to subzero temperatures, and she wrapped her arms around her chest. This wasn't supposed to be possible. After all the sacrifices made, she refused to believe someone was trying to open the gates to hell.

SIX

KNOCKING ON HEAVEN'S DOOR

It took a full minute for Keira to compose herself. Still holding onto the slimmest of hopes, she stared at the closed folder and asked, "Were the bodies found near the main altar at Mystery Hill?"

"How did you know?" Ryker's brows furrowed, and he turned to Deacon. "I thought you weren't going to brief the doc until I got here."

"I didn't."

Ryker let out a growl. "Does someone want to tell me what I'm missing?"

Keira pushed the folder back to him. "I'm going to need something each victim had on them when they died. Clothing, jewelry, a wallet. Anything, as long as it was in contact with them."

Ryker's eyes narrowed, and his mouth turned grim. She had the sudden urge to flinch. His unrelenting stare made her uneasy. He wasn't thrilled at being left in the dark. She met his gaze but faltered beneath his piercing scowl. How did the criminals he dealt with every day cope with this level of scrutiny?

"It's an hour's drive to the site," he said. "And it'll almost be dark when we get there. Are you sure you don't want to wait until morning?"

She crossed her arms and mimicked his posture. "Positive. If we delay any further, I won't be able to get the answers we need."

Ryker's gaze continued to bore through her. Unused to this level of scrutiny, she wilted. Mercifully, after what seemed an eternity, his gaze flicked to Deacon. She breathed a sigh of relief when he pushed his chair back and stood.

"All their personal effects are in evidence. We'll collect them on the way." Ryker paused and raked his gaze up and down her body. "However, I suggest that we swing by your hotel first. While I'm partial to heels and a nice pair of legs, I don't think your fancy clothes would fare well where we're going."

Her cheeks grew warm at his inspection. She uncrossed her legs and shot up from the table. "I'm not completely devoid of a brain. I didn't suggest I'd go dressed like this."

Ryker winked and grinned. Somehow, he knew exactly which buttons to push.

"Whatever you say, Doc." He indicated the door. "After you."

"Ryker will take you back to your hotel to save time," Deacon said as they shook hands. "Keep me in the loop. You have my number."

Back at the hotel, she raced up to her room, changed, and raced back out again in record time. Marcus was nowhere to be found, so she left him a message letting him know where she was headed. Just how long did it take to film one of his YouTube thingies?

As she exited the lobby onto the street, she spotted Ryker leaning against his car, chatting away to a group of women. Judging by the way the one closest to him reached out and brushed her hand against his arm as she laughed at something he said, they knew each other well.

A cynical smile tugged at the corners of Keira's mouth. Figures he would look right at home surrounded by groupies. Not that she could blame them. She had to admit he filled out his uniform perfectly. The problem was that he knew it.

She approached his little harem, and Ryker pulled away, smiling apologetically. "Sorry ladies, duty calls."

It was difficult to hold back a smirk as Miss Touchy-Feely pouted and batted her eyelashes at him. "Will we see you around later?"

His face non-committal, he replied in a voice so low she couldn't hear his reply. Miss Touchy-Feely's lower lip drooped even lower. The conversation clearly hadn't gone the way the woman expected.

Ryker nodded at the group, and they gave him a wave before wandering off.

"Ready, Doc?" he asked.

"Sorry to pull you away from your fans."

Ryker glanced over his shoulder at the women who were making their way down the street and shrugged. "It's all part of the job. We need to keep the peace between the Naturals and Supernaturals to make sure the communication channels remain open."

Keira muttered beneath her breath as she got into the car. "I just bet you do."

He opened the driver's door and bent his head down to look at her. "You know I heard that."

She feigned innocence. "Heard what?"

He chuckled. "And here's me thinking you had no sense of humor along with that stern school ma'am exterior and that rod stuck up your—"

A honk from a passing truck drowned out the remainder of his sentence.

It didn't take long for them to reach the Essex Sheriff's Office. Clearly, the man never met a speed limit he abided by. He retrieved the evidence box filled with personal effects of the dead Witches, and they were on their way.

The closer they drew to Mystery Hill, the tighter her nerves stretched. Her nails were about to draw blood as she squeezed her hands into fists to keep from fleeing the moving vehicle.

Ryker broke the silence. "Are you going to tell me what has you so rattled?"

"I'm fine."

"That's not what your jaw is telling me. In fact, if you grind your teeth much more, you won't have any left."

She stiffened. "I'm doing no such thing."

He tapped his ear. "You seem to forget my hearing is a little more developed than yours."

Instead of replying, she turned her head and stared out the window.

"The crime scene is two days old," he said. "It's been picked clean of evidence. What are you expecting to find out there?"

"Answers."

"Aren't you the font of information, Doc, and here's me thinking all you university professors know how to do is talk all day." With an audible sigh, he adjusted his hands on the steering wheel. "Suit yourself, but you'll have to tell me sooner or later."

With his need for speed, the forty-mile drive was over before she knew it. The highway was far quicker than the horse-drawn carts she remembered. After turning off the main road and onto a smaller one, they travelled a short distance until Ryker pulled into a small parking lot.

A low growl rumbled from Ryker's direction. Her head whipped around to face him, and she edged closer to the door.

His primal snarl had her on edge. "What's the matter?"

"The scene hasn't been released, so the gate out by the main road should've been closed. Stay here while I check the perimeter."

Before she could open her mouth to reply, he was out of the car and became a hazy, dark blur. He used his preternatural speed to race around the back of the large timber building that housed the Mystery Hill Museum. Or at least that was what the sign on the building indicated. She peered out the window and scanned the immediate area. The asphalt carpark, modern building, and chain-link fences that lined the road had her unsure of her bearings. Just how far away were the stones?

A dull double tap struck the window beside her, and she let out a muffled scream.

"All clear," said Ryker. "Let's go."

She exited the car and grabbed her tote bag, while Ryker retrieved the box of evidence. A gust of wind whipped around her legs, and a bouquet of familiar fragrances assailed her nostrils. The cleansing scent of pine mingled with damp earth covered in old fallen leaves and the spicy aroma of the tulip tree. Smells that marked time. Memories, unstructured and raw, flooded to the surface and bombarded her till she was paralyzed. After nearly two hundred and thirty years of being away from the place, it was the painful memories that pushed to the surface and dominated.

Ryker was almost at the small path that led around to the back of the museum before he realized she wasn't following. "You alright, Doc?"

She nodded curtly and shook herself out of her dark thoughts. She had a job to do, no matter how distasteful or how much she didn't want to be here. She didn't have a choice. If she did, she wouldn't be following a Vampire toward secluded woods.

She caught up to him and kept in step as they traveled down a dirt path leading them to their destination. The path led them to a thick wood, and they were surrounded by trees. Thick and lush, reaching up to the last drop of light before the day gave way to night.

But with each step, her heart beat heavier in her chest. "The trees are much larger than I remember."

"You've been here before?"

She faltered and half tripped over an exposed tree root. "Yes. A long time ago."

"Did your parents bring you as a child?"

Visions of her mother's smiling face as they wandered these woods swam to the forefront. "We lived nearby. But after my mother died, things became a little … suffocating, so my sister and I left."

"You live in LA, is that where your father took you?"

"No. My father died not long after my little sister was born. Our childhood was long gone by the time we decided to explore the world."

He gave her a sideways glance. "I don't think so. I've only been sheriff for seven years, but I've been here on and off for the past fifty. Believe me, I'd remember you."

Unable to help herself, she burst out laughing. Whether it was due to the overwhelming urge to flee or just how wrong his assumptions were, she wasn't entirely sure, but a dam burst, and she was unable to control herself.

Without meaning to, she said, "I left Salem long before you were born."

The moment the words were out of her mouth, she grimaced.

Nuts!

He stepped in front of her and cut off her path in an instant. His preternatural speed disturbed the dirt, and a cool breeze accompanied the small dust cloud that followed in his wake. "That's impossible."

He stood mere inches away as he scrutinized her. Even with the evidence box between them, it was a little too close for comfort.

She half turned to put space between them. "Why?"

"Well, for starters, look at you. You can't be any more than what? Early to mid-thirties? Witches age the same way as Naturals."

"If you say so."

This interrogation was too much. She navigated her way around him and continued up the well-worn path. For the remainder of the short journey, he kept pace with her, not once speaking. But the peace wouldn't last. She could literally hear the cogs in his mind working overtime as he cast curious glances at her.

The clearing came into view, and the weight of ghosts, long since gone, pressed heavily on her.

"You've gone pale," he said. "Are you okay?"

She visibly gulped and nodded her head. "I'll be fine."

She was far from fine when they stepped into the clearing. Unlike Salem, very little had changed. Most of the stones were still as she remembered. The chain-link fencing surrounding the clearing, and a small wooden viewing structure, were the only indication the modern age had turned the ancient sacred site into a tourist attraction.

The fourteen stone chambers and standing stones had baffled archeologists and historians since their discovery in 1826. She was surprised that it took the colonists that long to stumble upon the location. The more time marched on, the smaller the world became. Inevitably, the locals had discovered the gate of Issachar.

One of the smaller chambers had collapsed at some point, and boulders, unable to hold the weight of others, had finally given way. Over a hundred tonnes of stone now lay in a heap, filling the small cavity.

The Keepers Chamber was still in perfect order. She closed her eyes and recalled every inch of the six-foot-high and fourteen-foot-long tunnel that led into the side of the hill. She remembered the feel of the cold-quarried stone forming the inner chamber. Even all these centuries later, she still marveled at how its construction was possible. Like its sister in England, it defied all preconceived notions about early man's engineering capabilities.

In a small clearing before the Keepers Chamber lay the alter stone. Large. Gray. Unforgiving. And a witness to Human history as it unfolded. Memories, both good and bad, crashed over her in waves. This single, oversized rock was the reason her mother was ripped from them well before her time.

She sighed. The altar stone was also the reason she'd returned after vowing never to step foot in this place again.

The hint of a smile tugged at the corners of her mouth. For thousands of years, the sacred stones had only one name. Issachar. In the two hundred years since its discovery by the local population, it had been known as Mystery Hill Caves, Mystery Hill, and now America's Stonehenge. Both Stonehenge in Amesbury, England, and the American Stonehenge in Mystery Hill held the same secret. They were passages between Earth and Hell. In total, twelve ancient passages were spread across the globe. At each one, a Crossroads coven stood vigil to ensure the gates stayed closed and its prisoners stayed put.

Ryker raised the box he held. "Where do you want this?"

She indicated a large stone tablet balanced on three columns of small stones stacked on top of each other. "There should be fine."

She slipped the large tote from her shoulder and fished through her bag for the items she needed to get the job done. "I'll need some wood to start a small fire."

"Ten-four," he said before he disappeared into the woods.

She was pulling the first items out of her bag when he returned, laden with enough kindling and stout branches to start a small bonfire.

She showed him where to stack the wood. "What other cool tricks do you do?"

He wiped his hands and surveyed his handiwork. "Wouldn't you like to know," he said, waggling both eyebrows at her.

They danced over the rims of his shades, giving him a comical look. The banter was oddly comforting and gave her a sense of normality in a place that only held painful memories.

By the time she had prepared everything required for the ritual, the last of the sun was low on the horizon, and the forest had turned gray. Night was not far away. She arranged the firewood and picked up a small leather drawstring pouch. Her eyes fluttered closed, and she silently mouthed an incantation. Without opening her eyelids, she tossed a few pinches of red powder onto the small stack of dried branches. When she opened her eyes again, a fire was burning brightly.

"Doc's got skills," he said.

She dragged the evidence box closer to the fire and opened the lid to discover plastic evidence bags. Each bag had a name clearly printed, a signature, and a date. She pulled out a man's bloody t-shirt from the first bag.

Holding it to her, she again closed her eyes and said, *"Domine deduc me in sepulchrum tuum in locum."* She felt a tug and moved with it. The shirt led her to a smooth rock, and she positioned the stained shirt on it. *"Partis fabulam ut videam."*

She returned to the fire and placed another chunk of wood on the flames, repeating the process for each bag.

"You know, I could have saved you the effort," Ryker said once the last victim's possession had been laid where the spell directed.

As expected, they were resting on top of the low rock walls, which had been constructed in a rough circle around the altar stone.

She placed another stick on the fire and turned to him. "But then I wouldn't have been able to see."

He glanced around the clearing. "See what?"

She pointed to the circle. "Whatever happens, do not cross the lines that join them to each other."

With that, she opened her arms, palms upward, and chanted. "*Veneficas terrae, partis fabulam ut videam.*"

She repeated the chant a half dozen times before the air moved around her as the magic ebbed and swelled. She breathed out slowly. The power from Yggdrasil, the Tree of Life, had been drained. Not a lot, but enough to notice. Thankfully, the power to the gate was still enough to keep the cracks small.

At first, there were only flashes of images, each one grainy and out of focus. They formed and then disappeared, only to be replaced by others.

She frowned. It wasn't enough. She needed more magic.

Gracefully, she sank to her knees and placed her palms on the ground, then repeated the same incantation. A light sheen of perspiration broke out on her body with the effort it took to complete the spell.

Ryker's sudden sharp intake of breath told her when the incantation finally worked. She raised her head. Three bodies lay on the stone slabs. More accurately, a manifestation of the three victims. Gone were their possessions that acted as talismans to draw them back to their final resting place.

He approached the three-dimensional body closest to him and waved his arm through the apparition. "Why are they transparent?"

"Because it's only an echo of what has passed."

He shook his head. "You know, if you wanted to see their bodies, we could have just gone to the morgue."

"But that wouldn't show me how they looked before you found them. Photos of the scene can tell me only so much. I need to understand what sort of ritual was performed."

She rose from the ground and came to stand by the owner of the bloodied Def Leopard t-shirt. Her shoulders tensed. His throat had been slit, but something wasn't right. No blood dripped onto the stone and pooled in the small channel carved in the rock. If there was blood on his shirt and caked around the wound, it should be staining the stones beneath him. Perhaps she missed something with her spell?

"There was very little blood at the scene," he said. "We figure they were killed elsewhere and brought here postmortem."

All his previous joviality was now gone. In its place was the intense sheriff she'd glimpsed in Deacon's office.

A measure of relief allowed her to relax her shoulders. If they had been killed before being brought here, it meant her initial fears were unfounded.

Then she caught sight of a dark patch on the man's head, and her breath hitched in her lungs. In addition to the gaping wound across his throat, a two-inch circular gap in his crown exposed another wound where he had been scalped. She gulped and sent up a silent prayer.

Please, no.

She bent down and took a closer look at the markings carved into the Warlock's forehead. Her blood ran cold, and a shiver raced through her. The Order of Chaos.

Her worst nightmare was back.

Ryker bent to look at the markings. "The bastards took a knife to them. They all have that same circle carved into their foreheads."

Careful to keep her fears to herself, Keira pushed down the panic that made its way to her stomach.

"It's not a circle. It's a snake." She pointed to the wider chunk of skin missing at the top of the loop. "That's the head eating its tail."

"And that's significant?"

She nodded.

They moved to the next body, careful not to cross the invisible line that closed the circle and allowed the link to remain open. The light was dimming, but she made out a series of tattoos covering the woman's arm. As with the first body, the Witch's throat had been slit, and a portion of her head scalped.

Keira pointed to the inked skin. "Had she gotten it right, she might be alive today. But it takes many years to put a protection spell into the tattoo runes that won't turn on us. When completed, it's almost impossible to breach a Witch's defenses. Unfortunately, she didn't have the skill to do it correctly."

"Even if she had, it wouldn't have helped her. Their tongues were cut out." Ryker inspected the intricate markings. "Does that mean you have a set of rune tattoos like these?"

"Of course."

His gaze darted up and down the exposed skin of her arms. "Where are yours?"

"Away from prying eyes."

He grinned. "I'll just have to use my imagination then."

Mother Earth, how could one man have that much sex appeal?

She forced herself to ignore him and focused on the body. There was no way she should be having fantasies in the middle of such a gruesome scene. Get a grip. The man was a Vampire.

She leaned down to take a closer look. "That's odd." The Witch had a snake carved into her forehead, as did the Warlock. However, the jagged cut on the woman's cheek stood out. "What do you think that is?"

Ryker's vision was far superior to hers, especially now the sun had set.

"It looks like the letter 'C' with something coming out of it." He whistled. "We couldn't see that when we found the bodies. By then, it was just a large discoloration on her face."

Keira bent and drew an upside-down question mark with a horizontal line at the top in the dirt.

Her fingers shook as she drew. "Does it look like this?"

"That's it. What is it?"

She briefly closed her eyes, then stared at the altar stone in an attempt to push aside the panic bubbling up from the pit of her stomach. Without a doubt, the Order was back. And that could only mean one thing.

"Bad news," she said as she headed the short distance to the last body. As she stood over the small figure, her heart nearly broke. Unlike the first two, who were a little older, this was a girl still in her teens. "From the bruises and cuts over her body, she put up a brave fight."

Keira's breathing faltered when she looked up at Ryker. Etched into his face was raw and exposed pain. A little deeper, and she was sure he would begin to bleed.

He reached out to the apparition as if to smooth her matted hair. "Annie was the s-sweetest girl. She didn't deserve this. Neither do her parents." He sucked in a tortured breath. "I've lived a long time, but breaking the news to them was the hardest thing I've ever done."

Keira's throat ran dry at the level of emotion crashing around her, which was confusing. Since when did Vampires care about others?

"Deacon mentioned Annie was Crossroads," she said. "Which of her parents is also Crossroads?"

"Neither, they're both in the Le Fay coven. Because of her ability, Crossroads invited Annie to join about a year ago. While they didn't say too much, I think her parents, Zayne and Maize, were thrilled. Most covens are fairly secretive, but from my experience, Crossroads takes that to a higher level. The only thing I've worked out after all these years is that within the hierarchy of New England covens, Crossroads is at the top."

When he faltered on the last few words, the back of her eyes pricked. The pain in his voice cut the air like a knife.

"It sounds like you knew her well," Keira said.

"Annie was just like her folks. She only ever saw the best in people." He let out a self-deprecating laugh. "She even thought *I* was redeemable."

Keira rested a hand on his arm. "We'll find who did this."

He blinked, and a wall descended over his features. He moved to the first body and kept his back to her without speaking. His stiff shoulders signaled the discussion was closed.

She pushed away her inertia and focused on the sacrificed Witches.

By the time she'd inspected the bodies twice over, the moon had risen, and dancing shadows from the dying flames bathed the area in an eerie glow. She ended the echo spell, slumped against one of the standing stones, and placed her face in her hands as she focused on her breathing. She was both confused and terrified.

"From the fact the ghost bodies have gone and their clothes are back again, I'm assuming it's over?" Ryker asked.

She nodded, still trying to get her thoughts in order.

"Care to share?" he asked quietly.

"Annie was more special than you realized." She straightened and weighed her options. How much should she tell him? She reached for her amulet and played with its smooth surface as she struggled to find the right words. "All Witches share common magical abilities in potion-making, healing, illusion, and enchanting. But our real power comes from our kinetic magic; earth, water, air, and fire. If Annie was a Crossroads Witch, she was one of the rare few who are born every generation with the ability to tap into earth magic, the strongest of the elements. Earth magic is pulled from Yggdrasil, the Tree of Life."

Keira focused on the brightest star in the sky. This far from the blazing lights of the city, the sky was blanketed with pinpoints of light from suns millions of miles away. "When a Crossroads Witch or Warlock dies, their essence is absorbed back into Yggdrasil. It allows us to retain a balance in the strength and power we can draw from. The more powerful the Witch, the more power we can draw. However, when we pass, that power must return to the earth."

"I'm with you so far," he said.

She pointed to the crime scene. "The missing hair, tied feet, gouged-out tongue, and *oesobros* brand on the forehead are part of the ceremony performed to ensure power doesn't return to Yggdrasil. I suspect you also found nettles down their throats."

His brow crinkled. "But only Annie was Crossroads."

Keira shook her head. "I wouldn't bet on that. The thing that doesn't make sense is the missing blood. That's not part of the ceremony."

Her voice died on the breeze. The only sound was the crackling of the embers as the burning wood popped under the pressure of the heat.

Ryker scratched his forehead. "Let me get this right. You think another coven has done this to give them more power than the Crossroads Coven?"

She shook her head. If only that were the answer. Only one group possessed the knowledge to perform the ceremony. *The Order.*

She wanted to deny it. Surely there was another explanation. Her mind screamed until her ears ached from the sound. This wasn't supposed to be happening. Her mother died to ensure it couldn't happen. Yet, somehow, history was repeating itself.

Mother Earth, how could you do this to us again? Haven't we already given enough?

She hauled in a breath and released it slowly. There was no reason to panic. The Order might be back, but killing three Witches wouldn't cause the gate to open.

Squaring her shoulders, she met his intense gaze. "It's not another coven. I need to confirm a few things to be one hundred percent positive, but based on what I've seen here, the Order of Chaos is behind this."

He frowned. "Never heard of them. Are they an out-of-state cult?"

The burden of knowledge pushed down on her shoulders. "I would say they consider themselves more of a religion, and my guess would be they never left."

"Doc, you're not making any sense."

The truth had to come out sooner or later. She only hoped Ryker and Deacon had the manpower and the Crossroads coven possessed the strength to fight whatever war the Order was about to wage. "The Order worships Leviathan as their God. Leviathan was imprisoned in Hell for crimes against Humans, and the Order has spent the past five thousand years trying to break their God out of prison. The only thing stopping them is their inability to break down the gate to the passage between Earth and Hell. Through the power channeled from the earth through Yggdrasil, the gate to hell remains sealed."

Her voice faltered and she broke out in a cold sweat. "Without Crossroads' ability to harness that power Leviathan will return to wreak havoc on the earth. The lives of nearly eight billion people are dependent on the gate remaining closed."

SEVEN

WHEREVER YOU WILL GO

Ryker stood rooted to the spot and stared at her. Keira couldn't tell from his expression what thoughts were running through his head. His face was etched in stone. In the dim light, she could only work out that his intense blue eyes were fixed on her. With each second that passed, the silence became thicker and more uncomfortable.

A low growl finally broke the silence. "If you didn't want to tell me, you could have just said so instead of blaming it on a fairytale." He snatched the clothing from the stones, threw them into the evidence box, and headed down the path. His stiff gait as he passed her reflected his anger.

"It's fucking Roswell two all over again. Not on my watch," he mumbled under his breath.

Her mouth dropped at his scathing tone. Of all the possible reactions, this was not even remotely on the list.

She raced to catch up with him. "I was telling you the truth."

He halted and spun around so fast, she almost didn't stop in time. "Look, these were good people." His eyes flashed ominously as he towered over her. "I want to find whoever did this so their families can have some closure. And I don't need some delusional witch doctor blaming a bogeyman. People did this, whether a Supernatural, Gifted, or Natural, but a person, not some mythical monster. Are we clear?"

"I'm not saying a person didn't do this." She waved her hand. "I'm just saying the people behind this are trying to—"

"If you even try and float your nutbar ideas to the victim's families, I'll run you out of town so fast your broom won't be able to catch up with you. You were asked here to help us find out who did this, not scare people into thinking a fictional God is behind the killings. We barely survived the last hoax."

She was confused. How did he not know about his origins? Deacon knew the purpose of the Crossroads and the existence of the gate. Surely someone he considered his son would also know?

Over the years, she had met numerous Vampires and Demons. While it was typical for younger Vampires to be oblivious to the tumultuous past that had spawned them into existence, she had been confident someone with Ryker's responsibility would be more educated on the subject. Especially considering his connection to a Primordial Vampire. She was about to plead her case when his ringtone pierced the night air.

He threw an irritated glare at her as he answered. "Ryker."

When he turned his head away, she breathed a sigh of relief. She was on the brink of faltering beneath the weight of his unwavering stare. But her mind was in turmoil over his accusations and his dismissal of her as a lunatic.

"When?" he demanded.

Her head snapped around. From the tortured way the word was ripped from his throat, whatever he had just been told wasn't good.

"Where?" Their eyes met, and a heartbeat later, he nodded and said, "On my way. Make sure you keep the area cordoned off and let the medical examiner know he needs to get there ASAP."

Ryker barked out more orders and headed down the path toward the exit before he hung up.

She ran to catch him. "What's happened?"

"We've got another body. This time at Haverhill."

"Is it …" She trailed off, not able to give voice to the question that burned in her throat.

"Afraid so."

His resulting silence spoke volumes. A sour taste erupted in her mouth as she struggled to match his brisk pace along the darkened path.

As with the drive to Mystery Hill, the distance to Haverhill happened at breakneck speed with full lights and sirens. Keira gripped the seat the entire way, unused to weaving in and out of traffic at top speed as if they were on an Olympic downhill slalom.

She was so focused on not plastering her last meal over the windshield, she failed to notice where they were until they came to an abrupt halt.

"You are not to upset anyone, you hear?" he ordered as he reached for the door. "These people are scared enough without having someone come in and stir up a hornet's nest with a fantasy story."

She bit her tongue, but she was sorely tempted to let him know just how real the danger was. Problem was, he would block her access to the scene if she did.

She exited the car and counted to three before saying, "Fine."

"Why is it when a woman says that word, they never mean it?" he muttered as he headed up the small embankment that bordered the roadside.

A cluster of trees hid the hill from view. Around her, traffic had been diverted to a single lane, and yellow tape cordoned off the area. She hiked up the gravel driveway and stopped at a sign proudly boasting the Haverhill Historic Society. The slope of the land and the proximity to the river were oddly familiar. Not able to put her finger on it, she ignored the uneasy feeling and raced to catch up to Ryker. He was already speaking to two uniformed officers by the time she reached him.

The moment she neared, the conversation halted, and the deputies cast curious glances at her. At first, she thought Ryker intended to ignore her as he fired questions at his men.

But once they finished briefing him, he cleared his throat and nodded in her direction. "Dr. Wynter is the expert we've called in to help. She helped track down that Crucifix Killer in Nevada last year."

The taller of the two officers stepped forward and tipped his hat. "Deputy Leon Trudeau, at your service. Pleased to meet you, ma'am. We appreciate the assistance."

A snort from the older and stouter deputy caught her attention. He looked as though he'd just swallowed a whole lemon.

"You have to ignore my partner, Deputy Mitos, ma'am," Leon said. "He tends to be suspicious of all strangers."

The older man's eyebrows lowered and pinched together. "That's because you can always guarantee they bring trouble with them."

Ryker gave Mitos a pointed stare. "Deputy Mitos is an Essex native, and his default position is to blame the tourists, despite the fact the money they bring in pays his wages."

Mitos scowled. "That doesn't mean they aren't guilty. You mark my words. It'll be some goddam tourist, high on some goddam designer drug, who's gotten themselves caught up in all this paranormal shit. Too many horror movies, Facebook,

Tok Tick, Insta-thingy, and the other crap brainwashing apps their shit-for-brains minds live in."

Ryker rubbed his forehead. He'd obviously had this conversation with his deputy on numerous occasions. "And you're probably right. But we can't lock up every single tourist just on your say so."

Mitos harrumphed. "Can't see why not."

Leon chuckled. "I know you did things a little differently back in the old days. But today we need probable cause and what else … oh yeah … something we like to call evidence."

This was as far as Ryker's patience stretched. "Can we please focus on the scene?" He turned to Leon. "I want that medical examiner here now. A crowd is building up too near our crime scene, and there are far too many of them filming our victim. We need to remove the body before any of them get close enough to see how our vic died."

Leon nodded and pulled out his cell phone. "On it, boss."

Ryker faced Deputy Mitos. "Wilber, I need you to move the crowd back. They're too close. Take a couple officers with you and move the line back thirty feet." Without waiting for an answer, Ryker headed toward the cordoned-off area near the clump of trees. He halted and turned back to her. "You coming?"

Not needing to be told twice, she snapped into action and caught up with him.

"According to Mitos and Trudeau, our vic is Rose Banks," he said.

As they passed through the gates and the darkened clump of White Pine and Red Maple trees became more visible, her steps slowed. She stared at the giant oak that stood out from the pine and maple trees surrounding it.

She stumbled. "I thought you said we were in Haverhill."

"We are."

Her gut twisted into a tight knot. The girth of the oak was wider and much higher, but the uniquely shaped cavities and crevices were familiar. "But I recognize this tree, and it's located in Pentucket."

"That's right, Pentucket was renamed Haverhill sometime in the 1800s."

She brought her hands up to cover her mouth. Could this night get any worse?

He frowned. "Doc, you have to stop doing that. I don't know if you're about to throw up or if you've just seen a ghost."

She gulped and let her hands fall to her sides. "You're right on both accounts."

The moon shone through the canopy, allowing light into the wooded area. They circled the giant oak. Unwilling to look down just yet, she stared ahead as Ryker dismissed the officer guarding the victim.

He crouched and inspected the body. "Shit, you better take a look at this, Doc."

Unable to put off the inevitable, she crossed the short distance and peered through the darkness. She could make out a body on the ground but not much more. While lights had been set up a short distance away, they were yet to be switched on.

She squinted. "Unlike you, I do need some light."

"Sorry."

He stood and made his way over to one of the large halogen lamps.

The sudden brightness had her blinking rapidly to adjust her eyesight. When she looked down again, she understood what Ryker meant. Apart from the location, the body was in the same condition as the victims at Mystery Hill, including the scalping and the mark of a serpent carved into the woman's forehead.

Keira's hands trembled as she took a step closer. Any hope this new death wouldn't echo the ones at Mystery Hill flew out the window.

Ryker crouched beside the body. "Rigor mortis has set in, so I can't open her mouth, but I suspect we'll find her tongue has been cut out."

Keira scrutinized the large, jagged cut across the woman's throat. "The thing that's confusing me is the missing blood. It's not part of the ritual, and for the ritual to work, the sacrifice would have to be here."

"But that's impossible. If she was killed here, blood would have seeped into the ground, and there'd be splatter everywhere. The area is clean. The same as Mystery Hill. Rose was killed somewhere else and dumped here."

Keira disagreed, but she kept it to herself. "Did you know her?"

He nodded. "Not as well as some of the others, but I've seen her around town. Rose has … had a small farm outside of Danvers. The farm's been in her family since Salem was called Salem Village."

"I have to ask, is she Crossroads coven?"

"Not sure, but I don't think so."

Keira crouched and reached for the woman's arm just as one of Ryker's deputies shouted, "Hey, sheriff, the medical examiner's here."

She retracted her hand before she made contact with Rose's body. It wouldn't look good if they caught her touching the victim before the medical examiner did. She would determine if Rose was from Crossroads coven later. A mark on the inside of the woman's arm caught her attention. An image had been hastily drawn on the skin.

"Take a look at this," Keira said.

Ryker inspected the poorly drawn symbol. "That looks like a chain."

Things had just gone from bad to worse, if that was at all possible. "It is. She was sending us a message."

His forehead crinkled. "Message? What message?"

"Notice these broken links?" She pointed to the middle of the chain. "It means the chain is broken, and we have a traitor."

"Someone in the coven?"

"No. At least, I hope not. If that were the case, the symbol would have represented family. I think Rose is telling us she knew her killer." Keira stood and stared at the ancient tree that dwarfed them. "I am positive you'll find that Rose, as well as Sarah and Zac, are cloistered Crossroads Witches." Her throat was raw as she drew in a deep breath and let it out again. "We need to protect the rest of them before it's too late."

"What do you mean they're all Crossroads?"

"Look, I can't explain it right now, but I am pretty sure that only Crossroads Witches are being targeted. I'll need access to their bodies to confirm, but if I'm right, the Order has managed to identify the cloistered members."

Ryker shot up. "You're not making any sense."

She hesitated. Not sure whether she should be telling him the truth. "Crossroads covens exist all over the world. They always have, but they keep the identities of many of their members under wraps. We refer to these members as 'cloistered' and these members are a heavily guarded secret. That way, any direct attack on the coven by the Order will have minimal impact on the power being channeled to the gate."

"Shit!" He groaned as he ran his fingers through his hair. "You Witches will be the death of me. Why are there so many secrets with you?"

"Because we got sick of everyone trying to kill us." She couldn't help the hint of bitterness that crept into her voice. "And that includes Vampires."

"And you didn't do your fair share of hunting us down?"

An uneasy silence descended on them as they stared each other down.

He held up his hands in surrender. "Look, there's no point in opening up old wounds. It's in the past, and that's where it should stay."

She had to agree with him. No one was blameless for what had transpired throughout history.

A flashing light from somewhere in the distance caught their attention, and Ryker's phone beeped to indicate a message had arrived.

"The ME's wanting to do his job," he said after pocketing his phone. "Is there anything else you need here before I let him and the crime scene team in?"

She took one last glance at the site and shook her head. Whoever had done this knew what they were doing. Even with her powers, she wouldn't find any clues. Forensics were just wasting their time.

Within minutes, the ME took charge of the body and authorized Rose's removal for autopsy. Once done, the small contingent of crime scene investigators moved in, and Ryker handed the scene into their care.

While Ryker checked in with his team, she waited on the sidelines and studied the flurry of activity in the immediate area. Some locals were doing their best to work out what happened underneath the iconic landmark. She had to admit, whoever did this had done their homework. According to history, the Worshipping Oak was where early Puritans held their weekly services. Few people knew the tree also served as an altar for ritual sacrifices, and the large boulder that rested within its roots originally resided in Mystery Hill.

As much as she wanted to run from the impending disaster, it was not an option. The choice had been taken out of her hands. If the gate was under threat, she would stay and stop that delusional bitch from coming through.

Leviathan had another thing coming if she thought she could stroll through the gates without a fight.

Ryker returned and nodded at the exit. "I'm finished here. How about I take you back to your hotel?"

They made their way back to the small gravel road in silence. Her mind raced with questions, and Keira endeavored to put them into order. "We need to speak to the few coven members who have stayed out in the open, and we need the names of everyone in the coven. They must be protected at all costs."

"I can't do anything till morning. Rose's body needs to be officially identified and the next of kin notified. I'm not scaring the local population until we have more information."

She remained silent, unsure whether she was still welcome within his investigation. He had to let her stay. The only question was … how was she going to convince the Vampire sheriff that Armageddon was knocking at the gates?

They had cleared the road blockade and were headed toward Salem when Ryker finally spoke. "I noticed you touching the ground when you were doing your spell earlier. I'm guessing that you're an Earth Witch?"

She raised a brow and nodded. His observation skills were well suited for his job. She held on tight to the grab handle as they took another corner at record speed. "Believe it or not, you're one of the few people in a long time who's seen any of my spells in action."

He chuckled. "I hope that doesn't mean you're planning on killing me now?"

While she could hear the humor in his voice, the edge told her he was still suspicious of her. She pretended to think about it. "Jury's still out on that one."

He flashed her a mischievous grin. "That's good, cause juries just love me."

Her breath faltered. How could one man be so irritating one moment and so … so appealing the next. He really should come with a warning sign.

He turned serious. "I meant what I said before. We've all come here to start fresh and live our lives in peace. I took an oath to protect these people, and I take my job seriously. I won't stand by and have someone come in and waltz around spouting fables as the explanation behind all of this. From what you've told me, I think this is an old-fashioned power play. One coven trying to destroy another."

"I'm only after the truth."

While her magic didn't extend to mind-reading or knowing who was inherently good or bad, she knew he was being honest with her. He cared about what happened to those under his charge, and that included the Naturals as well as Supernaturals. Perhaps that was why she'd allowed him to witness what she was capable of. But right now, she didn't have time to dwell on why she trusted him. She needed to work out how she was going to persuade him to let her remain on the case.

Ryker adjusted his grip on the steering wheel. "I think the Witches would be more inclined to talk to one of their own kind."

"I'd have to agree."

He let out a growl from the back of his throat. "Look, Doc, you clearly think you have inside knowledge on what's going on here, and I could use your help, but I also think I'd be better off putting you back on the next flight to LA."

She held her breath and waited for him to finish.

"If I let you stay, I need you to promise you'll keep your hocus pocus ideas to yourself." He gave her a pointed stare. "Do we have a deal?"

She exhaled and nodded. "Deal. I won't mention my theory to anyone unless you give me the go-ahead."

"That's not exactly what I said, but it'll do."

The drive back to Salem was as breakneck as their drive out, and Keira doubted whether she would ever be able to eat again.

Marcus jerked the car door open the moment they pulled up to the curb. "Where have you been? I've been trying to reach you for hours."

She frowned. "You knew I was at the scene. Why didn't you phone me?"

"I did, about a billion times."

She reached into her tote and pulled out her phone. "You're exaggerating. It was only twenty-two." She frowned at the other number listed as a missed call. Why would Dayna be phoning? Her sister knew she would call her when she had answers. Cursing her sister's inability to listen, Keira ignored the missed call and focused on Marcus. "What's the problem, and why are you loitering on the pavement in your pajamas instead of in your room at this time of night?"

Marcus crossed his arms and scowled. "I would be in my room if I hadn't been evicted."

"What do you mean, evicted?" Ryker asked. He came around from the driver's side. "Those rooms are permanently reserved for Deacon. The hotel wouldn't dare throw you out, especially at night looking like that."

"They didn't," Marcus said through gritted teeth. "And because they're booked up, there's no other room available. This is a disaster. I was in the middle of editing."

Keira held up her hand. "Wait. You're making no sense at all. Who's taken over your room?"

"Someone with a truckload of Louis Vuitton luggage claiming to be your sister. Which is impossible because A, you would have told me you had a sister, and B, her Stella McCartneys so matched her Vans Old Skool sneakers, you can't possibly be related to her."

Keira's head dropped into her palms, and she groaned. "Mother Earth, how the hell can you do this to me?"

She froze when she heard her name called. Marcus and Ryker swiveled at the same time. Dayna sauntered up the street, her impossibly long legs accentuated by stilettos and a minidress that looked like it had come off a Paris runway.

Marcus pointed at Dayna. "That's her. She's the reason I'm homeless." He waved his arms. "And again, see the good, not boring, fashion choices. There was no way you two came out of the same side of the gene pool."

Ryker watched Dayna's approach. "That's your sister?"

She nodded.

He raised an eyebrow. "Your sister by blood, as in, same parents?"

She nodded again.

"And you're sure about that?"

She resisted the urge to roll her eyes. She was used to the effect her sister had on men. While the years changed, the opposite sex … not so much. Even Marcus, put out by Dayna's larger-than-life demands, was affected, and she detected a blush beneath his dark skin.

Dayna flew straight at her and enveloped her in a tight hug. "Where have you been?" She pulled away and held Keira at arm's length as she inspected her. "It's been so long. I missed you."

"We only just spoke the other day," Keira said.

"I know, and I know you told me to stay put, but I couldn't let you come here on your own. You're going to need my help."

Keira's gaze darted up and down the street. They were in a very public place, and Dayna was not known for her ability to be subtle.

Before Dayna said anything that could be taken the wrong way, she cut her off. "Dayna, I believe you've already met my teaching assistant, Marcus."

Dayna smiled and batted her eyelashes. "Yes, he was the darling boy who let me have his room."

Marcus scowled. "I didn't *let* you have anything."

"What happened to your last teaching assistant, Amanda something or other?" Dayna asked, ignoring Marcus' outburst. "She was far less emotional."

"She's now a research fellow at the Mayo Clinic," Keira replied with a huff. "Why are you here exactly?"

Dayna skipped over the question and arched a brow at Ryker. "And you are?"

"*Sheriff* Kincaid," Keira interjected, hoping her sister would get the hint and tone it down a few levels.

Dayna's smile widened, if possible, and she held out her hand as she gave him a once-over. "If you're the law around here, how does one go about getting arrested? Because I'm sure I can be all kinds of naughty."

Keira groaned. Of course, her sister would do the opposite. "Dayna!"

Without taking her eyes or hand off Ryker, Dayna said, "What? Just laying my cards on the table."

"Well, you can just put them back in the pack." Keira forced her voice to a lower level of panic. "We have work to do."

Dayna grinned and put an arm around her. "Oh, honey, you still haven't learned the art of multitasking, have you?"

Ryker let out a chuckle. "Are you sure you're related?"

Why did people keep asking that question? While Dayna was only slightly taller and colored her hair blonde, hiding the flaming red hair they'd inherited from their mother, they both possessed the same bone structure and eyes. How could people not see the resemblance?

She needed to take charge of the situation before it got out of control. "Look, I'm tired. How about we do this in the morning? Dayna, let Marcus have his room back. You can bunk with me."

Before Dayna could reply, Ryker interrupted. "Doc, I'll sort out something for Marcus. I suspect that you two haven't shared a room for quite some time, and I'm not sure the city could handle it if you did."

Dayna smiled at Ryker. "I knew I liked you."

"Are you sure you'll be able to find him something?" Keira couldn't leave Marcus out in the cold to fend for himself.

Ryker cocked his head and winked. "I'm the sheriff around here, remember? Besides, the Hampton Inn is just around the corner, and I'm sure they'll have a room available."

Dayna grinned and slid her arm into the crook of Keira's elbow. "Well, that's all settled then. Keira can see me to my room, and we will see you boys in the morning."

Keira shrugged at Marcus and mouthed "sorry" as she was being dragged to the hotel doors.

"Did you bring Felix? It's ages since I've seen him," Dayna said as they headed toward the lobby.

"No, one of the neighbors is looking after him while I'm away. And stop changing the subject. Why the hell are you here?"

Dayna shrugged her shoulders. "I told you. I'm here to help. When we get to the room, you'd better let me know what's going on. From your expression, it's not good."

While Keira was grateful to see her sister, she was terrified at the same time. She knew her sister. Dayna would demand details of the deaths. Except Dayna, like her, would know what was going on and why. Unlike her, Dayna's solution to a problem was anything but subtle and quiet. Keira needed to put a muzzle on her sister. Otherwise, Ryker would send them both packing.

The weight that descended on her when she realized how the bodies were sacrificed grew heavier. For tonight, maybe Dayna didn't need to feel that burden. Keira would give her sister one more night of freedom.

Their ghosts could wait till the morning.

EIGHT

GRIMOIRE

At first, Keira's mind ignored the insistent but irregular high-pitched beeps. She finally gave it up as fruitless, reached from under the covers, and blindly grasped for her phone on the bedside table.

She read the message and shot up in bed, fully awake. "Oh, *Mother Earth*, no!"

She reread the message from her sister and cringed.

>Where are you? With sexy Sheriff Vamp and cute TA. What is he, by the way? Can't work it out. In Café Luna, the coffee shop next door.

Dayna was downstairs with Ryker and Marcus. Who knew what she had told them. Keira scrambled out of bed and fell to the floor. During her troubled sleep, she'd become one with the bedsheets. Once she disentangled herself, she flew into the shower and, in record time, was dressed and out the door, bypassing the lift and racing down the stairs to try and minimize the damage only her sister was capable of.

She burst through the stairwell into the main lobby and bumped into stunned hotel patrons, nearly knocking them over. "I'm so sorry, please excuse me."

Once she picked up the startled tourists' bags, she raced out the main doors.

Outside, in the early morning sun, she didn't have far to look. Dayna, Ryker, and Marcus were seated at a table beneath the awning of a small coffee shop. As expected, her sister stood out by a mile in her white summer dress with bright, lime green flowers.

Keira stopped short and checked herself. Ryker and Marcus shouldn't think she was concerned. And she certainly didn't want to give Ryker any more reservations than he already had.

She nodded to Ryker and Marcus. "Dayna, why didn't you come and get me on your way down?"

Dayna's wide smile lit up her face. "I did try and text you, but the sun was calling, and I couldn't wait any longer."

Keira stole a glance at the men. "How lucky you bumped into Marcus and the sheriff."

Her chest tightened. How long had they been with her sister, and how much damage control did she need to do?

Dayna nodded. "Ryker's been an absolute teddy bear and let me in on all the local haunts to visit while I'm here." She winked. "You know, the ones the tourists don't know about."

Keira raised both eyebrows. "He has, has he?"

At least he hadn't escorted her out of town. *Yet.*

He leaned back and tugged on his cap. "Just doing my civic duty."

Although she couldn't see it, she was sure he was laughing at her.

"Perhaps you should just stick to the tourist spots," she said to Dayna.

Dayna waved her hand dismissively. "Oh, hush. I'm in no danger here, especially if the local law is around."

Ryker grinned as he pulled out the seat next to him and indicated for Keira to sit. "That may be the case, but I'm not so sure of my welfare where you're concerned. Something tells me you are more than a handful," he said to Dayna.

Dayna giggled as she reached for her cup and winked at Ryker. "Oh, darling, you don't know the half of it."

Dayna's light and carefree tone brought a smile to Keira's lips. She'd missed her sister. A waiter came to take her order before she could determine what Dayna might or might not have said to Ryker and Marcus.

"I'll have green tea and a slice of toast, thank you." Keira turned to Ryker. "Did the crime scene investigators find anything after we left?"

"Nothing so far. They're doing a final sweep before packing up and admitting defeat."

"What about the medical examiner? When is the autopsy scheduled?"

Ryker stiffened. Not so much that someone watching their conversation would notice, but just enough for Keira to know he was wary of something. "I don't think this is a conversation we should be having here."

Her eyes quickly scanned the immediate area. They were at an isolated table with no other customers sitting nearby. "Why not? No one can hear us."

"I can't discuss an ongoing case with civilians."

Dayna leaned forward and said in a fake stage whisper, "I think he's referring to Marcus."

Keira held back a smile. Her sister could never read the room. "Marcus was already vetted and approved for this case."

"Well, it's not me. The sheriff was just asking me what brought me here to Salem, and I told him it was to help my big sister." Dayna popped a slice of melon into her mouth.

Keira tensed and turned her head to face Ryker. He casually leaned back in his chair as if he didn't have a care in the world. "Oh? I didn't realize you interrogated tourists."

He shrugged. "I generally don't."

While his tone was friendly, she could feel the distrust.

"I think the smexy vamp is wondering why I turned up unannounced shortly after you, considering I didn't get an invite," Dayna said.

Keira's gaze snapped to her sister, then back to Ryker. "Don't tell me you think Dayna has something to do with this mess?"

Ryker held up his hands. "Whoa, I didn't say that. I told you yesterday. I protect my own. I just need to know how much trouble you two are going to bring me."

A snigger from Marcus caught her attention, and she pinned her traitorous teaching assistant with a hard stare.

He feigned innocence. "What?"

She crossed her arms and squinted at him. "You know hundreds of other grad students are waiting in the wings for your job? That side gig of yours doesn't pay all the bills."

Marcus snapped his mouth shut and sank onto his chair.

Ryker leaned forward and placed his arms on the table. "Look, I didn't come here to argue with you. I meant what I said last night. I need your help."

She blushed at the rashness of her outburst. "Oh?"

"From what you've seen, what are we dealing with?"

She stared at the wisp of steam rising from her green tea. After his reaction the previous evening, she chose her words carefully. "I would like to say that it's a psychopath serial killer, because that would be the preferable option."

"I'm hearing a 'but' in there."

Keira hesitated before speaking. She would deal with this case the same way she would if he were an FBI special agent, not aware that things do go bump in the night. "From the way the victims were killed, we are dealing with a religious cult. Very organized, very devout, and very capable of completing their mission, whatever it may be. Their victims are specifically targeted, and they will stop at nothing to find more victims who meet their criteria."

He fidgeted with his cup before speaking. "I spoke to a contact at the FBI. According to him, no one comes close to you when it comes to cults."

She shrugged. "I wouldn't go that far."

"As long as you keep your wack job conspiracy theories to yourself, we'll get on just fine. I've already got my hands full with a spate of missing persons, with the killings at Mystery Hill and Worshiping Oak on top of it, not to mention we're generally stretched at this time of year with all the tourists. Your help would go a long way toward alleviating some of the pressure."

Dayna let out a surprised squeak. "Worshipping Oak? Was someone killed at Worshiping Oak? Why would you neglect that pertinent piece of information?"

Keira groaned. She'd briefed Dayna on the four victims, but deliberately held back where the fourth body was discovered. Her sister was not stupid. Dayna understood the ramifications of a sacrifice at that location.

Before she could get Dayna to keep the knowledge to herself, Dayna's phone rang. She glanced at the screen and threw Keira an irritated look before swiping the phone off the table and standing.

"Saved by the bell, Sis. But don't think we won't be having words."

Dayna answered the call as she walked away from their table and stood far enough down the street, they couldn't hear her conversation.

Ryker adjusted his cap. "Look, Doc, I'm used to dealing with felonies and misdemeanors. Serial and cult killings are not exactly something we get every day, or decade, for that matter."

Careful to keep her expression neutral, Keira said, "The first thing we need to do is work out what sort of cult is behind these killings. If we can narrow it down, I can give you a profile that will help us find whoever is behind these murders."

"Where do we begin?"

Her hand came up, and her fingers played with her amulet. "I need to confirm all the victims were Crossroads."

"How will that help?"

"If they were, it will narrow down the organization behind the murders."

He nodded. "Okay, so we'll have a chat with Beatrice. She's one of the few Crossroads Witches I know of."

"No. We will speak to her, but not yet. I have another way to get a confirmation."

"How?"

"I need to take a look at the bodies."

Ryker reached into his pocket and threw some bills on the table. "Looks like we're taking a road trip to the morgue. I need to swing by my office first. How about I pick you up in an hour?"

"What did I miss?" Dayna asked as she returned from her phone call.

"Not much," Keira said. "Just working out a plan of attack on how I can best assist the sheriff with his case." She turned back to Ryker. "I'll be ready in an hour."

Ryker nodded at them, then headed down the street.

Dayna sighed as he made his way to his squad car. "I could stare at that tight butt all day."

Keira and Marcus made groaning noises at the same time.

Dayna turned back to them and shrugged her shoulders before sitting down. "What? I call it as I see it." She cast a glance at Marcus over her sunglasses. "I must admit, your butt looks a bit better in jeans than it did in those silly flannel pants you wore last night."

Marcus lifted a leg from under the table to show Dayna the material. "I should hope so. It's from Rag & Bone's new urban range collection."

"I thought I recognized it. I heard they flew right off the shelves."

Keira dropped her head into her hands. This was not happening. She had died and gone straight to hell. She shifted closer to Dayna and Marcus. "We've got more important things to think about than today's special at Nordstrom. Can we please focus on why we're here?"

Dayna scrunched her nose. "You always take the fun out of everything." She sighed dramatically. "Fine, have it your way. But from now on, make sure you don't miss things like say … another killing at a site of significant importance, if you know what I mean."

Keira drew in a deep breath. "I think the Order is back."

Her sister's eyes flew open wide. "You have got to be fucking kidding me!"

Keira's gaze darted around the café. Dayna's voice likely carried right around the block. "Not here. Let's go somewhere we can't be overheard."

Keira briefed Dayna and Marcus in her room. For once, Dayna remained quiet. Whether it was because she was too shocked to speak or because she struggled to find the words, Keira wasn't sure.

The room remained silent once she finished speaking. Marcus rubbed his jaw, deep in thought, while Dayna stared out the window onto the street below.

"So that explains why we feel the drained energy," Dayna said. "What I don't get is the missing blood. As far as I'm aware, that is not part of the ritual to stop magic from returning to Yggdrasil."

"Neither do I. I can't figure out what the Order is up to. Ryker thinks the bodies were killed elsewhere and staged at Mystery Hill and Haverhill, and, for now, I'm going to let him think that."

"Do you think it might be a ruse to distract the Crossroads coven from knowing what they are up to?"

Keira shook her head. "No. There's a reason behind the missing blood, and Leviathan is at the center of it."

Marcus woke from his trancelike state. "But I always assumed stories of Leviathan were just that, stories."

Dayna let out a self-deprecating laugh. "So did we. What I'd give to go back to being ignorant."

Keira dropped onto the edge of her bed. "As much as I agree with you, we know better, and the choice has now been taken from us. We must find whoever's behind these murders before someone else dies. And from experience, members of the Order could be anyone."

Dayna turned away from the window, her eyes filled with concern. "But if they've depleted our power, I don't understand how. We felt the drain when they made their first sacrifice. You know that yourself. And we have no idea who the Crossroads coven members are now. And then there is the matter of the cloistered members."

"Cloistered?" Marcus asked.

Dayna nodded. "Crossroads Witches have been targets throughout history. To protect themselves from being wiped out by our enemies, only a small portion of the coven membership is known to the outside world. The remainder, which are referred to as 'cloistered' are a heavily guarded secret. Every Crossroad Witch swears a blood oath to never reveal any of the cloistered members no matter the situation."

"It's not an oath they take lightly, and they will go to their grave to protect the identities," Keira said.

"Which begs the question, how are we going to stop Leviathan?"

Keira swallowed hard. The next words from her mouth were ones she never expected she would say. They went against the vow she took after she left Salem. "It should be fairly easy to track down the members who are known. We may have no choice but to reveal ourselves and rejoin the coven to bolster their power."

At first, Dayna said nothing. She eventually let out a slow breath before speaking. "What makes you think they'll believe us? For all they know, we're dead. We died a dozen lifetimes ago, and I hardly think this lot will let strangers in." She paced the room, then stopped and fixed her stare on hotel's bland artwork. "We may need to call in reinforcements."

Keira frowned. "What do you mean?"

"We could call in Crossroads Witches from the two gates we know about. I know a few of the Amesbury ones. I'm sure they would help if we asked."

"The problem with that plan is that it would mean we need to come clean with who we really are …" Keira narrowed her eyes. "Unless you already did?"

Dayna pouted. "Don't be a daft duck. We made a promise to each other, and I've kept it."

Keira shook her head. "I don't think we're there yet. We need to work out how to get the coven to speak to me. But I'm not ready for them to know who we are."

Discovering Salem Crossroads Witches they had never met in their midst was bound to be a shock.

"You knew it wasn't going to last. The gift was given to us for a reason."

Keira looked down at her hands resting on her lap. "Curse, you mean."

"What do you need Marcus and me to do?" Dayna asked.

Keira paused before replying. They had only one option. "We need the family Grimoire. It might help us understand why they took the blood."

Dayna twisted a strand of hair around her finger and frowned. "I knew you were going to say that. I'm assuming the book of spells is still where you left it?"

Keira nodded. "I have to go with the sheriff, so you and Marcus must retrieve the Grimoire without anyone noticing."

Dayna's brows furrowed. "But I don't understand. It's ours. It's only on loan to the library. Why can't we just go and pick it up?"

"We'd have to file the appropriate paperwork through legal representation, and that would take too long." Keira reached into her bag, pulled out her wallet, and scanned its contents. When she found what she was after, she pulled out three cards and handed them to her sister. "Marcus will know what to do, but only I can gain access to the area. You have to pretend to be me, and you'll need to make sure no one knows you were there or that the Grimoire was taken out of the building."

Dayna accepted the cards and leafed through them. "Okay, but I'm not sure I'll be able to pull off the boring spinster schoolmarm look." She gave Keira the once-over. "And please don't tell me I have to wear your clothes."

Keira raised her chin. "And what's wrong with my clothes?"

"Honey, we don't have that much time for me to list the reasons," Dayna said as she rested her hand on her hip. "Just as well I brought extra clothes. I had a feeling you wouldn't have packed properly."

Marcus made a T with his hands. "Time out. You know I'm still standing here." He turned to Keira. "Where exactly am I going? And why?"

She rubbed her forehead. This was only going to work if Marcus played his part. While her sister could pass for her visually, she would never be granted access to the place if they had the slightest suspicion about her motives.

"You're going to steal a book from the rare collections archive at Beinecke Library at Yale."

Marcus blinked at her. "Are you out of your cotton-pickin' minds?" He shouted as he waved his arms in the air. "If I get caught, I can say goodbye to my doctorate and any hope of an actual career. Not to mention my channel's ratings will go down the toilet."

"Oh, fiddle-faddle," Dayna said. "You won't get caught. You're with me. We'll be in and out of there before you know it, and no one will be the wiser."

Marcus choked at her words. "You're kidding me, right? I've known you for less than twenty-four hours, and you're the least quiet person I've ever met. You wouldn't know how to blend in if your life depended on it. Jocks during pledge week are quieter than you."

Keira shot up from the bed. "Enough. Marcus, we need this more than you know. I wouldn't ask you if it wasn't important. I need you to trust me on this one. I can't explain now, but I will as soon as we have more than five minutes to spare."

She spun to face her sister. "And as for you, leave Marcus alone. He's extremely gifted, and you will need him to get you in and out. I don't want to break in a new teaching assistant."

Marcus pinched the bridge of his nose. "What book is so important anyway?"

"The book of Hávarðr," Dayna said.

Marcus' jaw dropped. "I'm sorry, I don't think I heard you correctly. I could have sworn you just said the book of Hávarðr."

"I did. It's our family's book of spells," Dayna said.

"But that can't be right. The book of Hávarðr *was* one of the oldest and most powerful books of spells. It was lost during the Dark Ages. From memory, it was destroyed in a fire after a warlock attempted to steal it."

Keira glared at her sister.

Why on Mother Earth, would she tell him the book's true name?

She rubbed her forehead. The cat was out of the bag now, may as well let the rest of the litter out. "Yes, and no. At the time, it was the most powerful collection of spells. Rúna Hávarðr began the tradition of recording information on parchment around the seventh century. She then passed down her knowledge and her spells to her children, who, in turn, added to them and passed them to their children. Unfortunately, knowledge of this ever-growing and powerful collection of spells expanded, and there were countless attempts by other Witches and Warlocks to steal it.

"Just after the Vikings lost their final battle with the English at Stamford Bridge in 1066, our ancestor, Frig Skógr, a descendant of Rúna Hávarðr, lost her husband during an attempt by a local coven to steal the book. She was fearful the next attack would harm her young children, so she transcribed all the spells from the original book onto paper. At the time, paper had only just been introduced to Europe and was only used by scholars and royalty. No one suspected what she was doing or why. Once she was done, she bided her time and waited for the next attack. The Warlock was too stupid to realize that stealing the book had been too easy. As he stepped foot out of the house, the original copy of the book of Hávarðr burst into flames."

Dayna fidgeted with her bracelet. "The attacks stopped soon after word got around that the book had been destroyed. It was around this time that Frig moved to Amblesberie and was welcomed into the Crossroads coven guarding the gate at Stonehenge. Our very smart ancestor continued to follow tradition and record her most powerful spells. Each generation since then has added to it while making sure to guard its secrets."

The room fell quiet, and Marcus stared down at his sneakers. He finally raised his head. "Can I do a video on it for my channel?"

"Absolutely not!" the sisters shouted in unison.

By the time Ryker was due to return, Marcus had agreed to carry out Keira's hastily put-together plan. To give him credit, he succumbed a lot sooner than she'd expected. The fact that she promised him a tab at a bar of his choice and agreed to give him extra time off to finish his video may have swayed him more than her pleas. Once they rented a car and found clothing Dayna consented to wear that wouldn't attract too much attention, Keira waved them off.

She stared at the last spot she had seen them before the car turned the corner and slowly released her pent-up breath. "Mother Earth, please let them return with the Grimoire. Because I don't know what will happen if we have to face the upcoming storm without it."

NINE

CASPER'S DICTUM

Moments after Dayna and Marcus' rental car turned onto the main thoroughfare, Ryker's squad car, with its dented front fender, made its way toward Keira. How it only sported a single indentation from the way he drove was beyond her. The speeds he'd achieved the day before would put *Fast and Furious* to shame.

A woman behind Keira cleared her throat. "Excuse me. These are for you."

One of the waitresses from Café Luna held a cupholder tray with two takeaway coffee cups featuring the café's logo on the heat sleeves. The nearly transparent white shimmer gave her away as a Witch.

Keira stared blankly at the woman. "I think you're mistaking me for someone else. I didn't order anything."

The waitress laughed. "I know you didn't, the sheriff did."

Ryker's cruiser pulled up to the curb, and he flung open the passenger door. "Morning, Nita."

Nita's smile morphed into a broad grin. "Morning, sheriff. I see you're bringing on a better class of deputies."

Ryker chuckled. "I think Dr. Wynter here is a little too upmarket for us backwater folk. She's out from California to help us on the Mystery Hill case. That's all."

Nita's face dropped. "Oh, I see." She turned to Keira and gave her a sympathetic smile. "Folks around here are mighty scared. We appreciate any help catching whoever did this. You need coffee or good food, day or night. You just call me." Nita pointed to the café. "That's my café. Best coffee and best apple cider donuts this side of the Mississippi." She handed Keira the cupholder and pressed a brown bag into her other hand. "On the house. You and the sheriff just catch those murderers."

Before she had a chance to respond, Nita waved to Ryker, then spun on her heels and raced back into the café to deal with her customers.

Keira stared open-mouthed at Nita's retreating figure.

"I know things are laid back in LA," Ryker said. "But here in the real world, the clock is ticking."

She jolted out of her inertness, handed him the cups, and got in the car. No sooner had she clicked her seatbelt in place than they were peeling into traffic and navigating their way through the narrow streets to the city's outskirts.

"Green tea," he said, breaking the silence.

"Pardon?"

"I got you green tea. You ordered it before, so I assumed that's what you drink," he said as he reached for the second drink in the dual cup holder.

The nutty aroma of his coffee wafted through the car. Should she be pleased or worried that he paid attention to the small things?

He took a gulp from his steaming cup while weaving in and out of traffic.

"Should you be drinking and driving like that?" she demanded as she gripped the grab bar attached to the passenger door.

He flashed her a boyish grin and casually placed the cup back into the front console. "Doc, you're safe with me. In my one hundred-odd years of driving, I've not had a single accident."

"That's not what the dent on your car tells me."

He let out a chuckle. "That ding? That was the result of a troublemaker resisting arrest."

She hoisted an eyebrow. "And so you decided to hit him with your car? Great policing skills there."

"Doc, for someone as smart as you, you certainly have some missing cogs in that big brain of yours. You seem to forget that we have the highest population of Supernaturals in the country. That dent was the perp's body hitting the car after he'd tried one too many swings at me." Ryker shrugged. "The car just happened to be in the wrong place at the wrong time."

Not knowing whether to believe him or not, she chose to change the topic. "Where is your ME based?"

His half-snort, half-laugh let her know he was aware of what she was up to. "What? How about, 'I'm sorry, sheriff, I misjudged you and besmirched your stellar driving skills'?"

She held on tighter as he weaved through traffic and overtook another car. Likely, all the color had drained from her face. "I would, but I'd need my stomach to do that, and I think we left it about three miles back."

"Buckle up then. There's a way to go before we get to Boston."

Despite their speed, the drive took longer than expected. Much to Ryker's horror, they slowed to a crawl as they hit more congested traffic the nearer they got to Boston.

They finally arrived at the Boston City Medical Examiner's Office and made their way down the rabbit warren of corridors.

"Have you been in an autopsy room before?" he asked as they neared their destination.

She shook her head in answer to his question.

The double doors had a sign above the entryway that read "*Hic locus est ubi mors gaudet succurrere vitae.*" Keira did a quick translation, "This is the place where death rejoices to help those who live."

If nothing else, that alone would have told her what lay beyond. While she had seen gruesome images from the crime scenes she'd consulted on and had been witness to more than a handful of dead bodies, what happened to them after they were taken away was not something she was privy to. Most students doing forensic anthropology would have exposure to autopsies as part of their study. But she was not most students, and her knowledge of anthropology came from living history—not reading about it.

"In your line of work, I didn't figure you for an autopsy virgin." He halted his stride and reached into his pocket. He handed her a small bottle no larger than a lipstick tube. "If you rub a little of this under your nose before we go in, it might help."

The label read "Peppermint Essential Oils." She opened it and sniffed the contents. Jolting back at the sharp smell that shot up her nose, she quickly put the lid back on and blinked rapidly. "I think I'll be okay." She handed him the bottle.

He ignored her and reached for the door. "Keep it. You're going to need it." With that, he disappeared into the room.

She squared her shoulders and followed him through the door. The moment she stepped inside, her senses were overloaded by the white floor-to-ceiling tiles and stainless-steel countertops, slabs, and sinks. Four enormous tables lined the far side of the room. A large halogen light the pathologist could position as needed hung over each table. Stainless steel mobile trolleys with various-sized tools were scattered around the room. Some tools she had seen before. Others looked like torture devices from a horror movie.

A dead body lay center stage on each slab. A gloved pathologist placed the internal organs from one of the bodies onto a grocery scale. She gulped as she took in the body from which the tissue had been taken. A Y-shaped incision crossed the woman's shoulders to meet mid-chest and extended down to the pubic region. The skin, tissue, and muscles had been peeled back, and the ribs were broken off to reveal the organs they protected.

A putrid and rotting odor wafted up Keira's nostrils. Her stomach churned, and bile rose from the depths of her stomach. The only thing that stopped the contents of her breakfast from being plastered over the sterile room was Ryker's gentle shake as he placed himself between her and the horrifying scene.

"Hey, Doc, you okay?"

His voice penetrated her stupor. She mentally shook herself and met his concerned gaze. "Yes, sorry. It just came as a shock."

The medical examiner, dressed from head to toe in green scrubs, scowled at her. "Young lady, if you don't have the stomach for this, I suggest you get the hell out of my autopsy room. I will not have you compromising the evidence. This job is hard enough without you adding to it."

Not wishing to make a scene, she quickly apologized. "Sorry. I'll be fine."

She swallowed once again to make sure she was not about to projectile vomit over the irate medical examiner.

Ryker reached for her hand and pried it open. She was tightly clutching the small bottle he had given her. He opened it and poured some of the oil on his finger.

"Next time, might I suggest you listen to me," he said in a teasing tone as he dabbed the substance between her nose and upper lip.

His fingers were gentle as they lightly touched her skin. She froze as her stomach again made somersaults. This time, the overpowering smell of the morgue had nothing to do with the heat that flared up from the pit of her abdomen. She was acutely aware of just how physically close he had gotten to her. She swallowed hard and took a half step away from Ryker.

What was wrong with her? She was losing it.

He handed her the bottle. "Perhaps we need to start this again." He turned back to the older man. "Dr. Patterson, Dr. Wynter is the specialist who will be working the case with me. I understand you've completed a preliminary examination of the three bodies from the other night."

Dr. Patterson pulled off his surgical gloves, picked up a brown manila folder, and handed it to Ryker. He sighed. "Well, we have more questions than answers. I can tell you that much."

Dr. Patterson moved to the bank of lockers, opened the door on one of them, and slid out an enormous stainless-steel slab. He pulled the zipper down to expose the corpse of Sarah Tracey. "In each of the victims, the carotid artery was cut. I originally assumed that exsanguination was the cause of death, but I'm no longer one hundred percent certain."

"What do you mean you're no longer certain?" Ryker asked.

Dr. Patterson opened two more lockers and retrieved the bodies of Zac and Annie. "With precise cuts to the carotid artery, the victims would have lost consciousness in fifteen to twenty seconds and bled out in a couple of minutes. When the artery was cut, the force of the pressure would have the blood gushing out in all directions. There was no blood found on the body or the surrounding area."

"We assumed they had been killed elsewhere, cleaned, and staged at the dumpsite," Ryker said.

Dr. Patterson shook his head. "That was my original thought as well. However, blood in corpses pools to the lowest point in the body based on position. Based on lividity and the pooling, they died in the positions we found them in." His brows furrowed. "Which is impossible considering their hearts would have stopped beating after losing forty percent of their blood. With no heart to pump the blood, we'd expect to see at least six pints left. We'll need to do some more tests, but their throats could have been cut postmortem and not perimortem, as we originally assumed. However, we're sure the tongues were cut out peri, and we found *urtica dioica*, more commonly known as stinging nettles, lodged down each victim's pharynx."

Ryker hid his shock well.

Keira shrugged. She had warned him they would find stinging nettles in the victims' throats.

Ryker rubbed the back of his neck. "You think the blood was extracted by another method?"

"I don't know. I've not seen anything like it before. In order to drain that much blood from a body, you'd need to keep the heart pumping. And that's only possible in an operating theater"

"You're saying a doctor is behind this?" Ryker asked, his tone incredulous.

Dr. Patterson shook his head. "No. It could be anyone in the medical profession with the appropriate skills and equipment." He nodded at the folder in Ryker's hands. "The other odd thing is that all three victims' blood type was B positive."

Keira tore her gaze from the ghostly-looking bodies. "Why is that odd?"

"Because only nine percent of Caucasians have that blood type."

That couldn't be a coincidence. The sudden chill that fell across the morgue sent a shiver up her spine.

Ryker gestured toward the morgue drawers. "What about Rose Banks, the body that came in last night?"

Dr. Paterson reached for a tablet on one of the benches and tapped on it. "I haven't had a chance to do an autopsy yet, but my assistants would have taken blood samples already. Oh, here it is … her blood type was B positive as well." He shook his head. "Based on the photos, I would say it's linked to these three. The lack of blood is the most worrying aspect. I can't confirm cause of death until I run some more tests."

"How long will that take?"

"As long as it takes. We can't discount the possibility they were killed by another method, and the blood removed postmortem. That way, the death could have been more controlled."

Keira's fingers tightened around her amulet. "Did you find a paralytic in their system?"

Dr. Patterson's forehead creased, and he readjusted his glasses. "Yes, we did, a high concentration of curare. Too high to be synthetically produced. How did you know?"

She pointed to the open wound on Annie's head. "With this type of sacrifice, there's a lot of pomp and circumstance that goes with it. They would need the victim incapacitated but alive and conscious."

The medical examiner shook his head. "It never ceases to amaze me the way people can be so malevolent toward each other. I know I should be used to it in this job, but there's always another depraved person around the corner."

He picked up another file from the metal countertop and looked directly at Ryker. "Which makes the next bit more tragic. Not that it wasn't tragic enough."

Ryker took the file and read the name on the folder. He frowned, and his head snapped up. "Annie Mallick?"

Dr. Patterson's tone was somber. "She was about ten weeks pregnant."

Keira's chest tightened. Despite not having met Annie, she couldn't help but be affected. No words could describe the sense of loss. From her conversation with Ryker, Annie had been an exceptional young woman.

Ryker flipped through the bundle of pages stuck to the folder, but from the way his jaw muscles contracted, he was having a difficult time reigning in his emotions.

He cleared his throat. "Did you determine time of death?"

Dr. Patterson nodded. "Yes. I estimate death around seven p.m."

Ryker glanced up from the page. "What about the others?"

"That's the odd thing, as best we can tell, they all died around the same time, but we have no idea the order in which they died."

"Which means we are dealing with a small, well-organized group of perpetrators," Ryker said.

Dr. Patterson shrugged. "I've given you the 'how'. The 'who' is your job, sheriff."

Keira's heart thudded in her chest. From the ME's tone, their visit was over. She inched closer to Sarah's body, and her gaze darted around the room. How in the hell was she going to do this? She needed to confirm all four victims were Crossroads. The only problem was the ME. She had already made a less-than-stellar impression on him. What would he think if she suddenly whipped out four dead people's arms and cast a reveal spell? She attempted to make eye contact with Ryker and groaned inwardly. Of course, he would be nose-deep in the manila folder Dr. Patterson had given him.

Without looking up, he said, "If you discover anything else from Rose Bank's autopsy, please let me know ASAP."

A cold sweat erupted across her forehead. They couldn't leave until she knew if all four were Crossroads Witches. What could she use to attract his attention? When her gaze fell on the manila folders in Ryker's hands, her pulse sped up. *Paper.*

That she could work with. She focused on the folders and, in a whispered breath, said, "*Labi et cadere.*"

Ryker's expression was priceless when both folders suddenly slipped out of his hands and fell to the floor. "Son of a—"

"Whoops," she said.

He squatted to pick up the papers and place them back into the folders. She knelt to assist him.

When she finally got his attention, she pointedly stared at him and then at the bodies, hoping Dr. Patterson didn't notice her bizarre behavior.

He stood and threw an irritated glare at her, then turned to Dr. Patterson. "Before I forget, I'm going to need Rose Bank's personal belongings."

"They're bagged and ready for you in my office. I'll just grab them and be right back."

After the door closed behind the ME, Keira pulled out Sarah's limp arm and placed her palm on the woman's icy skin.

Ryker snorted. "Very subtle. Next time maybe give me some advanced warning when you're going to do your mumbo jumbo."

Ignoring him, she tightened the grasp of her free hand around her alexandrite crystal. She dropped her voice to a whisper. "Here goes nothing."

She hadn't used this particular spell in a few hundred years. Not to mention both parties were ordinarily alive.

At first, nothing happened. Not ready to admit defeat, she redoubled her efforts. Her pulse sped up when her fingers lightly tingled. She focused on the pale skin of Sarah Tracey's forearm. Faint shadows crossed the dead woman's skin, and a murky gray stain seeped out and spread across the arm like a vine.

Ryker drew in a deep breath. "What the—?"

She placed the arm back into the body bag. "She's a Crossroads Witch."

Her heart thudding in her chest, Keira repeated the process for Zac and then Annie. While she already knew the answer deep down, part of her hoped she was wrong. Her hands shook as she raced across the room to Rose, the woman sacrificed at Worshiping Oak.

Keira cast the reveal spell. Beads of sweat erupted on her forehead, and bile rose in the back of her throat. Her whole body rebelled as she fought to stay upright. Never before had she wished so hard to be wrong about something.

Ryker placed a gentle hand on her shoulder. "Doc, are you okay? You're not going to faint on me, are you?"

She hauled her erratic and panicked thoughts into check, but her body flushed hot and cold at the same time.

Her throat became sandpaper. "Crossroads. They're all Crossroads."

<u>TEN</u>

SPELLBOUND

They'd spent thirty minutes firing questions at the medical examiner, and now they were ready to head back to Salem. Not to mention the smell had started to overpower the peppermint that had temporarily masked the rotting odor.

Ryker remained deep in thought the entire way back to the car.

"Did you know she was pregnant?" Keira asked as they reached the car.

Ryker halted in his tracks. "What are you implying? I have my pick of women. Why would I try anything with a child?"

She groaned out loud. "Get off your high horse. I didn't imply anything. I was wondering if anyone knew she was pregnant. Besides, why would I assume you're the father? Vamps shoot blanks."

He grinned. "But very skilled blanks, I've been told."

Her eyes rolled skyward. "Oh, Mother Earth, I don't need to hear about your conquests."

He frowned. "You don't? But you might learn something. That spinster look can't be getting you much action. Unless you're going for sexy librarian, which I could get onboard with."

She rubbed her forehead. "How did we manage to go from a teen pregnancy to your sexual conquests so fast?"

"Mine? I thought we were talking about yours, or according to your sister, lack thereof."

She opened her mouth to retaliate, thought better of it, and snapped it shut. His mischievous grin told her in no uncertain terms that when it came to that particular subject, he would have an answer for everything.

"How about we get back on track?"

Once they were in the car, he sat staring at the steering wheel. "How am I going to tell her parents she was pregnant?" he said, more to himself than her. "She didn't have a boyfriend, or at least not one her family was aware of."

Keira leaned back on the seat and considered their options. "They have a right to know. You can't hold back the truth just because you think it will hurt them."

He turned the key in the ignition. "Most of the time, I love my job. Today is not one of those days." They were back on the highway heading north before he spoke again. "This curare, if it wasn't synthetic, where do you think they got it from?"

She welcomed the distraction. The number of near-misses as he resumed his fast-paced driving was unsettling, to say the least. "Curare is used as a muscular paralysis without impairing sensation or consciousness. Naturals have been experimenting with it for hundreds of years but could never get the formula right. Because of the problems they were having, they produced it as a synthetic drug."

"Who would know how to make it?"

She considered the question. Apart from her mother, she had never met another person with the same skills. "Even within the magical community, the knowledge is hard to come by. Unless you've got a tribe of South American Yanomami living in Salem, I honestly don't know, but I'm concerned. That, coupled with the ability to ensure the heart remained pumping until the last drop of blood, quite honestly scares me."

"Do you think it's another coven?"

As much as it pained her, that was something she had considered. Some Witches over the years have voiced their displeasure at having to hide their abilities from Humans and might have turned to the Order. "At this point, I'm not discounting anything. It would explain why there were no footprints at the crime scenes."

He made a noncommittal grunt. "I can't discount any Supernatural. It could have just as easily been Vampires or Were's. The more important question is why."

She tensed. Without help, he wouldn't believe what she had to say. "I think we better see Deacon as soon as we get back." She checked the time. To her surprise, it was midafternoon. "And I think we're going to need something more than tea and coffee to get the bad taste out of your mouth."

"What bad taste?"

She grimaced and reached for her phone. "The one you'll have once our little chat with Deacon is done."

Deacon answered on the second ring. "What did you find?"

"They're all Crossroads."

"You're sure about this?"

She gripped the door handle tighter as they took a corner a little too fast. "Yes."

Deacon drew in a deep breath and exhaled. "That can only mean one thing. What do you need me to do?"

"We're on our way to you now. But before we discuss the next steps, you have to do something you should have done long ago. I don't know why, but you've kept Ryker in the dark. That stops today. The Order is behind this, and they won't stop till they kill every last Crossroads Witch. He needs to know everything. Clear your calendar for the rest of the day."

"Yes, ma'am."

ELEVEN

RING AROUND THE ROSIE

Ryker struggled to hide his surprise. *Yes, ma'am?* She spoke to Deacon like that, and all Deacon said was, "Yes, ma'am?" Others had lost their life for less. What the hell was going on?

The doc was pissed at something. Thank God it was not directed at him. He had witnessed a lot of magic in his lifetime, but nothing that came near to what she was clearly capable of. A volley of questions bombarded his overactive mind. One after another until he simmered on a low burn, but as much as it went against his nature, he held his tongue and remained quiet.

He stole a glance at the striking woman in the passenger seat, holding on for dear life. A few wisps of flame-red hair managed to pry loose from the severe bun at the crown of her head. Except for her hair, the rest of her was meticulously in place. Her clothes, while expensive, were understated. Everything about her screamed, "Keep your distance." Which only made him more intrigued.

She was an enigma. In the short time he had known her, he occasionally saw beyond the walls she erected, but she deliberately underplayed her true nature. Unlike Dayna. He was still trying to understand how they could possibly be sisters. Sure, they looked alike. But where Dayna was a force of nature, Keira was in a league of her own, driven by an air of self-reliant confidence coupled with an aching vulnerability.

He had spent the better part of the day trying to reconcile her outward appearance and how she appeared to the outside world with the softer person he was sure hid in the shadows. Her quick wit had surprised him more than once. She took no prisoners. That was clear. And to be honest, he enjoyed pushing her buttons. The woman gave as much as she got, which only made him more curious about her motivations.

The problem was that he couldn't quite put his finger on the true nature of her character. It was entirely possible she was a compulsive liar and crackpot. After all, what sane Witch thought she was hundreds of years old and believed the Devil was real? He was about to break the silence when his phone beat him to it.

The caller ID on the dash said Leon Trudeau. "What can I do for you, Trudeau?"

"Hey, boss, you far away?"

His voice came through the car's speakers a little too loudly. Keira visibly flinched at the booming sound.

Ryker turned down the volume before he replied, "Could be a while. What's up?"

"The Historical Society wants to know when they can open to the public again. Mildred's been on my case all day."

"Have the analysts released the scene yet?"

"Um … not that I know of," Leon said.

Ryker shrugged. "Well, that's your answer then."

"They're getting quite antsy about it. Are you close to the station? Maybe you can speak to them when you get back."

Ryker understood why the society was champing at the bit to reopen. Being the height of tourist season, every cent counted. His deputy knew the rules, but it seemed enforcing them was another issue.

"I'm a while away. Get Mitos to deal with them."

"He did. It set Mildred off. I think she's going to lodge a complaint. She took exception to him advising her to take her cankles and silly bird's nest hat home."

Ryker chortled under his breath. He had to agree with Mitos' assessment of Mildred's water retention problem in the lower parts of her legs.

"But Mildred doesn't wear hats," he said, imagining how irate she must have been.

"She wasn't. I think she was just having a bad hair day."

Ryker swore. Wilber Mitos was, by far, his oldest deputy. He was a year shy of retirement, and it was well overdue. While he was a good law enforcement officer, his cantankerous nature ensured most people steered well clear of him. And those who didn't, wished they had.

"Look, Leon, you're an officer of the law. You're used to dealing with this stuff. Sort it out."

Leon released a deflated breath. "Sorry, boss, it's just been a little more manic than normal. I hope your day fared better. Did you get anything from the autopsy results?"

"I'll fill you in tomorrow. I'm not sure when I'll be back at the station. Just make sure you keep your partner away from Mildred."

"Ten-four, boss."

By the time Ryker finished his conversation with Leon, they were pulling into the small parking lot behind city hall. Keira emerged from the car, her posture stiff. If she was tense before, she was bordering on statue-rigid now.

"Are you okay?" he asked cautiously.

She stood tall and pulled down her suit jacket to straighten it, all the while not meeting his gaze. Her lips set into a grim line, she turned to face him.

He was rattled by the uncertainty and fear reflected in her eyes. Torn between reaching out to her to assure her everything was going to be okay and turning tail and running a mile, he settled for doing neither. If she was this nervous about the conversation, he was positive he was not going to like it.

A weak smile cracked through her rigid exterior. "Fine, just feeling a little ill from your inability to keep to the speed limit."

He wasn't fooled. The emerald-eyed Witch was trying to make light of the situation.

The end of the public opening hours at city hall drew near, so the building was relatively quiet, with only the employees wandering around the deserted floors. When they reached Deacon's outer office, the one he used for mayoral duties, Ananya, Deacon's petite, grandmotherly secretary, looked up from her monitor and peered at them over the rim of her glasses.

"Hey gorgeous, how's my favorite Ladakee today?" he said as he strode across the room.

Ryker had known Ananya since she was a child, and their banter was time-worn.

Her wrinkled face, weathered by time, scrunched into a scowl as she glared at him. "It was going fine until a little while ago. He's in a right mood." She nodded toward the closed door. "And it began just after he found out you were coming to see him."

Ryker hooked his thumbs into his utility belt. "Sorry."

Ananya folded her arms and sat back in her chair. "What have you done now? Whatever it is, you'd better fix it."

He shrugged, as much in the dark as Ananya. "For once, it's not me." He indicated Keira, who was standing silently beside him. "If you want to take it out on someone, I'd go with her."

"Me?" Keira demanded, looking exasperated. "I've got nothing to do with it."

Ananya leaned forward and peered over her glasses at Keira. "So, you're the stuck-up Witch."

Keira visibly stiffened. Ryker groaned out loud. Of course, Ananya would take what he said out of context. He should have kept his mouth shut.

"That's not what I said, and you know it."

Ananya waved her hand dismissively. "All I know is you were rude not introducing us before you ran off this morning like I said. I could have died before you got back. I'm not getting any younger."

She turned to Keira and broke into such a full smile that her pristine false teeth shone brightly against her dark skin. "My dear, as Ryker evidently has no manners, I will introduce myself. I'm Ananya Gupta, Deacon's long-suffering secretary. If there's anything you need to make your stay comfortable, just let me know."

"Pleased to meet you, too," Keira said. She looked questioningly between him and Ananya. "Ryker didn't mention we were supposed to swing by here this morning. I suspect he might have been too busy planning the new land speed record to remember."

Ananya burst out laughing. "I like this one," she said, looking pointedly at Ryker.

Instead of replying, he chose to ignore her. Ananya had been admonishing him for the exact same thing ever since she was a child, fresh off the streets of Calcutta, where he and Deacon found her.

"Can we go in?" he asked before the two women ganged up on him.

Ananya cocked her head, and she winked. "Yes, but considering Deacon's mood, I'm not sure of your chances for getting out alive, or not dead, in your case."

He made his way over to the door and held it open for Keira.

Deacon was deep in conversation when they entered.

Ryker closed the door, and they took a seat on one of the couches along the far wall. Keira appeared to be listening to the phone conversation.

He lowered his voice. "It's Japanese. Odds are, he's talking to the mayor of Salem's sister city, Ota." He stopped and tuned into the discussion. After a moment, he turned back to her and nodded. "Yep, he's speaking to Matsubara, the current mayor. Should be interesting to see what excuse he uses this time."

"Excuses?"

"Matsubara has been trying to get Deacon to come for an official visit."

"And what's wrong with that?"

He shrugged. "Let's just say Tokyo is not somewhere Deacon, or I, could ever step foot again."

"Let me guess. Girls, money, or your dangerous driving?"

He placed a hand over his heart, feigning pain. "You wound me."

"Which was it?"

He grinned. "All three, if you must know."

The sound of Deacon clearing his throat snapped his attention back to the reason they were there. Deacon was watching him intently. Something wasn't right. He could normally sense how Deacon was feeling. Right now, his walls were impenetrable.

Ryker gestured toward the phone. "You manage to put him off?"

"For now." Deacon exhaled, pushed back his chair, and stood. "We'd better get this over with."

Ryker was on high alert as Deacon made his way toward them.

"The only problem is, I have no idea where to begin," Deacon said.

He sank onto the chair opposite theirs.

Keira fidgeted with her pendant. "How about you start with how you knew my mother. I suspect Ryker is having difficulty taking my word on my age."

Deacon rubbed his temples. "To be honest, if I didn't know better, I'd probably doubt your word as well. It's unheard of for anyone other than Vampires and Were's to live that long."

The hairs on the back of Ryker's neck bristled. He couldn't have heard correctly.

"Wait. What?"

Deacon made a slight bow of his head at Keira. "I know ladies normally don't like divulging their age, but I'm sure you'll forgive me this indiscretion." Deacon turned to him. "I first met Annabeth Subrinski, Keira's mother, in 1665 in London. Keira was born a short time later, and her sister a short time after that."

Ryker's head jerked to Keira, who was still clutching the pendant around her neck.

Not possible!

But the moment her eyes met his, he knew it to be the truth. The weariness reflected in her expression gave it away. How had he not noticed it before? The look belonged to someone who had seen history unfold and witnessed the same mistakes repeated one too many times.

Deacon sighed and settled back in his chair. "We met during the great plague of London. Annabeth, always the healer, was ministering to the afflicted and fighting an uphill battle to teach the poor how to be more hygienic and quell the spread. You have to remember, London was a dirty, unkempt city at the time. Vermin were everywhere, and the city was imploding on itself. The rich didn't care. They'd already abandoned the city for their clean country estates."

"Why were you there?" Keira asked.

"The chaos allowed us to overindulge. It created a feeding frenzy for Vampires. We could feed at will. In hindsight, we were no better than the gentry who left the city in ruins." Deacon tapped a finger on his desk. "Would you believe many of us were employed by the parishes as searchers of the dead? Our duty was to inspect a corpse and determine the cause of death. No one noticed when we added to the count and declared it the result of the plague." Deacon let out a cynical laugh.

Ryker had heard parts of this story before and knew Deacon was remorseful for his past actions.

"The searchers were entitled to charge a small fee from relatives for each death they reported. We took the poor sods' lives and charged their family for it."

Keira sat forward. "Didn't they wonder why healthy people suddenly turned up dead from the plague?"

Deacon shook his head. "We were careful. As tempting as it was, we didn't feed on those who weren't ill. We chose people who were in the early stages of the disease, anything after that and our bodies would react violently to the tainted blood."

"How did you know my mother?"

"For a big city, we seemed to run into each other at every turn. At first, I was reluctant to go too near her. There was no denying who, and what, she was. I could feel it. Just as I can with you," Deacon said. He paused and shifted in his chair before he continued. "At the time, there was a heightened level of animosity between the different Supernatural races. The passage to hell had been sealed shut for so many generations that most Witches had no idea why they mistrusted Vampires. By then, it was a thing of legend. An ancient folktale to scare children. The only two groups who knew the real story were the Crossroads covens and the Primordial Vampires like me, who survived the culling."

Culling?

Ryker held his tongue. No doubt Deacon would explain it in due course. Deacon was one of the Primordial Vampires, the original of their kind. Besides being faster and stronger than a turned Vampire, only Primordials could turn a Natural into a Vampire. Holding his question, he focused on Deacon's explanation.

"Everything changed early one Tuesday morning as I was making my way down Market Lane," Deacon said. "The sun wasn't yet over the horizon, and, as usual, Annabeth was tending to those in need. I spotted her and was about to turn and leave when I noticed her shouting and pounding on the front door of a rundown building. A young child had somehow fallen partway out of the open window on the second story of the house. The moment she detected my presence, she demanded, in no uncertain terms, I scale the building and get the child safely back inside."

"What did you do?"

Deacon smiled and shrugged his shoulders. "I did what any sane person would do when being commanded by Annabeth. I did what I was told. After the boy was safely in his bed and the window was secured, Annabeth invited me for breakfast. That was the beginning of one of my most prized friendships. During the year that followed, I came to learn that she was one of the Amesbury coven Witches, the only Crossroads coven in England and one of the oldest covens on earth. She knew my past and didn't condemn me for it. I experienced such a sense of relief conversing with someone and not having to worry whether I was divulging secrets I'd sworn to keep. I could talk freely with her. I learned restraint because of our friendship. She made me understand that while I needed blood to survive, I didn't need to take a life to do so."

"About a year after we met, the plague slowed. I lost count of the number of bodies that littered the street. The stench still haunts me to this day. Finally, the death tally reduced enough that the Gentry returned to London. We saw the light at the end of the tunnel, but Annabeth was not so sure. She was convinced something else lurked in the shadows, and she was right."

Ryker leaned forward. The unfolding tale was fascinating. This was a part of the story he hadn't been told. "What happened?"

"The Great Fire of London," Deacon said. "It not only eradicated the disease, but also took the lives of most of the Witches and Gifted who hadn't succumbed to the plague."

Deacon faced Keira. "Your mother was devastated. It didn't matter how many lives she saved. She was convinced she should have done more. Once the ash settled, so to speak, she left the city and returned home. Not long after, she met your father, and she began a new chapter in her life. Over the next few years, each time I found myself near Amesbury I would make a point to visit and catch up with her."

"The last time I saw her, you were but a child, no older than five, and what a headstrong child you were." He chuckled at the memory. "Some of the coven were preparing to travel to the New World. They had received word the gate was unguarded, and a new protector was selected. Your mother."

"What happened?" Ryker asked.

"As with many of the indigenous populations at the time, the shamans protecting the gate were killed by the new arrivals, and a new coven was needed to take their place. One that would fit in with the local Puritans." Deacon slouched and rested his elbows on his knees. "I think she knew her fate before she left. 'When one remembers, no one is truly gone,' were her last words to me.'"

Ryker turned at a restrained whimper beside him. Keira's eyes welled with unshed tears. The rehashing of old memories was taking its toll.

"Is that why you came to Salem?" she asked in a broken voice.

Deacon rubbed his jaw and let out a frustrated sigh. "At first, I was in denial. I heard what happened to your mother, and I suppose I rejected the message it heralded. The next hundred years were a bit of a blur. I roamed aimlessly from continent to continent. I eventually returned to England and ran into Gemilla, one of the Primordial Vampires I recognized from my visits to Stonehenge and Amesbury. I think she must have assumed I knew more than I did. During our conversation, I discovered that alongside each Crossroads coven was a small coven of Primordial Vampires, appointed as guardians of the Earth Witches. Unbeknown to the coven, three of my kind stood vigil at each gate, watching over the coven, and had for a millennium."

The pained expression reflected on Deacon's face kept Ryker from firing questions. As much as it was against his nature, he held off from his natural investigative disposition and allowed his mentor to continue his walk down memory lane.

Deacon's face softened, and a faint smile emerged. "About that time, I stumbled upon this reprobate." Deacon jerked his thumb in Ryker's direction. "He'd been newly turned and left for dead by the Baroness Gabrielle duKent, his sire, bitch that she was, after he refused to kill an innocent family who had the misfortune to live in a house the baroness coveted. Once Ryker recovered, I took it upon myself to provide the guidance and the skills he would need to survive in the strange world where he now found himself."

"I wouldn't go that far," Ryker said, attempting to add a bit of levity to the situation. "I had plenty of skills and managed to teach you a thing or two along the way if memory serves. Don't forget about that lesson in Casablanca with that sultan's harem."

Keira snorted. "I'm not sure that's the skills he was referring to, and your sordid past is not something I'm interested in."

"Why not? I thought you brainiacs were always up to learning something new."

She ignored him and turned back to Deacon. "Is that when you came to Salem?"

Deacon fixed his gaze on a small stack of magazines. "I would like to say I did the noble and right thing, but that would be a lie. It took me another fifty years to get up the courage to set foot on American soil, and a few more after that to make it here. I discovered that, unlike the other covens across the globe, no Vampires guarded this coven. I have no idea if they ever did, and to this day, I wonder if things could have turned out differently if I'd followed your family and stood vigil as they tried to prosper in a foreign and strange land."

"Don't blame yourself. Mother chose to do what she did, and no amount of Vampire protection could have stopped her," Keira said.

Deacon stared at Keira for a long while, the conflict and self-loathing clear for all to see.

Ryker's thoughts reeled. So many things now made sense. While they had traveled extensively since their first visit to Salem, they gravitated back here regularly. He now understood Deacon's initial insistence they should keep their distance from the local Witches while at the same time knowing who each one was. What had him on high alert, with an uneasy feeling shooting through his body, was Keira's references to a passage and an implication that something sinister lurked behind the gate, waiting to push through at any moment. His need for answers now overrode Deacon's need to vent, and he opened his mouth to speak. He was cut off by Deacon, who rose from his chair and paced the room.

"The Witch Trials across the globe were orchestrated to deplete the Witch population. More importantly, anyone who could tap into Yggdrasil, the Crossroads source of power. We all knew it, and at the time, like fools, we thought it was not our problem. We were free, and that's all that mattered."

"Who is this royal 'we'?" Ryker demanded. "Because this is all news to me."

Deacon avoided eye contact. "Primordial Vampires. As with the Crossroads Witches, we chose not to hand down this knowledge to anyone outside those directly affected. We couldn't risk anyone trying to free Leviathan."

The fact that he was deliberately kept in the dark hit Ryker like a ton of bricks. "The bit that I'm still not getting is this secret you all seem to be hiding. Let's forget about the fact that you didn't trust me enough to share it with me in the ... oh … let's say anytime within the last two hundred years!"

Deacon raked a hand through his hair. "Ryker, you need to understand, I took an oath to protect us all. It was safer if you didn't know. What I failed to appreciate was that secrecy wasn't enough. Annabeth made me realize that unless we protect the Witch population, we are the authors of our own demise. If Leviathan breaches any of the gates, we will either be the first casualties or compelled to do her bidding. We would again be trapped in our minds, unable to do anything that she didn't command. In perpetual agony and torment as her will overrides our own."

Keira nodded. "Which is why we need to find the rest of the coven and keep them safe while we find the Order. They're behind these killings."

Deacon stopped his aimless wandering and faced her. "And you're sure about this?"

Ryker had had enough. He spoke many languages and had earned several university degrees over the years, just to pass the time. But for the life of him, they were speaking in tongues. Not one word made sense.

He bolted up from his chair and boomed, "Enough. Before you two go off on your little jaunt into whatever strange place you're headed, I suggest you put it in park and tell me what the fuck you're going on about. What is this gate? Who are you so afraid of? And what, or who, is this Order?"

He glared at Deacon and pointed at the chair he had vacated. "Sit." He turned to Keira. "I know, without a doubt,

I'm not going to like whatever you two are about to tell me. I suspect that it relates to whatever you were trying to tell me last night."

He headed for the wet bar and reached for a bottle of Glenfiddich and three glasses. "If it is, I'm going to need something to help me get through this."

He poured a shot into two glasses and filled his to the brim. He picked it up, took a gulp, and nodded to Keira. "You can begin by telling me about this damn gate."

TWELVE

BOOK OF GENESIS

Ryker took another drink and met Keira's startled gaze.

Something about the woman intrigued him. She was infuriating, secretive, and way too opinionated. Not to mention, a lot older than she looked. Since when did a nearly four-hundred-year-old witch look that appealing? Who the hell was she exactly?

Keira, unable to meet his unwavering, expectant stare, broke eye contact and looked away. He stood his ground. He needed answers. *Now.*

"I'm not getting any older, and apparently, neither are you, so I can wait as long as you can."

His voice came out harsher than he intended.

She reached for her drink and stared at the amber contents. "How well do you know the Bible?"

He shrugged his shoulders. "As much as anyone. It's a diverse collection of texts a bunch of religious faiths live and die by."

She cradled the drink in her hands. The clinking of ice in the glass rang through the silent room. She cleared her throat and broke the drawn-out, uncomfortable silence. "Biblical scholars look at the Bible in a different way than the average churchgoer. Besides its importance as a Human artifact written by more than forty contributors over a period of fifteen hundred years, it tells us a lot more than people realize."

She paused and finally looked up at him. Her expression was strained. "Most of Christianity's belief structure is focused on the New Testament, which depicts a forgiving and loving God. The Old Testament illustrates a darker, not-so-merciful God."

Not sure where she was going with this, he said, "I always wondered about that, between banishing, drowning, slaughtering entire cities, sending ten plagues, and killing first-borns, I could never work out how Christianity thrived and grew."

Deacon let out a dry laugh. "That's because it's based on Jesus' teachings and not the actions that came before."

Keira nodded. "You have to remember, the documented stories were written down hundreds of years after they actually happened. As with anything that is repeated verbally, through multiple generations, a little gets lost in the translation."

Ryker sat on the nearest armrest. He was still not sure where this was headed, but it looked like it was going to take a while to get to the point. "I'm with you so far, but I have no idea what this has to do with a gate."

"Most Christians know, and pretty much accept, that the fallen Angels were cast out of Heaven."

Angels? Heaven?

He scratched the back of his neck, trying to recall the story she was referring to. "It's been a while since I read the book, but if memory serves, the Angels staged a coup."

"That's right. God granted them free will. Some of the Angels believed they were more powerful than God. Lucifer was one of them. The power struggle escalated, and a third of the Angels were cast out when Lucifer failed to overthrow the Kingdom of Heaven. Leviathan was one of those who fell to earth when they were cast out. But her reason for joining the battle wasn't the same as Lucifer's. She was bent on revenge after God condemned her lover, Behemoth, to Hell for killing another Angel."

Ryker froze. She was talking like this actually happened. His head whipped around to face Deacon.

Deacon sagged against the leather seat. He stared at his hands for a moment before meeting Ryker's gaze. Dread washed over him at Deacon's expression. It was a combination of shame and resignation. What was he missing? He had never seen Deacon like this. *Ever.*

Deacon pinched the bridge of his nose. "I know this sounds far-fetched, but I assure you, every word is true. You need to understand the full story—from the beginning."

Ryker's stomach tensed, and he was suddenly thirsty. While this was absurd, he would give Deacon the benefit of the doubt. He owed him that much, at least.

He swept his arm in an encompassing gesture. "Please continue, Keira."

She let out a tentative smile and bit her bottom lip as if searching for how to go on. "Most of the fallen lesser Angels lost their wings and were the first Demons to walk the earth. The higher Angels retained an extraordinary amount of their divine gifts. The belief among the Angels that remained loyal to God, was that God hoped the Angels who fell to earth would realize the error of their ways, repent, and return to Heaven."

He would play along. "If God could banish them, surely that showed the Angels he was more powerful."

"If that was their only gripe, things might have turned out very differently. They were stuck on the belief that God loved Humans more than He loved his Angels. They were so jealous that after their banishment, they set out to break God's faith in His creation. What's more, they believed that Humans were inferior and not worthy of His love. So they walked the earth, proving their point. Corrupting one city after another. They fed off the sins they incited and reveled in the downfall of humanity."

Ryker jerked his head back. "So why didn't God intervene?"

Keira sank onto the soft couch. "For one, Lucifer and his cohorts never interfered with or broke the free will rule. They pushed boundaries but never forced anyone to do anything against their will."

She picked at a non-existent piece of lint on her trousers, her lips set in a grim line. "This wasn't enough for Leviathan, whose hatred festered and grew in proportion to her desire to corrupt. Once she'd crushed and annihilated her victims' dignity, she took their souls."

His mouth fell open. "That's possible?"

Deacon exhaled loudly. "There were a lot of things that shouldn't have been possible but were."

Keira threw Deacon a sympathetic smile. "Before anyone knew what happened, entire cities were under her control. Leviathan corrupted the citizens beyond salvation. They were reduced to puppets for her to command. She was like a disease spreading across the earth."

Keira visibly shuddered, and Ryker fought the urge to comfort her. "What did Lucifer and the others do?"

She met his curious gaze. "Lucifer and his cohorts knew God wouldn't stand by and see Humans reduced to being Leviathan's slaves with no free will of their own, so the fallen angels made a speedy exit and put a lot of distance between them and any city she ruled."

Her fingers curled into fists and then straightened again. The room fell quiet.

Ryker tapped a finger against his glass. That couldn't be the end of the story. "What happened then?"

Deacon and Keira stole furtive glances at each other, and an uncomfortable silence ensued.

Deacon was the first to break the silence. "The flood."

Ryker's eyes widened, and he nearly burst out laughing. "You mean *the* flood?"

"Yes, but it didn't happen the way you've been led to believe," she said. "The Book of Genesis was originally written in Hebrew. As with the English language, Hebrew words may have multiple meanings. The translation of text from one language to another can be tricky. Knowing how certain words were used at the time and within its culture prevents distorted translations. Unfortunately, this particular episode in our history is one example where the translations distort the real meaning."

Deacon snorted. "Think about it. Forty days and nights of rain cannot cause a flood whose waters rise to those levels. If that were the case, we'd have been wiped off the map long ago. Not a year goes by where it doesn't rain consecutively for that long somewhere across the globe. Texas is still there after forty-five days of rain. And Wales didn't float away into oblivion after one of their villages had eighty-five days of rain earlier this year."

"I'm guessing this is where the translation problems come in," Ryker said. "The current Bible has it wrong."

Deacon shook his head. "No, the Bible is right. There was a flood, but the translation of how it happened is incorrect."

Ryker splayed his arms. "Don't leave me hanging."

"A comet broke away from the Oort Cloud that surrounds our solar system, entered our atmosphere, and struck the Indian Ocean. The impact caused a series of mega-tsunamis that covered the majority of Mesopotamia before slamming into the mountains of Ararat in Turkey and falling back to leave a flood that lasted months."

"That was a bit of a coincidence," Ryker said sarcastically. "Of all the places to hit, the comet landed right near that hotspot."

Deacon raised an eyebrow. "Hmm … it was, wasn't it? Almost as if by divine intervention."

"And that would have been that," Keira interjected. "But … somehow, Leviathan and her followers escaped before the tsunami hit. They laid low but continued to weave evil. Everything she touched was tainted. Every person was doomed for eternity.".

Keira tapped a finger on her glass and appeared to be studying it again. "If possible, the belief that she was greater than humanity and should rule over them only compounded. Her hatred of Humans and God increased exponentially. She thrived on their suffering and servitude. Leviathan wanted to show God that His beloved children were nothing but cattle to be slaughtered and used as required if they didn't bow to her will. This time, she surrounded herself with people who worshiped her as their God and Savior. Her followers became The Order of Chaos. They only served to fuel her already out-of-control fire, and they carried out all manner of horrific crimes in her name." Keira's voice faltered, and she let out a shaky breath. "Leviathan settled in and ruled over Sodom and Gomorrah."

Ryker studied her with piercing scrutiny. Why he was shocked by this was beyond him.

"I'm listening."

Keira, again, picked at lint he was sure wasn't there. "Both cities rested along a fault line, and as fate would have it, one day a series of earthquakes opened the fault, basically creating a volcano. Tons of bitumen deposits were thrown into the sky. As they fell back to earth, they ignited, and a fiery burning mass engulfed the area, destroying the cities in the process."

"Fate, huh?" he said as he folded his arms across his chest. "Let's guess, once again, Leviathan escaped."

Her expression told him all he needed to know. Leviathan had evaded death a second time.

"Lucifer and the other fallen Angels knew she would be back. While they were more than happy to feed off humankind's sins, they knew the line should never be crossed. They waited for her next move before deciding whether to intervene."

Keira stared at a spot on the floor before looking directly at him. He tensed. Her face had taken on a tortured expression, as if she were in abject pain. He pushed back the urge to move closer and protect her from whatever was eating her from the inside.

"Leviathan's third assault on Humans was something no one expected," Keira said in a quiet voice. "By now, she truly believed she was a God. Like Him, she had her believers. What she didn't have was humanity. She wanted to create her own children, and so she did. She desired offspring who were stronger than Humans, and she wasn't about to make the same mistake as God. These children were to be devoid of free will, bending to her every wish and desire."

Her voice cracked, and her shoulders sagged. "She made her own creations, fashioned from Humans. Leviathan forcibly removed the essence of humanity, took their mortal bodies within a fraction of death, and breathed her own will into them." Her gaze darted tentatively toward Deacon. "The first Primordial Vampires. They were neither alive nor dead, and existed only to serve their master. She also gifted them with an innate need for blood with her life-giving breath. The havoc and chaos were absolute. Not satisfied with this, she then gave them the power to turn others to this non-dead, non-alive state."

Ryker's throat constricted, and a bead of sweat trickled down his forehead. He rubbed his brow.

This couldn't be true!

The stories were supposed to be superstitious fairytales.

Every nerve ending was in pain as he slowly swung his head to face Deacon. His friend's hollow eyes reinforced the revelation. Deacon stood and crossed to the window. He stared out onto the street below, deep in his thoughts.

Keira sighed, and her shoulders dropped. "Deacon, the rest needs to come from you."

The silence stretched on.

Deacon clenched his fists and turned back to face them. "In her maddened state, she hadn't realized, or cared, that we still existed. Trapped in our own minds, tortured every moment while she suppressed our will to her own. It didn't matter how much we fought or rebelled. We were unable to penetrate the walls that separated us from our bodies. We were forced to watch, unable to look away, as we did unspeakable things."

Deacon raked a hand through his hair. "I lost count of the men, women, and children who were discarded. The lives that were lost, the innocents who paid the price for simply existing. I am still haunted by their terrified eyes at the moment of death. Hoping, right up until the last moment, that salvation was coming. To be held prisoner, in your own body. To watch as your own hands take the last breath from someone. To feel your body hum when you take someone against their will. To feel Leviathan's adrenaline surge at every debased act you have committed in her name. We didn't even have the power to take our own lives. She controlled every action, and every movement our bodies made was only at her command," he said with bitterness in his tone.

Ryker blinked rapidly. An ice-cold chill welled up from his middle and spread across his body. A sudden crack in the glass he was holding jerked his senses back. He held on so tightly, he was about to shatter the crystal.

He opened his mouth to speak. Nothing came out. His throat barely gave him enough room to breathe, let alone his voice.

He cleared his throat and tried again. "Are you telling me the story Keira told us is true?"

Deacon, unable or unwilling to make eye contact, stared out the window, his arms held stiffly by his sides. "Every word."

Ryker's breath caught at the level of emotion in those two words. "With all that we have been through, why did you never tell me?"

"It wasn't a part of my history I'm particularly proud of. But I think you need to hear the rest of the story to understand why."

Ryker rubbed his eyes. The brain fog from the shock was clearing, allowing him to think more rationally. How had he not heard an inkling of this over the years? Even if Deacon kept this to himself, surely others were not as closed-lipped? Rather than let rip with a raft of questions, he chose to hold off. He needed more information. He needed to understand how the past impacted his present. He needed to know why the man he considered a father had lied by omission.

Keira stood and quickly moved to the wet bar. She poured a liberal glass of single malt into a new glass and returned to where he was seated. She handed him the glass. "I'm sorry if this is a shock to you. I assumed you already knew. But after our conversation at Mystery Hill, I realized Deacon not only kept silent about the purpose of the Crossroads coven but also kept silent about the Vampires' origins. This can't be an easy thing to wrap your head around."

He gave her a grateful smile and took the glass. He was going to need it to get through the history lesson. He took a deep gulp. "Then what happened?"

She sat across from him and darted a worried glance between him and Deacon before continuing. "Lucifer and the others knew they needed to intervene before God did. Leviathan was too powerful to kill. The only option left was to cast her down to Hell. At least then, she would be reunited with Behemoth. But they didn't have the power. Had this been Heaven, their domain, they might have been able to pull it off, but Earth was the realm of Humans and only Humans had that power.”

“By chance, Lucifer heard of a growing population of people with unique abilities. Some could heal the sick, while others could converse with nature or control the elements. What he discovered shocked even his jaded sensibilities. Without exception, everyone with these abilities was a descendant of a lesser fallen Angel, a Demon who intermingled with the Human population.”

Ryker lurched forward, nearly spilling the contents of his glass. Adrenaline tingled through his body at the implication. “Nephilim. You’re telling me that Witches are Nephilim?”

She nodded. “Magic had to start somewhere. Demons lost their power, but somehow a sliver passed to their progeny. Whether it was God’s intention all along, we’ll never know. But Lucifer saw a solution to his problems. While he couldn’t find a way to send Leviathan to Hell, the Nephilim could. In secret, he worked with them to enhance their skills and discovered the Witches who called their power from the earth through the Tree of Life had the capability to open a passageway between Earth and Hell.”

Ryker let out a hiss between his teeth. “This is the gate the Witches have been protecting?”

Their expressions confirmed it, and his mind whirled even faster. Again, he held his tongue. He needed to hear the entire story.

“Somehow,” she said, “Leviathan learned of the threat. Before too long, Witches were targeted by the Primordial Vampires. They were hunted and cut down without mercy. Knowing they needed to divide in order to conquer, the Witches dispersed across the globe to strengthen their skills, build the passages to Hell, and above all, ensure their survival.”

She took a sip from her scotch. Her face grimaced as the liquid ran down her throat. “It took many generations, but eventually the covens succeeded. There were now twelve entryways to Hell's gate. If one failed, another would be ready to stand tall."

"How did you get Leviathan in? I hardly think sending out invitations to her going-away party would work."

Keira shook her head. "No, that's where Lucifer and the others came in. After whispering in more than one pharaoh's ear, an army was amassed to take on her stronghold. At first, the battle was brutal, even though the army outnumbered her Vampires. But …"

Her voice caught, and a single tear trailed down her cheek.

His chest tightened at the apparent pain this was causing her. Without thinking, he leaned forward to wipe it away and caught himself in time.

Instead, he said, "But?"

She blinked to stop more tears from spilling and wiped away the runaway tear. "By pure luck, or accident, one of the Witches realized there was a link between Leviathan and the Vampires Leviathan controlled. But they needed to be near the Vampires to sever the connection. Working in groups of three, the Witches cast spell after spell. When they were cut down by the Vampire horde, another set replaced them and took up the challenge. Finally, after what seemed an eternity, the Vampires on the battlefield faltered. The connection had been severed. Leviathan no longer directly controlled their every move."

Deacon returned to his seat. "I cannot describe the weight pulled from us. We were deep in a field of blood and death. Chaos occupied every inch of ground. All I could manage to do was stand and stare at my hand, my fingers. Multiple lifetimes had passed since I was the one to flex them. To feel the simple act of opening and closing my fist. To be the one whose thoughts controlled one's own body. I felt…Human again."

Deacon leaned forward and rested his elbows on his knees. "And that's when the culling began. In our confused state, we were easy targets for what was left of the attacking army. The three Witches who broke the link were joined by others who reinforced the spell. It was the only way to ensure the connection couldn't be re-established before they succeeded in their goal.

"Somehow, one of us had the wherewithal to beg for mercy. Coming to our senses, a great number of us threw down our weapons and surrendered …" Deacon trailed off and shook his head from side to side. "To my horror, the majority continued to fight. I would like to think their minds were so far gone they knew not what they did. Even with our superior strength, it had been so long since our minds were required to think for ourselves. Our movements were slow and labored. In a heartbeat, the battle was over. We were surrounded by a sea of blood and thousands of headless Vampires scattered across the plains. As I knelt with my hands behind my head, I wondered if I too should have paid for my sins and died alongside the others."

Deacon's body slumped.

Unable to move, Ryker stared at Deacon. This was not the strong, unbendable man he had known for two centuries. This was a man haunted by his past, unable to forgive himself for past sins. Not sure how he could lessen Deacon's pain, but needing to do something, he retrieved the Glenfiddich, topped their drinks, and handed Deacon his glass.

"I'm sorry," he said as he laid his hand on Deacon's shoulder and squeezed lightly.

His words were inadequate, but at least Deacon would understand the intention. "What happened next?" he asked Keira.

She took a deep breath before continuing. "This time, Leviathan was unable to escape her fate. While Lucifer didn't participate in the battle, he was more than helpful in detaining her for the Witches. She was taken to Göbeklitepe. It took two days for the Witches across the twelve sites to open the gates. Leviathan and what was left of her Legion were pushed through. The Witches took another day to ensure the gate was sealed tight."

"How did you get her through? I hardly think she went willingly."

"No." Sadness once again fell over Keira's features. "She didn't go without a fight, and she swore revenge. Six Witches and two Primordial Vampires sacrificed themselves to ensure she went through that gate and stayed there. Right up until the moment the gate shut and sealed, she was hurling abuse at the Witches. Leviathan vowed she would return and cut them down. Her most chilling verbal attack was directed at the freed Vampires. She swore when she returned, she wouldn't give them the mercy of death. Instead, she would once again take away their free will and make sure they suffered for an eternity."

His brows drew together. "Why worry? She was locked in Hell."

"We were so focused on Leviathan," Deacon said, "we forgot about the Order of Chaos. In the aftermath of the battle and her capture, they were nowhere to be found."

Keira nodded. "We have no idea how big the Order of Chaos may have grown or even who they are. Since that day, Witches have remained at each of the gates, making sure she can't return and fulfill her promise."

Ryker leaned back and absorbed the information. Some things were not adding up. "But she *has* tried."

It came out as a statement rather than a question. He already knew the answer but needed the confirmation.

Keira's head dropped. "There have been a few attempts to unseal the gate, and the Order of Chaos has come close a few times to setting Leviathan free."

"What happened?"

Raw pain flittered across her face. "It was dealt with."

The strain in her voice spoke volumes. Whatever this "dealt with" entailed, the topic was off-limits. One that he suspected she wouldn't so readily yield to.

He moved the conversation to the other perpetrator in this mess. "And Lucifer, whatever happened to him?"

Keira's phone vibrated. She sighed as she glanced at it and stood up. "That's a story for another day. If you'll excuse me, I have to take this."

"Is there anything more I need to know about?" he asked once Keira left the room.

Deacon shook his head.

"In all the time we've known each other, not once did you think it might be a good idea to give me some sort of heads up on why we were here and why it was important we stayed?" Ryker held back the rage brewing just below the surface. "If I'd known, Annie and the others might still be alive today. Their blood is on our hands."

Deacon's normally stoic features broke. "Don't you think I asked myself that same question the moment Keira confirmed the Order was behind this? Everything I've done here was to make sure they were safe, and I've failed. I made sure the Crossroads coven could stay hidden. I built an entire community that allowed them to hide in plain sight, and still the Order found them."

Ryker struggled to hold back his annoyance. "So why would you lie by omission? I trusted you."

Deacon stood and made his way to the window. "At first, it was because I didn't think you could take on any more baggage. You hated yourself, and what you became, so much it consumed you. You'd been betrayed by a woman you loved. A Vampire who turned you against your will. One who then threw you to the wolves to die. You were broken. You needed to heal your mind as well as your soul. Not lose yourself in the knowledge of where we came from and just how depraved our history was." He tucked his hands into his pockets. "And once we eventually made our way here, it was too late. Too much time had passed.”

An uneasy twinge picked at Ryker. He didn’t want to remember. There were too many scars, some of which had just healed. “So how do we get out of this mess? I have no idea about who I am up against.”

“If the Order is behind this, we’re going to need Keira’s help. And if that necklace she’s wearing is what I think it is, she is far more powerful than you think. We won’t be able to do this without her.”

Ryker’s mouth set into a grim line. The Witch was a menace. She didn’t listen and had far too many opinions. “Truth or not, she can’t be going around declaring the Devil is real. It’ll set the place into a panic, and then you’ll see what end of days really looks like.”

“Cut her some slack. Her demons are just as fucked up as yours. This is the last place on earth she wants to be, but she came anyway. You have to find a way to work with her. We must protect the Crossroads coven. No matter what, Leviathan cannot be permitted to walk the earth again.”

Ryker reached for his phone and glasses. “So, no pressure then.”

Deacon stopped him before he walked out the door. “The Baroness Gabrielle duKent is the worst of us. You can’t live your life as though you are the same as her. You may be a Vampire, but your heart still beats. It can still love and feel the pain of loss. You erected a wall around the possibilities of ‘what if’ a long time ago. Don’t let Annie and her family be the only exception.”

THIRTEEN

BETTY LOU GOT A NEW PAIR OF SHOES

Keira was drained, both physically and mentally. This was not how she'd anticipated the week would unfold. She should be in LA, grading papers and listening to students try to explain why they hadn't turned in their assignments. Not be on the other side of the continent, reopening old wounds.

To be fair, she knew this day would come. As much as she denied it, the cards had been dealt a long time ago, and no amount of wishing would delay the inevitable. From her vantage point, she stole a glance at Ryker. His set expression gave nothing away. The sheriff-by-day and Vampire-by-night remained silent the entire walk to the car and the subsequent short drive to the hotel. Her only consolation was that his intense introspection eased his frantic and unpredictable driving skills.

Once they pulled up to the curb, Ryker made no move to exit the car or turn the engine off. His fingers gripped the wheel with such force that she could visibly see the strain on the steering column as it resisted his unyielding pressure.

"There's more to the story, isn't there?" he asked without looking at her.

A dull ache pulsed at her temple. The telltale sign of a headache was ready to wreak havoc on her state of mind. She blindly stared at her hands, which were clenched together on her lap. Not for the first time, she wished Ryker was not so good at what he did.

"Yes," she said with the smallest of nods.

He loosened his grip on the steering wheel. "Can I protect the Witches without knowing the full story?"

She lifted her head and turned to face him. His ever-present sunglasses gave nothing away.

He broke the uncomfortable silence as they regarded each other. "I get the feeling you're a little too raw at the moment. Whatever you're holding back is personal, and I get that, but I have a city to protect, and I can't do that if I'm kept in the dark."

"Knowing won't change anything," she said. While knowing wouldn't help him protect the others, it might change how he viewed her. Something she didn't want to face right now. Maybe he wouldn't see through her uncertainty. She tipped her head against the headrest. "I'm not trying to be difficult. It's just … it's not just my story to tell, and I've spent the better portion of my life trying to forget."

He placed his hand over hers and gave it a light squeeze before letting go. "Give me some credit. I can see how much this has affected you."

His sudden tenderness and lack of harsh judgment toppled her equilibrium. She had been prepared for his scrutiny and interrogation, and he made it quite clear that his loyalty to those he protected would always come first. She gave him an ashen smile and hoped he understood how grateful she was for not pushing the subject.

She glanced at the sidewalk in front of the hotel. Dayna and Marcus should have returned by now and undoubtedly would be waiting for her. "I know you've still got things to do, so I won't keep you. Just let me know when you manage to find someone in the coven who's willing to meet with me."

She quickly got out and closed the door, but Ryker exited the car as well.

"Where are you going?"

He donned his sheriff's baseball cap and tugged on the brim. "After what I now know, you're out of your broomstick if you think I'm going to leave you alone without making sure you're safely inside."

"I can look after myself."

A cynical eyebrow rose over the rim of his sunglasses. "I'm sure that's what the others said, and how did that confidence work out for them?"

"You can't just follow me around," she said as he made his way around the car. "You've got a job to do."

"Yes. To protect and serve. Right now, in order to serve the city, I need to make sure you are protected. I'm not leaving until I know you're with Marcus and your sister and that you'll stay that way until I come and get you in the morning. I'll station a deputy or two outside the hotel tonight."

He leaned down until he was only a few inches away from her. He pulled his glasses halfway down the bridge of his nose. The flash of steel blue, infused with a raging inferno, stared back at her. While his compulsion would work on a Natural, it rolled off her like water off a duck's back. The sudden display of unbridled power *did* let her know he was deadly serious.

Not wanting to test just how much mettle he was made of, she snorted and headed into the hotel, not looking to see if he followed.

They were halfway across the lobby when Dayna's voice rang out. "Sheriff, I've been very naughty. How about you arrest me, and I'll show you just how bad I can be?"

Keira groaned aloud. "Just once. Just once, can you not make such a public display like that?"

Ryker chuckled as Dayna closed the distance, rolling an overnight bag behind her.

"I don't know," he said. "I kinda like her brand of criminal behavior. It makes a welcome change from the drunken frat students who streak through the town every spring break."

"Your timing is perfect," Dayna said to her while giving Ryker the once-over. "We just got back."

Keira peered over Dayna's shoulder. "Where's Marcus?"

"Returning the rental. He'll be back shortly."

Ryker eyed where Dayna's fingers clutched the handle of her Louis Vuitton carryon. "You leaving so soon?"

Dayna frowned. "No." Then she followed Ryker's gaze. "Oh, my carryon …" Visibly flustered, Dayna appealed to Keira for help. "I've been shoe shopping, and you know how it is … Gucci, Louboutin, Jimmy, Steiger. Who can choose just one? I got a little carried away, and the carryon is easier than trudging around town with a dozen bags and boxes."

Ryker cocked his head, and his attention moved from the bag to Dayna. "In Salem? You went high-end shoe shopping in Salem?"

Dayna let out a nervous laugh. "Heavens no. Marcus and I drove down to Boston. It was such a lovely day, perfect really, for shoe shopping."

Marcus suddenly materialized beside them. "What was perfect?"

Keira's gaze shot to Dayna, who looked like she was about to have a coronary.

"Shoe shopping," Dayna said a little too quickly. "You know, the shopping for shoes we did today. In Boston. At the shoe shops … for shoes."

Marcus' expression was as confused as Ryker's. Keira needed to do something, and fast. Ryker was not stupid.

She was close enough to Marcus, so without making it obvious, she kicked him and said, "Dayna was just telling us that she bought so many shoes in Boston that she had to bring them back in a suitcase."

Would her pointed stare get through?

His face went blank. She fixed a glare at him and was thankful when his expression changed to understanding.

He placed his hands on his hips and glowered at Dayna. "Yeah, well, it may have been a great day for her. But I was the one who followed her from store to store, carrying all her crap. And I was the one apologizing when the shop owner wanted to kick her out for being too loud. We almost didn't buy any shoes today."

"That wasn't my fault," her sister declared. "That horrible man had no right to tell me I couldn't touch the shoes in any other section of the store."

Marcus clenched his fists. "We've already been over that. It was a special shoe shop. You were only allowed in the women's shoe department. You had to have a special invitation to the men's shoe department. They're special, temperature-controlled shoes. Just because you had access to the restricted women's shoes didn't mean you could try on every shoe in the goddamn store."

Keira grimaced. They were no longer talking about shoes. Something must have happened at the library. She stepped in between her sister and her teaching assistant.

"Okay, I don't think the sheriff here needs a play-by-play rundown of shoe shopping."

"Hmmm, I don't know about that," Ryker said with a drawl. "Much more of that drivel, and we might have heard what they were actually up to." She was about to protest when Ryker held up his hands. "Don't even try. You lot wouldn't make good criminals."

He hesitated. Whatever he was going to say, he didn't want the conversation overheard. "Until we know who's behind the killings, the three of you are to stay together. You're to go to Marcus' hotel, grab his stuff, and get back here ASAP. For tonight, you're all staying in the same room."

Keira opened her mouth to speak but snapped it shut when he glared at her.

"This is not negotiable," he said with a low growl. "I need to organize some protection for you without arousing suspicion. Until I do, you're safer together. Don't you think there have been enough deaths?"

Keira huffed. "But we can take care of ourselves."

Ryker pulled on the brim of his cap. "To be honest, I suspect you and your sister could take on any Supernatural and come out on top, but it's a risk I'm not willing to take right now. It's bad enough that my whole world just shifted on its axis today without anything happening to you three."

From his stance, he was not going to back down. Marcus and Dayna were glued to the exchange like spectators at a tennis match.

"Fine," Keira grudgingly declared.

She was not happy with the situation.

He raised a brow. "Fine, what?"

She leaned forward and spoke in a low voice that only he could hear. "You know, I could cast a spell that would make no amount of Viagra work on you."

His resulting grin only further infuriated her. "Go for it, Doc. It'll be your loss. You'd only be hurting yourself."

His cool breath sent a shiver down her neck, and goosebumps erupted across her skin. In less than a heartbeat, her pulse raced out of control, increasing her temperature by at least twenty degrees. *Mother Earth*, what possessed her to get that close to the flames? Unwilling to engage in a war of words with the man, she stepped back and gave a sharp tug on her lapels.

"Fine. We'll stay together tonight."

If possible, his grin only broadened. "I'll be back in the morning."

"Wow, that was sexy as hell." Dayna flapped her hand in front of her face as Ryker strode out the front doors. "Gotta love a man in uniform."

Keira resisted the urge to loosen the top buttons of her shirt. The temperature was way too hot for this late in the day. She let out a frustrated sigh and headed for the exit. How did one person get her so riled up so quickly? The man needed to come with a warning sign.

She motioned to her sister. "I'm hungry. Let's get Marcus' gear and get back here before it gets dark."

Dayna bowed and swept her arm before her carryon. "I think you're forgetting something."

Keira laughed. "Bring your shoes with us. We can't leave it here."

Despite her dismissal of Ryker's concern, they wasted no time in retrieving Marcus' belongings and returning to their hotel. Her nervousness must have rubbed off on Dayna and Marcus. For once, neither of them sniped at each other. They were in a town where the Order was hunting Earth Witches, and they were carting around one of the most powerful and sought-after books of spells.

Over the next hour, they didn't allow the Louis Vuitton suitcase to leave their sight. Once they were safely in her room and had smuggled in extra bedding, they all let out a sigh of relief.

Keira slumped onto the bed and stared at the suitcase. "I didn't think about the ramifications of bringing the book here."

Marcus opened the minibar and inspected its contents. "Well, it's too late to take it back. I'm about to drink, and I'm not going to be in a position to drive. Besides, I still have work to do on my video. This one is going to put me on the map. I can just feel it."

Dayna held out a hand for a bottle. "So how many followers do you have?"

He held out two mini vodkas in one hand and a tequila in the other. "A little over a hundred thousand."

"You anything like Zoe Sugg?"

"I wish."

Keira raised her eyes upward. Mother Earth, she needed a drink. "What planet are you both on? I tell you the Order is trying to bring Leviathan through, and you're chatting about popularity?"

Dayna waved her hand in the air. "Ignore her. She can spell fashion. She just doesn't know what it is. Never has, really. But I suppose she has a point." Dayna chose the tequila, took a drink, and let out an audible sigh. "Okay, what do you need us to do?"

Keira accepted the small bottle of vodka from Marcus and grabbed an orange juice. "We need to see if we can find anything in the Grimoire that can help us. It's been—"

She was cut off by a knock at the door. The three of them tensed until they heard the muffled sound of a man's voice call out, "Room service."

Marcus rubbed his hands together. "I'm starving."

Keira tipped the waiter and closed the door behind him, locked it, and placed the chain in its cradle. Confident they were secure; she made her way to the small table and eyed the large beef burger and fries on one plate, and the New York strip sirloin with jacket potatoes on the other.

She sat down in front of her Caesar salad. "Are you sure you have enough there?"

Marcus frowned. "It doesn't look like that much, does it? Do you think I should order something else?"

"You're fortunate you're good at what you do," she said as she tucked into her meal.

She had barely speared a second forkful of salad when Dayna tossed her knife and fork onto her plate, stood, and made her way to the suitcase.

"Who am I kidding? I must see it."

Keira stared at her salad for a moment, then carefully placed the utensils on the tray. If she was honest, she had resisted the urge to open the suitcase from the moment Dayna showed up with it.

"I guess dinner will have to wait," she said as she rose.

"Can you hear it?" Dayna whispered as they stared down at the distinct monogram Vuitton markings on the leather.

Keira nodded slowly. "It feels like it's singing to us."

Marcus squatted and leaned closer to the bag. "What are you two going on about? I can't hear a thing."

Her hands trembled as she reached for the handle. Once it was open, she took a step back, and they stood over the old, familiar book. She tentatively reached out, and her fingers brushed the rough brown leather. As her skin made contact with the uneven surface, pinpricks of energy danced up her fingers, turning them warm until a comforting fire ran up her arm and fanned out through the rest of her body. She briefly closed her eyes and reveled in the peace that settled over her.

Dayna touched the book, and a serene expression fell across her face.

They pulled the Grimoire from the case with agonizing slowness and rested it on the bed. The power seeping from the pages both terrified and reassured her. It bled into the air around them and hung like a mist. Thankfully, a powerful cloaking spell kept the true nature of the book hidden from anyone not belonging to Frig Skógr's bloodline. Otherwise, it would draw every Witch and Warlock for miles around.

Marcus made a whistling sound through his teeth. "Man. That has got to be the biggest spell book I've ever seen. There must be thousands of spells in there."

Keira flipped the book open and leafed through a few pages. "Right, first things, first." She nodded toward the closet. "You'll find them under the towels."

Dayna headed for the closet.

Marcus peered over her shoulder at the open pages. "What language is that written in? I thought it would be Latin or old English at least."

"Mother preferred Latin, just like her mother before her," Dayna said as she headed back to the bed with a handful of candles. "At that time, spells were written in a mixture of Gaelic, Norse, Old English, or Latin. It all just depended on what was most comfortable for the Witch."

Marcus looked closer, and his forehead crinkled. "But it's not in Latin."

Keira reached into her tote bag and pulled out her small pouch. "That's because it's cloaked, and we need to fix that." She set up the candles while Dayna retrieved her crystals. Once everything was in place, she let out a long breath and turned to her sister. "Are you ready for this?"

Dayna studied the white crystals in her hand. Her sister's face reflected the same uncertainty that she was sure was reflected in her own expression. "I'd rather be back in Ibiza with that DJ, but you can't have everything."

Keira picked up the small knife she had left on the bed and sliced into the palm of her hand. She flinched at the sudden pain and handed the blade to Dayna, who repeated the process and then tossed the knife onto the bed.

Marcus took a step back and visibly gulped. "Shouldn't you have sterilized that first?"

Keira reached for Dayna's bloody hand and clutched it tightly. They held their interlaced hands over the open book, and with one voice, chanted the spell they had learned a lifetime ago.

"Ostende te. Ostende nobis mysteria abscondis."

Marcus whispered through their intonation as he interpreted the spell, *"Reveal yourself. Show us the secrets you hide."*

They repeated the incantation, continuing to plead with the Grimoire to show them the spells handed down generation after generation. Their lifeblood entwined and pooled. Drop by drop, gravity took over, and the sanguine fluid fell and spread across the old parchment. Colors blended and bled as words danced across the open pages, dissolved, and reformed. The candles flickered and went out as the final words settled into place.

"I've seen some funky shit in my time, but this has to be the coolest," Marcus said. "That is just rad. Truly fucking rad. Way better than when I got to touch Kanye West's Nike Air Yeezy samples."

Keira opened the Grimoire to the first page. "We need to find something that will help us work out why they need the blood and give us some indication on how to find the Order."

She flipped through a half dozen pages before Dayna's hand reached out and stopped her. "The mark of the *Ouroboros*."

Marcus moved closer. "What's that?"

"It's one of the symbols the Order uses to identify their own." Keira turned her arm over and pointed to the fleshy part of her forearm. "When an initiate enters the Order, they are branded with it here. The pain is excruciating, but it's a rite of passage for these lunatics."

Marcus grimaced and scanned the open page. "Does it tell us how to find them?"

Dayna shook her head. "No. This entry is just about the different levels within the organization."

They studied the old parchments for the next few hours, pouring over each page lovingly as they traded stories from their locked-up bank of memories. Marcus was wise enough to remain quiet as she and Dayna shed tears for a long-forgotten life. A life that held promise for a future that was so very different from the one they lived.

Their mother's distinctive handwriting added to the family legacy which reached back so many generations they didn't bother to count. Memories came rushing back as she recognized her own writing near the end of the book. Keira still remembered when their mother declared it was her time to add to the Grimoire. She'd struggled for days to figure out what it would be. In the end, after yet another sleepless night, she'd decided on a spell she came up with to amuse Dayna as a child.

"You know I still use it." Dayna's voice caught as she spoke, and a tear fell down her cheek.

Tears clouded Keira's vision, and she wiped them away. "You do?"

"Yes, although I use brighter colors than you did to change my hair color."

With that, they both giggled. The sound was odd, considering the weight that hung in the room.

The next three hours of pouring over the pages yielded nothing.

Keira suppressed a yawn as she checked her watch. "I don't know about you two, but I could do with some sleep. We'll keep looking through the Grimoire tomorrow after we've rested."

After a bit of moaning about the sleeping arrangements, mainly from Marcus, they took turns in the bathroom and settled in bed a little after midnight. While they hadn't shared a room in years, she was comforted having her sister close by.

Dayna tossed a few times before turning back and facing her. "Do you think there's going to be more?"

"More what?"

"Crossroads who will die without their light living on?"

A lump lodged Keira's her throat. When they first experienced the disturbance in their power, she should have realized it was the light of a Crossroad Witch being extinguished in such a gruesome way as to not allow their power to return to Yggdrasil. Crossroads Witch's power was supposed to return to the Tree of Life for use by the next generation. Her voice wavered with uncertainty. "I don't know."

Dayna readjusted her pillow. "Apart from all the victims being Crossroads, you didn't tell us what happened at the morgue."

"Yeah, next time I get to go too, instead of shoe shopping with Imelda," Marcus said from his uncomfortable makeshift bed on the floor. "She wouldn't even let me check out the Bamba Fives at the bodega. Do you know how many views that would have given me alone?"

Keira let out a long breath. The rancid smell from the morgue would be branded on her for years to come. "Believe me, I never want a *next time*."

"So, what happened?" Dayna asked.

The room fell silent after Keira gave them a condensed version of the conversation with the medical examiner.

"That's so sad about the girl who was pregnant," Dayna said.

Keira stared into the darkness. The dim light from the alarm clock painted a streak across the dark ceiling. "I know. Ryker's pretty shaken up about it."

Dayna shifted and rested her head on her hand. "Hmmm … so, apart from the freaky dead people's bodies, how was your day with Mr. Vampilicious."

Keira made a disapproving noise at the back of her throat. "It's nothing like that, so you can keep your X-rated thoughts to yourself."

Dayna giggled. "Maybe it should be, after all, even you can't be blind to that fine—"

Marcus groaned. "Man. You know I really don't want to hear this."

The darkness hid Keira's scarlet face. "I'm not having this conversation, it's late, and I'm tired," she said in an attempt to divert her sister from the path she was traveling.

Dayna flopped down on her pillow. "Fine, but I think you're missing out there."

She dropped the subject, and the room fell quiet.

Keira had almost fallen asleep when her sister's voice broke into her near-sleep state. "From his parting words, I assume he knows?"

Her eyes fluttered open, and she forced her mind to wake up. "We had no choice. Deacon and I told him about the gate and the Order."

Another wave of exhaustion overcame her. This was not a conversation to have at this time of night. "Look, we're all tired. How about we deal with it in the morning?" She rolled over onto her side, hoping they both would get the hint.

Dayna lowered her voice to a whisper. "How did he take it?"

Would the torture never end? Keira turned her head into the pillow and let out a low moan. "As well as can be expected. He was angry, but now he just wants to get to the bottom of it," she whispered back.

"What do you think of him?"

"He's a fairly competent sheriff, as far as I can tell."

Dayna swatted her back. "That's not what I meant, and you know it. You can't continue to keep people out. I know it's hard to lose the ones you love when you've lived as long as we have, but locking yourself away from the joys of life is not the answer. Maybe while we're here, you can let down your hair a little and do something different? I'm sure the sheriff would be up for the challenge."

Keira groaned inwardly. This was why they hadn't shared a room in centuries.

Keira was ripped out of her sleep without warning. Whether it was the crack of wood as it splintered or Dayna's piercing scream, she would never know. It took her a second to realize something was going on and another second to scramble out of bed and reach for the nearest object that could be used as a weapon. The bedside lamp.

The silhouette of a man moved through their room. Marcus and Dayna squealed. Keira's heart thumped in her chest, and she readied her weapon to take a swing.

"I'm not sure that lamp will do much damage."

The light came on, and her shoulders slumped. "What the hell are you doing breaking into our room?"

The blood pounded so loudly in her ears that she was having difficulty hearing her own words.

Ryker adjusted his baseball cap and had the decency to look apologetic. "You weren't answering, and I was concerned they'd gotten you as well."

Her brows drew together. "As well as what?"

"Two more Witches have gone missing."

FOURTEEN

'I PUT A SPELL ON YOU

Keira got up as the first light of daybreak rose over the horizon. After the events of the previous night and their sudden relocation to Deacon's house, which turned out to be larger than the hotel they were staying in, she was unable to sleep. She finally gave up all pretense of trying.

She wandered over to the window and gazed at the massive lawn blanketing the clearing the estate was nestled within. It was as if someone had scooped out a portion of the forest and replaced it with a European country estate. Complete with majestic park-like grounds with both local and Mediterranean species of plants. The estate was accessed via a long driveway, which ensured the house was hidden from the main road.

Not that she imagined many people would have a chance to access the driveway or see the house, for that matter. The imposing gates would have most visitors steering clear. The gates were surrounded by two pavilions on either side. As they'd passed through them the previous evening, Ryker had pointed out that one was the caretaker's house, while the second was used as an apartment dedicated to the security staff and included a security post on the top floor.

Her muscles tensed when a movement caught her eye. When she recognized the two men patrolling the area, they relaxed again. Ryker had a small contingent of Vampires guarding them while he and Deacon returned to the search for the missing Witches.

They appreciated the gesture and the extra security, but she and Dayna took no chances. They'd cast protection spells over the rooms they used as soon as he left.

Marcus had taken himself off to bed, thankful he no longer had to sleep on a hard floor. He, and his Air Jordans, whatever the hell number they were, was likely fast asleep before they'd shielded the first room.

In the light of day, she wondered why they bothered. The house had state-of-the-art security and burly armed Vampires outside.

She dressed and made her way down to the kitchen. She wanted to be ready when Ryker returned. The sooner they found the rest of the Crossroads coven, the better. Who knew how far the Order would go to flush them out.

She was sipping a second cup of tea when Ryker's sheriff's cruiser made its way up the driveway. Guessing he might appreciate a coffee, she grabbed another cup. A few minutes later, she heard the distinct blips of the alarm being disengaged.

There was a moment's silence before wood splintered and glass shattered.

Her heart lurched in her chest when Ryker cried out, *"What the fuck?"*

Keira's gaze snapped to the candle flickering on the windowsill, and she grimaced. "Damn."

She blew the flame out and raced into the foyer, ringing with a string of ear-stinging curses. Ryker was lying amongst the broken pieces of the hall table. Fragments of ceramic from a large urn lay strewn across the marbled floor. A pool of water trickled away from the shattered vase and mutilated flower arrangement.

She rushed over to help him. "Are you okay?"

He looked up at her with a shocked expression. "What in God's name just happened?"

The chaos increased exponentially when the front doors swung open and two Vampires skidded to a halt, poised and ready to attack.

She froze, and her heart leaped into her throat. What if they thought she did this? She glanced around for something, anything, with which to defend herself.

Ryker waved them off. "Tim, Pete, I'm fine. Just threw myself across the room for no reason."

Neither Tim nor Pete looked convinced as they returned to their posts.

"I'm so sorry," she said once they were gone. "I forgot the protection spell was still active in this part of the house."

"The what?"

"We didn't want to chance anyone coming in without our knowledge, so we cast a spell to place a barrier in some of the rooms."

He brushed broken glass off the front of his shirt. "Next time, put up a warning sign, will you? That spell packs quite a punch." He reached over his shoulder as if trying to scratch his back, and his lips pursed together. "I think you'll need to pull it out for me."

She blinked twice and frowned. "Pull what out?"

He turned so that his back was now facing her. "That."

She gulped. A large splinter of wood from the table leg was embedded between his shoulder blades. The entire back of his shirt was soaked in blood and didn't look like it would stop.

"It's too low for me to reach," he said.

It took three attempts before the stake of wood, along with a large chunk of flesh, dislodged. The stake had pushed its way between two rib bones and widened the gap. The moment she removed it, they visibly settled back into place. How his ribs were not cracked as well was beyond her.

She cringed as his shirt soaked up the dark red blood. "That doesn't look good."

"It'll be all right. I've had worse."

"With that amount of blood loss, you need to replace it ASAP, and …" She peered at the open wound. "I think you need stitches."

"Stop fussing, Doc. It'll heal on its own."

He headed for the kitchen, then stopped short and raised his hands as if to ward off an incoming blow.

Her face heated. He already thought she was a nutbar. "You're safe."

The large gourmet kitchen opened to an even larger family room. She raided the drawers and cupboards.

"Take off your shirt," she said once she found what she was after.

He grinned at her. "Why, Doc, most girls at least try to woo me before they get down to business."

She snorted. "You wish. Just shut up and take it off so I can bandage the hole."

He pulled off his shirt and dumped the blood-soaked garment on the countertop.

Mother Earth!

His sheriff's uniform hid a beautifully toned and sculpted body. Her hands became clammy. Should she look away or continue to stare?

Her breath caught in her throat when her gaze took in the large scars crisscrossing his chest. He turned around, and her eyes widened at just how many more of them were across his back. *How the hell did he get those?* She quickly set to work. "I'll need to remove the splinters before I can clean the wound."

The room fell silent while she worked. She tried to be as gentle as possible, considering it was her fault he was injured. "You weren't kidding when you said you've had worse."

He shrugged. "Comes with the territory. You live long enough, you're bound to get into a few scrapes or—" He halted and hissed through his teeth. "Ouch! You trying to fix it or make it worse?"

She grimaced. She was not about to let him know how concerned she was about the damage. "Stop being a baby. That was the last one."

She cleaned and dressed the wound. "Did you find the missing Witches?'

He shook his head. "No. It looks like they just vanished off the face of the earth. Technically, their case falls within Salem PD's jurisdiction. But because we can't rule out whether it's related to the killings, Deacon and I thought it prudent to work the case without Salem PD's knowledge. And before you ask, no, we have no idea if they are Crossroads or not."

He wandered over to a second fridge and pulled out a bag of blood. "The missing Witches run one of the souvenir stalls on Main Street. All we know is they closed their stall at the usual time and were abducted on the way to their cars. No one saw anything."

Unconcerned at how closely she was watching what he was doing, he poured the contents into a mug. While her knowledge of Vampires was limited, she was sure one bag was not enough.

"What about video surveillance?"

"Big Brother only extends to the main roads. The cars were parked on secluded streets."

She stared at the coffee mug in her hands. The warmth from the cup gave her a measure of comfort. "What about Deacon? Did he get the members of the coven to give him the names of the others?"

"No, he's on his way home now. We're hoping you'll have more luck." He ran his fingers through his hair in a frustrated motion. "We need to catch these bastards before it's too late. At the moment, the missing women are not officially connected to the case, even though we know they most likely are."

Dayna breezed in and interrupted them. "Good morning." She halted midway across the room, and a broad grin crossed her face as she gave Ryker a once-over. "Oh my. A half-naked man in the kitchen. What a way to start the day."

Keira groaned inwardly. Normal people began the day with "Good morning" and "Where's my coffee?" Not Dayna.

Dayna gave Ryker a wink. "Had I known you have a topless policy, I would have dressed appropriately, or less, if you get my drift?"

Dayna glanced from Keira to Ryker and back again. Her eyes narrowed, and a suspicious expression settled into place. "You little minx, don't tell me I interrupted something naughty? Not that I can blame you, that body was built for—"

Keira's hands flew to her cheeks. No matter how much she might agree with her sister's sentiment about Ryker's physique, she was mortified at her sister's suggestion.

"Dayna! Nothing happened, at least not in the way you think. Ryker was hurt, and I tended to his injury."

Dayna's grin only widened, and she winked at Ryker. "Oh, I get it, doctors and nurses. Whatever floats your boat, I say."

Ryker, instead of denying the accusation, laughed out loud.

Keira slapped her forehead. "Give me strength."

"Was she gentle?" Dayna asked.

Enough was enough. Keira stomped her way across the room and forced Ryker to turn around. She pointed to the bandage soaked in blood.

"See? No sex. He was injured because of our protection spell."

Marcus sauntered in, still half asleep and rubbing his face. "Who had sex?"

If possible, Dayna's grin grew wider. "Keira and Ryker."

She glared at her sister. "What is the matter with you? Did we not clear that up?"

Ryker let out a chuckle and slipped an arm around her waist. "Secret's out now, Doc. There's no use in denying it." He turned to the others and grinned. "Although I should warn you, we got a bit carried away. You'd best wipe down the counter before you put anything on it."

Marcus froze, and his eyes darted to the cream pastry halfway to his mouth. He placed it back where he found it. "Maybe I'll stick with coffee this morning."

She pulled away from Ryker's grip and stomped her foot again. "Have you all taken leave of your senses?" She pointed to the counter. "There is no bodily fluid anywhere, and nothing happened between Ryker and me." By this point, she was almost screaming.

How on earth had this conversation degenerated so quickly?

The room fell quiet at her sudden outburst. Much to her frustration, Dayna burst into an uncontrolled fit of giggles. Her sister reached for the counter and held onto it to keep from falling. "Mother Earth, I haven't had that much fun in ages. You were always so easy to wind up."

"Wait …" Marcus said, his face full of confusion. "I don't understand."

Ryker handed Marcus a pastry. "Nothing happened. It's quite safe to eat."

Keira placed a hand on her hip and glared at Ryker and Dayna. "Could you have been more childish?"

Dayna brushed away her tears with the back of her hand but kept laughing. Each time she attempted to speak, she broke down again.

Ryker handed Keira a cup. "Doc, you need to loosen up." He bent his head closer to her. His breath caressed the shell of her ear. "You might find being reckless has its pleasurable advantages."

Goosebumps erupted on her hot skin. The man was too primal for her taste. A small, nagging voice at the back of her mind tapped its foot and said, *"So why does your body react every time he comes too close?"*

A smart retort flew to her lips, but she clamped her mouth shut before it could escape. The man thrived on banter. She wouldn't dignify his suggestion with a comeback. He was well aware of the effect he had on women, and she was not about to start something that just might backfire on her. Instead, she strode to the table and sat down. Dayna and Marcus joined her, and the conversation returned to the missing Witches.

Ryker brought them up to speed while he poured another bag of blood. Instead of joining them at the table, he pulled out a pan from the cupboard and placed it on the stovetop.

He broke half a dozen eggs into a bowl. "Anyone else want eggs?"

Keira's head whipped around to take a closer look at what he was up to. Why was he cooking? Her confusion at his actions must have shown.

Dayna shrugged and said, "Vampires have to eat. They just don't eat as frequently as we do. I suspect that it's been a while since he's had a meal." She turned to Ryker. "It's been ages since you've had some of the fresh red stuff, hasn't it?"

Ryker cocked a brow. "How did you know?"

She winked. "Meh, you pick these things up. Your wound is taking a while to clot."

Keira's earlier unease at the level of damage to him returned, and she looked closer at the blood oozing through the bandage and onto the clean t-shirt. "Now that you mention it, shouldn't the wound have healed by now? I thought Vampires had amazing healing abilities."

He shrugged. "I've been a little preoccupied lately and missed a few warm meals."

"But if you need the iron intake that you get from blood, shouldn't you be eating red meat?" Marcus asked.

Ryker poured the omelet mixture into the pan. "We can't eat meat. Our bodies reject it. Most of our nutrients come from blood. But we do need food to balance out the stuff we can't get from it. The diet to supplement our blood intake consists of foods high in protein and dairy."

Dayna pointed at Ryker's cup. "Cold blood won't help. You'd better get some fresh stuff. We need you fighting fit."

Ryker dismissed Dayna's concern and continued to cook his breakfast. Throughout the conversation, Keira remained quiet. She was stunned by the level of Vampire knowledge her sister possessed. While Keira knew they drank liquids other than blood, she hadn't paid enough attention to their other habits.

She silently studied her sister. She would let the matter rest, for now, but she would have a quiet conversation with Dayna in the not-too-distant future. Just what had she been getting up to in Europe?

Ryker had just taken a seat at the table when he cocked his head and froze.

Keira's pulse quickened, and her muscles clenched. Something had caught his attention.

An agonizing few seconds later, his shoulders relaxed, and he attacked his food with gusto. "Deacon's pulling into the garage."

She let out a breath but caught it again at a low growl from the front foyer. Damn, he didn't sound happy.

Before she could blink, a blur in the form of Deacon materialized near them. His posture was crouched, ready for attack. "What happened? Is everyone okay?"

"Depends on what you consider okay," Ryker said between bites. "If a huge hole in your shoulder is considered okay, then I'm just dandy."

Deacon relaxed and stood to his full height.

Would she ever live it down?

"I said I was sorry." She turned to Deacon. "I apologize about the furniture. We put a protection spell on some of the rooms, and Ryker came in before we lifted it. I'm quite happy to pay for the damage to the table and vases."

Deacon raised his hands to cut her off. "No need to concern yourself. I'm relieved you're all safe and unharmed."

Ryker's eyebrows shot upward, and he pointed at himself, his mouth full of food.

Deacon stared pointedly at Ryker. "Considering you're still alive and eating me out of house and home, I'd say you fall well and truly into the category of fine." He turned to Dayna and Marcus. "I'm sorry that my son's manners are lacking and that he has failed to introduce us."

Ryker swallowed. "Sorry, this is Keira's assistant, Marcus, and her sister Dayna. Meet Deacon, Vampire extraordinaire."

Dayna floated up from her seat and batted her eyelashes at the formidable Vampire. "Ryker, you never mentioned your father was all man."

Deacon blinked and backed away.

Dayna held out her hand. "I'd like to thank you for opening up your lovely home to us. If there's anything I can do to repay your kindness, just let me know. I'm sure I can come up with a few suggestions."

Keira suppressed a groan. They'd failed to warn Deacon about her sister.

FIFTEEN

STRAY CAT STRUT

"And you're sure she's your sister?" Ryker said as they peeled out of the driveway and headed north at speeds that far exceeded the normal limit.

Keira held on to the well-worn passenger grab handle. "You do know I'm not going to dignify that with an answer?"

He chuckled. "I've never seen Deacon at a loss for words. Mind you, I don't think she gave him a chance to say anything."

Keira held back a grin. Deacon did seem a little less intimidating. Her sister had the uncanny ability to put most people at ease. "She's always had that effect on people. They gravitate toward her. Even as a child, she shone like a diamond."

Ryker chuckled again. "She certainly sparkles. Despite being chalk and cheese, you both seem close."

"We are."

"That's what's confusing me. From what I can tell, she's been in the UK for nearly five decades. And before that, there were other long stints. Did you have a falling out?"

"No. Not really. We just needed space to do our own thing. Dayna wears rose-colored glasses. Always has. She has the ability to forgive easily and tries to see the best in people."

Keira froze. The words escaped before she could stop them. Normally, she shied away from personal questions and had spent a lifetime keeping people at arm's length. She let out a breath. Had returning to Salem weakened her defenses?

"But you don't?" he said.

She shrugged. "I see them for what they are. So-called good people can be just as evil as bad people."

He grunted in agreement. "And the longer you live, the more you realize just how true that is."

Her chest tightened, and she winced at the emotional pain. She looked out the window and forced the bad memories back down. She needed to change the subject before the ache overwhelmed her. She cleared her throat. "We just look at things differently, and we both needed our space to think things through."

He must have heard the finality in her words, as he wisely chose not to ask any more personal questions about her past. He flipped on the signal lights to overtake the eighteen-wheeler in front of them. "Diamonds are overrated. Sometimes the real gems are harder to find but well worth the extra effort."

Before she could ask him what he meant, he changed the subject. "At this stage, we have no idea if the two missing Witches were Crossroads. Hopefully, Beatrice can shed some light on that, but I wouldn't go holding your breath."

He was hoping the missing Witches were unrelated to the deaths of the others, but Keira didn't harbor the same wishful thinking. The Order would find, and destroy, every Witch in Salem if they had to. If they couldn't flush out the rest of the coven, they would eliminate anyone who could possibly be a threat.

He careened around another corner. "Beatrice's one of our more colorful locals. She runs a small bookshop in Salem."

"Deacon mentioned she's the only Crossroads member still out in the open."

He nodded. "She lives alone with at least thirty cats. The neighbors are always up in arms about the noise and the mess. My deputies refuse to serve her with court orders to get rid of the cats. When a deputy turns up, they end up having some sort of ailment or calamity afterward. From poison ivy rashes to temporary blindness and everything in between. There is nothing more vindictive than a cat lady without her cats."

"Those poor neighbors. They must be overrun by cats."

He chuckled. "No. I took care of it. The law's the law."

"What did she do to you when you delivered the bad news?"

"Nothing."

Her brows knitted together. "I thought you said—"

He grinned and cut her off. "Give me credit for some brains. I'm not going to put myself in harm's way. Instead of serving her with the papers, I just took the flea bags."

They pulled up to the old house, and she had to admit Ryker was not kidding when he'd warned her the place was run down. She was surprised the walls were still standing. The paint, unable to hold to the cracked and damaged weatherboard, let go and peeled away in layers. A quick inspection of the roof showed that more than one shingle was missing.

As they approached the well-worn and half-collapsed brown and gray picket fence, the noise and smell made it obvious why the neighbors were at odds with this particular house. A cacophony of at least two dozen cats drowned out any possible conversation. The noise and hisses from the felines only increased in volume when they approached the porch.

Ryker veered away from the front entrance and headed for the side of the house.

She sped up to match his pace. "Where are we going?"

"Front door doesn't work." He shrugged. "Besides, it's not so loud around the back."

As soon as they stepped through the small side gate, she understood what he meant. Unlike the front of the house, the back was not as overrun by cats. Two black tabbies sauntered around the backyard, but they were quiet and only flicked their tails in irritation at the intruders. The back porch was not as sparse as the front porch. Pots of ginseng, St. John's wort, and echinacea sat on the three steps. More pots growing medicinal herbs were scattered across the porch. Beatrice must be a healer.

He banged on the door frame. "Beatrice, you old coot. Open up!"

They stepped back and waited.

Footsteps shuffled from somewhere in the house, and a floorboard creaked. The screen door, half off its hinges, opened with a reluctant, high-pitched squeal as the rusty bolts resisted the movement. A weathered elderly woman in an oversized 1970s kaftan dress stood in the doorway and glared as if challenging them to get past her.

Her eyes narrowed. "I ain't gonna get rid of no cats, sheriff, if that's what y' here for."

Keira flinched. For a tiny wisp of a woman, Beatrice's voice belonged to a person much larger, and one that smoked at least three packs a day at that.

Ryker tugged on the brim of his cap in greeting. "And a good morning to you as well. Even though you're well over your limit, we're not here for the cats. We both know Deacon told you to expect us."

Beatrice let out a faint grunt and waved her hand dismissively. "Keep y' pistol in y' pants, Vamp. I'm not so old I can't 'member a conversation from two hours ago." The old woman turned her focus on Keira and gave her a lemon-faced once-over. "You is the upstart from Californi'a they brought in on this, is ya?"

"Yes, ma'am, that's correct."

Beatrice crossed her arms and tapped her foot on the weathered floor. "I'll tell y' what I told that confounded mayor. There ain't no others, and I ain't got no idea about this gate y'all harping on about." She turned to Ryker and waggled a wrinkled, bony finger at him. "You need to be finding this wicked person that's gone done and taken good people, rather than wasting time dawdling with the likes of me."

The muscles in Ryker's jaw tensed, and Keira heard his teeth grate. The old woman clearly got on his nerves.

"If we had more help from the people who know what's going on," he said through clenched teeth. "Perhaps two more innocent people wouldn't be missing,"

Beatrice stared at him without commenting on his outburst.

Keira stepped forward. They needed answers, and she was beginning to empathize with his predicament. The woman was starting to irritate her as well.

"Miss Sommers, you need to do a Calling of the Synod."

This grabbed the woman's attention.

Beatrice's gaze snapped back to her. "That's an odd choice of words, missy."

"Not really, considering the Order has massacred a decent portion of the coven, and we have no idea how many more deaths it will take to let Leviathan out."

All color drained from Beatrice's weathered face, and she stepped back into the house.

"I don't know what y' talking about," she said, faltering over the words.

The screen door slammed in their faces and left them staring at the faded wood on the front door. Locks clicked into place, and everything became silent.

Keira sighed. "I hoped it wouldn't come to this, but I guess we need a show of force. Stand back."

Ryker cocked his head. "If you're going to kick down the door, I think you're wearing the wrong shoes."

She reached into her tote bag, grabbed her crystals, and handed her bag to Ryker. "I won't need my legs."

She spun on her heels and headed down the stairs. As she did so, she scanned the area to make sure there were no nosy neighbors. The high fence and trees that surrounded the backyard ensured their privacy. Satisfied she wasn't in danger of being front page news of *USA Today*, she kicked off her shoes and stepped onto the lawn.

The mixture of grass, weeds, and dirt, prickled at her soles. She swung around to face the house, planted her feet, and steeled her courage for what she was about to try. She hadn't needed to tap into this level of magic for decades. A singsong chant flew from her lips as she stared intently at the front door. She clutched her crystals until they burned a hole in her clenched hand.

At first, nothing happened. She channeled the additional power required from the Yggdrasil, and a slight tremor shook the door. The vibrations increased, and Ryker scooted off the porch and well away from the house in a hazy blur. Another violent shake, and the rusted hinges gave way. Both the screen and front door broke off their frame and flew to the end of the porch. They landed against the railings with a loud thump.

Beatrice shrieked and shuffled up the hall toward them, calling out with an edge of panic in her voice.

"What are y' doin' y' chit?"

The old woman appeared in the doorway and held on to the frame for dear life. Her legs kept walking against her will. Beatrice's mouth gaped open when Keira locked eyes on her.

Satisfied that she had the other Witch's attention, Keira relaxed and let go. Her breath came out in uneven pants as she fought to bring her pulse under control. While the spell hadn't lasted long, it took more than a little out of her. Moving inanimate objects was one thing, a living, strong-willed person, another.

Now that her legs were no longer compelled to do someone else's bidding, Beatrice remained rooted to the spot. Her mouth moved in a fish-like motion as she stared at her, a wary expression on her face.

Ryker surveyed the damage and whistled. "You know, if you wanted the door opened, you didn't need to go through those theatrics."

Keira flashed him a warning, and for once, he understood and remained quiet.

Beatrice's hand came up to cover her mouth. "It's not possible," she mumbled from behind her palm. The air was thick with unanswered questions as they stared at each other. Beatrice's diminutive frame lost its rigid stance, and her hand fell away. "What coven are you from?" she demanded in a hoarse whisper.

"I think you know the answer to that."

A visible gulp was the only movement as the older Witch considered what she just said. "Which Crossroads?"

"That's not important for now. Of greater concern is making sure Leviathan doesn't come through the gate. We need to protect the coven Witches from any more deaths."

Beatrice's gaze darted to Ryker, and a look of uncertainty fell over her features.

"He already knows, and I trust him," Keira said. Witches seldom opened up in the presence of an outsider, let alone a Vampire. "If we are to survive, you and the rest of the coven will have to trust him too."

"Jolly green giants, I need a drink." Beatrice checked her oversized men's watch. "Is it midday yet?" Her gaze scanned the backyard. "It must be midday somewhere. Finland, it's dinner time in Finland, and they're bound to be having a drop or two. How about we join them?"

Keira let out a low groan and met Ryker's amused expression. He was leaning over the railing, enjoying the odd conversation.

"Beatrice," he said in a sing-song voice. "Pull yourself together. You're rambling."

She spun around to face him. Her dress billowed out with the sudden movement. "You're a thief. I know you is taking all my friends. So don't you be thinkin' ya is all high an' mighty."

Keira was starting to wonder about the woman's sanity. "The sheriff is right. You need to focus. There is a lot at stake here."

Beatrice turned back to her and peered more closely. "Who are you exactly? I ain't seen power like that in one as young as you." She frowned, and her lips pursed into a grim and defiant line. "Come to think of it, I ain't seen that much power called by a Witch on their own, full stop. How do I know you're not one o' them?"

Keira moved directly in front of the petite woman, slid off her suit jacket, and let it fall to the ground.

"Like this," she said as she reached for Beatrice's hand.

She twisted their arms around so their forearms faced the sky. As the light touched their skin, a wave of green and gold shimmered across their exposed flesh. Gray tendrils seeped out from the ridges of their veins and danced across their skin, forming a tattoo. The lines formed intricate shapes and weaved up her arm as if it were alive.

When Beatrice saw the tattoo, she snapped her hand away, as if shocked, and exhaled sharply. "It's not possible. It can't be."

"You know as well as I, anything is possible. I speak the truth. You've seen it with your own eyes," Keira said firmly. "Now, we need to protect our people and keep the gate closed."

Beatrice wrung her withered hands as another gust of wind billowed her shapeless dress. "I'm not sure they'll listen. After last night, the rest have gone into hiding. Even Eugene and Amy have the collywobbles. I wouldn't be surprised if they've gone and done the same."

"That's why you need to do the calling, they can't ignore that."

Beatrice shook her head, and a strained expression overtook her worried features. "It's been years since I had to. I ain't sure I even know how anymore. I ain't exactly the strongest in the coven, you know …" She trailed off. "And I sometimes forget things."

Keira placed a reassuring hand on the old woman's shoulder and gave her a warm smile. "You're Crossroads, and you draw your power from the Tree of Life, which is fed directly from the Axis Mundi. You are stronger than you think."

A stray cat sauntered up to Beatrice and wrapped around her legs. She scooped up the feline and hugged it. "Do you really think we can keep it closed? They gone an taken a lot of us. And some of the young'uns don't believe the story."

"Let me worry about that."

Beatrice clutched the cat closer and nodded. "Okay, I'll do it, but I can't guarantee it will work."

Keira reached into her trouser pocket and pulled out a crystal. "Here." She pressed it into Beatrice's free hand. "This might help you convince them. Let us know when they're here."

Beatrice grimaced. "That's gonna be a problem."

"Why?"

"They refuse to come anywhere near my place, and Eugene's allergic to cat hair."

Ryker let out an uncontrolled snort. "A Witch allergic to cats! That's one for the books."

Keira flashed him a dirty look. He was not helping the situation.

He ignored her look and tossed her the bag. "Get them to Deacon's office above the Blood Bank," he said to Beatrice. "It's very public downstairs, so no one will risk trying to take them out in the open. We'll also have enough privacy upstairs so you Witchy-poos can do your boil, boil, toil and trouble, and we can keep you safe. Just let us know when you can get there."

Beatrice's mouth set into a grim line as she considered the options. "I ain't sure they are gonna like outsider's privy to this." She glared pointedly at Ryker. "'Specially ornery cat thieves."

"They have no alternative," Keira interjected. "We need to protect the coven so they can protect the gate. You all took an oath. It's your purpose."

The coven would need Ryker and Deacon's help if they were to stop the Order from opening the gate. The sooner the local Witches came to terms with that, the better.

Keira reached out to Beatrice and gripped her arm lightly. "You will get them there, and there will be no discussion. There's too much at stake."

Beatrice's head bobbed up and down, and she visibly blanched. "Fine. I'll get them there, but that don't mean they gonna like it."

Keira nodded and followed Ryker, who had already headed around to the side of the house.

"Hey! Who's gonna fix my door?" Beatrice called after them.

The only reply she got was the meow of the tabby in her arms as it squirmed to jump to the ground.

The moment they passed through the side gate, the choir of cats living in the front yard screeched at them. Ryker clicked the latch back into place, and he shook his head at her. "You certainly know how to make an impression. I think the next time I come here with papers to serve, I'll just tell her you sent me, and she'll be handing the flea-infested cats over without a fight."

Keira rubbed her forehead. Beatrice had been left with a lot to think about. The old woman would no doubt attempt to perform a calling. But based on what she'd witnessed, she wasn't sure it would work. When she performed the reveal spell, Beatrice's marks that identified her as Crossroads were barely detectible. The woman's magic was almost nonexistent. Had her addled brain contributed to her diminished power?

"Do you know Eugene?"

Ryker lifted one shoulder in a careless shrug. "Tried him already, he's gone to ground like the others."

A cold chill snaked up her back. They needed to find the rest of the coven before the Order did. Mother Earth, were they really pinning their hopes on an elderly woman whose bat had abandoned the belfry? They needed another way to find the coven. But how?

An idea sprang to mind, and she drew in a sharp breath. There was another way, but Ryker was not going to be happy about it.

"We need to speak to Annie's parents. She might have let slip the names of the Crossroads coven members."

His hand froze on the car door as his smile faded, and a pained expression marred his face.

Her voice softened. "They're also our best bet to track down a link to the Order."

They drove to Annie's parents' house in relative silence. From the sedate and within-the-speed-limit way he navigated the road, Ryker was not looking forward to the visit. She didn't envy his position. To get the job done, he would need to put his personal feelings aside. He would be putting his friends under a microscope to determine Annie's timeline, not to mention the little issue of their daughter's pregnancy.

They could then narrow down who last saw or spoke to Annie. For so many people to disappear without anyone noticing, there was only one possible explanation.

Each victim knew, and trusted, their attacker.

<u>SIXTEEN</u>

LET SOMEBODY GO

Ryker's chest tightened as they approached the house. From the flutter of curtains, either Zayne or Maize had been alerted to their arrival.

The familiar surroundings brought back fond memories. He had been to this house so many times over the years that he'd lost count. Annie's parents were among the few people he trusted. While he knew and socialized with half of Essex County, he could count on one hand those he considered trusted friends.

He had met the Mallick family more than a dozen years ago, but it felt like yesterday. It had been pouring. One of those days where you just knew you were better off staying put. But Deacon was flying back from London, and Ryker had no choice but to venture out to pick him up from the airport.

He was almost at the highway when he spotted a car tipped over a steep embankment. It wouldn't have taken much more for the car to plummet into the gully below, hitting a few trees on its way, and taking the occupants with it.

He'd skidded his car to a stop and raced over to discover the driver unconscious, two kids in the back seat, and a distraught woman in the passenger seat trying to unlock her jammed seatbelt. Without thinking, he'd pulled the children to safety and managed to get both adults out before the ground gave way, and the car slipped down the embankment.

Zayne was still unconscious, and the paramedics would have taken too long, so he drove them to the nearest hospital and still managed to pick Deacon up in time.

He'd been eaten by guilt for not staying to ensure they were okay, so the next day he went back to the hospital. Turned out they knew who and what he was. That didn't stop little Annie from insisting a Vampire come for dinner once her daddy was better. And that's exactly where he found himself a week later. Even more extraordinary, after the initially uncomfortable part of the evening, he'd enjoyed himself. That was the first of many such evenings. As Annie grew and bloomed into a remarkable young woman with endless possibilities, so did his friendship with her parents.

How he had befriended a pair of Witches was beyond him. Over the years, he'd questioned it less and less, preferring just to accept the unconditional friendship and enjoy the limited time he ultimately knew they had. He'd celebrated their successes and each milestone as Annie and her older sister, Velvet, grew up. Outside of Deacon and Ananya, he considered them an extension of his family.

His guilt amplified with each step he took down the well-worn path. If he was such a good friend, why did it take him four days to see them after he broke the tragic news? *Because you couldn't face the fact that it was your job to protect her and you failed, that's why.*

A vice-like grip squeezed his chest. He had been living in fear, not capable of facing them again. How could he endure the condemnation that would be written all over their faces?

Keira touched his arm. "Are you alright?"

He mentally shook himself. Instead of replying, he pressed the doorbell and took off his hat. As the door edged open, he swallowed, but his parched throat felt like someone had dragged sandpaper down it.

Zayne's red-rimmed eyes were staring back at him without any sign of accusation or retribution. His friend was a man lost in grief. Wordlessly, Zayne stood back and waved them in.

Keira entered the house first.

As he passed the grief-stricken father, something made Ryker stop and place a hand on Zayne's shoulder. For a moment, they made eye contact. The pain emanating from Zayne was overwhelming. When Zayne's face crumpled, it took all of his effort to hold back the tears that threatened. Not knowing the words to say to a parent who had lost a child, Ryker tightened his grip on Zayne's shoulder.

In his very long lifetime, death had been a constant. Humans aged. Death came in all shapes and sizes, and more than once, by his hand. He'd learned the hard way to accept it, and until now, it had been easy. He'd grown up an orphan. Before Deacon, he had no concept of family. Until Annie, he never understood the pain of losing a loved one. How did Humans live with the anguish day after day?

Zayne wiped his eyes with the back of his hand. "Did you find who did this?"

"That's what we're here about."

They followed Zayne upstairs and down the hallway.

Just as he reached the last door, Zayne turned back to them. "Maize has been trying to channel Annie since this happened."

Ryker steeled himself as they walked into Annie's bedroom. Her scent was everywhere. Maize was seated on the edge of the bed, an old and tattered teddy bear clutched in her arms. She was slowly rocking back and forth, her lips moving, but the words were barely audible.

When she noticed she was no longer alone, Maize came out of her stupor. Her gaze rested on Keira, and she faltered.

"My baby's gone."

The broken way Maize cried out the simple sentence ripped through Ryker. He moved to the bed, sat beside her, and pulled her into a hug.

"I know, and I swear I'll get the bastards who did this."

Maize burst into tears, and her body convulsed as she wept.

He couldn't break down or show any weakness. They depended on him to keep them safe and mete out justice for Annie. A feeling of helplessness and grief washed over him in waves. They were family. No one did this to his family and got away with it.

Before his grief could consume him, he pushed it down and allowed the anger to set in. It fanned out from the pit of his stomach, and the flames, like wildfire, spread through every nerve ending in his body. He allowed the anger to burn white-hot. It was the only thing keeping him from disintegrating.

"You know she'd just been given an early acceptance to Northeastern?" Maize said through her broken sobs.

He pulled her closer. He couldn't find the words to comfort her. What words could possibly make this situation better? In the span of a few short days, someone had ripped the lives out of five good people. For what? So some misguided myth could live again. If what Keira said was true, the Order, a secret society, was in New England with the sole purpose of tracking down an equally elusive secret society. How had they gotten close enough to the Witches to discover their identities? Even he and Deacon didn't have that information.

A group of nefarious bastards were operating in his jurisdiction, under his watch, and he was clueless. *Fuck.* It was his job to know. The safety of everyone in Essex County was his responsibility. A responsibility he'd failed to carry out. He was now more than ever determined to find and kill every last man and woman in the Order. His resolve hardened. He would make sure they suffered tenfold before he allowed them the grace to die.

A single tear ran down Keira's cheek, and her eyes welled as she silently observed the distraught parents. He resisted the urge to wipe her tears away, as if that alone would remove any pain. Why he'd assumed she would be unaffected escaped him. But then, nothing about her was normal. And nothing about how he was drawn to her was normal either.

He cleared his throat and glanced around the bedroom, which, until recently, had been Annie's. Posters of her latest obsessions adorned the walls, and photos of Annie and her school friends were wedged into her mirror.

He cleared his throat a second time. "I know this is going to be hard for you both, but we've come to a roadblock and need some answers." He stood and nodded at Keira. "You might have heard that Dr. Wynter is working the case with me."

Maize blew her nose, but she was hovering between closing off and going on the defensive. The entire family of Witches would assume she was a Natural.

He took a step closer to Keira. "What you probably haven't heard through the jungle drums is that she's one of you."

Zayne and Maize's eyes widened, and they turned in unison to stare at Keira.

"What exactly do you mean by one of us?" Maize asked. "She's who the FBI sent. The last I looked, I wasn't on the government payroll."

Ryker shoved his hands into his pants pockets. "Technically, the doc is not here on behalf of the FBI. She's a Witch with the knowledge and experience to help us catch whoever is behind these murders. Not to mention, she's the only one keeping the federal authorities off our backs. And I don't need to tell you why we don't want them poking their noses into our business."

"We can see she's a Witch." Zayne's lips set into a grim line, and he looked fixedly at Keira. "How do we know this isn't a government trick?"

Keira stood her ground and didn't back down from his piercing gaze. "You don't. You need to take a leap of faith that I will do everything I can to help Sheriff Kincaid find the murderers and make sure no other families have to suffer like this. I am truly sorry for your loss."

Maize and Zayne continued to stare at Keira with suspicion.

Ryker ran a hand through his short hair. "I've seen what she can do firsthand, and I'll tell you right now, she can help."

Maize's shoulders slumped as if the wind had been taken out of her. "No one can help us. It's too late for that."

His mouth had a sour taste in it. She was right. Nothing would bring back Annie. Even if they got every last one of the killers, it wouldn't return Annie to the loving arms of her family.

"Where's Velvet?" he asked. Their eldest daughter no longer lived at home, but he assumed she would be with her parents right now.

Zayne made his way over to his wife and reached for her hand. "She's on her way to Virginia."

Virginia? What in blue blazes is the girl doing in Virginia?

Ryker's surprise must have shown.

"Maize has an aunt who wants to pay her respects." Zayne explained. "She doesn't trust planes and doesn't drive, so Velvet volunteered to collect her."

Maize interrupted before he could ask why they'd allowed her out of their sight. Especially when a bunch of killers were on the loose, hunting Witches and trying to open a gate to let a version of the Devil through.

"You said you had some questions?" Zayne prodded.

Rather than push the point and scare them, Ryker focused on the reason for the visit. "We're having trouble working out where Annie went after school that day."

Maize frowned and shook her head. "She was with Isabella and Rebekah. She was supposed to pick up some ginseng on the way home but rang to say she was spending time with her friends instead, and she'd be home around six."

He ran a hand through his hair. He didn't think Annie was in the habit of lying to her parents, but it appeared she had. "The problem is that her friends claim she went straight home."

Zayne and Maize looked at each other and then back at Ryker, showing disbelief and denial in every movement.

He had no way to sugarcoat this. "Was Annie seeing anyone?"

Zayne shook his head. "No. She broke up with that reprobate, Dan, last year and was concentrating on her studies."

Zayne had disliked his daughter's boyfriend from the moment she'd brought him home. While Ryker had to admit the boy was more brawn than brain, he was not such a bad kid. But after Dan was caught driving while intoxicated, his fate was sealed as far as Zayne was concerned.

Ryker shuffled uncomfortably. "I hate to push this, but are you sure she wasn't seeing anyone?"

"Positive," Zayne said.

Maize tugged on her husband's arm and fidgeted. She knew something. No longer able to put off the inevitable, he cleared his throat and prepared himself for their reaction.

"Zayne, Maize, I need to tell you something, but I think you both need to be sitting down."

Zayne sank onto the bed and waited.

How could he soften the blow? This would be the second time he'd delivered devastating news to them. He opened his mouth to speak, but words failed him.

"The preliminary autopsy results came back," Keira said.

Relief flooded through him. Somehow, she'd picked up on his pain.

Zayne's entire body stilled, and Maize's hand clutched tighter around her husband's. "And?"

Keira hesitated before speaking. "Annie was twelve weeks pregnant."

Zayne bolted off the bed. "She was what?"

His voice was so loud, the neighbors must have heard him.

Maize's trembling hands covered her mouth. "My baby."

Zayne shook his head and clenched his fists. "No. That's not possible. There must be a mistake."

Before Zayne could work himself up any further, Maize stood and rested a hand on his arm. "Calm down, Zayne." She studied Keira and then Ryker. "Are you sure?"

His stomach clenched as he nodded.

Maize let out a small whimper, then fell silent. She wandered over to the chest of drawers, reached out, and reverently touched a recent photo of Annie.

"I suspected she w-was seeing someone."

Zayne frowned. "Why didn't you tell me?"

"After Dan, and how much grief you put her through, I assumed the new boyfriend was someone you would disapprove of. Her grades weren't slipping, she wasn't missing school or her other commitments, so I let her have her little secret."

The conversation was on the verge of becoming a domestic argument.

Ryker cut in. "Do you have any idea who this secret boyfriend might be?"

"Perhaps Annie's friends know who he is?" Keira raised her voice in question.

"Do you think this boy was involved in what happened?" Zayne asked.

Ryker had an uneasy feeling about the secret boyfriend. Not telling her parents was one thing. Keeping it from her best friends was an entirely different matter. "At this stage, he's a person of interest. He may be able to give us a better idea of where she went that day or where they were. We need to understand how the killers got to all of the victims."

Zayne pulled Maize closer. Their shared strength was the only thing getting them through the grief. "Have you spoken to the other families yet?"

Ryker shook his head. "You're the first. We're headed to see Zac Cole's family next."

Maize hauled in a shaky breath and whispered, "So much darkness and sorrow, but at least their lights will live on."

"We couldn't find anything on her laptop or phone that would help." Ryker's eyes scanned the room. Perhaps something here might give them a clue as to whom Annie was seeing. "Did Annie keep a diary?"

Maize bit the inside of her lip. A habit when she was concentrating hard on something. "No, I don't think so."

"Do you mind if we look?"

For the next fifteen minutes, the four of them scoured through Annie's possessions. A sense of urgency charged the room as they rustled through each drawer and searched every nook and cranny.

Ryker replaced a large cushion from an oversized chair and scanned the room once more. Nothing. They had found nothing.

Keira closed the last drawer and made her way over to him.

"Do you really think she kept a diary?" she asked in a low voice.

He considered the question. "To be honest, I don't know. She never mentioned one, but I don't suppose a teenage girl would broadcast something like that."

"In my experience, teenagers need to share their secrets with someone, even if it is only on paper. So, yes, I think she kept a diary of some sort. We just haven't found it."

Indecision flitted across her face as she studied the grieving parents, who were still searching through the closet. She drew in, and slowly released a breath, as if she were about to jump off a cliff and didn't know if there was anything to catch her at the bottom.

She pulled Maize to one side. "I'm so very sorry for your loss, and at any other time, I wouldn't intrude on or invade your privacy."

Zayne stopped his rummaging to listen in.

"But in this situation, I don't think we have any alternatives. If Annie had a secret, we need to know what it was. Someone is targeting Witches, and we need to find them before anyone else dies."

Maize frowned. "I don't understand. That's what we've been doing, looking for a diary."

"If Annie kept a secret in this room, I could use my power to find it. But the secret I discover may not be her diary, and you may not like it.".

Ryker's brows lifted. *Now she tells us.* If she'd mentioned she had another trick up her sleeve, it would have saved them valuable time.

Annie's parents hesitated, then Maize nodded. "Do whatever you have to, as long as I get to see it first."

He took a step back. Who knew what would shoot out of nowhere. The woman was an enigma. The crazy cat lady was right. Never before had he seen the level of power she possessed. If he were a betting man, he would lay odds that he had only witnessed a fraction of what she was capable of.

Keira cast her spell, then gracefully meandered through the room, randomly touching Annie's belongings. A stray hair came loose from the tightly coiled bun at the nape of her slender neck. He suppressed a smile. Had she known, it would have been whipped back into shape. He fixated on her stunning red hair. The hue was somewhere between a vibrant red and a burnt orange. What would it feel like to run his fingers through her magnificent tresses?

He froze. Where the fuck was his mind at? An abnormally long span of time had passed since he'd bedded anyone. That shouldn't mean you start fantasizing about a colleague, especially a witch doctor with far too many opinions! Besides. She's way too old for you. He mentally shook himself and forced his attention back to what Keira was up to. From Zayne and Maize's expressions, they had no idea either.

She circled the room a few times while muttering some sort of spell under her breath. Then she stiffened, and her gaze darted to a clothes hamper next to the chest of drawers. She dropped to her knees and pulled on a wobbly floorboard. Much to their astonishment, it pried itself loose without much effort. Keira's hand disappeared through the hole and emerged clutching a small leather-bound book. She rose from the floor and handed the journal to Maize.

Zayne opened his mouth to speak, thought better of it, and rushed to his wife's side. Maize paled and dropped to the bed, not taking her eyes off Keira. Her hands shook as she placed the bear she had been holding on the bed beside her. The effort to keep calm was written all over her face. Annie's parents had been through so much, only to discover more anguish.

Maize lovingly ran her fingers over the hardcover as it rested on her lap. Her face full of sorrow, her eyes darted upward to her husband for reassurance.

Zayne placed an arm around her and rested his forehead against hers. Maize closed her eyes, and her chin trembled. She pulled away and flipped the cover. As she turned the pages, her brows knitted, and the wrinkles in her forehead deepened.

Zayne, who had been reading over her shoulder, mimicked her expression.

"What's the matter?" Ryker asked.

Zayne shook his head. "It's illegible. I don't understand, shouldn't whatever spell she cast on it dissolve the moment she …"

Ryker didn't need Zayne to finish the sentence. He already knew the missing word his friend was unable to say.

Died.

Any active spell that Annie had cast should have died with her. Even Ryker, with his limited knowledge, knew that.

Maize shook her head. "Normally, but she must have used a talisman to channel and maintain the power."

Keira stiffened. Something had sparked her interest.

"That was smart thinking," she said.

He was sure she wanted to say more but held back.

Maize handed Keira the small journal, and he made his way over to inspect the leather-bound book with her. Each page was full of letters and words. The letters he recognized, but the words they formed were unintelligible.

"Is there any way to break the spell?"

Keira bit her bottom lip. "If we find the object she transferred the power to, then maybe."

He frowned. They needed to find the last person who'd seen Annie alive, but right now, they were stuck. Annie had lied to her friends and her parents about meeting a boy. He could understand her not telling her parents, especially after Zayne's reaction to Dan, but surely she would confide in her friends? Something about this whole situation didn't sit well.

Keira looked to Maize. "Do you mind if we take the diary?"

Maize stared at the journal in Keira's hands. "No. I only ask that if you manage to break the spell, you keep anything that's not relevant private."

Keira gave her a small smile. "You have my word." Her expression grew apprehensive. "We have something else to ask. I assume you've heard we're trying to speak to the Crossroads coven?"

Maize's hands clasped tighter around the bear, and she nodded.

Ryker took a step closer. "Do you know who we could talk to?"

"We can't help you," Maize said. "Annie was Crossroads. Not us."

"We realize that. But Annie may have mentioned some names, or you may have overheard her speaking to the others? I know you wouldn't betray a confidence, but we're trying to stop this from happening again."

"I can't help you." Maize sank onto the bed. "I come from a long line of Le Fay Witches. Crossroads is one of the oldest covens in the United States. When it was clear Annie's powers were linked to the earth, the Crossroads coven invited her to join them. We were thrilled. What parent wouldn't be?"

Zayne choked back a sob. "She was learning so much more with them than she did in Le Fay."

Maize wiped her tears away and sniffed. "Annie took her role with Crossroads seriously. She never gave us names, and we would never ask. Apart from the members of the coven that we all know about, we can't tell you the names of the members we don't."

"What do you think?" Keira asked, as they headed back to the car.

Ryker studied the journal. "I think we need to find that boyfriend."

"I agree. And unless she told someone, or our mystery boyfriend steps forward, we need to break the spell."

He opened the car door. "Can you do it?"

She climbed into the passenger seat. "Probably, but it will take some time, and right now, we need to talk to the rest of the families."

"What about Dayna?" he asked.

"What about her?"

"Is her, you know, magic as good as yours? Perhaps she and your dreadlock wannabe influencer TA can work on it."

Keira turned to look out the window as she considered his suggestion. "That's not a bad idea and might just work."

He let out a snort as he turned the engine over. "Don't sound so surprised. I have been doing this for a while, you know. I may not have a broom, but I have my own set of skills."

By the time they dropped off Annie's journal with Dayna and Marcus and returned to Salem, it was nearly midday. Ryker had already warned Cecelia that they needed to speak with her about Zac's death. Both Cecelia and Zac worked at a high school south of Salem. Zac was the football coach and taught driver's ed, while Cecelia was the physics teacher.

They were polar opposites in every way. Zac was a Salem native who could trace his family back several generations. Cecelia was a petite refugee whose family perished on the killing fields of Cambodia. Zac was a Supernatural. Cecelia was not.

While Cecelia had no family to support her in her hour of need, she had more than enough friends in the community who rallied around her. The problem was that most of them were Naturals, and he couldn't have a conversation if they were around. The community survived on a policy of don't ask, don't tell.

A cat on the side of the road reminded Ryker of their early morning conversation with the lunatic. "We haven't heard from Beatrice yet. How long does it take to make a few phone calls?"

Keira suppressed a smile. "When I said she needed to do a calling, I didn't mean she was going to phone them."

"Oh?"

"A calling is done in the rarest of circumstances. It's a spell the upper members of the Synod feel. We generally can't resist the request. Once it's cast, each one will make contact with her for a time and place."

He chuckled. "You Broomhilders don't do things the easy way, do you? Have none of you learned how to text, Facebook, or Twitter?"

By mid-afternoon, the uneasy feeling that had begun when Ryker heard about Annie's lie and her unknown whereabouts when she'd gone missing, had escalated.

Zac had left football practice early, saying his wife was ill. This came as news to Cecelia.

The same scenario repeated itself with each of the victims.

Every one of them had lied about their whereabouts.

After dropping Keira at the house, he headed to the station to deal with the ever-increasing paperwork. He had only been in his office five minutes when Leon strode in.

"Hey, boss, we were expecting you earlier."

"I was following up on some leads. How are you doing with the missing girls?"

Leon dumped himself on one of the chairs in front of his desk. "Nothing. We got the warrant for their bank and phone records and came up empty. There've been no transactions since they were taken, and no calls in or out."

Ryker reached for a file and signed the forms in the places marked by the admin staff. "What about the traffic cam footage from Main Street? Any unusual activity?"

"Mitos is looking through it now." Leon leaned back in his chair. "If we don't know what we're looking for, it might take a while and be a waste of time."

Ryker gave his deputy a pointed stare. "It's procedure. We need to cover every possible avenue."

Color flooded Leon's face as he leaned forward. Ryker hadn't meant to snap, but he sometimes wondered about the officer's ability to think outside the rules he religiously adhered to.

"Sorry, boss, but I don't think we're going to find them alive. They've been gone nearly twenty-four hours."

Ryker stared out the door at the bullpen. Shift change was drawing near, and officers were coming and going as one shift handed over to the other. As much as he didn't want to admit it, Leon's unspoken implication was spot on. They hadn't received any ransom demands, and with nothing else to go on, these cases would likely change to a recovery rather than the happy ending the families were hoping for.

"Just keep on it," Ryker finally said as he picked up the next file and proceeded to initial and sign.

Leon jumped out of his chair.

"Yes, sheriff." The deputy halted at the door and turned back. "You never told us the autopsy results."

Ryker rose and stacked the folders he had completed. "I didn't? Must have slipped my mind." He handed Leon the bundle. "Drop these at Marsha's desk, will you? I'll brief you when I get a chance." He sat back down. "The ME couldn't tell us anything that we didn't already know. We'll need to wait for the full autopsy results to come back."

"That'll take weeks."

Ryker went back to his pile of manila folders. "That's what they tell me."

It took the better part of the next two hours to get through his backlog. After locking his office, he left instructions with the duty sergeant to contact him if they got a break in the two missing girls' case.

A flickering shadow in the audio-visual room stopped him as he headed for the exit. Curious, he peered around the door to discover Mitos watching traffic footage, all the while grumbling under his breath.

"Anything?"

Mitos scratched the back of his silver-white hair. "Nope. Just a bunch of weirdos, faggots, and skanks, and that's just the tourists. Don't get me started on the fucked-up locals."

Ryker cringed. "Watch your mouth, Mitos, or you'll be attending cultural sensitivity training again."

Mitos shrugged and went back to scouring through the video. "You and me both know that's a waste of time. I've taken that class so often, I could teach it myself."

Ryker ignored the comment and didn't say anything about how much money the department had wasted on Mitos going to sensitivity training over and over again.

As he reached for his keys, Mitos called out, "Just make sure you schedule me on the day that hot blonde with the big jugs and short skirt is teaching. At least I'll have something to look at."

"I didn't hear that," Ryker called over his shoulder as he headed toward the door.

"Sheriff."

"What is it now?" he muttered under his breath.

He turned back to the AV room.

"You going to be at the Witches Brew tonight?" Mitos asked.

Ryker glanced at the station's clock, which also displayed the date. "Shit. Is that tonight?"

Mitos chuckled. "Yep. See you there."

Damn. Once a month, the local first responders had a longstanding pool challenge. While he didn't compete, he was obliged to attend. After his station's abysmal loss the previous month, if he skipped out, that smartarse fire chief would never let Ryker hear the end of it.

He had no choice but to attend and make the best of a bad situation. Besides, he could do with a night out. Perhaps he could also top up on some warm blood. His accident that morning had proven his reserves were depleted.

<u>SEVENTEEN</u>

IT'S RAINING MEN

"Firemen!" Dayna squealed. "I love firemen. What time are we leaving?"

Keira threw up her hands. Of course, that's the first thing her sister would declare when surrounded by men. But she was not as eager to agree to Ryker's suggestion that they all have a night out.

She closed the Grimoire. The book contained a wealth of information, but they hadn't yet found anything that might help them track down members of the Order.

"Are you sure it's safe?"

"The place will be full of police," Ryker replied. "Not to mention fire and paramedics. Apart from here, it's probably the safest place to be."

Dayna crumpled her nose and glared. "Don't be such a party pooper. You're going, and that's final." She turned to Ryker. "How many firemen did you say will be there?"

Despite Keira's reservations, she agreed to go. It took Ryker a little longer to convince Deacon, who argued that he had too much to do.

Dayna pouted at Deacon from her place on the couch. "Fiddlesticks, all work and no play is not allowed while I'm here. Besides, if the local hosers don't measure up, at least I know there'll be one man in the place."

Ryker and Marcus snorted in unison.

"What am I?" Ryker pointed to himself. "Chopped liver?"

Marcus huffed. "Yeah, remember which man got you out of that libr-shoe shop in one piece."

Dayna raised her hands in the air to stop their objections. "Boys, boys, don't fight. There's more than enough of me to go around." She twisted a strand of hair around her finger, her expression absent as she grew silent before jumping up from the chair. "What's the dress code? I hope I've brought something that pops." She headed toward the door. "Are you coming, Keira?"

"What for?"

Her sister looked at her as if she'd grown an extra head. "To get changed, of course."

Keira glanced down at her dark suit. "What's wrong with what I'm wearing?"

"We're having a night on the town, not the southern spinsters' weekly bridge game." Dayna wrinkled her nose in distaste as she glared at her clothes. "Now get your A into G, and let's go."

Keira sighed and reluctantly trailed behind her sister. She hadn't packed anything suitable for a night out, and her gym gear might be a little *too* relaxed.

She was standing over her suitcase, staring at the contents, when Dayna sashayed through the door with a bundle of clothing.

"Try these on," she said as she tossed the clothing onto the bed.

Keira picked up a pair of jeans and arched an eyebrow.

Dayna placed her hands on her hips and tapped a foot. "I'll have you know they're Stella McCartney, and I paid good money to have them ripped like that."

Keira flipped over the jeans and gasped at the location of the holes on the butt.

"Just put them on." Dayna ordered. "Or I'll disintegrate all your clothes, and we'll see how fussy you are about what you wear."

"Fine." Keira shucked her dark trousers and pulled on the jeans.

A little spell should fix those rips up good as new.

They were the same size in clothing. Which, in their younger days, had been convenient. Their tastes had deviated when Dayna embraced the 1920s with gusto.

She inspected the tops Dayna threw on the bed.

"There's no way I'm wearing any of those," she said. "I'd like to leave *something* to the imagination."

Dayna made a disapproving sound in the back of her throat. "You should flaunt your assets, and I don't mean that over-developed brain of yours."

Dayna sauntered over and reached behind Keira's head. A tug on her hair, and a moment later, Dayna waved the pin holding her bun in place.

"Fine. I'll get you a top your Victorian sensibilities will approve of, only if you leave your hair down."

Before she could answer, Dayna rushed out of the room. "Be right back." A squeal of excitement reverberated through the room. "And I have the perfect CFM shoes for you to wear."

Keira frowned at the patent leather pumps by the bed.

"I don't know why I can't at least wear my own shoes," she muttered to an empty room.

The drive into Salem was at Ryker's standard pace. *Turbo*. The Cherokee was big enough for all of them, and she somehow managed to get stuck in the back seat between Marcus and Dayna.

Marcus fidgeted the entire way. "Man. This is not the way I thought this trip was going to go. I should have way more footage to work with by now. Instead, I've been cooped up in a museum all day."

"I'm sure you'll find more than enough to film tonight." Keira soothed, trying to get him to relax. "You might get lucky and find someone wearing sneakers."

He shook his head in mock horror. "Fat chance. A bar with a bunch of first responders? If there's anyone *not* wearing black combat boots, I'll wear Air Jordan fifteens for a week." He leaned forward and tapped on Ryker's shoulder. "What sort a beer they got on tap?"

"Not sure what they're promoting this week, but it's primarily local craft beer," Ryker said over his shoulder.

Marcus sat back with a grin. "Dude. Why didn't you lead with that? Maybe the night won't be a waste after all."

"I'll get Leon to introduce you around. He pretty much knows most of the people there, and I understand he is into his craft beers as well."

The Witch's Brew was bursting at the seams. By the time they arrived, things were already in full swing.

Dayna surveyed the room, and her face split into a wide grin. "Mother Earth, it's raining men."

Dayna turned back to Deacon and tucked her arm under his. At the sudden contact, he stiffened.

Keira was positive that few people made themselves that familiar with the formidable Vampire without his permission.

Dayna beamed up at Deacon. "Don't wander too far. I may need saving." She took another survey of the crowded room. "So, what are we drinking?"

Ryker visibly strained beneath the stress of holding back a smirk as Dayna dragged a man twice her size to the bar. Like Moses, the sea of people parted to allow them through.

What sort of reputation did Deacon have to warrant that level of avoidance? As she was about to ask Ryker to shed some light, Keira discovered he was beckoning to someone across the room. A tall, familiar face pushed through a small throng of people. She cast her mind back to the crime scene at Haverhill. Lester? No, Leon. Deputy Leon Trudeau.

"Hey, boss, we were wondering when you'd get here."

"I thought I'd invite Dr. Wynter and Mr. North along to show them that while we may not be a big city like LA, we have our own brand of entertainment." Ryker nodded at Marcus. "It might be a good idea for you to introduce Marcus around. He'll be here for a few more days and should get to know a few on the team."

Leon pushed his hands into his pockets and gave Marcus the once-over. "So, what's your poison, book boy?"

Marcus looked down and grimaced. "I should not have made that bet."

Leon's eyebrows drew together. "What?"

"Nice Stan Smiths. Do you have any decent craft beer?"

Leon's expression changed in an instant, and his eyes lit up. "Man, have you come to the right place. Follow me."

Marcus tossed her an inquiring glance.

She shrugged her shoulders. "Don't look at me. You don't need my permission. But if you end up in the same state you did last fall, you're fired. I will only be thrown up on once."

Marcus grinned at her teasing threat. "You won't fire me. You love me too much."

He bolted and caught up with Leon, and they disappeared into the crowd.

Ryker draped an arm over her shoulder. "Looks like you're left with me, Doc. The kids have flown the coop."

Warmth spread through her body at the familiar way in which Ryker touched her. Too startled to move, she remained still.

He raised two fingers and nodded at the bartender. "My guess is that you're a white wine kind of gal."

She tried to put some distance between them and failed. "A chardonnay will be fine if they have it."

Ryker spotted an opening at the bar and propelled them toward it. Just as they reached the seats, the bartender placed two tall glasses in front of them.

She eyed the lagers. "You must be thirsty."

He gave her a subtle wink and slid one of the glasses over to her. "This one's yours."

Her brows furrowed. "But I didn't order a beer."

"I know." Ryker picked up his glass and took a few gulps. "Your sister thought it would be a good idea if you tried something new. I figured a beer would be a good place to start." He shouted over the noise, "Relax, it's been a shitty week, and she's only got your best interest at heart."

She scanned the room for Dayna. It figured her sister would rope in others to torment her. The place was wall-to-wall with people. Somewhere in the milling crowd was her conniving sister. A very dead one if Keira got her hands on her.

A small group eager for refills jostled her. Before she was trampled under the rush, Ryker pulled her out of the way, and once again, she was pressed against him.

She stared at the zipper on Ryker's leather jacket only to realize when she fell into him, she had clutched his white t-shirt. She released her grip and attempted to straighten the stretched fabric.

"Sorry, I didn't mean to make a mess of your shirt."

Ryker placed his hand over hers and maneuvered them so that he was nearest the crowd. "It's only a shirt." He released her and reached for their beers. He handed one to her. "Now, I'm here to educate you on our local vintages."

She stared at the tall glass and held back a shudder. Her last attempt at trying beer was in the 1950s, and only then to fit in with the locals when she'd passed through a small town in rural Australia. She squared her shoulders and reached for the brew.

Ryker burst into laughter and shook his head. "Anyone would think you're headed to the gallows. You really do need to get a life, don't you?"

Her eyes flashed, and she raised her chin. "I'll have you know I lead a very full existence. I've traveled practically everywhere. I have a fulfilling career, a great apartment, season tickets for the ballet, and I—"

His laughter erupted once again. For the life of her, she couldn't work out what set him off this time. He cocked his head and gave her a penetrating gaze. Not used to that level of scrutiny, she looked away. Something told her he was astute enough to see into her very soul.

Needing something to do, she took a sip of the cold drink. The taste was oddly sweet—nothing like the bitter palate from her memory. She tried it again and let the flavor settle on her tongue before she swallowed. Strawberries. It tasted like strawberries.

Before she knew what was happening, she'd emptied half her glass. When she looked up, Ryker was grinning from ear-to-ear and sporting a self-satisfied expression.

She squirmed. "Don't start. I know what you're thinking, and you're wrong. I was thirsty, that's all."

"I wasn't going to say a thing." He reached for a lock of her hair and caressed the strands between his fingers. "You know, I've wanted to do that all day."

Her body quivered. She was both hot and cold at the same moment. While he was doing nothing wrong, his touch felt intimate. She regarded him as he concentrated on her locks. The Vampire was easy on the eye. She would have to be blind not to recognize his sensuality. And from the accident in the hallway that morning, she knew firsthand that his attractiveness extended throughout his body.

"Apart from the hoity-toity you surround yourself with," he said, "do you ever get off your broomstick and allow yourself to have fun?"

He was still playing with her hair, but he was studying her reaction. She forced herself to remain calm and unaffected by his proximity.

On the outside, she was the epitome of strength and every bit as cool, calm, and collected as ever. Inside was a different matter. Her arms and legs turned to jello, and her pulse raced out of control. It was the beer. She was just not used to the barley. She gulped down the rest of her drink. Hopefully, it would give her the strength to push down the improper and erotic thoughts and have a conversation with him.

"Well?" Ryker prodded.

She slammed the glass onto the bar with a little more force than she intended. "Firstly, I don't have a broomstick."

The corners of his eyes crinkled at her outburst. The man was enjoying her discomfort.

"And secondly, I have fun."

"Are you sure about that?"

She crossed her arms and nodded.

"And exactly who is it that you have *fun* with?" he asked in a low earthy tone that rippled through her.

"I—" She faltered, a lie balancing on the tip of her tongue.

Damn it! How the hell did the conversation get so out of control?

"So, it's just you and your broomstick then?"

Certain her head was going to explode, she rubbed her forehead. "I think I need another drink."

Ryker leaned over the bar and ordered another round. While they were waiting, she watched Marcus at the other end of the bar, deep in conversation with an off-duty paramedic. He'd always had a way with people. To be fair, when he wanted to, he got along with most people, no matter their walk of life or background. Among his many talents, the one that marked him as Gifted was his empathic ability. He could read a situation and know the right thing to say at the right time.

She nearly jumped out of her skin when someone tapped her on the shoulder. "Hello, Dr. Wynter. I didn't see you in the café this morning."

She spun around to find Nita, the owner of Café Luna, behind her. "I'm no longer staying at the hotel."

Nita smiled. "The rumor mill is actually correct this time then. You're now out at the Eastridge Estate?"

She nodded. "That's small towns for you. Nothing is sacred."

Their drinks arrived, and Ryker grabbed her by the arm. "The game's about to start."

Before he could pull her into the crowd, she gave Nita an apologetic smile. "Sorry. But we will be back to the café. You were right, the apple cider donuts are the best I've ever tasted."

Not sure how they did it without spilling a drop, he navigated them across the jam-packed room and maneuvered them into a prime position to watch the game.

The sheriff's department won the toss, and a cheer went up from the crowd. She couldn't get over the level of competitiveness between the two departments as they hurled friendly abuse at each other. The game was fire against police, with the paramedics as referees.

After watching Ryker's team sink the first four balls and then miss the next, she was curious about the rules of the game. "So how do you win?"

"Have you not played before?" Ryker asked.

She shook her head.

He slipped an arm around her waist. "Just as well I'm a great teacher. Did you know the game evolved from a lawn game similar to croquet played during the fifteenth century in Europe?"

Without waiting for an answer, he appeared to make it his personal mission to turn her into an expert on pool in a single evening.

Every now and then, one of Ryker's officers would stop and introduce themselves. After the first five, she didn't bother trying to keep track of their names, but it struck her just how close Ryker was to his men. It was obvious they respected and looked up to him, even Mitos, the gruff and rude shlumpy one.

The teams were evenly matched, which only exacerbated the rivalry. To her surprise, she enjoyed the evening and ended up being as vocal as the remainder of the sheriff's department supporters. When she thought about it, it had been a long time since she had so much fun. But no way would she admit that fact to Ryker. She would never live it down.

A couple of times, Dayna, the social butterfly that she was, floated by. Her sister would wink and blow her a kiss as she disappeared back into the crowd, but it had been a while since she last saw Marcus. She scanned the throng of people.

Ryker lowered his voice so that only she could hear. "You know, you should smile more often. It takes at least three hundred years off of you. Too much more, and you'll be impossible to resist."

She lifted her face to him. The teasing tone he'd adopted for most of the evening was gone. In its place was a timbre she couldn't quite identify.

The moment she met his intense gaze, her smile froze, and her breath caught in her throat. His eyes bore through her as they intensified and became hypnotic, sapping the strength from her. The raw desire burning in his eyes set her body on fire. The heat was all-consuming and weakened her resolve to be unaffected by him. His head lowered, and his breath fanned across her face. With a gentle push of his finger beneath her chin, he angled her head. She held her breath, waiting for his lips to meet hers. Her entire core was reaching out to be tasted by this Vampire.

"Hey, babe. You ready?"

They sprang apart at the intrusion. Her fire extinguished as fast as it had exploded when a tall, leggy blonde gave her a once-over before turning her focus on Ryker.

His lids snapped shut. When he opened them again, his simmering gaze had returned to normal. All evidence of the desire from a moment ago was gone. Shut off as fast as it had ignited.

Keira let out a slow breath to settle her erratic pulse, not sure if she was relieved or furious at the sudden intrusion.

The woman stood on her tiptoes and curled a hand behind his neck, then planted a sensual kiss on his collarbone. Had Keira not seen it herself, she wouldn't have believed it. Jealousy, green and vile, ripped through her as the woman tugged Ryker with her.

"Come on, babe, what are you waiting for?" the woman asked. "I'm back on shift in twenty."

Ryker glanced at the blonde and then back at her. "Will you be alright by yourself for a few minutes?"

Keira blinked. How did he go from whatever they shared, to racing off with a bimbo for a quickie in the parking lot?

Numb, she shrugged and forced her voice to stay steady. "I'll be fine."

She turned back to the game and pretended to follow the action with the rest of the audience.

EIGHTEEN

SOUND OF SILENCE

Keira's emotional defenses were back in place by the time Dayna materialized by her side. Deacon followed not far behind.

"Having fun?" Keira asked brightly.

Her voice came out normal and reflected none of the tumultuous emotions flaring inside her.

Dayna bobbed her head and wiggled in time to the music that blared over the sound system. "Everyone is so nice. Especially the firemen." She giggled. "They want to take me for a ride in their big truck this week."

Keira groaned. "You're not going to sleep your way through the entire Salem Fire Department, are you?"

Dayna hit her in the shoulder. "No, silly, not *all* of them."

Nothing in Deacon's expression indicated a reaction, but he'd clearly heard every word.

"I hope she didn't make too much of a spectacle of herself," Keira said apologetically after Dayna raced off to get another drink.

"It was entertaining, if nothing else."

Keira fidgeted with one of her rings. Why had she agreed to come?

Deacon craned his neck to scan the packed bar. "Where's Ryker?"

Her gaze darted to the pool table, and she pretended to focus on the game. "Umm, he ducked out for a few minutes. He said he'd be right back."

"Deidre found him, did she? I was worried she wouldn't, and he'd go another night without."

Her brow rose. She would never understand Vampires. Deacon sounded like he was overjoyed Ryker was tripping the light fantastic with a cheap skank.

Mother Earth, she was starting to sound like Dayna. She moved the subject well away from Ryker's libido and into safe territory.

"Have you seen Marcus around?"

"Last time I saw him, he was over by the bar."

The game was drawing to a close when Ryker pushed his way through the crowd. From the way he was hurrying, he was agitated.

The bad little Witch inside her smirked. Performance anxiety?

He stopped and spoke to two men, who grabbed their jackets and headed out the door. Her pity party came to an abrupt halt. Something had happened. From his expression as he stormed toward them, she knew it was serious enough that his game face was back. He was all business.

Deacon stiffened. "What happened?"

Even Dayna turned serious.

Ryker raked a frustrated hand through his hair and shook his head. "I just got a call from the duty sergeant. He sent out a car to investigate a complaint." The muscles in his face tightened, and he looked at her. "They found Beatrice Sommer's body. It looks like she was severely beaten before she died."

Fear ripped through Keira as his words sank in. "Didn't you have a car outside her house?"

"Yes. He followed her to Patty's, her sister's, and that's where she was supposed to stay for the night. Somehow, she got by him and went back to her place. To feed those damn cats, I bet."

Her mind went into overdrive. Why would the Order risk killing a Witch who was under surveillance? What was so important that they would risk getting caught?

Ryker's phone went off, and he answered before the second ring. He barked out orders and let the unfortunate soul at the other end of his tirade knew, in no uncertain terms, that if animal control didn't round up the cats before they contaminated the site, there would be hell to pay.

"I need to get out to the crime scene. I'll drop you home first." He scanned the room. While the bar was not as full as it once was, it was still crowded enough to make it difficult to find someone. "Where's Marcus?"

"I'm not sure." She stretched her neck to look over the bar area in case he was loitering in one of the dark corners with someone. "I haven't seen him in a while."

"If you ask me," Dayna chimed in. "He's found a warm bed for the night and is doing much better than any of us." She reached into her small bag and fished out her phone. "How about we call him? It might be easier than sending out a search party and a lot less embarrassing if we walk in on something."

She punched in his number and waited. She pulled the phone away from her ear and stared at the screen. Her lips twitched. "How rude. He didn't pick up. I'm going to have words with that boy."

Ryker spotted Leon a short distance away. "Trudeau, have you seen Marcus?"

Leon shook his head and shrugged his shoulders. "Sorry, boss, he hooked up with one of the paramedics, and I haven't seen him since."

"Shit." Ryker growled. "This is all I need." He turned to Keira. "We can't wait any longer. I'll have Trudeau round him up and drop him home."

Her gaze wandered over the room again. Where the hell was Marcus? Something was not right. Marcus was many things, but irresponsible wasn't one of them.

She pursed her lips. "He wouldn't leave without telling me. Dayna, can you try him again?"

A commotion behind the bar stopped Dayna. Two of the kitchen staff were visibly distressed and in the middle of a frantic discussion with the bartender. They were close enough to see the shocked expressions but not close enough to hear their conversation.

A small group of patrons gathered near the doorway to the kitchen. One of the cooks held a crying woman to his shoulder while the rest threw furtive glances at each other.

Her pulse skipped a beat. From the protective way the staff rallied around her, the woman was clearly traumatized. The bartender broke away from the two men and scanned the room. When he caught sight of Ryker, he mouthed a few words and jerked his head toward the back.

Ryker's body stiffened.

"You understood what he said?" she asked.

Ryker nodded, and his eyes narrowed as he listened to whatever he was being told. He spun around, and his gaze darted to the small groups around them.

Ryker's voice boomed over the noise. "Barret, Trudeau, Mitos, Wilenski."

In an instant, the four men were in front of him. Curious, a few of their compatriots followed behind.

"We have a ten-fifty-four in the alley behind the building. Secure the scene and make sure no one goes near it."

Not having to be told twice, the four raced out the door.

Ryker turned to Deacon. "Keep Dayna and Keira here. Do not let them out of your sight. You spot one broomstick, and you have my permission to burn it." He stopped midstride and anchored his gaze on her. "You know that broomstick remark was aimed at you, right?"

She glared at him. "I'm not stupid. There are too many Naturals in the room. Why would I try any magic?"

Ryker turned deadly serious.

He lowered his head until they were almost cheek to cheek. "You look for Marcus the old-fashioned way. If I hear you risked exposure to locate him, I will run you out of town so fast your runes won't be able to keep up."

The warmth from his proximity vanished as he straightened and raced out the door.

How did he know she was considering risking magic? They would need to scour the building the old-fashioned way.

She turned back to Dayna. "Look under every table. He's probably passed out on the floor somewhere."

Dayna nodded and took a step before turning back to Deacon. "What's a ten fifty-four?"

"Homicide."

Keira faltered at Deacon's answer, and she nearly tripped over her feet. Homicide? Terror consumed her, and she forgot to breathe. A burning sensation grew in her lungs until she hauled in a breath before slowly releasing it. The tightness in her chest remained as her lungs filled again. This was what a heart attack must feel like.

She spun on her heel and sprinted across the room as fast as her stilettoes would allow. Exiting the building, she skidded to a halt. Which way? Choosing the left, she took off like the Devil was behind her. But with each step closer to the small crowd gathered in the poorly lit alleyway, her mind screamed.

"Don't let it be. Please don't let it be."

She rounded the corner to the back of the building and spotted Ryker standing by the dumpster. He turned, a look of surprise on his face, and hollered at the officers nearest her.

"Stop her! Don't let her come any closer."

Leon stepped in her path and grabbed her by the shoulders. "You can't go in there," he said through gritted teeth.

Her heart beat faster, and she fought to break free. Using all the strength she had, she brought her heel down on Leon's foot. Not expecting the attack, the deputy's grip faltered enough for her to escape. She deftly evaded the second officer who tried to catch her.

As she reached the dumpster, she ran straight into Ryker, who blocked her path. He wrapped an arm around her waist and turned her away from the body discarded on the far side of the garbage bin.

"You don't want to see this," he said as he pressed her face against his shoulder.

She pushed against his chest and squirmed in his arms.

"Let me go." Her voice came out as a desperate cry. "It's not him. It can't be."

Ryker relaxed his grip, and she pivoted before he could change his mind. Her brain closed down the moment she laid eyes on the broken body of her teaching assistant and friend. His head was twisted in an unnatural position. Marcus' eyes stared back at her lifelessly. His contact lens had fallen out, and the purple and orange eye of a Gifted stared back at her.

The initial shock gave way to a tsunami of grief and denial as a heart-wrenching "*No*" ripped from her lips.

Her legs buckled, and she shivered uncontrollably. "No, he can't be dead. You've made a mistake."

This was not happening. Someone was playing a cruel joke. Any moment now, Marcus would sit up and scare the living daylights out of her. She would get pissed at him for scaring her, and, as usual, get over it a short time later.

Get up!

Ryker caught her as she collapsed. He turned her away from the dumpster and pulled her into his chest.

"He's gone," he whispered into her hair.

His gentleness was her undoing. Ryker confirmed what she already knew but couldn't accept. She was consumed with pain as the tears erupted, and her body convulsed with anguish.

Movement was happening around her, yet it sounded far away. Not that it mattered. Keira was unable to hear anything over the dull buzz hovering over her, refusing to budge and refusing to let her concentrate. What day of the week was it? It was Friday … was it still Friday? She had never liked Friday. It was too close to Monday.

Shapes came in and out of focus while she sat on the bottom step of the grand staircase in Deacon's foyer and debated the day of the week. She was okay with Friday the thirteenth though. It got too much bad publicity if you asked her. Her hand grew cold, and her mind focused on the source. The veil lifted piece by piece. She was holding a glass of water.

"… should relax you."

She frowned. Whatever had been said, she only caught the tail end. She looked up and shook her head to wake up from the nightmare.

"I'm sorry, what did you say?"

Dayna held out her palm. Two small white pills rested side by side. "I said to take these."

"What is it?"

"A sedative. The good kind."

Keira tossed the pills into her mouth and washed them down with water. She inhaled, filled her lungs, then let it out slowly. The image of Marcus' broken body swam to the front of her mind, and she let out a half-sob. She had lived a dozen lifetimes, but nothing prepared her for witnessing her friend's body violently ripped from this life decades before he was due.

Dayna took a seat next to her. Her forehead puckered, and her eyes turned glassy. "It doesn't get easier with time, does it?" She took a deep breath and fidgeted with her bracelet. "You'd think by now we'd be used to it."

Keira turned and stared into space. This had to be a dream. He couldn't be gone.

"How am I going to tell Queenie?"

Her voice broke with the effort not to shut down.

"That's his grandmother, right?" Dayna asked gently.

Keira nodded, and her eyes prickled at the effort not to break down again.

"Queenie's a New Orleans Witch I met just after I returned from Australia. She's the one who encouraged me to teach again. She even helped me find a hacker to manipulate my qualifications." She took a labored breath. "This is going to devastate her."

Unable to withstand the pain any longer, she let her body mourn in the only way it knew how. Her shoulders slumped, and her body shook with each sob as it tore out of her too-tight chest. She wept until her body was too exhausted to shed any more tears. She replayed the events of the evening over and over until she was physically ill. They hadn't planned on being there. What made him a target?

"He was just a boy. His life hadn't started yet." She turned to Dayna. "Why? Why did they do this?"

Dayna pulled her into an embrace. "Oh, honey, you and I both know people don't need a reason. Bad shit happens to good people, and the worst is reserved for those who are virtuous."

The truth of her sister's words wasn't lost on her. They had lost so many loved ones over the years. Unable to withstand any more hurt, she'd withdrawn and refused to get close to anyone for fear they might be gone at any moment. Marcus and his grandmother had been one of the rare exceptions to her rule.

This was in direct contrast to Dayna, who surrounded herself with friends and lovers. Keira had always wondered how her sister went through life, losing a piece of her heart with each move or death.

How could she face Queenie? How could she face herself? She shouldn't have let him come. If she'd said no, he would still be alive.

A slow-burning rage at the injustice rose to the surface. She pushed away her tears and pulled herself upright. Her lips set into a grim, determined line. "Well, it's about time that changed. I have no doubt whatsoever that the Order is behind this." She clenched her fists so tight that her nails cut into her palms. "That was the last innocent they'll destroy for their cause. We've lost too many of the people we love, and it's damn well going to stop. The gloves are coming off. If they want a fight. I'm going to take it to them.

Dayna fell quiet and wrapped her arms around her knees. "You sound so much like mom just now. Do you remember when she took old man McAlister to task for how he mistreated his livestock?"

Keira cocked her head and stared off into the distance. Many things had worn with time, but memories of their mother remained clear.

She let out a mournful smile. "She always stood up for those that couldn't."

Both she and Dayna fell quiet. Her mind wandered back to a time when her biggest concern was finishing her chores so she could play with her friends. If only life remained that simple.

Dayna broke the silence. "What do you think she'd make of all this?"

Keira rested her elbows on her knees and placed her chin in the palms of her cupped hands. "I've been wondering the same thing lately. I can't help but feel she knew this was coming. We've never understood her last words or the reason for our curse."

Dayna let out an exasperated snort. "You know, most people would consider biological immortality a blessing, not a curse."

Keira pressed her lips together and held back a retort. She and Dayna never saw eye to eye on that particular topic.

Dayna yawned and stood up. "I'm going to get some beauty sleep. I'll take another crack at it in the morning and see if I can find anything in the Grimoire that might help, and I'll keep working on that diary." She placed a hand on Keira's shoulder. "Are you going to be okay?"

Keira threw her sister a weak smile. "I'll be fine. You go up."

Dayna was almost at the top of the stairs when Keira called out, "If you manage to unlock the journal …"

"You'll be the first to know. I'm not that ditzy. See you in the morning."

The foyer lapsed into silence the moment Dayna disappeared from view. The light that glowed whenever she was around made any space feel dark when she left.

Keira's throat became dry as she held back the grief that descended over her the moment her sister departed.

Dayna was right. Losing loved ones to death didn't get any easier with time. That was the reason she strived to not to make any connections. The lump in her throat grew as her mind drifted back to the moment she saw Marcus' body. She couldn't shake the memory of the lifeless eyes staring back at her. A pale comparison to the man he was and the promise of who he had the potential to become.

Her cheeks grew damp as tears once again escaped and ran free. Too upset to sleep and unwilling to meet the nightmare awaiting her, she made her way to the lounge and curled up on the window seat that overlooked the front of the property. Now and then, she detected a movement as their protectors kept vigil while Ryker and Deacon dealt with the aftereffects of the two murders.

The decision to return her and Dayna to the safety of the house was not something she'd willingly agreed to. Ryker had forcibly placed her in the car and threatened to lock her up if she didn't see reason. Remembering some of the adjectives she hurled at him, she cringed. They must all think her mad.

She chewed on her thumbnail as she paced the room. Each minute seemed to last hours as the time passed with agonizing slowness. The suspense was killing her. Had he discovered who did this? Did they get all the evidence?

She groaned inwardly. "Get a grip. The man knows what he's doing."

Knowing it would be hours until he cleared Beatrice's and Marcus' crime scenes did nothing to quell her desperate thoughts. One thing was clear though. The Order wouldn't stop until they'd slaughtered every last Crossroads Witch.

NINETEEN
RIDE OF THE VALKYRIES

Brother Superior Amos's expression froze as he stared at—and right through—his second councilor, Noel.

Inhale.

Exhale.

Inhale.

Exhale.

His gaze flickered in and out of focus and fixed on a non-existent spot on the wall in the distance. He reached into his happy place, and Wagner's Ride of the Valkyries swept him away in its beauty. His soul soared as Brünnhilde carried a terrified, half-unconscious Sieglinde past him and onto her ultimate sacrifice. If he didn't focus and calm down, he would be short another second councilor, and Noel would be missing a head.

The last notes died and faded, leaving him mourning the piece's lingering crescendo. With reluctance, he returned to the matter at hand.

Inhale.

Exhale.

Inhale.

Exhale.

Now that his body and mind had calmed enough to deal with the situation in a manner befitting someone of his rank within the Order, he released his rigid control and allowed his limbs to move. A sharp pain rushed through his joints. He was not getting any younger, and his bones objected to the harsh treatment. He reached for his upside-down crucifix and prayed for guidance.

My Lady Leviathan, grant me the strength to not kill every last fucking one of them.

The youngest generation of the Order was incapable of following even the simplest of instructions. Amos would happily gut the one in front of him, but he was quickly running out of second councilors, and time was running out. He took another deep breath and glared at Noel. At least the imbecile had the fortitude to look shamefaced at his actions.

"You do remember what we are working toward?" he hissed.

Noel bobbed his head but kept his eyes on the ground. "Yes, Your Grace."

"And correct me if I'm wrong, keeping the authorities from sniffing around is one of your primary objectives."

Another bobble, and Amos resisted the urge to decapitate the boy. They would see how well he bobbed his head when it was rolling on the ground.

"Then please explain to me, how, out of the seven hundred thousand people who live in Essex County, you managed to kill the one outsider whose connections could bring in the FBI, State Troopers, and the National Guard?"

Noel flinched at the icy accusation.

"Was there no other local you could have harassed and maimed instead?" Sarcasm dripped from every syllable. He reached for his crucifix to keep his rage under control.

An incoherent mumble was Noel's only reply.

"Well? What sorry excuse do you have for destroying hundreds of years of work?"

"I had no choice, Your Grace. He recognized the *Oroboros* on my arm."

Slack jawed, Amos stared at Noel. "Of course he knew what it was, you dolt. He studies anthropology and European myths. It would have been a waste of a hundred thousand dollars if he didn't."

"No, I think he knows about *us*. The Order."

"What makes you think that?"

The imbecile at least had some grounds for his actions, flaky as they might be.

Noel shrugged. "I just had a feeling. He was acting a little strange after he saw it."

"So instead of following him, you took it upon yourself to kill him, and dump his body right there for all to see?"

Noel's head bobbed once more, and a muscle ticked along his jaw. "I'm sorry, Your Grace, I panicked. My only wish is to serve. But I'm sure he was on to me."

Sure? Where was the positive, the *knowing* in all this? Where was the interrogation? The slow death? Amos raised his hands in disgust. The youths of today were sloppy and had no sense of tradition.

"When our Savior returns, she will decide what to do with you. Let's hope she's as understanding as I." In his anger, Amos had forgotten the university professor working with the sheriff's office. "What about the woman he was with? The professor? Is she a threat? If he was on to you, what makes you think she wouldn't be as well?"

Noel shook his head. "She's as clueless as the rest of them. Her assistant, Marcus, was with the professor's sister over the last few days. D-Dayna. Her name is Dayna. Deacon has them holed up at his estate, and no one can get close."

"I suggest you find out about this *Dayna* then."

Needing to get back to more important matters, Amos dismissed his second councilor and headed for the door. Dusk had settled in. They needed to resume the ritual, which would allow them to fulfill their destiny.

Noel scurried after him. "Did you manage to get the information from the Witch, Your Grace?"

Amos shook his head. Bats had taken up squatter's rights in the old woman's head years ago and evicted the three remaining brain cells soon after. By the time he was through with her, she couldn't remember her own name, let alone the names of the others.

"We can't wait any longer. We'll need to flush them out."

Noel cocked his head. "We've tried that, and they went to ground."

A sly smirk tugged at the corners of Amos' mouth. "This time, we will have help. Did you secure the extra blood?"

Noel remained in step with him. "Yes, Your Grace."

Amos sighed. He only hoped it was enough. The Crossroads Witch's blood had made this possible. That and the mistake Annabeth Subrinski made when she meddled with their last attempt.

"What about the hosts for tonight's arrivals?" Amos rasped.

"They have been subdued and are being transported to the site."

A rush of excitement quivered through his aging body. The Lord Leviathan's return was in their grasp. An achievement no other Brother Superior had accomplished. The sacrifices made for her return were insignificant. No matter how many Witches they needed, it was a price he was willing to pay.

Leviathan would return, and the Order would once again resume their rightful place.

TWENTY

THEIR LIGHT WILL LIVE ON

Keira wiped a tear from her cheek before she entered Deacon's kitchen.

As expected, the call to Queenie had been tough. She'd expected Queenie to blame her. After all, she was supposed to look out for Marcus. Instead, Queenie's only concern was getting Marcus home so he could rest alongside his ancestors.

Queenie and Marcus' parents would be on the next plane to Boston. Her grandson wouldn't be alone on his last trip home to New Orleans.

Keira gazed out the window, and unease stirred.

Their bodyguards were usually close by when Ryker and Deacon were not at home. "Where are Tim and Pete?"

"I made them some coffee. They're having it at the outside table." Dayna looked up from the cookbook she was pouring over. "How was it?"

Fresh tears threatened, and Keira blinked rapidly. "The local police had already broken the news." She cleared her throat. "I couldn't give her any of the answers she was after."

Dayna rose and put her arms around Keira. "Oh, honey, don't beat yourself up over that."

Her vision blurred. If she had just said "no" to bringing him along, he wouldn't have been caught up in the Order's mayhem. He would still be alive today.

She squared her shoulders. "We have to find a way to put an end to this. They're not going to stop the killings until we do."

Dayna pulled away from her, concern reflected on her face. "You don't know the Order was behind Marcus' death. It could be a coincidence."

"Dayna, this was no coincidence." Keira's body tensed. "Marcus stumbled onto something, and his life was forfeited because of it."

"How many of them do you think attacked Marcus?"

"Likely only one. Any more, and someone would have seen something. What I'm more concerned about is whether the killer was police, fire, or paramedic."

Dayna's mouth fell open. "Or it could have been someone who worked there. Not all the customers were first responders."

Keira stared pointedly at her sister.

Dayna's shoulders dropped. "Fine. The obvious thing is that the Order infiltrated the first responders." Her head jerked. "But you already knew that."

Keira shrugged. "It's the only thing that could explain how they got to so many victims without a fight. The murderer was either someone they all knew or someone they trusted. Who would suspect someone in uniform?"

Her sister sank onto a chair. "There goes my ride on the big red truck."

She groaned. Of course, that would be Dayna's takeaway from this revelation.

Dayna's irritation didn't last long, and she changed the subject. "Did Ryker or Deacon have any luck this morning?"

"No. Ryker is knee-deep in two crime scenes, so Deacon went door to door to search for any of the known Crossroads Witches. As far as their neighbors are aware, they've left town to visit a sick relative."

"What, all of them?" Dayna said.

"Yep. They all told their friends and neighbors the same thing. It makes sense, really. No one would question why they suddenly up and left. And each one of them has their phones off, so we can't even get a subpoena to ping their location."

Dayna chewed on her thumbnail. "How many more do you think it will take before Leviathan breaks down the gate?"

Keira's stomach tightened. "It won't come to that. We'll find the coven before the Order does."

"With the power of more than half a dozen Crossroads Witches prevented from returning to Yggdrasil, I can feel the drain. If their lights can't live on, I don't know how we're going to get the power we need to keep the gate closed."

Keira jerked around. "What did you say?"

"I don't know how we're going to keep the gate closed."

She was suddenly breathless. "No, not that. The bit about their lights."

Dayna frowned. "I'm not following. You told me you saw the bodies at Mystery Hill. Their powers were unable to return to the earth."

A flush of adrenaline tingled through Keira's body.

"Their lights will live on," she repeated in a hoarse whisper.

Dayna's eyebrows knotted together. "You know you're not making sense."

"When Ryker and I met with Annie's parents." Keira paced the room. "Maize said, *their lights will live on.*"

"That's understandable. You said yourself that they weren't told the full details of how she died. They think her soul and power have returned to the earth through the Tree of Life, and she now resides with the ancestors."

Keira stopped short and swung around to face her sister. "No. Don't you get it? Only Crossroads use that prayer. Annie was Crossroads. Not Maize. It's also not public knowledge that all three victims from that night were Crossroads. So how would Maize know to say *their* lights will live on?"

Dayna gasped. "She knew. Maize is Crossroads. She's one of the cloistered."

Keira raced to her bag and rummaged for her phone. She needed to speak to Ryker. They now had a name. One was all they needed to get to the others.

Keira gripped the car's grab bar. No wonder people called it an "Oh Jesus!" handle. Ryker was breaking all speed limits to get to Maize and Zayne's house, and her stomach was paying for it.

"And you're sure about this?" Ryker repeated.

She gulped. "Yes."

"How can you be so certain?"

"After I spoke with you, I called Ananya. Earth Witches can be born from Witches of other elements, but it's more common for an Earth Witch to produce Earth Witches. I needed to know Maize's family history, and I figured Ananya would either know it, or know someone who did."

"And?"

"Maize was born in Nebraska, but her mother was born right here in Salem. And she is from a very long line of Crossroads Witches. Their family goes back to the 1600s. I knew her great-great-great-great-great-great-great-grandmother."

He parked outside the house. "I think you're missing a few greats in that."

She shrugged. "I know, but I can't be bothered doing the math for generations across three hundred and fifty years."

They exited the car, and she took a calming breath.

Ryker placed a gentle hand on her shoulder. His touch was oddly comforting.

"Doc, if you're sure about this, you have nothing to worry about. I'll take your lead on this one."

She gave him a wan smile. They couldn't afford any more deaths. In order for Maize to admit she was Crossroads Keira had no choice. She would have to perform the reveal spell to confirm Maize was Crossroads. But the spell would also unlock Keira's secrets and bring them out into the open. After two hundred years of running, she was about to reveal her own connection to Crossroads and the Salem coven. A connection that would have more questions than she was willing to answer.

A younger version of Maize opened the door before they reached the top stair to the verandah.

Ryker removed his cap. "Afternoon, Velvet. Your folks in?"

Velvet's lower lip quivered. "They're in the living room."

His hands outstretched, Ryker stepped forward. "Aww, sweetie, what's happened?"

Keira's stomach churned, and her gaze darted through the open door. Had there been another killing?

Velvet flew into Ryker's embrace. "Oh, Uncle Ryker, they just told me I was going to be an aunt. You have to find who did this. They must pay for what they did."

Uncle Ryker? Mother Earth, he really was part of this family. Why she was shocked was beyond her. From the moment she met him, the man had been full of surprises.

Ryker set Velvet at arm's length. "That's why we're here."

Velvet sniffed. "Mom mentioned you're working with a Witch."

"Velvet, this is Dr. Keira Wynter," Ryker said.

She gave Velvet a sympathetic smile. "I'm so sorry for your loss."

Velvet nodded and pulled away from Ryker. "Thank you." She motioned toward the doorway. "Mom and Dad are in the living room."

The moment they entered the room, Maize jumped to her feet. "Do you have news?"

"Yes, but not the kind you're expecting," Ryker somberly announced.

Zayne moved across to Maize and draped an arm around her shoulder.

Ryker appeared to collect himself. "Beatrice Sommers was found dead in her home."

Maize cupped her cheeks. "No."

All color drained from Velvet's face, and she let out a low cry. Zayne pulled Maize closer. His expression reflected the horror on Maize's face.

Keira moved to the large bay window. Rays from the sun poured through the glass and bathed the room in a bright glow. A stark contrast to their current mood.

"How?" Maize sobbed.

A bead of perspiration erupted on Keira's forehead. "*How* is not important. The *why* is what we all need to be concerned about."

Maize frowned and glanced between her and Ryker. "I don't understand."

She fingered her amulet, and her stomach lurched. What if she was wrong? This could get very awkward. Her gaze flicked to Ryker. His dark glasses covered his eyes, but his comforting smile and nod gave her the boost she needed.

She held out her hand. "Maize, I need to show you something, but you'll only see it in natural light."

Maize's frown deepened.

Ryker stepped forward. "I know you don't know the doc here very well, but you need to trust her."

"Do you?" Zayne asked. "Trust her."

Ryker pushed his hands into his pockets. "To be honest, when I first met her, I thought she was a nutbar."

Despite not being able to see his eyes, Keira could feel them boring into her.

"But now, I would trust her with my life. And I think you should too."

Maize tentatively pulled away from Zayne and slowly edged her way over to Keira. Maize was wearing a sleeveless top. At least that would make this less awkward.

When Maize stood before her, Keira extended her arm. Maize slowly raised hers as if to shake hands. She grasped Maize's wrist and twisted their clenched hands to expose the underside of their forearms to the light.

Maize gasped aloud and attempted to pull away. When their skin rippled, she stilled, her gaze riveted on the display.

Small trickles of ink spread out of their veins. Like vines, they grew and danced, leaving intricate patterns across their skin as they formed a delicate design spanning both forearms.

Keira frowned and stared intently at the shapes. *Something's not right.* She inspected the patterns again. While hers grew and disappeared up her sleeve to grow across the rest of her body, Maize's halted just below her shoulder.

She'd expected that from Beatrice. The older woman's sanity had been suspect, and with it, her powers. But others within the coven? Why was Maize's power so underdeveloped?

His eyes full of concern, Ryker leaned against the doorframe. "Is everything okay?"

How had he picked up on her shock? She had been careful to keep her emotions in check. She pulled her arm away, and the vines retreated as quickly as they had appeared.

"I'm fine. We're just getting acquainted."

Maize kept staring at her arm. "I-I don't understand. You're Salem Crossroads. You can't be. How?"

"I am, and it's a story for another day."

Velvet took tentative steps toward them. "Mom, did you see how far up and across her body it went? I've never seen anyone with that sort of power before."

And with that, Velvet confirmed that she was also Crossroads. Keira wasn't surprised that both of Maize's daughters were. And while Zayne may not be, he would undoubtedly be aware they belonged to Crossroads.

"Look, there's no way to sugarcoat this," Keira said resolutely. "Annie and the others were killed by the Order. We don't know what they are up to, but we *do* know it will be something related to opening the gate."

Maize went pale, and she took a halting step backward. "It can't be. Not after all this time."

"The Order?" Velvet rubbed her forehead. "But that's just an old myth to scare kids when they misbehave."

Keira shook her head. "I wish that were the case. But the Order is very real and very dangerous. They nearly got Leviathan through the gate almost four hundred years ago, and I believe they are making another attempt."

Ryker cleared his throat. "Zayne, Maize, I think you need to sit. There's something about Annie's death I didn't tell you."

The room fell quiet, and a heavy weight descended around them like a mist as Ryker spoke. Once Ryker fell quiet, Zayne rose and crossed to the window, his back to them.

Keira's chest tightened when Zayne's shoulders shook. The grief for his lost child was all-consuming.

Maize, eyes red-rimmed, held on to Velvet's hand like a vice grip. "We have to protect the rest of the coven before the Order gets to them," she said in a broken whisper.

Ryker squatted until he was eye level with Maize. "That is what we're here for. Somehow, the Order knew Annie, Sarah Tracey, Zac Cole, Oggie Truscott, and the others were Crossroads. We've had more Witches disappear, but we have no idea if they are Crossroads or not. The others have gone to ground. We don't know who we need to protect."

Keira bit her bottom lip. It was now or never. "When we met with Beatrice, she was going to do a Calling of the Synod. I need to meet with them. We have to bolster the spell on the gate, and I can't do it myself. And more importantly, we need to make sure the coven is safe."

Maize shook her head. "We didn't get a calling. But to be honest, I don't think anyone in the Synod has ever done a calling, let alone anyone in the coven."

Ryker straightened to his full height. "I don't care how you get them together. We need it done ASAP. Time is running out. The Order has been a step ahead of us the entire way. I don't think we can stay under the Feds radar if anyone else dies."

"If you can't get the coven to work with us," Keira grew somber. "More Witches *will* die."

TWENTY-ONE

WITH A LITTLE HELP FROM MY FRIENDS

An instant after Deacon called Ananya's name and disappeared into his office, the petite woman popped her head out of a room at the far end of the corridor. "Be right with you, dearies."

Ananya reappeared a moment later and ambled toward them, resting her hand on the small of her back. "Rain's coming. I can feel it in my bones."

Ananya's wrinkles multiplied when she gave the small gathering a sympathetic smile. She shook her head and clicked her tongue. "I'm sorry for your loss, Keira. Such a tragic waste."

The backs of Keira's eyes stung, and she held at bay the tears threatening to push past her eyelids.

Ananya turned to Dayna and peered over the rims of her glasses. "You must be the sister?"

Dayna nodded and beamed at Ananya. "That's me. I'm so pleased to meet you. From what Deacon's told me, you're the one really in charge around here."

Deacon's diminutive secretary laughed. "He did, did he? Well, at least he knows which side of the bread his butter is on." Ananya cocked her head and winked. She raised her voice at the office Deacon had vanished into. "But that doesn't mean I'm working next Wednesday. Apocalypse or no apocalypse, I'm going to that bingo tournament, and you can take your own damn calls."

Keira glanced toward the stairs that led to the ground floor and the fake blood bank. She was a little nervous the others would arrive ahead of schedule, and she wanted Dayna out of sight before then. "Did Deacon tell you what we need?"

Ananya nodded. "It's all set up. No one will know you're here." She motioned for Dayna to follow and turned, only to stiffen and reach for her back once more. "Or it could be that I just need a hip replacement."

Dayna appealed to Keira. "Don't forget, if you need anything, you call."

She pushed her sister in the direction Ananya headed. "And you make sure you stay out of sight."

The sooner Dayna was away from prying eyes, the more comfortable she would be. While she could understand Deacon's reluctance to leave her alone, even under the protection of his Vampires, she didn't want Dayna spotted by the wrong people.

"Chillax, sis, or you'll accidentally set fire to something," Dayna said as she and Ananya headed down the corridor.

Ananya halted abruptly. "She can do that?"

Dayna nodded.

"Where were you when I wanted to burn down that monstrosity the neighbors put up in their front yard?" Ananya tsked. "Come on, blondie, let's get you sorted."

"I'm not sure my sister does house calls, but I can give you a recipe for a magic Molotov cocktail that might do the trick."

"Dayna!" Keira chastised her sister. "Remember what we talked about?"

"What?" Dayna tossed innocently over her shoulder.

Ananya tucked her arm into Dayna's elbow. "How close do I need to be to throw it? I'm not as young as I used to be."

"That's the best part, it's on a delay," Dayna said as she patted the older woman's arm. "You have as much time as you want."

"Let's get you settled, and you can tell me more."

Keira rolled her eyes and headed for Deacon's office. Her sister knew better than to give a wiry old lady access to explosive devices. From Deacon's expression when she entered the room, he'd heard the entire conversation.

She glanced over her shoulder. "Just how serious is Ananya about getting rid of the thing in her neighbor's yard?"

Deacon put his pen down and leaned back in his chair. "On a scale of one to ten, I would put it at twenty-five. I've already bailed her out of jail for poisoning a tree blocking part of her driveway. She's feuded with them for the past decade."

Keira frowned. "Perhaps I should make sure Dayna doesn't put any ideas in her head."

"No, don't worry about it. Your sister knows what she's doing. I warrant she'll give Ananya a long list of things she can do without getting caught."

"And you don't mind?"

Deacon shrugged. "When she's not meddling in the neighbor's lives, she's meddling in mine. So the more ideas Dayna gives her, the better."

Keira wandered over to the window and scanned the busy street below. The blinds blocked her view, so she pried the slats apart for a better look. "Do you think they'll come?"

"Maize promised they'd be here. Ryker has kept Beatrice's death under wraps, so I can't see any reason they wouldn't."

Her gaze fell on a passing police cruiser, and her pulse quickened. How far away was Ryker? Since their meeting with Maize two days ago, she hadn't seen much of him. His hands were full with two additional deaths, and he had been working around the clock. If she were being honest with herself, she missed him.

Ryker had surprised her with his out-of-character compassion for her grief. His unexpected tenderness confused her. From her meager experience, Vampires wore their cold and haughty attitudes like a cloak. Never letting anyone see beneath. The more time she spent with him, the more she realized just how little she knew about his race. She also realized the more time she spent with him, the more he featured in her dreams.

Nah. It was probably just the sedatives Dayna had given her.

As though on cue, Ryker strode in and tossed his cap and glasses on Deacon's desk. "It's showtime. They're here."

Keira took a deep breath and slowly let it out. This time, her erratic pulse and the butterflies in her stomach were not because of Ryker. Maize was able to persuade the Synod to meet with them.

Now the moment had arrived, was she prepared? She'd walked away from the coven over two hundred years ago, vowing never to return. During that time, she'd hidden who and what she was. In a matter of a few days, the number of people who'd discovered she was not only an Earth Witch, but a Crossroads Witch at that, had grown exponentially.

She froze at the light knock on the door and drew her shoulders back. She could do this. One by one, the members of the Synod filed in. As the final two stepped through the door, she stole a glance at Ryker. It took every effort not to smirk at his dumbfounded expression. While Maize had warned her that one of Ryker's ex-deputies was Crossroads, but the revelation had clearly come as a shock to him.

Once the ten senior members of the coven making up the Synod were in, Ananya closed the door. Her job was to make sure no one else entered the building.

A nervous murmur settled over the room when the Synod realized both Ryker and Deacon were present. Voices rose in a wave as the members looked to each other for support. Some accused Maize of betrayal. Others threatened to leave.

Ryker raised his hands, palms up, to settle the escalating panic. "No one's going anywhere. I suggest you all take a seat."

No one moved.

Ryker shrugged his shoulders. "Suit yourselves." He waited a couple of beats before he continued. "The night before last night, Beatrice was found dead in her home. Any one of you could be next."

A look of fear rippled through the Synod as the information sank in. Nita Metz, the owner of Café Luna, clutched the woman next to her before dropping onto the nearest couch.

"I think you need to tell them how," Maize said in a broken voice.

His face reflected his reluctance to discuss the details of such a horrific crime, especially with the group who were targeted.

Maize pulled Violet closer. "Don't hold anything back, Ryker. They need to know."

All eyes turned to him, waiting to hear what he had to say. "She was beaten to death by members of the Order. We suspect she was tortured to reveal the names of other Crossroads members."

One of the Synod members turned to Maize, and his nostrils flared. "How could you lead us here, knowing it's not safe? Our being here has given them the ammunition they need."

Keira's head was beginning to ache at the bickering.

"Enough!" Deacon's voice boomed across the room, and everyone stopped mid-argument.

He leaned menacingly over the desk, his face dark and foreboding. The civilized veneer dropped, and he showed them just how dangerous an ancient Vampire could be. His eyes blazed and bore into each person around the table.

"In the matter of one week, you have lost nine of your coven. Instead of allowing us to protect you, you have chosen to ignore the fact that you have a responsibility to not only yourselves but to humankind. This will not be allowed to continue. From this point onward, until we have dealt with the Order, marshal law prevails for you and your families."

From their straight, tense postures, his knowledge of what was after them was the last thing they expected.

Nita swung her head around to face Maize. "Why would you risk us like this?"

Maize pointed in Keira's direction. "Dr. Wynter is one of us. I think she can help."

Nine pairs of eyes swung around to face her.

A man she hadn't seen before shifted his weight from one foot to the other. "We know she's a Witch."

Keira braced herself, knowing what was coming next. The us Maize was referring to wasn't that she was a Witch.

Maize shook her head. "No, that's not what I meant. She's Crossroads. And I don't know how, but Salem Crossroads." Maize gestured to her forearm. "Her markings cover her entire body, and my *teeth* felt a vibration when she linked with me for the reveal spell."

Nita's brows shot up. No one uttered a word. Were they even breathing?

"Don't all speak at once," Ryker said. "I can't keep up with the speed at which you are all talking."

Nita's voice shook. "But … but …" She turned to Deacon and Ryker. "And how is it that you know about our true purpose?"

"There's a lot you don't know," Deacon said. "What is of the utmost importance is your safety. Your numbers were dwindling before this tragedy. We can ill-afford to lose any more of you."

Maize rubbed her forehead. "I'm not even going to ask what else you know." She looked to the others as if seeking some confirmation on how to proceed. Her shoulders sagged, and she let out a long breath. "What do you need us to do?"

"We need to protect the coven, and the coven needs to protect the gate."

"How are we going to do that?" Nita demanded.

Deacon stepped forward. "The Vampires will protect the coven with our lives."

"And my sister and I will teach you how to protect yourselves and the gate," Keira said.

She looked down at her wrist and contemplated the blunted power she'd detected in Maize and Beatrice. While she had seen similar trends in other Witch covens, she hadn't expected the same deterioration in a Crossroads coven. What would she discover if she performed the same ritual with the others?

The coven's power was weak at best. If this was the level of energy focused on the gate, how long would it be before the reserves from the past wore away, leaving them all vulnerable? In the end, she had no choice.

She couldn't let her mother's sacrifice be for nothing. "Which one of you calls the most magic?"

From the way everyone turned to Maize, she had her answer. Her stomach dropped. If that was the best they had, it was a wonder Leviathan hadn't already breached the gates.

She turned to Nita. "What about you? Where do you fall?"

Nita's cheeks reddened when the Synod members focused on her. "Um, in the middle, I'd say."

Keira held out her hand to Nita. "I need to show you something."

As if sensing they needed privacy, Ryker made his way to the window, donning his glasses on the way. Deacon followed Ryker's cue and copied his actions. Ryker opened the blinds, and sunlight streamed into the room.

When her skin touched Nita's, Keira invoked the incantation, and the familiar tattoo spread over their arms.

"I've never seen one grow that much," Nita said in awe when the vine inched up Keira's arm. "Mine has only ever reached my elbow." Nita tipped her head and looked at her. "How far does it go up?"

"If I let it, it covers my entire body."

A snap of the blinds caught her attention, and she could have sworn Ryker muttered, "That, I have to see."

She ignored him. She had bigger concerns than his untimely commentary. "What about the coven members who were killed? How far up did theirs go?"

Maize bit her bottom lip and scrunched her nose as she considered the question. "Annie was about three-quarters up, like mine and Velvet's, and the rest were mainly around elbow height. Why?"

Keira's breath caught. The reduction in power was worse than she thought. "At a minimum, the Crossroads mark should cover both arms."

She bit back her panic at the implications. While on one hand the deaths of the Crossroads Witches hadn't depleted as much power from Yggdrasil as the Order had expected. But, it also meant the power charging the gate was no where near where it should be.

"What about that hum I felt?" Nita asked. "Were the vibrations related to the mark?"

"That's the link the person you are touching has with Yggdrasil. The stronger the vibration, the stronger the link. I can barely detect your connection."

Nita darted a glance at the others. "Why do I feel like that's a problem?"

Problem was an understatement. "Because to keep the gates shut, you have to be able to draw more power. And if you haven't been channeling power to the gate, I have no idea how the gate is being kept shut."

The room fell quiet as they contemplated her words.

"How do we fix this?" Maize asked.

"You'll need to go back to school. And fast."

TWENTY-TWO

ONCE IN A BLUE MOON

Keira cleared her mind and allowed her magic to reach out. The corners of her mouth flicked upward when it took a little longer than the previous attempt to hit the edge of Maize's spell.

Maize had finally managed to cast a protection spell wide and strong enough for it to work on another person.

The Crossroads Witches in Salem had more ability than she'd given them credit for. "Try focusing your thoughts a little narrower, and visualize the area it needs to cover," she said in a low voice.

Maize closed her eyes and scrunched her nose. A sheen of perspiration erupted on her forehead. This time, the surge of energy Maize emitted sent tiny magical shimmers through the air.

"Do you think you're ready to try it out again?" Keira asked.

Maize nodded, then opened her eyes, the strain still evident on her flushed face.

Keira called out in a loud voice, "Okay, Ryker, you're up."

She couldn't hold back a grin when he grumbled from the other room. He stood just outside the door, then took a tentative step into the room and scanned the immediate area with a grim expression. He took a second step, and nothing happened. His face relaxed, and he entered the room. Before anyone could blink, he was physically repelled backward. A curse escaped his lips.

Maize shot up from her chair. "Did you see that? I did it! I can't believe it worked." Her expression quickly turned to concern, and she rushed to Ryker. "I'm so sorry. Are you okay?"

Ryker waved her off. "I'm fine. Stop fussing." He raised a brow at Keira. "Were you helping out this time?"

She shook her head.

"It doesn't pack the same punch as the doc's," he said to Maize. "But it certainly does the trick."

Relief flooded through Keira. "The real test is determining if the spell only targets the person you want to repel. If Zayne can enter the room without being stopped, then we can call it a success."

Ryker slapped Zayne on the back, and a devilish grin spread across his face. "Your turn to be a crash test dummy."

Maize's husband gulped, and his gaze darted to the doorway. "Are you sure?"

Keira shrugged her shoulders and grinned. "There's only one way to find out."

Ryker pushed Zayne toward the door, and Maize grimaced as her husband put one foot in front of the other. The closer he moved to the spot that stopped Ryker, the more he faltered.

"Come on, Zayne," Keira prodded.

Squaring his shoulders, he moved forward at a snail's pace. Ryker blew out an exasperated breath and shoved his friend into the room. Zayne almost lost his balance and rushed forward to right himself. By the time he was steady, he was well beyond the barrier that had repelled Ryker.

"Mom, you did it!"

Velvet jumped up. Until now, the Mallick's remaining child had stayed quiet, absorbing the magic Keira taught both Velvet and her mother.

Instead of the expected triumph, Maize's eyes glazed over. "It's my fault." Her voice came out in a broken whisper. "If I'd kept to the old ways, Annie would still be alive."

Keira reached out and rested a hand on Maize's arm. "You can't think like that. From what you've told me, it's been a few generations since the coven has been at full strength. You couldn't have done anything different than you did."

The tears fell and Velvet rushed to her mother's side.

Velvet's anguish weighed heavily on Keira. Her own loss was still a little too raw. Holding back her grief, she focused on what they still needed to achieve.

"Maize, you need to concentrate on making sure you keep Zayne, Velvet, and the others safe."

Maize let out a shaky breath and nodded. "That's my only focus."

Ryker gave Keira a pointed stare, tapped his watch, and nodded toward the door.

She clapped her hands. "I think that's enough for today. I want you both to keep practicing. Each time, try to push the barrier farther. Between the two of you, your home will be a fortress."

"Are you sure we'll be able to do it?" Velvet asked.

Keira gave her an encouraging smile. Like her mother, Velvet had untapped strength that just needed to be cultivated.

"To be honest," Keira began. "When I first discovered how low your reserves were, I had my doubts. But now, I think you'll be just fine."

Ryker put a hand on Zayne's shoulder. "Casey and Eugene will be here shortly with the change of guard. Make sure Maize has a rest before she starts working with them."

Zayne nodded. "Let's just hope Nita has enough strength to work with the others. When you took her across to Mark's, she was looking a little exhausted."

Keira cringed. Their exhaustion was her fault. After discovering just how weak their magic was, she'd assessed their capabilities. She was relieved to discover they were capable of a lot more magic than their current skill level indicated. With that in mind, she and Dayna had resolved to teach them as many defensive spells as they could in the limited time they had.

She had pushed them hard over the past week.

"Did you mean what you said back there?" Ryker asked as he dropped the car in gear. "That they'll be fine?"

Ryker peeled out of the driveway, and Keira clutched the door handle with one hand and her seat with the other. "It all depends on whether the rest of the coven has that same spark. As far as I can tell, it's been three generations since the coven was at full capacity with their powers."

"So why the change?"

"I've seen it before. In the past, we were able to live in isolation. Now, not so much. Being in constant contact with Naturals has caused Witches to use their powers less frequently. Plus, Supernaturals have integrated into society. Our power is like a muscle, if unused, it becomes ineffective and weak."

In the seven days since discovering the identities of the coven members, she and Dayna had spent the better part of each day working with Maize, Velvet, Nita, and a select few of the other

Crossroads Witches to help them learn the skills they had never been taught. During the evenings, Maize, Velvet, and Nita worked with the others in the coven to pass on the teachings they had learned.

Maize absorbed the lessons and was by far the fastest to increase her range and strength. Most likely due more to her motivation to protect her remaining daughter and husband than anything else.

Keira stifled a yawn. Unable to keep her lids open, she let her head lean onto the headrest and allowed her eyes to flutter closed.

The car decelerated, and Ryker's hand squeezed one of hers. "You okay?"

His touch sent a dance of sparks across her skin.

She kept her voice as even as possible. He didn't need to know how much his physical touch affected her equilibrium.

"Just a little tired," she said without opening her eyes.

"Doc, I know you think you're doing the right thing, but you can't carry on like this. Look what it's already doing to you," he said with a low growl.

"I'll be fine."

His disapproving tone spoke volumes. "You're overdoing it. How about you skip the dawn trip up to Mystery Hill tomorrow? You've been doing it every morning for a week. Even Dayna is worried about you."

"I can't. Until we can build up the Crossroad Coven's power back to where it should be, you know I have to reinforce the binding spell on the gate. The Order expected to do a lot more damage when they murdered Annie and the other Crossroads Witches."

"I understand why you are doing it, but you're putting too much of yourself into the binding spell each day, and it's taking too much out of you."

She brought up her hand to cover another yawn.

"Keira, when was the last time you slept?" Ryker persisted.

"I sleep just fine."

He snorted. "Liar. Deacon says you've been pacing all night. Tonight, I'll leave one of the deputies in charge. I'm staying home. Even if I have to tie you to the bed and knock you out, you are getting some shut eye."

He accelerated, and she fell back against the seat. She was a grown woman. Not a child.

She drew her lips into a thin line and glared at him. "You wouldn't dare."

He threw her a wink, and his face broke into a grin. "We'll have a slumber party in your room tonight. And if you normally sleep in your birthday suit, don't go changing just cause I'm there. Might be my chance to work out where those runes of yours are hiding."

Keira's anger immediately evaporated. Her face heated, and a swarm of butterflies set flight in her stomach. A part of her wanted him to do more than just find her runes.

She raised her chin, not wanting him to see just how much his words affected her. "You will do no such thing."

He chuckled. "You should know me by now, Doc. I never make a threat I don't follow through on."

Her body was now on fire. How the hell had she gone from exhaustion to anger and then to a quivering mess so quickly? She needed to change the subject before he picked up on just how erratic her thoughts had gotten.

"Did you get any more from that missing Witch who turned up?"

The sheriff's office, already pushed to capacity, was again overloaded when one of the missing Witches reappeared, wandering aimlessly along a local highway. To top it off, the department had received a rash of reports on missing tourists who had turned up a day after they supposedly disappeared.

His mouth clamped into a thin line. "No. Dissociative amnesia. She can't even remember being abducted. The hospital examined her, and there is no physical reason for the memory loss."

"Where is she now?"

"Home. She checked herself out against doctors' wishes."

That was odd. If Keira had lost her memory, she would want answers. "What about the other Witch who was taken?"

"No sign."

She snapped her head around to face him. Something in his tone didn't sit well. "So what's the problem?"

"What makes you think there's a problem?"

She raised a brow. "You."

He chuckled. "I didn't realize I was that obvious."

She shrugged. "I could tell you were distracted when you came to pick me up. What's the issue?"

"I don't know. Something just doesn't feel right. She's got bruises all over her arms and face. From the chafing around her wrists and ankles, she was bound for quite some time. I can't see how she got away."

"How long do the doctors think it will take for her memory to return?"

"That's the strange thing. She's lying."

That got Keira's undivided attention. "Are you sure?"

"It's not anything obvious. My gut is telling me something's not right."

"How often are your instincts wrong?" she asked.

"This decade or this century?"

She fixed him with a hard stare.

"Fine, this century then." Ryker squinted, and his eyes traveled upward as if in thought. "Oh yeah, that's right, I remember now. Never."

She glared. "And you couldn't have started there?"

"Where would be the fun in that?"

"Fine." She turned back to the matter at hand. "If you have no proof, what are you going to do?"

"The only thing I can. Keep an eye on her until she slips up, and then find out what she's hiding."

They drove the remainder of the journey in silence. Ryker retreated into his troubled thoughts. Despite his erratic driving, she even managed to doze.

Ryker gently shook her awake once they arrived. He opened the passenger door and bent to eye level.

"I can carry you if you're too tired," he said with a broad grin.

She immediately snapped awake and pushed him away. "I have legs."

Her face grew warm when he stepped back and muttered, "Don't I know it."

As they walked toward the house, he stopped abruptly and sniffed the air. "Can you smell that?"

She lifted her face and inhaled. "No. What is it?"

"I'm not sure, but it's coming from inside."

The moment they walked in the door, she scrunched her nose. "I can smell something now. What is that godawful smell?"

Deacon was making his way down the stairs. "I think that might be dinner." He sniffed the air and grimaced. "Dayna decided she would prepare a meal for us this evening."

Keira balked at his words. "Cook? Dayna doesn't cook."

"When that aroma made its way upstairs, I suspected as much," Deacon said as he reached the bottom step.

She groaned. "Have you checked on her? How does she even know how to turn on an oven?"

"Give her some credit." Ryker headed to the wing that housed the kitchen. "You've said it yourself, it's been a while since you've lived with her. She might have learned in that time."

Keira pushed past him and raced to the kitchen. "Not my sister. Even my mother gave up trying to teach her how to cook."

When she entered the room, she skidded to a halt. It was worse than she thought.

Ryker's mouth dropped open. "What the fuck happened here?"

Dayna, dressed in black tasseled shorts and a bright pink t-shirt with her flaming red hair in pigtails, was shimmying across the kitchen, her hips gyrating in time to whatever music was playing in her earbuds.

They watched in stunned silence as she broke into an air guitar performance. Her hair fell over her face as her head shook in time to the music while she danced barefoot through the kitchen. What was more disconcerting was the condition of the usually immaculate kitchen. As with everything about Deacon, it had been pristine. Even the stainless-steel garbage bin under the sink shone. The keyword being *had*.

Containers, jars, and boxes mixed with scraps of vegetables and meat covered every inch of the granite kitchen counter, and something gray and sticky dripped onto the floor. The tile was blanketed in a layer of flour, mixed with her sister's footprints.

Ryker snorted. "Her cooking may be questionable, but there's nothing wrong with her Metallica rendition."

Dayna chose that moment to spin around to a very captive audience.

Keira didn't know who was more surprised. Her sister at being caught unaware or Deacon at the condition of his kitchen.

Dayna pulled the buds from her ears.

"Busted." She broke into a mischievous grin. "I also do requests."

Keira surveyed the mess. "What did you do?"

"I decided to treat everyone to a home-cooked meal."

"But nothing's in the oven or on the stove." Keira rubbed her forehead. "And what's that smell?"

Dayna sniffed the air. "Oh, that. I was trying to remember one of Mother's brews."

"And the food?"

"I got everything prepped, sort of, but I couldn't work out the dials, so I improvised. Dinner is on its way. I hope you all like pizza."

Keira surveyed the damage and sighed. "I'll wash. You dry."

By the time they'd returned the kitchen to its original immaculate condition, the pizza had arrived. From the stiff way Deacon accepted the delivery, Keira guessed this was the first time the ancient Vampire had fast food turn up on his doorstep.

Dayna took a bite of her pizza. "How did the training go?"

Keira eyed the opened pizza boxes haphazardly spread over the dinner table. "A lot better than yesterday. I expect within a couple days, Maize, Nita, and Velvet will be able to place a protective ward around their own homes, rather than relying on the ones you and I have set. What about you?"

"Pretty much the same. Some are picking it up faster than others. But they'll get there in the end."

Keira agreed. "They need to learn a lot more, but we'll limit it to key spells to get them through this crisis. But considering the security standing vigil outside their houses and their spells, they are the safest they've been in decades."

"Pop, you're looking a bit casual there," Ryker said.

They were halfway through their meal, and from his sly grin, Keira had a feeling Ryker had been biding his time, waiting for a lull in the conversation.

Deacon stiffened. "Whatever are you talking about?"

"Since when do you own a pair of jeans, let alone a t-shirt?"

Dayna giggled and raked her eyes up and down the swarthy Vampire's form. Her expression reminded Keira of a feline playing with a particularly juicy mouse.

"Don't you think he looks delicious? It took me hours to convince him to put them on."

Keira had to admit, while Deacon cut a fine figure in the suits he usually wore, this new look was appealing.

Deacon shifted uncomfortably in his chair and mumbled something under his breath. From Ryker's sudden chortle, he had no difficulty hearing what Deacon said. "That, I would like to have seen."

Deacon's focus on his glass of chilled blood was a little too intense, and her curiosity took over. "What?"

She bit into a slice of pepperoni pizza. It had been a while since she'd indulged in fast food, and she found herself enjoying the flavors.

"Your sister threatened to give him a magical wedgie if he didn't."

"That had nothing to do with my decision," Deacon said. "I simply decided to try them out. The festival is only days away. The committee has pressed me into judging the bake-off. I hardly think a suit would be appropriate for the occasion."

Dayna clapped her hands in glee. "I love festivals. What's this one in aid of?"

"Summer solstice and Strawberry Moon."

The moment the words passed Deacon's lips, Keira dropped her slice of pizza. A chill rushed through her body, and nausea overwhelmed her.

Her gaze snapped to Dayna.

Her sister's face had lost all color.

Dayna's normally happy expression was replaced with one of pure, unadulterated terror.

Keira was pulled out of her escalating panic when Ryker reached over and placed his hand over hers. "What's the matter? You both look as though you've seen a ghost," he asked.

His cool skin over her warm hand sent a row of goosebumps up her arm. The touch was both calming and sensual.

"W-What are the chances?" Dayna stumbled over the question.

Keira held back a snort. Knowing their luck, probably quite high. She shot up and raced to the kitchen bench to grab her phone.

Mother Earth please don't let it be so.

She cursed when Google confirmed it was.

"How close?" Dayna asked.

"Jupiter and Venus are going to be in perfect alignment."

Dayna took a few labored breaths and shook her head. "No. No. It can't be. How did we miss it?"

"Would someone tell us what the hell is going on?" Ryker demanded, his voice booming across the room.

Keira glanced toward Dayna before speaking. "There are certain planetary alignments which Leviathan and any number of demigods have unprecedented access to their source of power. A full planetary alignment with the sun gives her full power. Thankfully, that won't be for another two million, or four hundred billion years, depending on which scientist you believe. While two or three planets aligning will give Leviathan limited access to power, it isn't enough to worry about."

"What does that have to do with the summer solstice?" Ryker asked.

"A planetary alignment is not the only celestial event that does this. When the solstice coincides with a full moon as well as a perfect alignment with at least two of the bright planets, it also means that Leviathan will have access to her power."

The room fell silent, as Ryker and Deacon absorbed the information.

"Exactly how much power will she be able to tap into?" Deacon asked.

Dayna pushed her plate away, the pizza long abandoned. "Not as much as a full alignment, but enough for us to worry about."

"How do we stop it?" Ryker asked.

Keira hauled in a deep breath. In her single-minded focus to protect the Crossroads Witches she had failed to look beyond and recognize the true danger. "Even with her power, diminished or not, she needs the Order to help unlock the gate. We stop them. We stop her."

TWENTY-THREE

O FORTUNA

Amos shifted uncomfortably and tugged at his ceremonial robe. The fabric clung to his body as sweat soaked through his once-crisp starched linen shirt. The heat was all-consuming. The longer this went on, the harder it became to breathe. The ancient stones were in the middle of a clearing in a vast wooded area, and yet he had never felt as smothered or as claustrophobic.

He was also more than a little vexed. Each time a Legion awakened after taking over the host's body, they looked less than their best. Even though it was the middle of the night and visibility was limited, he still wished to look presentable and worthy as he greeted his Lord's personal army. As the one who finally freed her, she would elevate his position, and the Legion would be his to command.

He inhaled, and his nose protested at the vulgar odor invading his nostrils. The musty and acrid smell that settled around them like a glove morphed into a putrid stench the hotter it became. The change in aroma signified the first part of the procedure was almost over. *It was about time.*

When he stumbled on the way to summon the Legion, Amos hadn't realized just how long the process would take.

Nor how uncomfortable. They'd repeated the ritual enough times to understand the squirming prisoner would, within a matter of minutes, begin to convulse as the newly emerged essence of a Legion claimed the body and destroyed the host's mind.

Noel nodded at the struggling prisoner. "Why do you think they wanted someone like him?" His whisper cut into the silence. "And why did we need to use so much of the dead Witch's blood?"

Amos studied the well-muscled prisoner and shrugged. Fahim, the Legion who last emerged, insisted on choosing the host for the next arrival as well as instructing them to use four times the blood during the summoning ceremony. When pressed as to why, the only answer they got was, "It is the will of Leviathan."

Since they had very little choice in the matter, Amos volunteered Noel's services to take Fahim on a shopping trip. He was more than surprised when they returned. It took four men to carry the tranquilized prisoner from the vehicle to the extraction site. Based on Noel's expression, the man wouldn't have been his first choice either. Their new host was at least six feet tall and built like one of those testosterone-fueled wrestlers the younger members of the Order watched on the idiot box. From the massive shoulders and arms bulging through the beige t-shirt, the man's muscles had muscles.

"I don't think I can take much more of that godawful smell," Noel said as the stench around them rose to intolerable levels.

The gray mist seeping from the enormous solstice standing stone finally separated from the rock, and a sudden rush of color pulsed through it. Both he and Noel took a step back at the same time.

"What was that?" Noel screeched.

Amos regarded the incorporeal creature floating above the stone and attempted to hide his shock. *Red.* The gray smoke was surrounded by a red aura that pulsed with a hint of black. A cold chill ran the length of his spine. He'd not seen this before.

The mist that painstakingly seeped from the sacred stone drifted toward the sacrificial altar stone where its new host lay bound and gagged.

"How long do you think this is going to take?" Noel asked as he peered into the dark.

Amos gritted his teeth. They had been through this enough times for the idiot to know the answer. "Perhaps you'd rather be the one on the rock?"

Noel frowned. A moment later, his face relaxed as he shook his head. "No, I mean, when do you think we will have enough Legion here to do the job? The site is still cordoned off, but there is pressure on the sheriff's department to release it."

Amos rubbed his hand over his face. They needed access to the stones. Thus far, they had unfettered access to Mystery Hill. The reopening of the sacred site would be a disaster for their plans. This year's summer solstice also coincided with a full moon and the conjunction of Venus and Jupiter. An event that only occurred once every five centuries.

This was one of the few occasions when they would have access to Leviathan's power. If they failed, they would need to wait another five hundred years for their next chance to summon help to free their beloved Leviathan. The last time they tried, they were bested by a single Witch. This time, he would destroy any magical being that stood in his way.

"Should I tranq him again?" Noel inquired.

Amos glanced at the man whose body was about to become a host to a warrior in a sacred and holy war. The tranquilizer had worn off, and the prisoner struggled against his bindings. The man's eyes bulged at the glowing cloud hovering over his body. He rebelled against the ropes, his muscles visibly bulging with the effort to avoid the colored and pulsating smoke.

Amos shook his head and smiled. Why did they always do that? How stupid must they be to think they could break free?

The next part would take a few minutes. He pulled earbuds from his concealed robe pocket and placed one in each ear. He selected Carl Orff's *O Fortuna* from his phone's playlist and watched as tendrils of vapor broke away and drifted closer to the man's face.

O Fortuna,

velut luna,

statu variabilis,

Realizing what was about to happen, the man thrashed his head from side to side. The veins in his temple bulged a deep purple as he sought to escape.

semper crescis,

aut decrescis;

vita detestabilis

Amos tilted his head, and the corners of his mouth twisted upward. As usual, he had chosen the most appropriate musical piece for the occasion. The first dramatic bar unfolded, and the chorus of voices entwined with the full orchestra in a crescendo of power and anticipation. He tapped his foot in time to the marching beat.

nunc obdurate

et tunc curat

ludo mentis aciem,

The Legion's incorporeal form dipped lower, and its smoky tendrils reached for the man's face, slithering like a snake ready to pounce.

egestatem,

potestatem,

dissolvit ut glaciem.

With minimal hesitation, the tendrils of smoke entered the man's nose and ears in a flurry of movement. The cloud shimmered as the red and black smoke pulsed once again. The man's body contracted. His back arched off the slab in a savage thrust.

Sors immanis

et inanis,

rota tu volubilis,

Amos stepped forward and tore away the tape over the man's mouth.

status malus,

vana salus

semper dissolubilis,

Before a scream could rip from his lungs, the tendrils filled the man's mouth and throat with a gray cloud.

obumbrata

et velata

michi quoque niteris;

An eerie red-yellow light glowed from the man's eyes as the Legion forced its way into the unwilling donor.

nunc per ludum

dorsum nudum

fero tui sceleris.

Unwilling to let go, the body shook uncontrollably. One last stand before the inevitable.

The turmoil and pace of Amos' beloved music assailed his senses, and euphoria drenched his soul. The man's agony fueled him, sending every nerve ending to the heights of bliss. Amos reveled in the man's pain. The escalating tempo further enhanced the experience. Rapture drenched his soul. If only *he* was the one inflicting the pain. "*I am, in a way,*" he reasoned. If not for me, the Legion wouldn't have been able to emerge.

A blast of energy pulsed through the host's body. The ongoing struggle held Amos at the precipice of an emotional climax. Each thrust, each spasm as pain lacerated the host from the inside out, only served to push him further over the edge.

Sors salutis

et virtutis

michi nunc contraria,

est affectus

et defectus

As the tempo rose, so did the struggle. Their victim was a worthy opponent. He lasted an agonizing breath longer than the others. The weak, who simply released their souls to the inevitable without putting up a fight. This one clawed onto life with everything he had. He fought back with every fiber of his being. Even when it was clear he would lose the battle, he kept resisting. The stronger will would survive, and the Human was weakening.

At long last, the mist fully entered the man's body. The final assault began. Even in the dim light from the torches, Amos watched the veins redden and swell as the sacrificial heart furiously pumped blood through the donor's body. The added strain of defying the invading essence had sent his vital organs into overdrive.

Hac in hora

sine mora

corde pulsum tangite;

sternit fortem,

mecum omnes plangite!

Amos closed his eyes as wave after wave of music crashed over him. Each rapturous note sent ripples of pleasure through every nerve ending. As the music erupted into its final crescendo, his breath caught as wave after wave of euphoria swept through his body in tempo with the orchestra.

All too quickly, it was over. He sighed as he pulled the buds from his ears. With the last note, so too was the battle for the host. The body now lay still. The life of the man, whoever he was, was no more.

"Quick, check his pulse," Amos ordered.

The Legion had better survive. They had forfeited too much sacred blood to get this far.

Noel raced over and placed two fingers against the Legion's neck vein. At first, his mouth set in a grim line, then he nodded. "It's steady." He stood back and looked down at the Legion. "Now what?"

"Now we wait."

His second councilor ambled over and took up vigil beside him.

Amos clenched his jaw. "Aren't you forgetting something?"

Noel's forehead puckered, and his gaze darted from the standing stone and back to the prisoner. A few chosen acolytes stood guard on the outskirts of the circle.

Amos let out a frustrated growl. It never ceased to amaze him just how stupid this generation was. "The restraints, you dolt, get them off."

Noel slapped his forehead with the back of his palm. "I knew that."

But still, he didn't move. "What are you waiting for? An invitation?"

When Leviathan gave him back his youth, he wondered if she would grant him powers. He would use them to turn Noel into a sloth, and he would still be the stupidest of his kind.

"Your Grace, Your Grace, I think you need to see this," Noel screeched from his vigil near the new Legion.

Typical, Amos couldn't even enjoy a five-minute rest, and some other disaster needed tending to. He opened his eyes and pulled the buds out of his ears. By his count, only five minutes had passed. From experience, he still had a while to go before the Legion awoke.

Movement from the altar stone caught his attention. *Already?* He thrust the buds into his pocket, bolted up, and checked his robes. He patted his hair—what little was left—into order.

"How do I look?" he asked Noel.

Instead of answering, Noel looked at him with owl-like eyes and blinked in quick succession.

Amos pushed his second in command to one side. "Oh, never mind, get out of my way."

By the time he reached his destination, the Legion was sitting up.

"Welcome," Amos said with a low bow. "I am Brother Superior Amos. Devoted servant to the great God Leviathan and keeper of the ancient scrolls."

The Legion ignored him and scanned the immediate area. "*Ayin acuppah?*"

Amos' brows knitted. He had no idea the meaning of the strange words.

"*Ayin acuppah?*" the Legion asked again.

Noel leaned forward and raised his voice. "We no understand. Speak-e-da E-n-g-l-i-s-h?"

Amos groaned. "He's not deaf, you imbecile!"

They were well out of their comfort zone with this new arrival. The other Legion took nearly an entire day before they spoke. This one had barely awoken. Just who was he?

The Legion stopped his search of the area and turned his attention back to them. He pierced them with a cold stare.

Amos was caught off guard by the flash of yellow-red around the Legion's irises. He cleared his throat. The otherworldly being was making him nervous.

"C-can you understand us?"

The being gave a curt nod.

"He understands us," Noel said excitedly. "He nodded,"

Amos rolled his eyes. "Yes, that's generally what a nod entails, you dolt." He returned his focus to the Legion. "We do not know how to speak the ancient words. You will need to communicate with us in English."

From his discussions with the other Legion, they could access their host's memories, which included language.

"Men," the Legion demanded in a hoarse voice. "Where are my men?"

"They are safe. We couldn't risk exposure. I temporarily returned them to their hosts' lives before they could be missed."

Leviathan's soldier glowered.

Perhaps if Amos mentioned the other Legion, this one would be a little less angry. "Fahim agreed it was prudent."

The Legion pushed himself off the slab and rose to his full height. "I will see him now."

Amos tilted his head to look up at the Legion and gulped. He was more than six feet tall, and from this distance, the Legion's sinewy arms could crush him in a heartbeat.

"As you wish." He swept his arm in the direction of the path to their waiting vehicles. He bowed. "How should we address you?"

"General Zahir."

Amos blanched, and his knees nearly buckled.

General Zahir was the right hand of their Lord. Could there be more than one by that name?

Amos' mind whirled in a panic. Bringing through Legion was one thing, but to have the legendary leader of Leviathan's army in his presence was another thing entirely. The general was her avenger, the one who meted out punishment at Leviathan's will. He was not sure whether he should be elated or worried.

The general wandered around the stone structures. He paused before a small tomb, the one the locals referred to as the oracles chamber. He reached out and placed both hands on the rock wall. Words Amos didn't recognize floated into the night, and the Legion's body tremored in a spasm.

General Zahir pulled away and stared at the wall. "You disposed of the Witches?"

"Yes, the ones that we knew of."

"You failed. There is a new layer of magic on the gate."

The moment the words were out of the general's mouth, Amos tensed.

Those Witches were going to be the death of him. It should have been a simple job to track the Crossroads Coven Witches down and kill them. How were they evading them? He threw a withering glare at his second councilor. Another example of Noel's incompetence.

The general extended his arm and touched the rock again. "Strange."

"What?"

"The magic is old."

Amos blinked. "But I thought you just said it was new?"

"Magic was laid across the gate recently. The source of the magic is old. Strong." The general strode down the path leading to the exit. "After I meet with Fahim, you will take me to your slaves. I need hosts for my men," General Zahir said without breaking stride.

Noel frowned. "Slaves? What sl—"

Amos stared daggers at the idiot, who took the hint and stopped mid-sentence. "Much has changed since you walked the earth. We no longer keep slaves. It is frowned upon."

The general halted. "That cannot be. Who does your bidding? Who are in service to our God? How can you have power and standing without slaves?"

Amos pinched his nose. A headache was brewing. "It's a long story. For now, we need to get new hosts from the tourists who won't be missed. How many do we need?"

"Five score."

He nearly choked on the number. "One hundred? We need one hundred more Legion to free Leviathan? We don't have time to get that many through the gate."

"That is your doing. The new-old magic requires additional Legion. By my calculation, it will take four solar turns of the sun to meet our needs."

"How? It took nearly a day to get you through, and we don't have enough blood left for those numbers."

"We require five score to break the barrier and open the gate for Leviathan to take her rightful place as ruler and God of the earth."

"Perhaps his Babelfish translator is on the fritz," Noel pondered.

"Just shut up, will you!"

"Shut what?" The general peered down the dark path. "There is nothing open."

Amos flashed a glare at Noel and attempted to appease the Legion. "Please forgive me, general, but I was speaking with my soon-to-be demoted second councilor. We are a little concerned about how we are to bring that many Legion through."

"You still possess the ancient Leviathan cross?"

"Yes."

"And the Witch's blood?"

"Yes, but—"

General Zahir resumed his march down the well-worn path. "Then we have what we require. The cross will strengthen the blood's power. Enough Legion will come through before the allotted time. We are unsure why you did not simply use the cross in the first place."

General Zahir's comment gob smacked Amos. The cross, an ancient and revered artifact, had been the symbol of their belief for thousands of years. But the scriptures contained no mention of its magic.

"Much knowledge has been lost over the millennia," he said as they finally broke through to the clearing that led to the parking lot. "I was not in possession of this information." He led the way to his car. "It will take us thirty minutes to reach our destination. Fahim awaits you at the estate."

Zahir cocked his head and raked his gaze across the parking lot. "Where are the chariots?"

Noel let out a snort. "Why do they all ask that?"

Amos raised his eyes skyward. Turning Noel into a sloth was too good for him. But first, he needed to eradicate that Witch before the host quota tripled.

TWENTY-FOUR
TIME TO SAY GOODBYE

The sound of female shouts caught Keira's attention, and she spun toward the shrill outburst.

One of Ryker's deputies struggled with a woman whose blue eyeshadow overpowered everything else on her overly-made-up face. The woman was dressed in jeans molded to her stick-thin body. How did she not topple over from the amount of hair product caked to her frizzed hair?

The woman ripped her arm away from the deputy. "I ain't no thief. That husband-stealing bitch ain't nothing but trailer trash. That bracelet was mine."

Keira turned back to the laptop monitor and ignored the chaos in the station. From the little she'd witnessed of the freak show, as Deputy Mitos put it, she no longer wondered why so many law enforcement offers were jaded. After dealing with some of the less-than-stellar citizens traipsing through the station, she, too, would find it hard to see the goodness in people.

In the three days since discovering the significance of the astrological alignment, neither she nor Dayna had slept. The Order was taking advantage of the summer solstice. The question was, how? They were on borrowed time, but she couldn't work out how Leviathan was planning on coming through. The gate remained locked, and the cracks were holding.

She focused on the copy of the medieval text on the monitor. Access to the university's rare archives came in handy.

Ryker appeared in the doorway a short while later. "Mitos said you'd arrived."

She nodded. "I finished early, and Eugene dropped me off to save you a trip."

Ryker handed her one of the coffee cups he was holding. "Bypassed the green tea. Thought you might need the caffeine."

"Thanks." She had drawn blanks from the archive. "I think we should go to Mystery Hill and check again."

"There's no need. You were there this morning, like you've been every day. I have Leon and his team checking on the site throughout the day and night. Apart from a few new scuff marks around the site from curious teenagers, there's nothing."

Frustration crinkled her eyes. "Something doesn't feel right. There are only two days before the summer solstice."

"Are you sure you're not overreacting? You can't find any indication the gaps are big enough for the Legion to come through and take form?"

She shook her head. "I'm positive. Traditionally, our powers become stronger around the solstices. When the solstice coincides with a full moon as well as an almost perfect alignment with Jupiter and Venus, that power is compounded. But it also means that Leviathan becomes stronger. We know the Order are trying to release Leviathan. Only I have no idea how they plan on accomplishing that goal."

He rubbed his forehead, and a dark scowl took over his expression.

Since their discovery of the celestial alignment of the Strawberry Moon, they had seen very little of the cocky and charming Ryker. If she were honest, she missed the banter.

"Okay," he said. "How about we look at this logically. What are the possibilities?"

She rested her chin on the palm of her hand and stared at his desk as she sifted through the options. "The Order must know by now that killing the coven won't remove the wards and spells keeping the gate closed. They only have two options available to them. The first is to have the coven open the gate, which they'd be stupid to even think was an option."

"What's the second?"

Option two stumped her and Dayna. "Leviathan has help from this side of the gate, and whoever that is needs to share her source of power. And a considerable amount of it. Which is impossible as that would mean Legion. And the gaps are too small for them to come through and rematerialize." She rustled her hair in frustration. "And now we're back to where we started. Nowhere."

"You're positive the Order doesn't have the ability to open the gate or make a dent in it?"

"The Order lost their power the moment Leviathan was sent to hell. But with the summer solstice coinciding with the Strawberry Moon, some of the Order may have some of their power returned. But it will be weak, with no danger of unlocking the gate. Only the Legion's power would be capable of damaging the gate. Like I said before, they are trapped in hell with Leviathan, so they pose no threat to us."

He tilted his head to one side. "How sure are you? Is there any way they could have escaped?"

"I don't see how. But they clearly know something we don't. The sacrifices. There's a reason. The blood. *Something*. I just don't know what."

"Another gate, perhaps?"

"Maybe, but not this one. My mother died making sure they couldn't get through the cracks."

Ryker fell quiet and crossed to the large glass wall separating his office from the station's bullpen. He gazed at the organized chaos of his team and remained deep in thought. He pushed his hands into his pockets and turned back to her.

"I know neither you nor Dayna want to talk about what happened to your mother. But understanding the event might give us a clue on how to find who's behind this and what they're up to."

Her lips tightened "I can't see how."

Ryker was across the room in two strides and pulled a chair beside her. He sat face to face with her. "So far, I've not pushed you for anything you're not comfortable discussing. I've let you deal with things on your terms. If we had more time, I wouldn't do this. But I am running out of choices. I think your gut is right. There's something we're not seeing, and the only way forward is for me to understand what happened in the past."

Keira stared at her hands. He was right. She was too close to this, and a fresh set of eyes could help. She looked up at him and bit the inside of her lip. Hundreds of years had passed with so much water under the bridge.

"I don't know where to start."

He leaned forward, and a compassionate smile spread across his lips. "Maybe start with how you found the cracks?"

She closed her eyes and took a deep breath. Slowly letting it out, visions of her mother's loving face surfaced. Her smile was filled with the same joy and zest for life Dayna had inherited.

"The beginning of the end started with the Salem Witch trials. We knew something was amiss when Puritans began accusing their neighbors of being in league with the Devil. Like a disease, it infected even the most level-headed of them. They arrested over two hundred people. Some of them were nasty individuals, but they were not Witches. It wasn't until it was too late that we realized the Order was behind the false accusations. They wanted to build an army and couldn't have locals getting in their way. You can imagine how helpful they were in offering to buy any property when the family wanted to escape the insanity."

"And you had no idea they were behind it at the time?"

She shook her head. She often wondered how they'd missed the signs. "Once the trials were over, we thought things would go back to normal. How wrong we were."

"What happened then?"

"About a year later, we felt, rather than saw, something putting stress on the gate. My mother had the foresight to take a closer look. Until then, the cracks were minute fissures, barely detectable. We didn't know what to make of the discovery. A force was at play. We just didn't know what or why. Our overconfidence was almost our undoing. Only after three days of scouring through the ancient texts, did we realize what was happening under our noses."

She shifted in her chair. These were memories she rarely revisited. "We were blind to the fact the Order was on our doorstep. Somehow, they discovered that if they could bring Leviathan's Legion through to our world, they, in turn, would have the power to destroy our locks from the outside, while Leviathan chipped away from the inside."

"In a few short days, the fissures had become large cracks, almost big enough for a Legion to fit through. Even worse, their power was growing exponentially. The summer solstice was almost upon us. That year it also coincided with a full moon and—"

"Let me guess, Jupiter and Venus in close alignment?" he said.

She nodded. "That's correct. The Strawberry Moon. We wouldn't be standing here today had it not been for the perfect alignment. The Star of Bethlehem is the harbinger of a great shift in the earth's energy. I doubt we could have summoned enough power to hold her in."

"How did you stop her?"

"We did the only thing we could. We poured all our energy into closing the cracks. Nothing we did worked. They had gathered too much momentum and were destroying our wards before they got a chance to solidify. And we had no idea where they were. They managed to find a direct link to the stones without physically being at the site."

She touched her pendant. "To this day, I'm unsure what happened next. Time had run out. The solstice had come and gone, and the full moon was only a couple of hours away. We were desperate and fighting a losing battle. My mother announced she needed to speak with someone and that we were to guard her body. At that point, we didn't question her command. She had always been the most powerful, and her ability far exceeded any others within the coven."

"Do you know who she spoke with?"

"No." They had speculated, but nothing had ever been confirmed. "We constructed a circle of protection, and she put herself into a trance while we maintained her link to us. She wasn't gone that long, but when she came to, tears were streaming down her face. Before breaking the circle, she reached for Dayna and me and held us tight. I knew something was wrong. The grief rolled off her like a musty aroma. When the circle broke, she addressed the coven. She was resolute in her decision. Dayna and I were equally resolute in trying to talk her out of it."

"And that was?" he nudged gently.

"According to what she had just learned, only one thing could close the gaps and stop Leviathan's attempts. We didn't need to remove the gaps. We just needed to make them small enough that they couldn't send themselves through. Turns out, it was easier said than done. Someone would have to pour her magic into a single deadly incantation that would take her soul as payment. And by someone, I mean my mother."

Keira clenched her fists. "Despite knowing it was a death sentence, no one tried to talk her out of it. Not one of them. They acted like we were about to perform a simple, common spell. And nothing Dayna and I said swayed her."

Her throat grew sore, like a rock had lodged itself halfway down. She swallowed and struggled to remain in control. "Time is evil. It gave me minutes to say goodbye to my mother and an eternity to mourn her sacrifice. Not a day goes by that I don't ask myself if there was another way."

His cool hands rested over her clasped ones. His thumb made tender, circular motions on her skin. "Based on what little I know of your mother, there was no other choice. She wouldn't have made that decision unless it was the only way."

The painful memories surged to the surface and repeatedly stabbed at her emotions until they were raw. Keira couldn't hold back the floodgates. She still smelled the lavender in her mother's hair as she'd hugged her goodbye.

Keira's breath caught and set fire to her throat at the memory of her mother's touch when her calloused hands cupped her face.

"You must be vigilant," she'd said. "They will try again."

"Mother, I don't understand. Your shield still holds, and the gaps are still too small. Help me understand."

He didn't push her. He let her work through the memories, his touch giving her strength.

Keira hauled in a deep breath and wiped away the tears. "To complete the ancient magic, Mother required a direct connection to the coven's source of power, the Tree of Life. She needed to be tethered to the earth until she built up enough power and was ready. She couldn't do both, so the coven had to provide the link.

"Time was running out. We only had minutes until the birth of the full moon, and Leviathan's power was at its peak. Dayna, myself, and the rest of the coven resolved to give my mother the best chance of succeeding, so we provided her with a tether to the Tree of Life. Layers upon layers of magic were entwined to create a chain that wrapped around Mother, anchoring her to each of us, to the earth, and to the source of our power.

"As our spell grew in strength, my mother chanted words in a language we had never heard. Soft at first, then faster and louder. One moment everything around us was chaotic, the next, the world stopped. The wind died as if all the air had been sucked from it. The birds ceased their chatter, crickets followed in the silence, as if they knew what was about to happen and stood vigil, awaiting the outcome of the battle for humanity.

"At first, nothing. Then, the slightest of tugs on the chain. Like a fish teasing a fisherman, it nibbled at the connection."

She briefly closed her eyes, and her voice wavered. "None of us were prepared for what came next. A violent tempest tore through our bodies without warning, and I felt like I was being torn limb from limb. But the tortured scream from my mother scared me more than the pain roiling through my body.

"We watched helplessly as lightning flared from the earth and repeatedly struck my mother. Bolt by bolt, it burst free, and like a whip, it lashed at her body. She was suspended in midair, her arms stretched out wide, her head thrown back.

"Each time the current from the earth ignited, white pulsating ropes of energy flowed from the earth to her body, vibrating with enough force that my mother appeared out of focus. The vibrations increased with each new strike, and a few of the coven Witches collapsed, unable to withstand the power. Those of us who remained did our best to carry the extra load. To this day, I can't tell you how long it lasted. It could have been minutes. It could have been hours. I was watching my mother sacrifice herself in the most painful way possible. At some point, the screams stopped. In its place was a low hum of energy that pulsed like a heartbeat and became brighter with each passing moment. The tethering chain we valiantly held was wrapped around my mother's legs. My body ached from the strain of keeping it under control."

She hauled in another deep breath. "The extra power came out of nowhere, and she disappeared in a blinding, explosive light. The only thing left behind was her amethyst necklace. The amulet had broken in two and fallen to the ground. One half in front of me and the other by Dayna. I've never experienced such power. It radiated in all directions. Everything was affected by the pure raw energy. This all happened in the middle of the night, but it was almost as if the noonday sun had appeared in all its glory. The ball of blinding light rose higher and higher before plummeting downward and sinking into the earth with such force that we were all swept off our feet. Even as I fell, I knew Leviathan's plan had failed. My mother had sealed the cracks. But before we could take a breath, two small white orbs from the stone flew toward Dayna and me."

She fell quiet and fingered the amulet. The only thing she still carried from her mother. In the moments before losing consciousness, she'd felt their mother's love, warm, strong, and unconditional, sweep through her body as her familiar voice whispered in their ears, *"My gift to you until we can be reunited."*

"We awoke two days later. A decade passed before we suspected what my mother's final gift was, and two decades more before we accepted it. We ceased to age. I look the same as I did the day my mother sealed the cracks and saved humankind from a fate worse than death. As with everything, Dayna saw the positive and readily embraced her gift. I, however, view it as a curse."

"What about the rest of the coven?" His voice broke into her reverie. "How did they react?"

"At first, things stayed the same. But eventually, enough years passed that those coven members present that day were well and truly gone. We felt like strangers to the coven. While they said nothing, we knew they were wary of us. I couldn't blame them. We failed to age like typical Witches. With nothing to tie us to the place we'd called home for one hundred and fifty years, I severed ties with the coven and vowed never to return. I lost my mother, plus too many friends to old age. I couldn't face another person I loved dying while I stayed behind with only their memories as a constant companion."

She blinked to clear her watery vision. When she left Salem, she had locked her heart away from the possibility of ever being hurt again, and she'd left the key behind. It was the only way for her to go on with her sanity intact.

"Until your call, I'd never been back."

Ryker tucked a stray hair behind her ear and rested a hand on her cheek. "I can't pretend to know your grief or the pain of losing your mom. I grew up not knowing my parents or a mother's love. The only family I've known is Deacon and Ananya. Your mother sounds like a remarkable woman, and I would have liked to meet her."

She gave him a half-smile. "I'm not sure what she would have made of you."

He winked and cocked his head. "She would have adored me. What's not to like?"

She let out an unladylike snort. She was not about to admit he was probably right.

Ryker turned her hand and studied her palm. With the lightest of touches, he rubbed his thumb across her lifeline. "From what Deacon tells me about Annabeth, I don't think anything would have changed her mind. She did what she did to save you and Dayna. That her sacrifice also saved the rest of us was a happy coincidence. There is no point in second-guessing or blaming yourself for what happened."

She chewed on her bottom lip. Now that she had unburdened herself, her shoulders didn't feel as heavy. "Did you learn anything?"

"I learned that you are more like your mother than you think," he said softly. "If you're okay with it, I'd like to speak with Deacon about how the Order was able to worm their way into Salem back then undetected. I have a few questions that he might be able to answer. You never know, the past may help us work out where they may be based now."

He stood, but before he let go of her hand, he gazed down at her. "Closing your heart to the outside world doesn't stop the pain. It just postpones it and sets us up for a fall."

Before she could question his meaning, he strode to the door and shouted across the bullpen, "Mitos!"

Mitos hastened over. "Yes, boss?"

"Where's Trudeau? I'm still waiting for his update on the team guarding the crime scene at Mystery Hill."

Mitos shrugged. His expression reflected his indifference. "He got waylaid. Another tourist went missing from a local B&B this morning, and he's taking their statement. I don't know why we bother. He'll just turn up in a day or so, just like the others. Waste of time, if you ask me."

"Why isn't the desk sergeant taking the statement?"

"Fucked if I know. I've certainly got better things to do than deal with whiny tourists who've lost their boyfriend and have too many holes in their nose." Mitos shuddered. "This generation is going to hell in a handbasket. You wonder why there's a steel shortage? It's cause these shit-for-brains retards stockpile the stuff in holes in their bodies. If you ask me—"

"Did you and Trudeau go out to Mystery Hill this afternoon?"

Mito snorted. "Leon took that fuckwit Binks with him."

"What did Binks do to deserve that?"

"He managed to trip and spread the entire contents of his lunch over me. That goddamn curry stains like a bitch. Leon couldn't wait for me to change, so he took the retard with him."

"Can you let him know I'm after him?"

Mitos turned away. "Sure thing."

As he disappeared out the door, Ryker called after him, "Oh, and Mitos …"

The deputy poked his head back in the doorway.

"Have you booked the cultural sensitivity training yet?"

Mitos scrunched his face. "They said they'll let me know when a spot opens up. For some reason, they can't schedule me with Betty what's-her-name, the one with the big jugs. Apparently, there's some sort of conflict or something."

Keira shuddered when Mitos left. "How is he still on the force? He must be an HR nightmare."

Ryker grunted and rubbed his right eyebrow before he answered. "You have no idea. The man's been on the force for nearly forty years and is a born-and-bred local. I couldn't get rid of him if I tried. No matter how much he irritates me or how much of a headache he makes for me, I need him."

"I thought he was Human?"

"He is, but he's seen a lot over the years. Not once has he questioned it. I'm not sure whether it's because his mind explains it away or he's just in denial, but he's the voice of reason whenever any of the Human deputies think they've seen something they shouldn't have."

Her brows rose so high she was sure they disappeared into her hairline. "Mitos? The voice of reason?"

"I suppose that's a bad choice of words, but his political incorrectness bullies them into thinking they were seeing things." Ryker leaned back in his chair. "Once he retires, I'm not sure if we'll get away with the very thin veil we hide behind in this office."

He checked his watch. "I'm almost done here. How about we grab an early dinner, my treat?"

Before she could answer, her phone rang.

Dayna's voice came out in a rush. "Where are you?"

"At the station. Why?"

Dayna held a muffled conversation with someone else before replying. "Don't go anywhere. Ananya is going to drive me over."

"Where's Deacon?"

"He's at a city council meeting. This can't wait for him."

"Dayna, you're scaring me. What's going on?"

Dayna hesitated before replying, "I've managed to unlock Annie's journal."

Finally, something's going right. "How?"

"I went through her social media accounts and the photo albums her family supplied and found a common theme. A stuffed toy."

Keira recalled the tattered bear Maize had been clutching. "It's not a gray bear, is it?"

"Yes." Dayna paused before she said, "And there's something else."

Keira tensed. Her sister's voice didn't sound reassuring. "Why am I suddenly worried?"

"Because I know who the boyfriend is, and I'm pretty sure he's the one who killed her."

Keira's head shot up and her gaze slammed into Ryker's. "Who?"

Dayna's voice was barely audible. "I'd rather not say over the phone."

"I'm assuming you heard that?" she asked Ryker as soon as the call ended.

He nodded. "I'm not happy she's traveling without backup."

"She's with Ananya."

His brows knitted into a frown. "I know she comes across as a battleax, but she's a sixty-nine-year-old woman who's five foot nothing. Not exactly what I'd consider great protection. I'll call Tim and Pete, make sure they go with them."

Keira reached for the phone. "Maybe you're right."

After a heated discussion with her sister, who refused point-blank to wait for their bodyguards to return from their patrol of the estate, she and Ryker had no choice but to cool their heels and wait for their arrival.

Relief spread through her when, forty-five minutes later, Dayna waltzed through the door with Ananya hot on her heels.

Keira had spent forty-four of those minutes pacing back and forth in Ryker's office like a caged lion.

"Can't stay long. It's my bingo night," Ananya declared as they stepped into the room. "There's a thief that's trying to take my title."

For once, Dayna wasn't sporting her trademark smile. Instead, her gaze darted around the room as if nervous and wanting to appear as unobtrusive as possible. *Something was wrong*. Dayna went out of her way to be noticed, not blend into the background. That was Keira's default position, not her vibrant sister's.

Dayna closed the door behind her. Without saying a word, she stretched up to close the Venetians covering the window to the station's bullpen. As soon as they were closed, she reached into her oversized tote bag and pulled out the familiar journal. She placed it on Ryker's desk. Her hand disappeared into the bag, and she pulled out the stuffed toy and placed it next to Annie's diary.

Dayna stared at the book without moving. Something was troubling her sister, but she knew her well enough to wait for her to speak first.

They jumped at a knock on the door. Without waiting for a response, Deputy Leon Trudeau poked his head into the room. "You were after me, boss? Whoops, didn't know you had visitors."

"Not now, Trudeau. I'll come and get you when I'm ready," Ryker said sharply.

Leon glanced at the room's occupants and grimaced. "Sorry." He closed the door.

Dayna flipped the journal open and flicked to the page she was looking for. Ryker leaned forward, and Keira moved around to the side of the desk to get a better view. Dayna positioned the bear closer to touch the book. She reached into her pocket, pulled out her crystals, and mouthed a silent incantation.

"Hell's bells, would you look at that?" Ananya shrieked.

The shock of witnessing the writing on the page suddenly melt and swirl was evident in the old woman's tone.

Annie's words eventually settled and reformed.

Keira scanned the page, and her chest tightened with each passage. *No. It can't be!* Ryker's expression reflected the same disbelief. They turned the page and continued reading. Once they finished, the room fell silent.

Ryker bolted up and was at the door in an instant. He scanned the outer office. Not finding what he was after, he called out, "Mitos, where's Trudeau?"

"Changing room, I think."

Ryker turned back to them. "Wait here. I'll be right back."

Her blood boiled as the shock wore off. With the identification of Annie's killer, they had also discovered who was responsible for Marcus' death. The need for revenge rushed to the surface, and she bolted for the door.

"Where are you going?" Dayna called.

"To stop Ryker from killing Trudeau. I want a piece of him first."

TWENTY-FIVE

PASS THE DUTCHIE

Keira was ready to breathe fire. The two-faced pond scum of a deputy had looked her in the eye and expressed his sorrow for her loss. And he had the audacity to do so minutes after taking Marcus' life. She wanted her piece of flesh just as much as Ryker.

Before she cleared the doorway, Ryker burst out of the small hallway leading to the changing rooms.

His expression perfectly matched hers as he scanned the bullpen. "Where the hell is Trudeau?"

The venom that laced his booming voice stopped the entire station in its tracks. Everyone whipped around to face the enraged sheriff. Even from the opposite side of the building, she could see the fury as flashes of red bled into the blue of his irises. If she were closer, she was sure she would hear his teeth grind against each other. His jaw was so ridged, she was surprised he could move it at all.

"He was in the changing room, I swear," Mitos said. For once, he refrained from any derogatory remarks.

She couldn't believe her ears. They had lost Marcus' killer and their only lead to the Order. He had just been in the building.

Ryker took a deep breath and hissed as he let it out between clamped teeth. The entire station, including the members of the public at the front counter, were fixated on the sheriff. He was barely keeping himself together. A far cry from the laid-back and congenial man they were used to.

"Jessie-Pearl, get him on the horn and tell him I want him back here now."

The heavily pregnant station's dispatcher nodded as she swung her chair back to her desk. "Unit thirty-two, what is your ten-twenty? Over."

A few confused looks passed between the officers, but no one was game enough to speak. Apart from the static noise from the two-way radio, the room was silent.

"I repeat. Unit thirty-two, what is your ten-twenty?" Jessie-Pearl slowly turned back to Ryker. Her hands were clenched together so tightly over her bulging stomach that her knuckles were white. She visibly gulped. "He's not answering."

Keira only hoped that in her frightened state, Jessie-Pearl's waters didn't burst. Most of the staff wore the same confused expressions.

From the little she'd gleaned during her time here, Ryker had the communities' and his officers' backs, and they knew it. They saw him as a fair and just sheriff. Not one of them questioned his mysterious background or the fact that he never appeared to age. Since he had taken the badge, crime was at an all-time low. They felt safe. Windows and doors were rarely locked. For him to be so public with his anger and to almost lose control of the thin veneer that separated the beast from the civilized man could only mean one thing. Trudeau had done something they needed to be concerned about.

The three civilians waiting to speak to an officer edged their way out of the station's door.

Ryker scanned the room again. "Where's Binks?"

Heads swiveled in all directions.

"He's not on patrol," Jessie-Pearl said, her voice coming out in a tiny squeak. "I saw him about ten minutes ago."

A low growl escaped the back of Ryker's throat. "Mitos."

"Yes, sheriff?"

"I want a roll call now. If I don't have a list of the names of the officers who are unaccounted for or ignoring their radios on my desk within five minutes, you will be taking missing person reports for the rest of your life. Am I understood?"

"Yes, sheriff."

Ryker cast his narrowed gaze across the room. "Trudeau is considered dangerous and a person of interest in the deaths at Mystery Hill and the Witches Brew."

A dull buzz erupted at Ryker's words.

"And unless the rest of you are statues, I suggest you get back to work."

Ryker stormed down the hallway and disappeared.

The officers and staff snapped out of their stupor, and the station resumed its hive of activity. Everyone returned to what they were doing before Ryker's outburst.

"You heard the sheriff, you fucktards," Mitos hollered. "Sworns to the briefing room. Jessie-Pearl will account for the rest of you."

How had they not seen what he was up to? The more Keira thought about Leon, the more her blood boiled. He was a murderer who played them all. White-hot fury rose from the depths of her soul, and she had a sudden desire to destroy something. Anything.

A gentle touch on her arm brought her back from the brink of eruption. She turned to see Ananya making strange faces as her gaze flickered downward.

She turned back to Dayna. Her sister's eyes were like saucers. A hand covered her mouth.

"For Heaven's sake, girl," Ananya said in a voice low enough the others wouldn't overhear. "Look down at your hands."

Keira glanced down, and her heart stopped mid-beat. Floating, as if they were natural and normal to be there, were two glowing orbs resembling small balls of fire. Each one cupped in the palms of her hands. What the hell?

Until that moment, she thought she was clenching her fists, not clenching two mini-suns. She appealed to Dayna for some sort of explanation. When she looked down again, the orbs were gone. Mindful she was in a public place, she checked to see if anyone else in the station had noticed the apparition. Satisfied they were too busy, she threw a grateful look in Ananya's direction and raced into Ryker's office.

Dayna slammed the door behind the three of them.

"I assume that's not supposed to happen," Ananya said as she rustled through Ryker's desk. "I'm sure he's got some of those drugs to calm your nerves. You know, the stuff he keeps confiscating from teenagers. Pan, I think it's called."

Dayna's hand fell away from her mouth, and her face lost all color. "Pot. It's called pot. If you find some, I think we all might need a tote."

Too stunned to speak, Keira shook her head, not sure which way was up.

Wide-eyed, Dayna stared at Keira's hands. "It shouldn't be possible."

Not only was it impossible, but it was also outside the laws of nature. An Earth Witch couldn't call on the fire, water, or air elements.

Keira held her hands in front of her face and inspected them. They looked normal, not at all like two fiery balls that had manifested themselves only moments before.

"I don't know how that happened."

"What were you thinking at the time?" Dayna asked.

"I was too angry to think."

Dayna's eyes widened. "What would have happened if you'd used them?"

Too terrified to voice a reply, Keira remained silent. But they both knew the answer. People would have been hurt. No doubt about it, the two fireballs were weapons. She'd somehow manifested a fire element from its source.

Lighting a candle with her mind was easy. She used earth elements to set the wick alight. The flame was the result, not the source.

She looked at her hands again and shook her head. "I don't want to think about it."

Dayna opened the filing cabinet and rifled through the files with a sense of urgency. "We need something to calm us down. He must have it stashed somewhere."

"I'm fine. It's not like I'm angry now and balls of fire will fly around the building like comets."

"It's not for you," Dayna said as she checked Ryker's jacket. "Shit just got serious."

Ryker stormed into his office and cut off all conversation. "Trudeau, and who knows how many others, are missing. He's also helped himself to extra weapons and ammo from the armory."

"They've armed the Order?"

A sharp pain manifested behind Keira's eyes. This was getting worse by the moment.

Before she had a chance to take a breath, Mitos knocked on the door and walked in.

"Jessie-Pearl has accounted for all the off-duties. Trudeau, Binks, and Worthington are unaccounted for." He turned to go, then, as if thinking better of it, turned back. "Do you really believe he killed Dr. Wynter's colleague and all the others? Maybe he's just stepped out for donuts?"

Ryker tossed a deputy's shield and nametag on the desk. "I found this in the locker room."

"That's just fucked up on so many levels." Mitos scratched his head. "I guess I won't be going to Bingo tonight."

The sound of someone clearing their throat caught their attention. Jessie-Pearl peered around the doorway, her wrinkled forehead and questioning eyes an indication she was still a little wary of approaching Ryker.

"Sheriff, the phones won't stop, and there's a line of people at the counter."

"What's happened?"

Mitos huffed. "It'll be those skitzo tourists wanting to report a missing person. Just tell them to get a grip. Their friend will turn up within twenty-four hours."

Jessie-Pearl shook her head. "No, Brad just called in a ten fifty-four."

Ryker rubbed his forehead. "That's all I need."

"What's a ten fifty-four?" Ananya asked no one in particular.

Keira frowned and looked toward her sister. "Dead body."

Deputy Brad Simons appeared relieved when Ryker and Keira walked into the Stop'n Bite Diner. "Don't mind telling ya'll, this one takes the cake. Ain't seen nutin' like it before."

Ryker glanced around the eatery. "Where's the victim?"

The deputy jerked a thumb over his shoulder. "Far side of the counter. I called in the ten fifty-four the second I realized there weren't no breathing."

The man's body lay crumpled on the floor. Apart from an ashen color, not a hair seemed out of place.

Ryker squatted and took a closer look. "What happened?"

Brad pushed up the brim of his Stetson with the finger of one hand while tucking his thumb into his belt buckle with the other. "It's the darndest thing. According to Mary-Anne, the owner of this here establishment, the other customer never laid a finger on him. They was arguing one minute, then the customer who started the disagreement gave our vic here the evil eye, and he dropped dead."

"Where's the other customer now?"

The deputy shrugged. "No one knows. Everyone gave him a wide berth when he left. Ain't no one want to mess with something like that."

"Witnesses?"

The deputy pointed at a small group of customers cowering in the far corner of the diner. "Take your pick."

"And no one else was hurt?"

"Just this guy."

Ryker motioned toward the emergency truck parked outside the café. "What's with the paramedics?"

"Oh that, that's on account of Louise, one of the waitresses, having herself a little episode. Louise done gone and got herself all worked up. They were called in to give her one of those injections to settle her nervous disposition."

Ryker straightened and studied the small group of customers who'd witnessed the bizarre incident. "Have you taken their statements yet?"

"No. I was holding off till the cavalry arrived."

Ryker nodded at the huddled group. "You get started there, and Doc Wynter and I will see what we can get out of Louise."

With that, he strode to the door.

"What do you make of it?" Ryker asked when she caught up to him.

"Something's not right. There's not a mark on him."

He opened the door just as his phone rang. "Kincaid."

She stopped short when a curt *"when?"* came out loud enough to startle the rubberneckers behind the police tape. Ryker swore under his breath and thrust his phone into his pocket.

"What's happened?"

"There have been two more reported incidents similar to this one. Both times, someone literally dropped dead."

"What about the missing tourists?"

"They're disappearing faster than we can write the reports."

What did the Order hope to gain from this level of destruction? She only hoped that Dayna's divination to locate Leon worked. They had his badge to help them narrow down his location. If anyone could do it, her sister could. Keira had never mastered that particular piece of magic. Dayna, however, was exceptional at scrying. You never wanted to piss off a Witch who could find you no matter how far you ran.

Keira indicated their dead diner customer. "Then we have to assume the Order is behind this?"

He looked at the slender woman rocking back and forth on the curb. "I suspect Louise will be able to shed some light on the situation."

Louise wrapped her arms around her knees and rocked violently. Whatever had occurred had driven her into a mild hysteria.

Ryker moved around in front of the visibly distraught woman. "Louise, I'm Sheriff Kincaid. I realize you've had a bit of a shock this evening, but I was wondering if you're up to answering a few questions?"

Louise stopped moving and looked up at him. Dark splotches where her mascara had smudged made her look like a forlorn baby panda.

She bit the bottom of her lip and nodded. "I'll try."

"Can you tell us what happened?"

Louise's gaze darted around the immediate area. Her expression became uncertain.

Ryker beckoned for Keira as he sat beside the young waitress. She took Ryker's lead and sat on the other.

"You're Gifted, aren't you?" he asked in a low voice.

Louise nodded.

"What's your gift?" Keira asked.

Louise rested her chin on her knees and pulled her arms around her legs tighter. "I see auras. I know people's souls." She blinked and nodded at Ryker. "I know what you are, sheriff." She swung her head to her. "And you as well."

Keira held back her curiosity. She couldn't help wondering why Louise chose to live in Salem and not in a small, remote part of the country. Of all the talents a Gifted person could have, seeing auras was the most common, and it was both a gift and a curse. Many successful diplomats over the centuries had been aura-reading Gifted. But many Gifted shied away from large populations, unable to cope with knowing a person's soul before meeting them.

Louise dropped her head to her kneecaps. "You know, you can tell a lot by people's auras."

Ryker placed a hand on her shoulder. "And what did you see in the diner?"

"I've never seen anything like it before. Like it was being sucked right out of him." Louise shivered and expelled her breath in a whoosh. "His life force. The real freaky thing was that the man who did it didn't have an aura. Every living being has an aura. Why couldn't I see his? He just ate that poor man's soul like it was a freshly baked peach pie."

A chill shook Keira's body, and she broke out in goosebumps. She had never heard of that sort of ability. Taking a life that way was not possible. Or at least, until now, it hadn't been.

Ryker stood and helped Keira to her feet, then drew her aside. "What do you think?"

Louise was clearly too distraught to continue, and they were reluctant to push her over the edge.

"I don't know what to think. None of what she said makes sense. No one, and I mean no one, can just rip a person's essence from them like that."

"Could it be a rogue Witch doing some sort of mumbo jumbo spell?"

She considered the question for all of two seconds. "No. We can't tap into that sort of power. If we want to kill someone, it will be with a potion or poison. Aside from that, we use the same methods as everyone else."

He grinned. "At least it's not a Vampire. When we take out a person, you can bet your last dollar that blood will be involved."

The county coroner's van pulled up, and a wiry middle-aged man jumped out of the vehicle before it came to a complete stop.

He rushed over to Ryker. "What do you have for me?" He turned back to the younger man driving the vehicle and yelled out, "A little faster would be nice. We don't have all day."

His assistant closed the door of the van and raced toward the back. The coroner turned back to Ryker and adjusted his glasses.

"We're still trying to piece the crime scene together," Ryker said. "But it looks like our vic got into an argument and dropped dead. My guess is that he had a heart attack or stroke. Remember that Atherton case a few years back? This one feels the same."

The coroner cocked his head. "Three in one day? What the hell is going on, sheriff?"

"Full moon tomorrow night. Maybe that's affected them."

The coroner didn't appear convinced. "You and I both know the crazies don't need a full moon."

Her stomach tightened. She had to agree with the coroner's sentiment. All these murders were not coincidences. What in God's name was going on? What power had the Order tapped into?

As soon as the coroner and his assistant disappeared inside, Ryker reached for his two-way radio and scanned through the channels. In the short time they'd been in the diner; the body count had risen. Five fatalities, each with the same story. The victims suddenly dropped dead after talking to a stranger. But it was highly unlikely that two deaths in Ryker's jurisdiction in Essex County, one in Salem, and two in Laurence had all resulted from the same killer.

The uneasy feeling turned into bricks sitting at the bottom of her stomach.

"We're going to have a major disaster on our hands if we don't get in front of the story," Ryker said as he again reached for his phone. "The press is going to have a field day."

"Who are you phoning?"

"The old man, he's bound to be getting pressure from the governor. That weasel sheriff in Laurence County married the governor's sister. He's bending the governor's ear every chance he gets."

While Ryker was deep in conversation with Deacon, Keira wandered back to the diner. The unfortunate man who'd had his aura ripped from him was now in a black body bag. Officers were keeping spectators well away from the scene. For all intents and purposes, it looked like a typical police crime scene found anywhere in the country.

The hairs on the back of her neck stood on end. Nothing could be further from the truth.

Ryker clamped a hand around her upper arm and pulled her away from the window. "We've got to get back to the station."

Stumbling to keep pace with him, she struggled against his tight grip on her upper arm. His grim expression added another brick to the pile already at the bottom of her stomach.

"What about the other crime scene? Don't we need to get to it?"

"I train my officers to do their jobs without me having to hold their hands. We need to get back now."

"Why?" she demanded as they reached his squad car.

"Because there's only a skeleton staff on duty at the moment."

"And?"

Ryker opened the door and halted for a moment before he got in. "Deacon will meet us there."

Mother Earth, why was he not making sense? She opened the door and bent down to look inside the car.

"What aren't you telling me?"

"I told Deacon about what our aura reader said." Ryker started the engine. "We've got to get back to the station. He'll meet us there." He growled and flashed an angry glare at her when she remained still. "Doc, get in the goddam car!"

Not wanting a repeat performance of his earlier outburst, she threw herself into the car. "Fine, but you still haven't explained the urgency."

"Legion. Deacon said the only thing that can suck out a person's soul like that is a Legion. Dayna is on her own with a lilliputian secretary who's seen better days, a pregnant woman who I am sure is having quadruplets, and a desk sergeant who walks with a limp."

TWENTY-SIX

THE GIFT

For once, Keira had no problem with Ryker's excessive speed. If he was not already pushing the vehicle to its limits, she would have cast a spell to press the accelerator to the floor. The moment the tires rebelled at the sudden screech of brakes as they pulled into the station's parking lot, she was out the door. She imagined the worst, and with Dayna not answering her calls, each scenario that played out was more horrifying than the previous.

She raced inside. "Dayna!"

Jessie-Pearl looked up from her monitor and froze, a muesli bar hovering halfway to her mouth.

Keira halted in her tracks. She didn't know what to expect, but a peaceful and quiet building was not close.

"I'll phone you back." Jessie-Pearl and placed the handset on its cradle. "Is everything all right, Dr. Wynter?"

The door swung open, and Ryker materialized beside her. "I've checked the perimeter. Did you find them?"

She shook her head and turned to Jessie-Pearl. "Where are my sister and Ananya?"

The dispatcher pointed to Ryker's office. "They haven't come out since you left."

"Is everything okay here? Where's Jobson?" Ryker asked, referring to the desk sergeant.

Jessie-Pearl leaned back in her chair and placed her hand over her heavily pregnant stomach. "She ducked out to get us some pizza. Why?"

Not waiting for the answer, Keira made a beeline for the office, relieved at not finding any of the thousand scenarios that had played out in her head during the mad dash.

When she pushed open Ryker's office door, an odd, sweet smell blew into her nostrils.

"What the—?"

Dayna was sitting, or rather, lounging, in Ryker's chair with her feet on the desk. Ananya was in a similar position on the couch. They were both doing a good imitation of hyenas with their raucous laughter. Tears rolled down Dayna's cheeks while Ananya held on to her stomach.

"Stop, Dayna, my sides hurt too much."

Keira waved her hand in the air to clear out some of the smoke that hung in a low cloud formation. "What the hell is going on?"

Instead of answers, all she got for her troubles was another round of laughter. She placed her hands on her hips.

"This is not funny."

Her outrage only set them off again.

A low growl erupted from beside her. "This is a sheriff's station, not a teenage frat house."

Ryker strode across the room, opened a window, then glared down at Ananya. "This is your doing, isn't it?"

Ananya swung her legs off the couch and sat up. The twitch in her jaw betrayed her struggle to keep a straight face.

"And why would you assume it was me? I'm just an old woman."

Ananya fidgeted under Ryker's death stare. She pursed her lips together, scrunched her face, then pointed at Dayna. "It's her fault. She made me do it. I thought it was a herbal cigarette."

Dayna whipped her legs off the desk and bolted upright. "Don't you go blaming me, you wrinkled old hag. You're the one who found the stash."

At that, both women burst out laughing again.

"I told you he'd blame me," Ananya said between breaths. "Even when I was a kid, he'd accuse me of stealing stuff from his room."

Dayna faced Ryker and stuck out her tongue. "He's just a big meanie."

"That's because you did steal my stuff." Ryker towered over the diminutive secretary. "You were caught red-handed every time."

Ananya harrumphed and stood. "Now you're just exaggerating. I got away with it sometimes." She raised her chin. "I'm peckish. I think I'll go see if there's any food in the kitchen."

Once the petite, older woman exited the room, Keira swung back to face her sister. With Dayna not answering her calls, she'd panicked. Anger now replaced the fear.

"How could you be so irresponsible? We're in the middle of a disaster, you don't answer your phone, and you sneak a joint with an elderly woman. You were supposed to be scrying for Trudeau."

Dayna's nose crinkled. "As usual, you're overreacting. My nerves were wound up so tight the scrying wasn't working. I just needed something to relax me enough to focus properly."

Keira counted to ten. That was typical Dayna, never considering the ramifications of her actions.

Ryker placed a hand on her arm and gave it a gentle squeeze. "She's fine. Nothing's happened to her."

At his words, the stress she'd experienced the entire drive to the station popped, and her temper deflated.

Dayna leaned forward and grinned. "Sheriff McSexy is correct. I'm fine, so fine, in fact, I'll even let you join the party." She looked over at the desk and frowned. "Where did that old biddy go? She's taken the party with her."

"Crap!" Ryker said with a low growl. He turned and headed out the door. "Ananya, where the hell are you?"

Dayna raised her voice and called out, "If you find any food, can you bring it back with you?"

Keira folded her arms over her chest, tapped her foot repeatedly, and stared at her sister.

Dayna, who had begun to stack some of the files on Ryker's desk in a neat pile, looked up.

"What?" She shrugged. "I'm hungry."

Deacon arrived not long after Ryker scrounged a tube of Pringles for Dayna. The chaos that had gripped the city and outlying counties died down as quickly as it had erupted. The day shift slowly returned to the station to clock out for the night, and Mitos was charged with driving Miss Ananya home.

As expected, he did so with very vocal and flowery complaining. Much to their surprise, the deputy was Ananya's arch-nemesis at their weekly bingo nights. They left the station accusing each other of cheating just as Dayna began to scry for the missing deputy once more.

Deacon closed Ryker's office door once Ananya had left the building. "I think it best we are not overheard."

The room fell silent with all eyes focused on Deacon.

"I believe the Legion are behind the recent unexplained deaths," Deacon said.

"I don't understand how that's possible," Dayna said, an edge of alarm in her voice.

Not that Keira could blame her sister. Even she was struggling not to break out in a cold sweat.

"There's no other explanation," Deacon said. "The upper ranks of the Legion are the only beings that have ever possessed that sort of power."

Keira grimaced and shook her head from side to side. "The gaps are not big enough to let in Legion. What's more, if they were coming through, it would be at Mystery Hill. We've been there every morning, and the site's been checked on throughout the day, every day."

"Trudeau," Ryker said with a groan. "The team monitoring the crime scene are the same men who disappeared with him. Which means they had unrestricted access to the stones, except during the short time we were there each morning."

Dayna let out a little squeak, and all eyes turned to her. She was holding her pendant at arm's length. The crystal had attached itself to the map they'd hastily spread on the desk. Which could only mean one thing. Dayna had found where Trudeau was hiding out.

"Where is he?" Keira asked.

Dayna's voice came out in a broken whisper. "Mystery Hill."

Ryker reached for his sheriff's baseball cap. "We'd better get out there."

They were about five miles from Mystery Hill when Ryker pulled off the road and tucked the vehicle out of sight from the road and behind a clump of trees.

They exited the dented squad car, and Keira peered into the darkness. The road was not well lit, and an overcast night blocked the moonlight.

"Okay, then, lead the way," Keira said.

Ryker chuckled. "We won't be walking, or at least you won't be."

"I don't understand. Why not?"

Deacon approached Dayna. "If we walk, it will be at least an hour's journey, probably more, through bush and uneven ground. Ryker and I can get you there in a fraction of that time."

Dayna let out a squeal.

"Hold still, big boy." She hurled her body at Deacon's back and settled in for a piggyback ride. "I could get used to this."

"Doc, it's your lucky day." Ryker turned his back to her. "Hop on board."

She stumbled away. "You can't be serious."

He grinned. "Don't be shy. Just wrap your legs around me and hold on real tight. I promise to be gentle with you since it's your first time."

Uncertain, she looked over at Deacon and Dayna. Dayna was teasing him and prodding Deacon with her heels. The next instant, they disappeared in a plume of dust.

"Unless you can find that broomstick of yours, we need to go," Ryker said. From the low timbre of his voice, he was not only serious but impatient.

He crouched, and she wrapped her arms around his shoulders. He stood, pulling her legs up until they were straddling either side of his waist. She pressed her face close to his neck and couldn't help noticing a faint smell of licorice beneath his masculine scent. Her body heated up and a flash of desire ripped through her. She held on tighter to his firm chest and stopped herself from pressing her lips to his neck.

Mother Earth. What the hell was wrong with her?

She was mortified. How did one man make her go from one extreme emotion to another in a heartbeat?

"It'll get a little bumpy. Just don't let go."

The journey took a little more than ten minutes. The coolness of the night air whipped through her hair as they sped through the underbrush of the forest. More than once she jammed her eyes closed as they ducked and weaved to evade trees and low hanging branches. Her heart thumping in her chest at every near miss. She couldn't, for the life of her, figure out why piggyback riding had been so enjoyable as a child but so uncomfortable as an adult. Not to mention nauseating. Although she had to admit, the closeness of their bodies caused a series of hot flushes each time she was forced to mold herself tighter to his body.

For his part, Ryker never appeared to break a sweat. The unbridled power in his muscles tore them through the forest faster than she believed possible. It was another reminder of just how much Vampires outmatched the rest of the races in speed, agility, and strength. Despite this power, she had no reservations. She was safe with Ryker. Check that, she was physically safe with him. Her erratic emotions when she was around him was another story.

To reduce the chance of being seen, they circled the clearing and approached from the north side of the woods. Keira had never been so thankful for the clouds blocking the moonlight. The darkness afforded them the ability to get much closer than they otherwise would have.

Deacon and Ryker set them down, and they cautiously moved closer.

Keira held her breath and sent out a silent prayer as she crawled forward along the uneven ground covered by dirt and moss. When they reached the top of a small embankment that provided a direct line of sight to the clearing, her breath exhaled in a whoosh.

Crap.

Based on the light emitting from the direction of the stones, any hope that Deacon had been wrong evaporated. The night air sent a cold shiver down her spine.

Ryker let out a string of curses that would have made a sailor blush.

Keira looked at her sister. *This can't be good.* She narrowed her eyes and peered into the light.

"What do you see?"

As much as she tried, they were still too far away to make out anything tangible.

They crept closer, and her heart thumped against her ribcage. The sight was worse than anything she could have imagined.

Fifty people circled the ancient site, facing into the woods as if they were providing a human shield. They stood like sentries, an arm's distance between them. Small fires spread around the site, providing a dull but eerie glow. Three people stood near the altar stone.

Keira adjusted her position for a better view and drew in a sharp breath. Someone was strapped to the stone. Leaning over him was a mountain of a man who could have given Arnold Schwarzenegger a run for his money. His shoulders had shoulders.

"That much muscle on one person is just not natural," Dayna said in a whisper.

An older, smaller, and wiry man with thinning hair stood next to the muscled Arnie double. The long, dark robe he wore reminded Keira of the monks during the Spanish Inquisition. He clutched something around his neck.

Most likely a satanic cross. The cross associated with Leviathan. The older man had to be a Brother Superior within the Order.

Arnie pulled out a knife and held it up to the night sky.

Dayna whipped her hand before her mouth, holding back a whimper as she leapt to her feet.

"He's going to kill him," she said in a muffled voice. "We need to do something."

Keira was about to tell her sister to get down when Deacon yanked her to the ground.

"It benefits no one if we rush in without a plan."

The knife plunged downward.

Keira looked away at the last moment. When she turned back, the sacrifice victim was sitting up.

"What in the hell?"

He had been cut free. The sacrificial lamb was now standing toe to toe with Arnie, who rested his hand on the other man's shoulder.

"It's a sign of respect and greeting," Deacon said in a low voice.

Ryker stiffened. His features were set in stone. She could feel the rage washing over him in waves.

She understood why. At least two dozen prisoners were on their knees, bound and gagged. Their hands tied behind their backs, they knelt on the outer rim of the large circle of sentries. Another small contingent of armed men guarded them.

But the prisoners and the guards were not what caught her attention. A familiar face set her teeth on edge. Former deputy Leon Trudeau, along with another man, pulled one of the prisoners off the ground and dragged him to the altar stone.

She clutched Ryker's arm. "Promise me one thing. When you kill him, make it as painful as possible."

Ryker covered her hand with his, and squeezed it lightly. She didn't need the words to know he had made her a promise.

Leon threw the prisoner onto the altar stone. The man valiantly resisted, and it took two sentries to overpower him.

"What are they doing?" Dayna asked.

Ryker rubbed his jaw. "I have no idea, but whatever it is, I don't like it."

Arnie, the muscle man, stepped forward the moment Leon moved away. The robed man followed, and they stood over the body in the same manner as before. They poured something into the prisoner's mouth and then stood back.

Ryker stiffened. "Is that what I think it is?"

Deacon, lips pursed, nodded.

Keira frowned. "What?"

"It's blood," Ryker said.

Dayna let out a little gasp.

Keira's heart thudded in her chest. What was going on down there?

The prisoner convulsed, and his back arched high off the stone. Even from this distance, the agony on his face haunted her. But from what? Nothing was touching him.

She took a closer look at the sentries guarding the perimeter, then back at the guards hovering near the prisoners. The three groups were distinctly different. The prisoners were cowering in fear for their lives. Their armed guards were a little too cocky as they pushed around their charges. But the staunch barrier of sentinels worried her. Their lack of movement and emotion as they stood vigil set the hairs on the back of her neck on end.

Possible reasons for the missing blood and the prisoners kept churning through her mind. She eliminated all but one of the options, and a heavy weight crushed her. There was only one logical reason.

"No. No. No. Please let me be wrong," she pleaded desperately. "It's not possible."

"Stop scaring me." Dayna's voice dropped to a whisper. "What's not possible?"

"Somehow, they've found a way to come through without their bodies. The Legion are taking over a host's body."

Dayna bit her bottom lip, and her eyes grew wide. "But … but that's not possible."

"Ockham's Razor. There's no other explanation."

Keira forced her attention to the unfolding drama within the circle. The man on the altar was now limp. The muscled man droned an incantation. She could only assume he was chanting to allow the Legion a path to consume a Human host.

Ryker squeezed her hand. "Are you sure?"

"Honestly, it's just my best guess."

"Your eyesight is better than ours," Dayna said as she looked between Ryker and Deacon. "Can you see anything that would confirm our suspicions?"

They shook their heads.

"Without knowing for sure," Deacon said, "we are at a tactical disadvantage. We'd need to assess their capabilities outside of their own bodies. I can't imagine they would have retained all their skills. However, I suspect they would still be far stronger than a Human."

"There must be a way to work it out," Dayna said.

Keira had a sudden thought. "Maybe there is. Louise said they didn't have auras. We just need to use our magic to replicate the ability to see a person's aura. But how?"

Dayna crawled closer to her. "I have an idea. Do you remember the reflection spell in the Grimoire? The one that reveals the true self? Perhaps we could modify it to see auras?"

"I think that would work, but the spell will take both of us." Keira reached into her back pocket and pulled out her onyx crystals, then took stock of their surroundings. "We need to work out what to use. There's no water to allow us to see the projection."

"A mirror. We could use a mirror instead of a body of water. It might do the same thing."

"Good idea, but where are we going to find a mirror in the middle of the woods at this time of night?"

"No problem, I have one in my bag—" Dayna let out a groan and brought her hands up to her face. "Which I left in the car. And it has my crystals."

Deacon stood. "That's not a problem. I'll be there and back in a few minutes. Where in the car is it?"

"How could I have not brought them with me?" Dayna said. "I know better than that. Instead, I leave them on the back seat of a car for anyone to steal."

She was about to tell Dayna to calm down when she stopped mid-movement. At first, she was sure it was her imagination. But from the looks on each of the other's faces, it was a mass hallucination.

On the ground, in front of Dayna, was a woman's bright pink leather tote bag. One minute it was just dirt and leaves, and the next, a bag appeared that had been locked in a car five miles away.

"What just happened?" Ryker spoke first.

Keira looked up at her sister. From Dayna's shocked expression, she was as mystified as the rest of them.

"Have you ever done that before?" Keira asked.

Dayna tentatively reached out her hand to touch the bag, then snapped it back. "It's real."

"I'll take that as a 'no' then."

Ryker tapped it with his boot. "I don't think it'll explode, but you never know."

Deacon peered over the small mound of dirt they were hiding behind. "I suggest we worry about this later. We have enough on our plate already."

Keira crawled closer to Dayna. "Deacon's right. We need to work out how to modify that spell."

It took them less time than expected. From a lifetime of experience, they knew what changes needed to be made to the spell.

Keira clutched her crystals and willed them to help her channel the power they would require. They remained silent as Dayna pulled out a small mirror and placed it on the ground. Even with the minuscule light from the fires, they couldn't see a reflection. It was still too dark.

She retrieved her white crystals and placed them around the mirror in alternating colors to ensure their magic was fused and amplified. The spell in the Grimoire was for a single person. They needed to perform it for at least sixty.

She took a deep breath and said, "Ready?"

Her sister nodded. "As much as I will ever be."

In a low voice, she began the incantation, "*Tenet hodie, in nocte lucet.*"

Dayna joined her magic to the spell. "*Silebit ventus, et lucis estis.*"

As one voice, they weaved their magic. "*Quæ abscondita est, iam,*

in nos videamus,

et verum se referunt ad nos,

removere a negotio extra velum."

This close to the stones, the power surged through her in full force. The familiar energy was a warm comfort on a chilly night. Unlike her previous attempts at this level of magic, the flow was faster and …

She faltered with her incantation and just as quickly recovered.

The power she called on was stronger and more intense. That was not possible. Their source of power had been depleted, not increased.

Pushing the questions to the back of her mind, she focused on the small mirror. A faint glow faded in and out as if it were a beacon, always in motion, always searching. Close up, they were able to make out the images that materialized on the reflective surface.

"Are you seeing this?" Ryker asked Deacon.

Deacon's low growl indicated he had, and he was not happy about it. Once she was sure the spell was locked, she focused on the image in the mirror, which reflected the immediate area around the stones.

Both she and Dayna leaned in at the same time. "I can see what it is, but it's too small for me to make out any individual forms."

"What did you want to know?" Deacon leaned closer. "We can be your eyes."

"If we got the spell right, you should be able to make out an aura around each living being. It usually manifests itself as a colored glow."

There was a brush against her side as Ryker inched forward. "We can see it, but what are we looking for specifically?"

Keira recalled the conversation with Louise, the waitress from the diner. "If any of them are Legion, they shouldn't have an aura."

Dayna started. "All creatures have auras."

"Or so we thought." Keira turned back to Ryker. "We also need to know what's happening on the altar stone."

The Vampires peered into the small mirror. Their faces gave nothing away as they scanned the image.

Ryker sat back and studied the unfolding events around the stones. "We have a problem. The prisoners all have auras, and we can see the ones around Trudeau and the others, but I can't see any around the little army."

His grim tone sent a wave of panic through Keira, and she looked across at Dayna.

"How many?" Keira asked.

"I'd say about fifty-four of them and counting," Deacon said.

She bowed her head and held her breath. This was worse than she thought. They were through. How was the Order creating their army?

Ryker's hand slipped around hers, and he tugged at it lightly. "There's more."

When she looked up, he was inches from her.

"There's some sort of mist seeping out of the large standing stone. It's floating toward the prisoner on the alter and streaming into him. The more it goes in, the weaker the man's aura is becoming."

The last nail in her coffin. They had found a way. How was this even possible? They shouldn't have been able to come through the gaps and transfer their minds to a Human host.

Dayna's expression was grim. "It's only a matter of time before they are strong enough to bring Leviathan through."

"We can't let that happen." Keira crept closer to the site. "If we assume they need to transfigure all those prisoners before they can bring Leviathan through, how much time do you think we have?"

They spent another agonizing twenty minutes watching two entities, a life and a Legion, struggle for control of the same body. For her, it felt like twenty hours. By the time the tragedy was over and another victim was strapped to the altar, they calculated they had forty-two hours until the Legion began their assault on the gate.

The timeline coincided with the full moon and the summer equinox. When the Legion would be at the peak of their power.

They needed a plan, and they needed it now.

"We don't have enough Vampires to take on that many Legion." Deacon stood. "Time to regroup and consider our options."

"We need to take another look at the Grimoire," Dayna said as soon as they were far enough away not to be heard. She held out her arm and lifted her thumb. "Can I hitch a ride, big boy?"

If Deacon noticed the grim set to her mouth that belied her light words, he didn't say anything. Once she had her arms around his neck, they were gone.

Ryker touched Keira's cheek. "You okay?"

She raised a brow. "Just peachy. I've just discovered the end of the world is the day after tomorrow. My mother's sacrifice bought us another three hundred years and nothing more. Oh, yeah, my sacrifice is next, and who knows how much time that will buy us? A day, a week? Nothing?"

Ryker cupped her face with his hands. He tilted her head up until she had no choice but to meet his steely gaze. His eyes bore into hers with an intensity that frightened her.

"I do not want to hear you say those words. Ever. Do you hear me? We'll find a way to stop this, and it won't include any idiotic heroics on your part."

"That's not your call. Leviathan can't be permitted to get through. You know that as w—"

Ryker's lips crushed against hers with such savage force that her arms fell limp at her sides. His hands dropped from her face, and he molded her against his hard frame. With very little effort, he teased her lips apart. Ripples of pleasure surged through her body as his tongue skimmed her trembling lip. One moment he was demanding, the next teasing.

A desperate, sultry moan escaped her throat as he deepened the kiss. Pure, unadulterated lust rose from her core and set her alight. Her arms came awake and wrapped around his neck. Their dire predicament was temporarily forgotten as her iron-tight control over her emotions shattered. All she could feel, all she wanted to feel, was this frustrating man who had stripped away her restraints, layer by layer, until she was raw with desire.

Mother Earth.

The hunger of her response scared her. Never before had she given in to her desire as wantonly and with such wild abandon. In the past, she'd chosen her partners carefully, without any danger of either of them becoming emotionally involved. Her vow to protect her heart never wavered. Until now. As much as it pained her, she needed to stop. His kiss was too potent, like he was branding her. Combined with his tangy taste and male scent, she was ready to sink to the forest floor and finish what the kiss promised.

She trailed her hands over his shoulders and rested her palms on his chest. It took all her effort to resist the urge to rip the shirt off his body and run her hands over his bare skin. Would his chest taste as divine as his lips? She fisted the fabric of his shirt and pushed him away.

While he would come out of this unscathed, she was in great danger of being scalded permanently. She would be just another notch on his bedpost after he sated his desire, while she'd wallow in chocolate cake and ice cream.

Who cares? You may not live beyond this week.

She froze. Their predicament thrust itself to the forefront, and she pushed away.

"We need to stop," she said, her voice coming out in a breathless pant. "We can't … I can't do this."

His breath was ragged, and a childish satisfaction pricked at the back of her mind. At least she was not the only one affected by the kiss. He pulled her back to him and bent his head down until they were almost cheek to cheek, his breath warm against the shell of her ear.

"Make no mistake. We will be finishing this."

The graveled words uttered against her flesh sent a fresh wave of goosebumps over her skin.

He turned his back and crouched. "Let's find a way to kill these bastards, and it will not include any of your ridiculous plans to sacrifice yourself."

She rested her hand on his shoulder, savoring the feel of his muscles rippling through his shirt. To save him, to save her sister, to save humanity, she'd risk everything.

Even her life.

TWENTY-SEVEN

'I HOPE YOU DANCE

The moment the front door to Deacon's mansion opened, Keira and Dayna raced upstairs. They needed to take another look at the Grimoire.

Dayna sat beside her and studied the passages as they considered each spell. "Maybe we can use the strengthening spell to increase the Vampire's abilities."

Keira shook her head and turned the page. "Won't work. That spell is for strengthening something that's broken. Bones, a chair leg, a window. Vampire abilities are not broken."

Dayna cleared her throat. "So, uh, what took you two so long to get back to the car?"

This was not idle curiosity. Keira reached for her amulet and fingered it nervously. "We were right behind you."

"If you say so." The room was quiet for all of ten seconds before Dayna said, "So why did you look so guilty?"

Keira groaned inwardly. Her sister was like a dog with a bone.

She'd spent the entire ride back to the house trying *not* to think about that kiss. The more she tried to forget, the more her body remembered. The feel of his lips against hers when he lit

306

every nerve ending. She hadn't experienced that kind of bliss in a long time. Her face heated as she recalled just how aroused she had become in such a short time.

Dayna grinned from ear to ear. "So, you did get up to something. You're blushing."

Not able to meet her sister's intense gaze, she turned back to the Grimoire. "I am not."

Dayna giggled. "Methinks the lady doth protest too much. Are you going to tell me what happened, or can I use my imagination? Even with his Vamp skills, there's no way you had enough time to do the deed. That leaves so many options." She tapped a finger against her bottom lip. "What would get my straitlaced sister all in a fluster?"

"Oh, for Mother Earth's sake, it was just a kiss, so you can get your mind out of the gutter."

Dayna squealed, jumped on the bed, then fell to her knees with a bounce. "I knew it. I knew it. So how was the tonsil hockey with Sheriff McSexy? Was it hot? What am I saying? Of course it was. The man knows what he's doing, and from your particular shade of scarlet, he's very good at it." She clapped her hands. "I want details. Details, I tell you."

Keira snatched the Grimoire out of harm's way. "You can speculate all you like. I don't kiss and tell."

Dayna scrunched her nose in a childish sulk. "Not fair! You spoil all my fun. Well, you leave me no choice." She jumped off the bed and headed for the door. "I'll just have to ask Ryker. I'll get him to rate your ability. Even you can't stuff something up as simple as a kiss."

At her sister's threat, Keira dropped the Grimoire on the bed, then raced toward the door and flung herself between the exit and Dayna. "You will do no such thing. It was a one-time thing that shouldn't have happened."

Dayna snorted. "Poppycock. You're deluding yourself. You two are a ticking time bomb. Give me some credit. I'm neither blind nor stupid. I'm just surprised it took that long." She paused. "Actually, I'm not. It's you we're talking about."

"Look, there's nothing between us. You know as well as I do that it can't work."

Dayna rested a hand on her hip. "Last time I looked, he's a man and you're a woman. *Just.* You both have bits made to work together. Have you seen his bits yet? It's been a while since I've been with a Vamp, but let me warn you, they are like the Eveready Bunny. They go on and on—"

Keira covered her ears with her hands. "Dayna, enough! I'm not having this conversation."

Dayna raised her hands, palms up. "Fine. I'll let it drop for now. But just let me say this—whatever crap you have going on in that head of yours, you need to rethink. Our mother raised us to get the most out of life. When are you going to start?"

Keira opened and closed her mouth in a fish-like motion. This was not the time nor the place to have this discussion. Instead of replying, she headed back to the Grimoire.

"We should be focusing on Leviathan, not trivial matters like kissing. None of this will matter if that gate opens and Leviathan's army decimates millions; continent by continent."

Dayna snorted. "Suit yourself, but don't consider this conversation over."

Keira flipped open the book and muttered, "I wouldn't be so lucky."

She resumed leafing through the pages, but her heart stopped in her chest when her gaze fell on writing she hadn't noticed before.

Despite only recently reuniting with the book, she knew it well. The smell of the worn leather that protected the secrets within, the feel of each page under her fingertips as she brushed them across the words. Each of her ancestors' scripts, her mother's clear script, Dayna's flowery contributions, and her own careful writing. Each held a memory, some happy, some not.

"Dayna, have you added any spells to the Grimoire?"

Over the past few days, they had poured over the book many times. How had they missed this new writing?

Her sister stood in front of the large dresser mirror, her long locks bunched on top of her head as she turned from side to side. Dayna let her hair fall over her shoulders.

"No, why?" Her hands swept over her tresses, and blonde was replaced by shocking pink. Dayna swiveled around to face her. "What do you think?"

She took note of Kiera's shocked expression and stopped. "What's the matter?"

"I think you'd better take a look at this."

They counted five new spells and a message addressed to them. Keira was unsure what was more concerning, the fact they hadn't noticed the pages before or that the pages were penned in their mother's hand. She clutched at the amulet around her neck.

"How did we miss this?" Dayna whispered.

Keira scanned the page, her eyes faltering at the first sentence. "We didn't."

My dearest daughters,

If you are reading this, it heralds Leviathan's imminent breach of the gates to this world. For only then will these words be revealed along with five spells. As I do not know the manner in which the attack will take place, I can only hope the spells will help you fight her and the masses that worship at her feet. Be resolute and mindful. There is power in strength, not numbers.

This missive is not the form I expected my last words to you would take. My intention was to live well into senility with my grandchildren and family near. However, daughters, fate has intervened and written another path I must travel.

Do not think ill of me, children of my heart, for I will be with you always. If not in body, in spirit. We are standing at an impasse, and I must put an end to it. I believe it is because we failed to admit our weaknesses and thought ourselves too superior to underestimate the danger that lurks beneath the surface. Evil knows no bounds and will always find a way. My daughters, you must be vigilant.

The decision I make today is the only course of action. I must cease the Legion's ability to walk through the gate.

We will win this battle, but the war still wages. She will never stop. Her hatred for Humans is too intense to allow her solace in her reign over the underworld. I know not the outcome, but sure as the sun will rise each morning, Leviathan and her army will not stop in their quest to wreak havoc on earth.

As I write these, my last words to you, my tears fall to the page in grief. I do what I must to protect you. If things unfold as I expect, the Legion will not be able to walk through or march between the worlds unless the gate is open. As long as the gate remains closed, their bodies will never again set foot on the earth. With my last breath, my dearest daughters, lights of my heart, I will leave you with two gifts.

The first is the gift of time. You, as I, have a purpose. What yours will be, I cannot say, but you will age with the earth itself. This is a gift, a burden, and a prison. No doubt, by the time you read this, one, if not all three of these states will have come to pass.

The second gift will not manifest itself until needed. The elemental laws will bend, and you will be able to draw upon earth, fire, water, and sky. Which of these elements you harness will depend upon your ability to command them.

Use this power wisely. It is given for a single purpose. To protect all living things, both Natural and Supernatural. I know what I ask of you, dear daughters, is a heavy weight to carry. It will not be an easy journey. I only hope you walk it together and feed upon each other's strength. You are mightier than you think and deserve every goodness that life has to offer. Remember to have faith in those around you, and when you get the chance, I hope you dance with joy under a full moon.

When the time is right, an Angel will endow you with your final two gifts. What they are and when, I am unsure, but know this: He will only show himself when He sees fit and not before.

I can only hope that, with time, you forgive me for leaving you in such an abrupt manner. Have courage. You are the children of my womb and daughters of the earth. Know I love you with every fiber of my being, and even in death, my love will remain.

Your loving mother,

Annabeth

As she read through their mother's words, tears streamed down her face. It was as if she were standing beside them, guiding them forward. She blinked to clear her vision as Dayna wept quietly, her hands clenched on her lap as her body convulsed in silent sobs.

Keira moved across the bed and wrapped her arms around Dayna. The moment she did, Dayna rested her head into the crook of her shoulder, and the floodgates opened. They were never given the chance to say goodbye. One moment she was there, full of life and vitality. The next, gone.

When she was spent, Dayna pulled away and wiped her eyes with the back of her hand. She reached for a box of tissues and blew her nose.

Keira smiled. Everything else Dayna did was gentle and feminine. Her delicate manners didn't extend to blowing her nose. The trumpet of Jericho blew with Dayna.

"Well, that at least explains the balls of fire and the bag," Dayna said between blasts. "But I still don't understand how she knew. And who's this person who is going to show himself?"

Keira rubbed her face with her hands. They were the same questions running through her mind. She didn't see any answers forthcoming in the near future.

"I don't know, Dayna, but maybe there's an answer in one of the spells she left."

"Hopefully, there's one to smite the Legion who have taken over a person's body."

Keira sucked in her bottom lip, and her shoulder sagged.

Dayna's eyes widened, and she looked as if she were about to break down again. "Surely we'll try and save the hosts?"

As much as they might wish otherwise, the poor souls who had the misfortune of being taken as hosts were gone. Short of divine intervention, nothing would bring them back.

"Are you certain?" Dayna implored, reading the dower expression. "Maybe there's still something left?"

"This is going to end in one of two ways. Either we will have to explain nearly one hundred dead tourists and locals to the world…"

"And the other?"

"Leviathan will turn those hundred into millions."

Dayna clenched her hands. "Well, we'll just have to stop that skanky bitch then."

"One step at a time. First, we need a plan."

When they emerged downstairs three hours later, Keira was surprised to discover Ananya carrying a tray across the foyer toward the large front living room.

Dayna called out as they reached the bottom step, "Hey, you old tart. I thought you'd gone home."

Ananya gave Dayna a toothy grin. "I heard the others were headed over, and I couldn't leave my boys when they needed me the most."

"What are you talking about? What others?"

"They just arrived. I've made a nice pot of tea for everyone," Ananya said over her shoulder as she disappeared through the door.

She and Dayna followed, none the wiser. The moment they stepped into the room, Keira stopped short. The Crossroads Synod milled around the lounge in small groups. In addition to the Witches, there were at least a dozen people she had never seen before.

"I figured we were going to need them," Ryker said as he materialized at her side.

Deacon nodded toward the far corner. "We also have every Vampire in the area, and more will be here tomorrow. That includes at least ten Primordial Vampires."

She recognized Tim and Pete, her Vampire bodyguards when Ryker or Deacon were not around. They were talking to at least a dozen other Vampires, one of which she was sure was Dracula Bond from the blood bank. The others she had seen before, but their names eluded her.

As they spoke, Maize joined them. "We also have the strongest Witches from some of the local covens. I figure every bit will help."

Keira stiffened.

Maize raised her hands. "Now, hear me out. We may not have the strength we should have, but each member of the coven made the same oath as you. We've kept the Crossroads secrets, and that includes from other Witch covens. I know the other covens don't have the ability to help us with the gate, but from what you've told us about the Order, we are dealing with a bunch of deranged Humans. I made a judgment call and reached out to the other covens. They were more than happy to help."

Zayne stepped forward and placed an arm around Maize. "They took our baby girl. I have as much a right as anyone here to seek revenge. While I may not have the correct magic to fight what's coming through that gate, I and the others can certainly deal with the scum who got us into this mess in the first place. And …" He took a deep, shaky breath and looked pointedly at a tall man in wireframe glasses who could have passed for a librarian. "It turns out that many of the older covens knew Crossroads was protecting something, just not what."

There was a murmur of agreement from the other Witches in the room.

Speechless, Keira looked around the room. While she had no choice in the matter, the other people in the room did. They didn't ask for this fight, nor were they expected to lay down their lives to keep a deluded god from wrecking vengeance. But from their determined expressions, that was precisely what they were hell-bent on doing.

Maize broke the silence. "How are we going to kick their arses?"

A throat clearing caught their attention, and she swung around. Deputy Wilbur Mitos stood in the doorway, shuffling from foot to foot.

Mother Earth! How much had he heard?

Ryker was the first to recover. "What are you doing here?"

"I've come to help."

Ryker hesitated. "Help with what, exactly?"

Mitos let out a snort. "I've lived in this godforsaken zoo all my life." He crossed his arms over his chest. "The people around here are about as retarded as they come. There's too many chinks, i-ties, towel heads, fags, girly-boys, and general fuckheads for my liking, but they are my retards. Fuck with them, and I'm going to have something to say about it."

Ryker stiffened and adopted a menacing pose. "I'm still not sure why you're here."

Mitos threw up his hands. "I know what you all are. Always have. Don't know what's going on, but I know shit's about to hit the fan. Whatever it is, I wanna help. I ain't no walking freak show like you bloodsuckers, and the only magic I know is how to make food disappear off a plate in record time, but I do know how to use a gun, and I know every inch of this goddam state."

From his determined stance, there was no budging him. Keira was surprised, but not nearly as much as Ryker. The sheriff clearly hadn't been as careful around his deputy as he thought.

Ananya thrust a cup of tea into Mitos' outstretched hand. "That doesn't mean I'm letting you win at Bingo next week. If there is a next week."

Ananya ensured everyone was not about to dehydrate. Several people gathered around the table.

"You were about to tell us about the plan, Keira?" Ryker hitched a thumb into his utility belt. "And it better not include a part where you catch a bullet for the rest of us. Tell *us* how *we* are going to stop the end of days."

She grimaced at his menacing tone. "It's less of a plan and more of an educated guess."

Besides the spells, their mother had imparted as much information on the Legion and Leviathan as she knew. Most of it they already knew, but the new facts gave them a vague idea of how they might go about fighting the threat. And with all the additional Witches and Vampires, they might have a chance of winning.

By the time she and Dayna outlined what they needed to do, sunrise was only a few hours away.

"I suggest that everyone get a couple of hours' sleep," Deacon said once they were done. "We still have a lot of work to do before tomorrow night, and it won't help if you are fatigued or below par. Those of you who don't live local and don't mind doubling up, we have enough rooms for everyone."

He turned to her and Dayna. "Do you think you could place a protection spell around the property? I'd like to give everyone a break and time to recharge."

She nodded. Even though the Vampires didn't require as much sleep as Humans did, they would need to gather their strength and feed.

Ananya rose from her seat.

"I'll show everyone to the spare rooms upstairs." She rounded up the Witches, and Deacon addressed the Vampires. "You're welcome to use the guest house. Should you require sustenance, you'll find it amply stocked. I will notify those standing guard to join you."

Before Keira followed Ananya and the others upstairs, Maize reached out and hugged her. "No matter what happens, Keira, I want you to know that we appreciate everything you've done for us. Without you, we would have never understood what we lost. We're stronger because of you. You're the reason we have a chance to fight this thing."

The room fell silent. Only Keira, Ryker, Deacon, and Dayna remained. She sank onto one of the leather couches.

"I'm also responsible for too many deaths. If I had worked out what the Order was up to, Marcus, the Witches, and all those tourists would still be alive today."

A low growl vibrated across the room. The next moment, Ryker stood over her and tilted her chin up to meet his intense gaze. "You're not to blame yourself for what might or might not happen. Leviathan is responsible for all of this, not you. Never forget that."

Dayna nodded. "He's right. Our mother may not have had a choice, but you read her words. We do. We have the tools. We just need to work out how to use them." She placed a hand on Deacon's arm. "If you show me to the guest house the other Vampires will be in, I'll place a protection spell around that first." Dayna turned back to her. "I'll do upstairs if you take care of down here?"

Keira nodded. She may as well make herself useful. Sleep was the furthest thing from her mind.

Dayna reached for Deacon and tugged him out the door. "Come on, big boy, I need my beauty sleep, and then I need to work out what to wear into battle with an army of Zombies and an evil Goddess." A short silence was followed by a little squeal. "Oh, you must try on that gray polo neck, you'll look so dapper, and it'll be easy to move in when you're breaking their necks."

Deacon responded with an indignant growl. "You will go nowhere near my wardrobe!"

She and Ryker relaxed and broke into laughter.

"And you're sure she's your sister?" Ryker said, his eyes full of mirth.

"Of course she is. We look alike."

"She could just be a doppelgänger."

Keira gave him a blank stare, but she knew what he was up to. Surprisingly, it worked. She was less panicked and more focused.

Ryker shrugged. "Okay then, she's your sister." He held out a hand. "Let's make a start on that protection spell down here."

She took his hand, and he pulled her into a standing position. "You go ahead. You heard Deacon. You need to feed. I'll finish up here once Dayna's finished the guest house, then go to bed."

She headed for the small candle that had taken up a permanent position by the window over the past few nights. Before she got too far, Ryker blocked her path.

"You do know that sort of speed makes one dizzy," she said as she attempted to move around him.

"Moving at that speed doesn't affect me."

"I wasn't referring to you."

Once again, Ryker blocked her from moving around him.

She placed her hands on her hips and glared at him. "What are you doing? Are you trying to irritate me?"

His mouth twitched into a half-grin. "There are many things I'd like to do to you, Keira. Irritating you is not one of them."

She physically pushed him to one side and marched over to the candle. Once she finished the protection incantation, she turned, only to bump into his solid chest. Her heart thumped out of rhythm at the sudden shock. She took a step back and looked up. His expression was unreadable as he regarded her.

"What?"

"Promise me you won't take any unnecessary risks tomorrow night."

She wilted under his unrelenting stare. The intensity was unsettling. "I'm not planning on committing suicide by Leviathan if that's what you're thinking."

"If what you said about the message your mother left you is true, you don't need to do what she did to beat them."

Keira cocked her head. "I'm aware of that."

"Just making sure. Dayna needs her big sister. Who's going to keep her grounded?"

She let out a half-laugh. "My sister can take care of herself. Haven't you worked that out by now?" Finally managing to get around him, she crossed to the door. "Let's get the other rooms done, and we can all get some rest."

"I want you to come to bed with me."

The words were spoken so quietly that she nearly missed them. She stopped in her tracks. Without turning around, she said, "What did you say?"

A gentle hand rested on the nape of her neck, and goosebumps erupted across her skin at the contact. Exerting very little pressure, he brought her around to face him. Her breath quickened at the intimate movement.

"Doc, as much as I'd like to find out where those runes of yours are, you need to rest. I want to make sure you do. If that means I need to be in bed beside you to make sure that happens, it's a sacrifice I'm willing to make." He dipped his head and grazed her lips with his. He lifted his gaze. "And I wouldn't bother fighting me on this one. You'll lose every time."

She reached for his hand. "No argument."

At least she had the satisfaction of shocking him, if his expression was anything to go by. He wasn't expecting her to give in so easily. If she were honest, she simply needed to feel safe.

He led her upstairs into the cavernous chamber he claimed. As if reading her mind, Ryker rummaged through a drawer, threw her one of his t-shirts, and pointed to a door on the other side of the room. By the time she changed and returned, he was propped up in bed, reading a thick police file. Still fully clothed.

Nervous, she hovered and carefully folded her clothes, conscious that the shirt only came down to mid-thigh. While it covered more of her than Dayna's everyday wear, she still felt exposed.

Without looking up, he said, "You have ten seconds to get in bed. Otherwise, you won't like how I make you get in."

Not needing to be told twice, she rushed to the bed and slipped beneath the covers, grateful he was still on top. She rolled over on her side with her back to him and closed her eyes as she willed her heart rate to slow.

He turned out the lights a short while later, and his weight shifted on the bed. An arm reached around her waist. He chuckled when she stiffened at his sudden touch. "Relax, Doc. I said I wanted to make sure you slept. This way, you can't sneak off when I'm napping."

Despite his cooler body temperature and a closeness that rattled her somewhat, she hadn't been as comfortable and secure in years. Whether it was his promise to keep her safe or her utter exhaustion, she didn't know or care, but she fell asleep in record time.

Her whole body relaxed into the strength of his embrace, and her eyes drifted shut.

How she felt safe with a Vampire was a strange experience in itself.

While Vampires were nothing like the creatures depicted in urban myth, they were, without a doubt, extremely dangerous.

TWENTY-EIGHT
HURT

The scent of cinnamon wafted into her last thread of sleep, and Keira pulled the covers closer. Her eyelids were heavy, and she couldn't gather the strength to open them. It wasn't time to wake up, was it? She had just fallen asleep.

The sound of rain punctured her foggy brain, and she rolled over with a loud groan at the effort. From under the sheets, she reached for her phone and read 6:15 a.m. Why did she feel so tired?

The dull brain fog lifted. The reality of their current predicament, as well as where she was, smashed across her in waves, and she sat up in record time. *Damn it.* She was only supposed to nap for one hour, not three.

A cup of green tea had been left on the bedside table, sending tendrils of steam into the air. At least that explained the cinnamon. She regarded the vacant spot beside her and groaned inwardly. Ryker's bed. She had given in and slept in his bed.

Three hours ago, she should have marched straight upstairs. She should have told him he was a little presumptuous. She should have done any of the thousand things that had run through her mind. Instead, she'd followed him, thankful that for once, she didn't need to make a decision.

She pushed her hair off her face and sipped the hot tea. What she thought was rain was the shower running in the adjoining bathroom.

Was the shower big enough for two?

The thought was out before she could stop it. Her mind was heading into very murky territory. Over the years, she had shied away from emotional attachment. If there was any chance her heart might get involved, she cut off all ties. The only way to protect herself was to keep an emotional distance. This time, if she allowed anything to happen between her and Ryker, she wouldn't walk away unscathed.

She smashed her face into her pillow. How had she allowed herself to get into this mess? The man was far too tempting to ignore. If they got out of this alive, it was a foregone conclusion she would allow him to find her runes. But she had no illusions. She would be just another conquest for Ryker. She was going into this with her eyes wide open. At least she could nurse her wounds back in LA, well away from Salem, Essex County, and its very sexy sheriff.

At the idea of not seeing him again, an uncomfortable twinge pricked at her, and she shook off the implications. She sat up and scanned the room. Where the hell were her clothes? Even after sleeping in Ryker's t-shirt, it still smelled of him. Mother Earth, why hadn't she refused his invitation? The practicalities of her unwise choice sprang to mind the moment she'd stepped into his room three hours earlier. Sleeping attire for one.

"Sorry, did I wake you?"

She nearly spilled her tea. Deep in her thoughts, she hadn't heard Ryker appear in the bathroom doorway. He was toweling his hair dry. A worn pair of jeans sat low on his hips, and the muscles on his bare chest rippled.

She quickly averted her gaze. A half-naked Ryker first thing in the morning was a little too much eye candy when the end of the world was nigh. "Ummm, no, it wasn't you. I just couldn't sleep anymore."

He threw the damp towel onto a small armchair and crossed to the bed. "Did you know you talk in your sleep?"

She pulled the sheets tighter around her body. "I do no such thing."

He shrugged. "Have it your way. But what does *cerebrum fluctus* mean?"

She froze. "Where did you hear that?"

He couldn't have overheard the private conversation between her and Dayna the previous night.

"I told you, Doc, you talk in your sleep."

She smoothed out a non-existent wrinkle on the bed covers. How much should she tell him, if anything? She cleared her throat.

"It's one of the spells that appeared in the Grimoire and was used by the Witches to disrupt the control Leviathan held over the original Vampires. We think it might be key to helping us now."

He scratched the back of his neck. "But Leviathan doesn't have Vampires under her control. Just Legion who have taken over Human bodies."

Keira leaned forward. "I know. But if we can work out what link she has with them or how they can take over the body of a Human, we might be able to adjust the spell accordingly."

He didn't look convinced. "That doesn't seem like much of a plan."

She placed her now-empty cup on the side table.

"Unfortunately, that's all we've got." She pushed the covers down and swung her legs off the bed. "Somehow, between now and tomorrow evening, the Crossroads need to learn the five spells my mother left us. I need to determine what the fire, wind, and air Witches are capable of, and Dayna and I need to work out how to use our new powers, or more accurately, how to call on them without killing ourselves or everyone else."

"And what's the plan for after lunch?"

She stared deadpan at him. "You know you're not remotely funny."

He grinned. "Oh, but I am. You're just in denial because you're finding it difficult to resist my charms."

Before she could respond, he closed the distance between them. "Good morning, by the way."

He pulled her into him and brought his lips down to hers in a crushing kiss.

Mother Earth could the man kiss. All too quickly, it was over.

He reached for a gray shirt he'd left on the bed and yanked it over his head. "I'll let you freshen up in peace and meet you downstairs."

If Ryker had any sense, he would finish what he started. He ran a hand through his hair and glanced back at the door to his wing of the house. He fantasized about getting her in his bed far too often lately. And what did he do when she was finally there? He left without finishing what he knew they both wanted.

No matter how much she denied it, she wanted him just as much as he wanted her. He groaned aloud. This was as fucked up as it got. They were heading into a battle that could change the world as they knew it, and he was more concerned about making sure that when he found her runes, she was totally focused on them. Not on what she needed to do to save nearly eight billion people. Just thinking about where the runes could be hiding sent his temperature skyward. He needed another shower.

He detected movement as he approached the main living area. Thankful for the diversion, he followed the noise and was not surprised to find Ananya placing a tray in the oven. He made his way to the fridge that held their supply of blood.

"Hey Ladakee," he said, using her pet name since she was a young girl.

Ananya wiped her hands on her apron and smiled. "Good morning. I've just put another batch of biscuits in the oven for you and your guests."

He smiled appreciatively. Despite knowing they could fend for themselves, Ananya was forever making sure they ate sufficient protein and were being fed properly. She had even pointed out healthy Human donors over the years. Ananya was convinced they would fall ill from tainted blood.

She whipped up a batch of pancakes while he drank. "I don't suppose you know where Keira is?"

At her unexpected question, he nearly choked on the blood. "Why?"

Ananya shrugged her shoulders. "Just curious. She didn't come upstairs with the rest of us last night, and I got a little worried. Dayna didn't seem concerned. She was sure Keira was with you."

Ananya's casual comments didn't fool him. She was more than curious, and the not knowing was killing her.

"So?" she nudged.

"So what?"

Maybe she would get the hint that he didn't want to discuss the topic.

"Was she with you?"

He banged the empty cup on the countertop. "Yes, if you must know. But you can rest assured that her virtue is still safe, if that's what you're worried about."

Before he could say anything further, Ananya giggled. "You must like this one."

"You haven't raided my contraband stash this early in the morning, have you?"

Ananya waved him off. "In all the time I've known you, you've never brought a woman home." She clicked her tongue. "I never thought I'd live to see the day you had a female in your bed, and you didn't take advantage of the situation."

Instead of replying, he poured himself a second cup of chilled blood and wandered over to the door that led to the back patio. Much as he didn't want to admit it, Ananya was right. In all his years, not once had he brought a woman home or even desired to do so. Oh, he'd had his share of women. More than he could count or remember. But always on his own terms and well away from what he considered his home at the time. He must be slipping in his old age.

He had vowed never to let a woman get inside his head or defenses again. Painful memories of Gabrielle rose to the surface, and a cold hand clutched at his scarred heart. The hate he felt for her knew no bounds, even after all these centuries. She'd played him and betrayed him in the basest way possible. He had been so besotted with her that he'd ignored the signs that something was not quite right with the beautiful baroness.

Laughter from inside the house jolted him back to the present. He cocked his head and listened. Keira and Dayna had joined Ananya and were discussing pancake toppings.

He jammed his hands into his jeans' pockets. His fascination with the red-haired Witch was nothing more than that—a fascination. She was an itch he needed to scratch. He desired her. He wanted nothing more than to explore all that he knew bubbled beneath that prickly surface of hers. But that was it. It was physical, nothing else. Once this crisis was over and she was gone, he would go back to his old life and forget her.

When he stepped back into the house and met her warm smile, warmth flowed through him, and his resolve faltered.

TWENTY-NINE

PROTECTORS OF THE EARTH

As Ryker and the rest of their little army made their way downstairs, the odd sight of Witches, Vampires, a grumpy deputy, and an old Asian Indian woman who forever fussed over them didn't escape his sense of humor. Those who had gone home would be back within the next few hours, bringing the rest of the Crossroads coven members as well as the strongest Witches from the air, water, and fire covens. He was sure there was a joke in there somewhere.

"What the hell is all this pansy crap?" Mitos grumbled as he stared at the array of food on the countertop.

Ananya clicked her tongue against the roof of her mouth. "Hush, you old fart. There's bacon and sausages keeping warm in the oven. You can get them yourself. I'm not your maid or mother."

Mitos grabbed a plate and grumbled under his breath as he wandered over to the oven.

Ryker shook his head. Even if he lived as long as Deacon, he would never understand the strange little man.

The atmosphere was subdued, and most of the guests ate without much conversation. Did they regret their decision to stand against Leviathan? To their credit, not one Witch made a move to leave and evade whatever was about to befall them.

When Keira chuckled at something Dayna said, it dawned on him why. They each had a vested interest. The Witches had an innate, overriding need to keep their loved ones safe and alive, which drove them to risk everything. A need stronger than self-preservation—and just as deadly.

Keira caught him studying her. She cocked her head and raised an eyebrow.

Not wanting her to see where his thoughts had led him, he gave her a wink and one of his cheesiest grins as he leaned against the countertop. He nearly burst into laughter when he received an exaggerated eyeroll in return. She was one of the few people who saw beneath the façade he showed to the rest of the world. Had he slipped and let his guard down with her, or was she that perceptive?

Keira poured herself a cup of green tea and joined him.

"Do you think we're ready for this?" she said as she looked around the room.

He shrugged. "We have to be. There's too much at stake to back down now."

Keira drank the rest of her tea and placed the cup on the countertop. "We'd better get this show on the road then."

Before she joined Dayna and the others outside, he reached for her hand. "No matter what, I've got your back."

Her expression was soft but unreadable. "I know."

The pure trust she had in him sent an unfamiliar warmth spreading through his chest. He no longer knew which posed a greater threat to his safety, Leviathan, or the maddening, provoking, and stunningly beautiful woman before him.

After breakfast, Ryker dispatched Tim and Pete to Mystery Hill. Arrangements had already been made to keep the summer solstice celebrations away from the ancient site. Even so, they needed to keep an eye on the Legion. Both Keira and Dayna were adamant that Leviathan couldn't possibly come through before the moon was at its peak. He, however, was taking no chances.

A car pulled off the main road and onto the estate's gravel driveway just as they gathered outside to review the hastily drawn-up battle plans.

"Stay here," Deacon said to the small group of Vampires that had gathered.

He indicated for Ryker to follow.

They rounded the corner to the front of the house as a silver S500 Mercedes drove through the main gates.

Not recognizing the car, Ryker frowned. "Friends of yours?"

Deacon chuckled. "A very old one. And a boon for Mercedes-Benz cars since the late 1800s." When the car came to a stop near them, he said, "I see he's still traveling with that Nubian princess."

A shiny bald head emerged from the car. The Vampire's sleeveless black vest, black pants, and army-style, steel-capped boots gave him a distinct air of discipline. Without a doubt, this was one of the Primordial Vampires Deacon had called upon.

The Vampire's smile was wide as he approached Deacon. "My friend, it has been far too long."

"I agree, Bayek, far too long."

Ryker held back his surprise. Deacon had spoken often of Bayek, a Primordial Vampire he shared a history with, but he hadn't mentioned Bayek was one of the Vampires he'd summoned. From his thick accent, Ryker guessed that Bayek was Egyptian. The fact that he was Primordial implied he was ancient Egyptian.

As Bayek embraced Deacon, two other people exited the car. A beautiful, ebony-skinned woman, and a tall, slender man.

Bayek gestured toward his two traveling companions. "May I present Hakim. I do not think our paths have crossed before."

Deacon nodded at the man in greeting.

Bayek indicated his second companion. "Makeda, you already know."

Deacon bowed his head and kissed her hand. "If possible, you grow more beautiful every time I see you, Makeda."

Ryker had to agree. The ebony-skinned woman was flawless.

"I see you can still lure the flute off a snake charmer," Makeda said with a light laugh. "And I agree with Bayek. It's been far too long. A pity it had to be under these circumstances."

Bayek extended his arm. "You must be Ryker. Deacon has told me much of you."

Ryker accepted Bayek's proffered hand. "We appreciate you coming such a distance on short notice."

"I do not yet know the full story, but if what little Deacon has told me is true, I am only sorry we couldn't have been here sooner. We may have been able to track down more Primordial Vampires to assist."

Makeda nodded toward a group of Witches. "I understand the Order of Chaos has found a way to release Leviathan from her prison. How are you so confident the Order will succeed this time?"

"First, they knew exactly how to deplete the Crossroads' power and how to kill Crossroads Witches to do it."

"There is also the matter of the Legion," Deacon added.

Bayek stilled. "What of them?"

"They are here. Some of them, at least. More are being brought through each day. It will only be a matter of time before they can break down the gate and free Leviathan."

Bayek grew somber. "I do not need to tell you, my old friend, that this cannot be allowed to happen."

"I am fully aware of this."

Bayek tugged on his vest as though it needed to be straightened. "Take me to these Witches. I wish to see if they possess the same mettle as their forebearers. I have no desire to walk into a battle we have no chance of winning."

Deacon called Keira and Dayna over.

Ryker bristled at the way the Primordial Vampire devoured Keira with his intense gaze as she drew near. His annoyance was only made worse when she held out her hand, gave a short nod of the head, and said, "*Nane atoouri. Tahir mmoc nwien.*"

Bayek chuckled and turned to Deacon. "I like this one. It has been a long time since I've heard my mother tongue, and hearing it from the lips of one so beautiful only makes it more pleasing." The ancient Egyptian took Keira's hand and lifted her fingers to his lips. "My dear, the honor is mine."

Ryker had the overwhelming desire to rip her hand from Bayek's clutches and put some distance between them. A lot of distance.

Deacon cleared his throat. "And may I present Dayna Sanderson, Keira's sister."

Bayek released Keira's hand reached for Dayna's.

Ryker breathed out a sigh of relief. He would need to keep a close eye on the new arrivals. He didn't trust them. Especially the slimy Bayek, who took far too many liberties for his liking.

"I see the rumors are true," Makeda said. "You two are what remains of the legendary Annabeth Subrinski,"

Bayek shrugged. "That is yet to be determined. There is a likeness, but that can be falsified."

Bayek placed his hands behind his back and proceeded to circle Keira and Dayna with a slow and steady gait that made it look like he was gliding. "Before Annabeth and the other Witches arrived in the new world to keep vigil over this gate, it was protected for thousands of years by shamans from the various Native American tribes. That all changed the moment Christopher Columbus stepped foot on the Americas. When the last Native American protector passed into the afterlife, the sacred stone of Issachar sought out its new protector, your mother. If you are indeed her daughters, you will know where and what the stone is."

How were they supposed to know that?

Keira and Dayna were looking at each other with brows furrowed together.

Keira's hand flew to the amethyst hidden under her top.

She turned to her sister. "You don't think it's this, do you?"

Dayna's face went from confused to shocked in a heartbeat. "It can't be that, can it?"

Keira pulled the pendant from beneath her top at the same time Dayna held up her hand, revealing a smaller but just as beautiful purple gemstone on a bracelet.

"It split in two when she was taken from us," Dayna said.

"Two protectors?" Bayek peered at the stones, and a satisfied smile spread across his features. "Just as alive and bright as I remember it on your mother."

"Protectors?" Keira and Dayna said in unison.

Bayek nodded. "Each stone in the Breastplate of Judgement chooses its protector. I have never heard of dual protectors. But we cannot always understand the will of God." He straightened and looked directly at Deacon. "It appears we are to go into battle. How many are you?"

"We have thirty Vampires. Of the Witches that have sufficient magic to join the battle, there are twenty-two earth, twenty from fire, seven from water, and fifteen from air. The rest will keep things running in town to make sure we are not missed and arouse suspicion."

"Not great odds." Bayek said. "We will need more Primordials,"

Deacon nodded. "I have been making calls all night. I can only hope they will arrive in time."

"Vincent LeGrande?" Bayek lifted his voice in question.

"He and two others boarded a plane from Mexico City this morning. He has promised to reach out to more."

Bayek turned to Makeda. "I think a few calls are in order."

Makeda nodded and returned to their car.

Ryker glanced across at Keira. Gone was the tight bun he was accustomed to. In fact, despite the gravity of the situation in which they found themselves, she was relaxed and a calming presence to the other Witches. Strands of hair escaped her ponytail. Every now and then, she would attempt to tuck them behind her ear. This was a very different professor than the one he'd met just a few short weeks ago.

He cleared his throat. Not sure of how his next words were going to be received, he chose them carefully. It had played on his mind since Deacon and Keira's revelations about their connection to Leviathan.

"I think we need to tell the Vampires everything. They deserve to know their history, and how we began. They are going into battle with a half-truth. If they are going to risk their lives, they need to understand why."

The group fell silent, as if stunned.

Deacon was the first to recover. "Ryker has a point. We have hidden our origins for too many millennia, and it has made us complacent."

Bayek let out a deep, audible sigh. "In our need to hide our shame, we neglected to ensure the next generation of Vampires were prepared should Leviathan return. I think it is time we rectify our mistake."

Ryker was both relieved and surprised, but he kept his emotions to himself. He had expected resistance from the Primordial Vampires.

"I agree." Deacon faced Keira and Dayna. "But that would mean revealing the Crossroads' involvement in our history."

Fuck. In his need to be transparent with the Vampires, he had forgotten that the story also involved Witches. The Crossroads Witches were even more secretive than the Primordials.

Dayna pushed her hands into her jeans' pockets. "I think that horse has bolted already." She appealed to Keira. "But it's your call."

Keira reached for her pendant, deep in thought. "Right now, only two things are out in the open. One, Leviathan is an evil bitch who has spent thousands of years plotting her escape from Hell. And two, Crossroads Witches are the guards of Leviathan's prison. If you had asked me this question a few months ago, I would have said that even this is too much information. Countless lives have been devoted to keeping Leviathan trapped and not to mention ensuring the coven remained invisible." Keira's hand dropped away from the pendant. "But that silence may have contributed to our downfall. How are we going to forge a future when all we're doing is repeating the mistakes of the past? Both the Vampires and the Witches deserve to know our shared history, no matter how painful it is. They need to understand what is truly at stake. And we're only going to get through this if we can trust that we have each other's backs. So yes, I think it's about time we come in from the cold."

Relief flooded through Ryker. Without all the secrecy, it would be easier to protect her.

"I would say you are wise beyond your years." Bayek held his hands behind his back and glanced at Deacon then at him.

"But I suspect, considering your true age, that wouldn't sit well. With time running out, there is no time like the present."

Ryker nodded. "I'll get everyone together."

Once the rest of the Primordial Vampires arrived, they collectively agreed to tell the younger Vampires how their race was given birth and what they went through to escape. While the majority were nowhere near as civilized and absorbed into society as Deacon, Ryker, Bayek, and his associates, they had a single view when it came to Leviathan. They valued their freedom too much to allow her to rule them again.

Ryker stuffed his hands into his pockets as the small crowd dispersed. "That went well. Considering."

Keira tucked a stray strand of red hair behind her ear. "Did it feel like some of the Vampires weren't as surprised as others?"

"It appears some Primordials have been more transparent with our heritage than others. Which explains why we've had more Vampires than expected turn up to help. At least none of those kept in the dark for millennia backed out."

Keira let out a snort. "That may have more to do with the fact that Vampires have no desire for anyone stronger to rain on their parade. You've been the predominant predator on earth for millennia, and none of you are about to let your reign end without a fight."

Ryker lifted his hands in supplication. "I won't argue that point."

"The main thing is that whatever help the Witches need, the Vampires will supply it. A common enemy makes all the difference."

Deacon and Bayek came to stand beside them. Small groups of Vampires and Witches huddled together, digesting the major bombshell just delivered to them.

"At least they are talking, truly talking," Bayek said. "We can only hope it will strengthen their resolve and help us win this."

"And this time, my friend," Deacon began. "We will start and end on the right side of the war."

Ryker adjusted his cap. "We can't go into a war without a plan. I suggest we stop listening into others' conversations and focus." He raised his voice and called out, "Unit leaders to me."

Once they gathered, Deacon retrieved large stones from the rockery and dropped them on the ground.

Ryker drew a circle in the dirt around the stones. "The Legion, in their own bodies, are as strong as Primordials. But we have no way of knowing whether they still retain that strength while in a host's body."

He pointed to the large rock that Deacon had placed in the center of the circle. "To stop the apocalypse, we need to get Keira, Dayna, and Maize to this spot unharmed. And we need to make sure they stay there."

Mitos frowned. "In what universe is that gonna happen? I thought you just said about a hundred or so of these freakazoids are guarding the stones. How are we gonna get them from there to there? I hardly think they'll give us time to get our weapons in place. And even if we did manage to get the three of you in there, how are we gonna stop the rest of them from attacking you?"

Keira stepped forward. "Once we're within range, Velvet and the other Crossroads Witches will cast a protection spell on the inner circle."

"How can you be sure they can't breach it?" Zayne asked.

Keira turned to Zayne. "It's our best guess at this point if the barrier will hold. We have no idea how much magic they possess nor how much strength they'll place on the barrier, but it will take all of the Crossroads Witches to reinforce it once it's under attack."

"I don't understand," one of the Fire Witches said. "You placed a protection spell on the house. It only took two of you, and you didn't need to keep it active."

"You're right, normally it wouldn't, but with the added pressure and magic thrown at it, the barrier will need to be kept active and recharged. In addition to feeding the barrier, Dayna, Maize, and I will be siphoning the bulk of the Crossroads' power, as well as power from the Yggdrasil, for our assault on the Legion."

The Crossroads Witch gasped. "Isn't that dangerous?"

Keira nodded. "Very, but it's a risk we have to take. Based on what we've just learned, the Legion's power comes directly from Leviathan. That power can open the gate from this side."

"Alone, we don't have the strength to defeat her," Dayna said. "But combined, we may have a chance."

The Witches became quiet as they considered the ramifications. Until this moment, Ryker hadn't appreciated the danger of the plan. He would pull Keira aside and question why she had omitted that pertinent fact when she first floated the idea.

He crouched and circled an area. "With the exception of the Brother Superior, the rest of the Order is here, standing guard over the prisoners." He looked up at Steve, one of the Fire Witches and an Essex County firefighter. "This is where you and your team come in. The Legion will be too distracted to notice their prisoners being freed. As far as we can tell, the Order will have minimal powers, as they can only access their magic fully if Leviathan is on earth. We know they're armed, but you will be as well."

Mitos grunted and pointed to Steve. "I'm with them. I've got a bone to pick with that former fucktard partner of mine." He readjusted his hat and squinted at Ryker and Deacon. "What I wanna know is how fifty of you bloodsuckers are gonna take on ninety-odd zombies. I ain't so confident with those odds."

"You let us worry about that," Deacon said. "Just get those prisoners out of there and take care of the guards."

Once they each knew what they needed to do, a renewed purpose set in. For the next day and a half, the fire, air, and water Witches practiced the spells they needed to achieve their part of the plan, while the Crossroads Witches learned the new spells Keira and Dayna's mother left for them.

In between training sessions, the sisters were drilling the fire, water, and air Witches to discover how they drew from their power base. They repeatedly attempted to re-channel and repeat their newfound ability to use fire, water, and air magic, but nothing they tried worked.

Keira downplayed their lack of progress, but Ryker knew they were concerned. Neither sister would reveal just how dependent they were on the new powers for their plan to succeed. Each time he asked, Keira would dismiss his concerns.

Midafternoon on the night of the Blood Moon, all the Vampires had arrived and were fully briefed on what to expect. As the day drew to an end, their mood became somber. Each person was deep in their thoughts as they readied themselves for the battle.

The time to leave for Mystery Hill arrived sooner than expected. Ryker gave Steve last-minute instructions, then made his way to the patio. What, in God's name, was taking Keira so long? She had rushed into the house for additional supplies a while ago, and no one had seen her since.

Maize, Velvet, and Zayne huddled together in an embrace a short distance away. Maize's eyes were red-rimmed as she kissed the top of Velvet's head and gently ran her hand down her daughter's hair. Zayne's hand rested on the small of Maize's back, and he looked as if he, too, was about to shed tears.

None of them knew if they would survive the night. Yet this didn't discourage their determination to defeat the evil that threatened all they knew. The evil had already taken one of their children, but they would fight to prevent it from taking another.

Ryker looked away from the private, tender scene.

His chest ached as he studied the other Witches and Vampires. Each of them was doing this to protect the ones they loved. A lifetime ago, he'd longed for a family. A son to carry on his name, a daughter to cherish, and a wife he could love and respect. The wish had eluded him, pushed beyond his reach the moment Gabrielle walked into his life.

He swallowed his melancholy thoughts and concentrated on the here and now. He would make sure Zayne, Maize, and Velvet came out of this in one piece. They had suffered enough and had already paid a high price for Leviathan's attempt to return.

Just as Deacon pulled out of the driveway with Dayna and Mitos, Keira finally exited the house. Her hair glistened and sparked in the late afternoon sun as if on fire. She hung the strap of her bag over her shoulder, took a deep breath, and let it out slowly as she came closer.

"You okay?"

She gave him a wan smile and nodded. "As okay as I can be."

He reached out and pulled her toward him. "Keira, I need you to promise me there will be no heroics. If there's any danger to you, Maize, or Dayna, you high-tail it out of there. You hear me?"

She scrunched her nose as she returned his concerned gaze. He knew her well enough to know she was working out how to respond without lying. "I promise I won't do anything that is not absolutely necessary."

In that instant, he knew if he lost her, he'd lose a part of his soul.

THIRTY

HEART OF COURAGE

By the time they arrived at Mystery Hill, the summer solstice sun had set, and the Strawberry Moon hung low and majestic in the evening sky. The glowing light painted across the sky resembled the color of honey. Its amber color lent it an ethereal radiance that had fascinated people since the dawn of time.

Keira closed her eyes and raised her face to the moon. Her body came alive, as if it were already siphoning energy from the earth. Every nerve ending shivered and twitched. Her legs ached to race through the forest. Her fingertips pulsed, and she longed to discover just how much power she could tap into.

A light touch at her elbow brought her back to the present, and she swiveled her head toward Dayna.

"Can you feel it?" she whispered.

Dayna nodded. Even in the dim light, the energy pulsed behind her sister's energetic and expressive eyes.

"I know you said we would feel the extra power with the Strawberry Moon, but this is unbelievable," Maize said in a low voice.

Keira and Dayna had experienced this phenomenon before, but the intensity of the surge in energy was that much stronger so near the gate.

Keira peered around the giant tree they had taken refuge behind and studied the clearing around the ancient stones. Small fires flickered with enough light to provide a clear view of the Legion. As with their previous visit, Arnie, the muscled Legion in charge, and the robed older man she'd identified as Brother Superior in the Order of Chaos, were focused on the ceremony to bring Legion through the gate and into a host's body.

The Legion were scattered around the outer third of the clearing nearest the tree line. Their arms were crossed at their chests, each hand resting on the opposite shoulder. Their heads faced downward, and a low hum resonated throughout the woods.

From their expressions, both Deacon and Bayek recognized the hum. The Legion were channeling power through each other to begin their final assault. That same technique had been used across the eons to bring cities to their knees and allow the Legion forces full reign to decimate Leviathan's enemies.

Keira rubbed her arm and looked around. Where were the Vampires?

Her question was answered when a small gust of wind whipped up the dry dirt at her feet. She was relieved when Ryker, Deacon, Bayek, and Vincent, another Primordial Vampire, appeared, deep in conversation.

"I agree with Deacon," Ryker declared. "If we separate the Legion, we have a better chance of getting the three Witches into the clearing."

Deacon cleared his throat. "It is agreed then. Ryker, you and the other Vampires will attack the Legion and force them to separate into smaller groups. Once there is a sufficient path, Bayek, Vincent, and I will escort the three Witches into the clearing." He held up a hand. "And before you object to not escorting them yourself, Ryker, we have no way of gauging the Legion's power. While turned Vampires have exceptional strength and speed, it is nothing like that of a Primordial. Do you really wish to jeopardize their safety, as well as the lives of everyone, should Leviathan succeed this evening?"

"My old friend is correct," Bayek agreed. "We will protect the Witches with our lives, as will all those who have joined us."

Ryker looked as though he was going to argue the point but hesitated before nodding. "Very well."

"Is everyone in place?" Bayek raised his voice.

Vincent stepped forward. "The Crossroads coven is hidden well away from the clearing but still has a line of sight as requested."

"What about the other Witches?"

Ryker indicated the north. "They are on the far side, ready to free the prisoners when they are given the go ahead. Are the Vampires in place?"

Deacon nodded. "Vampire teams are ready on the north and east."

"And two other teams, south and west," Bayek said. "Ready to begin on our command."

Ryker moved to Keira's side. "Are you ready to take on a horde of Legion and their deranged God?"

She shook her head, then nodded. "Can you ever be ready for something like this?"

"I'll take that as a yes, then," he said with a wink. He turned to Deacon, and his face turned to stone. "Keep them safe,"

Deacon squared his shoulders. "We have this. Fear not. They will be guarded with our lives. We understand more than you what is at stake."

Ryker's intense gaze on her as he prepared to return to his team caused her pulse to race. "You remember what I said, Doc. No heroics. You need help. You call me."

He pulled her into a standing position. His arm curled around her, and she found herself pressed hard against his chest. His lips found hers in a crushing kiss. As quickly as it began, he pulled away. A gust of air, and he was gone. Her heartbeat skyrocketed out of control. She didn't know whether to be mortified at the very public kiss or grateful she had something to hold onto as they went into battle.

Deacon checked his watch. "Two minutes. Be ready to move to our position. Once the others have diverted their attention, we'll take you into the middle of the clearing."

She huddled with Dayna and Maize and crouched low to keep out of sight. Deacon and Bayek blended in with the night to check on the Legion.

Dayna elbowed her. "Well, that was hot. When this is over, you and Sheriff McSexy will need to get a room before you blow the state up with that repressed tension."

Maize let out a slight giggle. "He is easy on the eye, but don't let Zayne know I said that."

"Pfft." Dayna waved her hand dismissively. "There's no harm in window shopping. You don't need to buy. I'm sure Zayne does it all the time."

"Will you two quit it," Keira hissed.

They looked up as a throat was cleared. Deacon, Bayek, and Vincent stared down at them. Her face grew even warmer. The Vamps had overheard the conversation.

"It's time," Deacon said.

He reached out to Dayna and pulled her into a standing position.

With as much stealth as possible, they made their way to their assigned positions. They needed to be extra vigilant to stay out of sight given the full moon.

The minutes dragged on and felt like hours. The inactivity made Keira acutely aware of the energy pouring into her body with the force of a waterfall after a heavy rain. She struggled not to fidget. From Dayna and Maize's uncomfortable twitching, she was not the only one.

Almost in unison, the teams began their assault. At first, it looked like the plan would work, and a quiver of excitement rippled through her. Legion separated and stalked toward the Vampires nearest them. Her hopes came crashing down when only a handful took the bait. The Vampires and Legion snarled as they jockeyed for an advantage and the best opening to attack. A Vampire was the first to leap towards the Legion nearest him. The Vampire's clenched fist slammed into the Legion's chest, propelling him backwards and into the Legion behind him. The Legion quickly recovered his balance, hissed at his attacker and hurled himself at the Vampire. As if a dam had burst, the small group of Legion rushed the Vampires and an all out brawl ensued. But still no further Legion broke ranks to assist.

Bayek cursed under his breath and shook his head. "Most unexpected."

Deacon studied the teams embroiled in battle and the Legion that remained at their posts. "They are too coordinated for my liking. Leviathan has managed to get one of her generals through." He glanced back at Vincent. "Change of plan. Bayek and I will clear a path. Only bring the Witches through when it's safe."

Before she could object, the two Primordial Vampires disappeared in a blur. By the time she looked up, they had entered the fray and joined in the chaos.

Following the swift-moving battle was a challenge. The grunts, growls, and pained shouts as fists and legs made contact drowned out any conversation. But once her brain caught up, she was able to follow the Vampires and Legion as they tore their opponents apart limb from limb.

She peered into the dark woods surrounding the clearing. Somewhere, just behind them, the Crossroads Witches had begun channeling their power so that she, Dayna, and Maize could tap into it. Every nerve ending was enhanced by the additional magic surging toward her, making it difficult to focus.

"Are you alright?" Dayna asked.

"I'm fine. I was just wondering where all the power has come from. It's like someone has returned the stolen magic and added to it. I've never felt this much energy before."

"I wouldn't overthink it," Dayna said as she turned back toward the clearing. "Just be thank—" Dayna let out a small cry.

Keira spun around. Deacon had just taken down a Legion, but three others were about to attack his position. Her heart leaped into her throat. She was unable to look away as the Legion descended on him. The host's boardshorts and summer boat shoes were a stark reminder that just a few days ago, the original owner of the body was a carefree young man on vacation. She sent out a silent prayer that their guess was correct, and the Primordial Vampires were much stronger than a Legion in a Human host's body.

The first Legion rushed Deacon, and he stepped to one side at the last moment. At the same time, Deacon spun to face the nearest walking corpse, and with a roundhouse kick, his booted foot crashed into the Legion's torso, sending the Legion flying. Before Deacon rebalanced, the third Legion rushed him, and a full-body slam pushed him to the ground. Quickly recovering, Deacon circled the Legion that had just attacked him and waited for his moment to strike.

Her pulse sped up when two more Legion moved closer and looked to attack Deacon. But Bayek disposed of his attacker with a final, crashing blow and rushed to Deacon's position. Together, they took the Legion head on.

Dayna clenched her hands into fists. "I'm not sure this is going to work."

Keira had to agree. The enemy was so confident in their abilities that they simply readjusted their positions around the clearing rather than sending out their entire battalion. Some of the Legion fighting the Vampires had left the battle and returned to their original positions.

"There must be another way," she said, doing a quick calculation of their opposition.

While the Vampires had disposed of some Legion, they had yet to clear a path. She flinched when Tim was set upon by four Legion. He put up a good fight but was outmatched through pure numbers, not ability.

Please, someone help him. Terror ripped through her when one of the Legion punched a hole through his chest and ripped out Tim's heart. With a cry, he crumpled lifeless to the ground. She brought up a hand to cover her mouth. The battleground was pure chaos.

Maize let out a cry when a gunshot rang out in the night, followed by another series of gunshots.

She whipped toward the sound. The men from the Order guarding the prisoners were taking potshots at any Vampire who came near them.

Dayna's hands flew up to her cheeks. "We need to do something."

"I know, but what? We don't have the physical strength to fight our way to the center."

The outer two-thirds of the clearing was full to the brim with Vampires and Legion, but the inner third of the circle was empty. The ceremony to transfer a Legion from hell into a living host required space.

Dayna clasped her hands and squeezed them together. "We have to find another way. This will be all for nothing if we can't stop Leviathan."

Keira opened her mouth to answer, but Dayna was gone. Her sister was there. Then she wasn't. She checked to see if Maize or Vincent had seen what happened, and her eyes opened wide. Her sister stood four hundred feet away, a short distance from the altar stone.

Panic welled from the pit of her stomach. "No, no, no, no, no!"

Dayna was alone and unprotected, surrounded by nearly one hundred Legion. She took a step forward and called out, "Dayna!"

Strong hands pulled her back before she took another step.

"There is nothing you can do," Vincent said sharply. "Deacon and Bayek will get to her. We can't risk both of you falling into their hands."

The panic threatened to debilitate her as the group of Legion nearest her sister recovered from the shock of a woman materializing in their midst.

The Legion advanced menacingly.

Keira struggled against Vincent's grip. "Let me go. I need to get to her."

Deacon, seeing Dayna's predicament, let out a guttural growl and snapped the neck of the Legion he was fighting. He rushed toward her, but his path was cut off by another group of Legion, making it impossible for him to reach her in time.

Dayna swung her body around so that she was facing their direction. Her petrified expression was clear. While she could see her sister, Dayna didn't have that luxury.

She fought against Vincent's grip. "I said, let me—"

A strange sensation shimmied through her body, and the words died on her lips. She brought up her hands. They were vibrating so quickly that her fingertips blurred. *What the—?* The pressure on her shoulders lifted, and when she looked up again, she was standing a few feet away from Dayna.

Just as quickly, her stomach churned, and nausea hit her. She held back the bile that threatened to projectile vomit and focused on two Legion bearing down on her sister. She knew with certainty what would happen if they reached her.

Whether it was fear or a desperate need to protect Dayna, she instinctively raised her hand, and a blue-white ball of fire shot out of her palm and hit one of the Legion square in the chest. He propelled backward with such force that he took out another one in his flight, and they landed in a crumpled heap on the ground.

She hurled another sphere of fire at a second Legion and incapacitated him. "Dayna, I don't know how you did it, but get Maize here, now!"

She gritted her teeth, and her arm swung around to face another Legion moving toward them. "We need to set the barrier. I don't know how long I can keep this up."

Four more Legion turned their focus on her and Dayna.

Dayna scrunched her face and called upon her new power. Her effort was rewarded when Maize appeared next to them.

Maize's face lost all color, and she clutched at her stomach. "I'm going to be ill."

Keira hurled energy balls at the Legion and moved closer to her sister and Maize. "We don't have time to be sick. We need to get the barrier up."

Maize nodded and took a deep, visible gulp. The three of them chanted. To her surprise, the wall locked into place before they finished the chant, and the noise from the raging battle dimmed to a low murmur.

In the immediate area cordoned off from the outside world, she counted three bound and gagged prisoners, the Order's Brother Superior, Arnie, the head Legion, and ten Legion henchmen.

They were effectively cut off from the rest of the Legion, as well as the Vampires. They no longer had any protection, and the outcome of the battle against Leviathan now rested solely on their shoulders.

In less than two minutes, they had teleported across a war zone, killed or badly maimed half a dozen Legion, and erected a protective wall around the inner third of the ancient site. Not bad for a couple of three-hundred-year-old women and a grieving mother who had only just tapped into her true power.

"Do you think it will hold?" Maize said as Legion after Legion raced at the wall only to be repelled back when they came into contact with the barrier.

"Yes, but for how long is the question."

Dayna took an involuntary step backward as one of the Legion moved closer, clearly learning from his downed fellow soldiers' mistakes to be careful. "Ladies, I think we need to put up our personal barrier before they get any bright ideas."

They quickly moved close enough to erect another barrier. This time, one that would encircle the three of them and protect them from those remaining in the inner circle. Their magical barricade locked into place just as the Legion ran at them. It held, and he flew backward and bounced against the ground.

Maize gasped for breath. "That was close."

The failure only further enraged the Legion, and he quickly rose and moved to make another attempt. While the original host reminded her of a bookish librarian, complete with pocket protector. The Legion that had taken the unfortunate man as a host didn't share the same level of intelligence. If he couldn't get through the first time, what made him believe it would work if he repeated the exact same action?

When he landed in the same place a moment later, she snorted. Idiot.

Now that she had a moment to breathe, she pulled her onyx crystals from her pocket and took a quick look around. The chaos beyond the barrier was now a distorted, angry hum. The speed at which some skirmishes took place made it challenging to follow the action.

After ensuring they were safely ensconced in the middle, Deacon, Bayek, and Vincent joined the fight. To her right, the fire, water, and air Witches, with Stephen and Mitos leading the way, began their assault to free the remaining prisoners.

Keira grinned when one of the Order's disciples dropped his sidearm and cradled his hand to his chest, a look of agony plastered on his face.

What do you know? Mitos' idea worked. The Witches couldn't safely get near the Order because Trudeau had raided the sheriff's office weapons cache. The Order could take on a tank if required. They needed a way to separate the Legion from their weapons. But how?

Mitos, with his usual politically incorrect flair, had asked, "Can't you freaks turn lead into molten lead? Make it too hot to handle and burn the fucknuggets?"

He may have failed at sensitivity training, but he was a font of good ideas on the battlefield.

Satisfied the prisoners were now safe, she, Dayna, and Maize arranged their crystals in a large circle. They stood on the outer rim, an equal distance apart. She tipped her head, gazed at the stars in the night sky, held out her hands, and reached up as she chanted, "*Illam Terra parens aestivum solem, lunam offertur. Ad nos praeditos canalibus. Iubeo instar Huc Concede nobis praecipere fluxus*."

Dayna repeated the process, followed by Maize. Finally, in unison, they intoned the ancient incantation that would allow them to draw magic from Yggdrasil and from the other Crossroads Witches.

Maize blinked. "Did it work?"

Keira nodded. She could feel the additional power surge.

As they prepared for what would come next, she scanned the battle for a glimpse of Ryker. He was in the thick of things. He and another Vampire had teamed up and were now protecting each other's flanks as they waited for the Legion to come at them. She flinched as a Legion flew at Ryker and knocked him off his feet. In quick order, he was up and paid his attacker back in kind.

"He'll be fine," Dayna said when she let out a barely audible cry at the large gash on Ryker's shoulder and down his arm. Dayna nodded her head in the direction of the altar stone. "It's him you need to worry about."

She tore her focus away from the chaos. The massive Legion they'd dubbed Arnie had successfully brought through another Legion to take over a host's body. She sent up a silent prayer for the victim. No matter how this evening turned out, his life was over.

Arnie turned his attention to them. A shiver of fear snaked down her spine when his piercing gaze rested on her. The air rippled as his energy reached out to push against their protective barrier. Without a doubt, he was powerful.

Dayna froze. "Mother Earth, did you feel that?"

Arnie's eyes opened wide when another push failed to break through the barrier. He advanced on them, his stride confident, his expression calculated as he studied each one of them in turn.

"I know not what you hope to achieve, but it will fail. You are mere Witches against the mighty Legion. Cease this foolhardy behavior and submit to us now. Our Lord and Master may be lenient and overlook your transgressions."

He held out his hand and tested the boundary. With a deceptively casual air, his fingers trailed along the surface, inciting a slight ripple with his touch.

When Maize let out a slight whimper, Keira gave her an encouraging smile. "Have faith. It will hold."

Arnie attacked with force, launching his body at their barrier. The power of their magic propelled him backward. His shocked expression was enough for her. While he might have the power to summon the Legion from hell, he lacked the strength to reach them. They were safe. For now.

Enraged, he snarled at them from behind the barrier. "You're no match for General Zahir, the right hand of our Lord Leviathan and general of the Seven Legion armies. You will fail."

Keira stared unblinkingly at the general.

She sauntered to the edge, inches from his wrathful presence. People who referred to themselves in the third person irritated her.

"I'm sorry, am I supposed to be impressed?"

He let out a vicious bellow and bared his teeth. "Witch, I will have the utmost pleasure making your death particularly painful and prolonged. I will ensure you bear witness as your friends die in agony. I will present them to Brother Amos as a gift for his loyalty. He takes special delight in inflicting pain. He is something of an artist, or so I am told."

As General Zahir stormed back to the stone altar and snatched another prisoner off the ground, Dayna called out. "Nice chatting with you. Sorry I couldn't talk longer, busy stopping your evil bitch puppeteer from coming through."

Keira drew more power from their link to Yggdrasil. A wave of heat rushed through her, and she cringed. The burning energy now surging through her body was agony.

It was time.

As one, they began the arduous task of breaking the Legion's connection to Leviathan. The surge danced and teased as it flowed from the earth up through their bodies and out into the night sky. The combination of shared power they were drawing from the Witches was heady and thick. She could almost taste the different flavors as they flowed through her. Never had she considered her magic having a taste, but with the mixture of shared magic, as it combined and melded together, it tasted metallic and earthy at the same time.

Despite the energy surging through her, nothing on the battlefield changed.

Amos, the Order's Brother Superior, carved a symbol into the prisoner's forehead. The man screamed as blood trickled from the wound. From the glint in the old man's eye and his cold smile, Zahir hadn't been lying when he said Amos had a predilection for inflicting pain.

She blinked a few times to clear her vision. Was the Brother Superior listening to music? She could swear there were earbuds in his ears connected to something in the pocket of his robe.

As he approached the victim to begin the ceremony, General Zahir glared at them, a sneer on his face. She expected him to say something, but he turned back to his prisoner. She tapped into her power and focused on severing the connection with renewed purpose. The general halted his efforts and let out a loud growl. He spoke to Amos, then flexed his muscles, the veins bulging on his neck as he redoubled his efforts.

A feeling of satisfaction rushed through her. Something was not going right with his parasite summoning.

"It's working," Maize called.

Keira grinned as a heavy weight lifted off her shoulders. Perhaps this would work after all. "Yes, but disrupting a single transfer is not enough. We need to sever the link between Leviathan and her disciples to give our team a chance."

They turned to the battle raging beyond their sanctuary. Her heart skipped a beat. More dead Vampires lay on the ground. Some she recognized, others she didn't. She scanned the area and breathed out a sigh of relief. Ryker and Deacon were holding their own.

Another angry growl cut through the noise, and she turned toward the source. Zahir stood halfway between the altar stone and their position. His hands clenched into fists, his bloodshot eyes bore into them.

"He doesn't look happy," Maize said, her voice strained.

His expression saturated with fury, Zahir stalked them from behind the barrier. "What have you done? If you think this will work, you are deluding yourself. You have not stopped us. You have merely delayed the inevitable. All you have done is seal your own fate."

"Settle down, big boy." Dayna mocked the general. "If you put much more strain on that stolen body, it's likely to have a coronary."

Zahir's eyes narrowed, and his rage overflowed.

He turned away, and his voice boomed across the clearing. "Get them."

At least two dozen Legion broke ranks from the battle to follow his order. General Zahir's army either shared telepathic abilities with him, or had very well-developed hearing.

The remaining Legion within the inner area began an assault on their personal barrier as those trapped beyond the larger wall began their attack.

Dayna winked. "Someone's got rage issues."

"Focus," Keira ordered with an edge of irritation. "We need to siphon more power. We've slowed them down, but it's not enough."

While both barriers had held thus far, how long they would last was anyone's guess. Most of the power they channeled was focused on severing the connection. Even with her advanced abilities, her body felt like she had just run a marathon. She checked to see how Maize was faring. The woman's brows were furrowed, and her mouth was set in a grim line. Her hair was matted to her sweaty forehead.

"Are you okay?" she said.

Maize nodded. "I'll be fine." She stiffened her shoulders and pulled them back, but the rapid rise and fall of her chest indicated she was anything but fine. "I probably won't be able to move for a week after this, but it will be worth it to see these bastards suffer."

Dayna sent Keira a pointed look but addressed Maize. "Don't be a martyr. Make sure you let us know if it becomes too much."

She understood the message Dayna silently conveyed. Between the two of them, they needed to draw the bulk of the power. Maize couldn't take much more. To make matters worse, Zahir was correct. Whatever they were doing had only slowed, not stopped, the process.

The general resumed his chant. Amos joined him. The man strapped to the slab was losing his struggle. The incoming Legion's consciousness would overpower him at any moment, and the man would be lost forever.

She redoubled her efforts and sank to the ground, one knee bent, the other resting on the uneven dirt and rock. She placed her hands, palms down, on the earth and breathed in deeply. She ignored the prisoners' agonized screams as they echoed around the clearing.

The three women continued to siphon power as they chanted in unison. A jump in energy coursed through her. It jerked her body into an arch, and she fought to control it. Her heart thumped against her ribs as she forced the energy out and focused on severing the connection.

She could now see the faint strands of energy linking the Legion to General Zahir. A second, stronger strand weaved its way to the large standing stone on the far side of the clearing. The entire area resembled a giant spider's web, magnificent in its complexity and chilling in its purpose.

She gasped when the truth hit her. The cracks. Leviathan had found a way to tether her power to the cracks, and through them, the ancient stone. The cracks in the gate were too narrow for Leviathan to break free, but if the fallen angel managed to tap into the entire Crossroads network of gates and tether her power to those, Leviathan could break the protective connections. At the same time, she'd gather enough of her own power to emerge from hell.

No wonder the general still expected to bring Leviathan through with a depleted army. He didn't need the numbers. He needed to feed his power grid. Like a worn car battery, it could recharge if sufficient energy passed through it.

They needed to stop Leviathan from connecting with their power before it was too late!

Now that Keira knew where they needed to concentrate their attack, she barked out instructions to Dayna and Maize. Dayna, without hesitation, mimicked her position and channeled more power from Yggdrasil. They needed to up their game before it was too late.

"It's like a spiderweb," Dayna said.

Keira kept an eye on the thickest strand. "Focus on the main standing stone. Push everything you have toward it."

At first, there was no visible change, but they maintained their relentless bombardment of the stone. It took a few minutes, but her breath caught when she detected a flicker in the web. Slight at first and then more pronounced.

"It's working!"

Zahir must have detected the change in his power levels. He renewed his effort to break through the barriers.

Dayna smirked when one of the Legion nearest her pounded on their protective wall. "Nice try, but we've made sure your kind can't get through."

Keira ignored General Zahir's outburst and remained glued to the stone. The web wavered but didn't appear to be in distress. They needed more energy.

A flash of black, followed by a woman's cry of pain, caused her to falter. She spun her head around and locked eyes with Maize. Standing directly behind her was the black-robed Brother Superior, his expression triumphant. They had been so focused on the Legion, they had forgotten that Amos, a Human, was in the inner circle.

Maize wavered and sank to her knees, her face etched with shock.

Dayna shrieked. "Naturals, we didn't think to ward our personal barrier against Naturals."

Amos smiled, and with a yank at something behind Maize, he raised his arm. Clutched victoriously in his hand was a dagger dripping with blood. Before Keira could react, he plunged the blade downward a second time.

She reacted instinctively, and a ball of energy flew from her hands. Its blue-white glow in stark contrast to the dull orange tinge from the fires dotting the clearing. The force of the energy propelled Amos backward in a blaze of light as the orb shattered on impact.

She raced to Maize, who was on her knees, her eyes wide and her face pale. Maize's mouth opened to speak, but nothing came out.

Dayna crawled over to inspect the damage. Her face grew pensive, and she hauled in a deep breath.

"Oh, Mother Earth." She dropped her head as if unwilling to see the wound. She glanced around frantically. "She needs medical help. We have to drop a portion of the wall to get her out safely."

A single tear trickled down Maize's cheek as she shook her head slowly. "It's too late for that."

Keira's heart clenched as the strain contorted Maize's face into a study of controlled pain. The wounded woman's gaze drifted off into the distance, somewhere over her shoulder, and Keira turned to see what Maize was looking at with such sorrow.

Zayne, who had been watching the unfolding drama, was held back by Mitos. His shouts were distorted through the thickness of the barriers. But she could feel, rather than hear, the distress in his voice as he fought off Ryker's deputy. She turned back in time to see Dayna attempting to remove the dagger embedded in Maize's back.

"No, don't."

Dayna froze.

"It's probably the only thing keeping her alive. If you remove it, she'll bleed out."

Dayna snapped her hand away as if burnt and scrambled around to Maize's front. She reached for Maize's hand. "What can we do? We can't leave her like this."

Maize gave Dayna a weak smile and coughed. A spray of blood ran out of her mouth with the exhaled air. "I won't be able to keep the spell complete for much longer."

Keira stilled. The magic running through Maize was the only thing keeping her alive. The strands of webbing from the Legion were regaining strength, an indication their spell was unable to retain its full power without all three of them actively charging it.

Maize coughed again, and her head lolled toward Dayna. "You need to get Velvet here now. You must have a third Witch to help you finish the job. She's the only one left with the capacity to take on this level of magic."

Dayna's face fell. "I … I don't think I can do it again."

"You must," Maize said as she clung to Dayna's arm. "You know more than I what is at stake."

Maize tensed, and she let out a hiss through her teeth. The combination of the injury while still retaining the energy surging through her body was taking its toll.

She needed something to dull the pain. A long-forgotten spell emerged from the depths of Keira's memory, and she reached over to take Maize's weight.

"Dayna, get Velvet here now!"

She glared at her sister, willing her to move quickly as she began the words that would ease the agony surging through Maize's body and causing it to shake. Tears flowed from Dayna as she visibly brought herself under control.

With the energy flowing through their bodies, everything was enhanced, including their emotions. She understood why Dayna was not confident she could use her newfound magic. With all the current flowing through them, it was difficult enough to concentrate on the spell to break Leviathan's connection to the Legion. Let alone add another layer to transport a living being from one place to another in the blink of an eye.

Keira cradled Maize to give her as much comfort as possible with the little time she had left.

After a few seconds, Dayna wrinkled her face in concentration and then shook her head. "I can't do it."

Keira glared at her sister and wished she could shake her by the shoulders to get some sense into her. "Yes, you can, and you will. We've come too far to fail. Look around you. Too many have given their lives to ensure Leviathan does not step foot in our world again. We will not be the ones who fail them. Get Velvet here now, before it's too late."

Dayna rubbed her hands up and down her thighs as she glanced toward Maize, who was fading fast. She squared her shoulders and pressed her lips together. Before she had a chance to take stock of the battle that had moved up a notch, Velvet materialized beside them.

From her tears and strained expression, the young woman had seen everything.

A familiar feeling of grief rose within Keira, and memories bombarded her mercilessly. She knew exactly what Velvet was feeling. A long time ago, against the same foe, in this exact place, she had lost her mother.

No words would console Velvet or make the pain any less consuming. Keira avoided looking at Zayne, where he was being physically restrained for his own safety. She blinked rapidly as Velvet rushed to her mother's side.

"Mom!" The raw agony ripped from Velvet's throat.

Maize pushed away from Keira and righted herself as she placed her hands on either side of her daughter's face. "Honey, mourn for me later. Right now, you must take my place. This is your legacy."

A sob caught in Velvet's throat as she shook her head and whispered, "I don't know how."

A calmness fell over Maize as she gazed lovingly at her daughter. "Yes, my love, you do. You have such a capacity for greatness. I can see that now. Just open yourself to the possibilities, and the three of you will triumph."

A jolt of pain stiffened Maize, and she slumped backward.

Keira eased her collapse to the ground. Maize held out her hand to Velvet. The moment mother and daughter's fingers touched, the transfer of power rushed from one body to the next, causing Dayna to let out a whimper.

The transfer increased, and Velvet shook uncontrollably. As the pent-up energy flowed through her, Velvet was rocked backward. Even in her weakened physical state, Maize held on tightly to her child's hand.

"I can't take this." Velvet's voice came out as a pained cry. "It's too much."

Dayna crawled across to Velvet. "Don't fight it. The more you resist, the more painful it is."

Dayna talked Velvet through the transition. The tremors ceased as she opened herself up, and the power flowed freely from mother to daughter. Through their shared connection, she felt the life ebb from Maize as the seconds passed.

"Tell your father I will love him even in death."

"No," Velvet said between sobs. "You tell him. You can't leave us."

Maize held her daughter's hand with both of hers. "I am with Annie now, and we will always look over you both." She tensed as the final burst of energy left her body. "Promise me you'll strive to be happy."

Maize's muscles relaxed as the life left her damaged body and her soul moved on.

"May your light live on," Keira said in a broken whisper.

She gently lowered Maize to the ground and pushed away the rush of grief that could very well be their undoing.

Velvet refused to let go of her mother's hand.

"Mom, no. Mom!" she screamed, repeating the words over and over again as though her force of will alone could bring her mother back.

THIRTY-ONE

SPELLCASTER

Keira's soul ached at the inconsolable sobbing coming from a broken heart, mingling with the low chant from the soulless one. Throughout the chaos, the general hadn't once halted his mission. How had he known they had a flaw in their personal protective bubble? What had they said that triggered his suspicions? Was the blood from Maize's death on their hands?

Unable to process her sudden doubts, Keira held her tears back, sniffed, and placed a hand on Velvet's shoulder. "We need to finish this, or your mother died for nothing."

Velvet, still sobbing, stood and wrapped her arms around her middle. "I don't know what to do. What if I fail her?"

"Then don't fail. This is what you were born to do. You come from a long line of Crossroads Witches. You may lack knowledge, but if you dig deep inside and call on all those who came before you, you'll know what to do. Open yourself up and let them guide you."

She took a deep breath and let it slowly exhale. This is what the general was aiming for. If he couldn't get to them directly, he was making sure they were otherwise occupied with self-doubt and grief.

They couldn't, they wouldn't, let that happen. No matter what it took, they needed to push beyond their pain and let it strengthen rather than consume them. Too much was at stake to admit defeat now.

Velvet wiped away the tears. Her voice wobbled as she took one last look at her mother. "Okay, let's do this."

She and Dayna moved Maize's body away from the crystal circle and said their last goodbyes. Maize's death affected her as much as Marcus' had. For so many years, she managed to keep her distance. In a span of a few short weeks, she had opened herself up again and allowed people in.

She not only let a Vampire inside her defenses, but she also opened her heart to make way for a friend, a friend she would mourn longer than she had known her. Maize had been a pure soul, loving, and easy to like.

Keira wiped the tears from her eyes. She couldn't lose any more. Knowing what now needed to happen, she took her place around the crystal circle.

"Channel your anger and sorrow, let it amplify your magic. We cannot give an inch of ground to those bastards."

Without fanfare, they began the ancient chant and drew the additional power they needed to regain the ground they had lost. Inch by inch, the power returned and became explosive energy.

Not only could she feel the sorrow in the power shared between the three of them, but it was now infused with the power siphoned from the other Crossroads. In their grief, the coven gave every last drop of energy they possessed.

As they began their renewed assault on the standing stone, channeling a link to Leviathan, she risked a glance at the outer edge of the woods. What remained of the Crossroads coven had emerged from their hiding places. They stood in plain sight of the Legion.

The fire, water, and air Witches had freed the prisoners and were now the only thing standing between the Crossroads coven and the Legion.

Mother Earth, they were exposed. Her stomach churned as if she were going to be sick. With their focus on the Legion, the Vampires failed to notice the coven was now out in the open and at risk. Even with all their good will and determination, the fire, air, earth, and water Witches were no match for a horde of Legion.

"What is it?" Dayna cried.

She nodded toward the exposed Witches. "I don't know what the hell they are thinking."

Dayna let out a groan. "Shit. Shitty, shit, shit. Our next assault on Leviathan's power will make it obvious that more than three Crossroads Witches are involved."

"This wasn't part of the plan," Keira called over the noise of battle. "The moment General Zahir realizes those Witches are exposed, he'll go straight for them."

The link to the standing stone faltered, and Keira called out a warning to Dayna and Velvet.

"It's slipping. The link. Focus on the link."

They resolidified the link and continued channeling power to the invisible strands that connected Leviathan to her army.

Once Keira was satisfied they'd fought back the lost ground, she nodded toward the Legion. "The fire, water, and air witches will try and protect them, but the Crossroads coven won't stand a chance."

Dayna's eyes brimmed with fear. "We need the Vampires to protect the Crossroads coven before that happens."

Mother Earth! They were too late. General Zahir pointed toward the group of Witches on the outskirts of the clearing. As if they had a hive mind, the Legion turned in the direction he was pointing.

Fear ripped through her as the Legion abandoned their attempt to breach the barrier. They pushed their way toward the exposed Witches. She shuddered to think about the carnage if the Legion got past the Vampires.

Some of the Vampires noticed the abrupt departure and raced toward the Witches. The fight that had been dispersed across a wide space was suddenly concentrated in the south of the clearing.

"They don't stand a chance, not with those numbers," Dayna said, half sobbing.

Keira's throat constricted when a Legion broke through. He attacked the first Witch he reached. In a brutal heartbeat, the Witch was dead and discarded on the ground as the Legion lurched for his next victim. A plume of fire blocked the Legion before he took three steps.

Two Fire Witches focused on the billowing smoke. Flames erupted from the Legion's shirt and pants. He growled and kicked, waving his hands against the smoke. A third fire Witch joined and added her magic to the flames. The Legion howled as he succumbed to the raging inferno. He finally collapsed, the body of his host now burnt beyond all recognition.

Dayna screamed as another Legion hurled himself at the Air Witches creating a barrier between the Legion and the Crossroads. They crashed into a heap on the ground. The Legion grabbed the nearest Witch by the throat and crushed her neck. Before he could reach the next Witch, Bayek snatched him from the pile of bodies and tossed the limp host in the opposite direction from the Witches.

Velvet's scream joined Dayna's and pierced their bubble. A Legion breached the Vampires' defenses and attacked the Crossroads Witches. A flash of terror rushed through her when two Legion set upon Ryker, who had come to aid the fight. The scene descended into pure chaos.

Bodies littered the ground, and more were joining them. When a third Legion flew at Ryker, her terror escalated. How many had lost their lives already? How many more would die before this was over?

Something inside her snapped, shattering her inertia.

This ended now.

She crouched and placed her palms on the ground. Both Dayna and Velvet followed suit. The effort to contain the sudden build-up of energy made it difficult to breathe, and her words came out in an uneven pant.

"This is our last chance. Make it count."

She steadied her gaze at the standing stone and chanted. Dayna joined her. Velvet, a quick study, added her voice to the singsong mantra as they began their final assault. Layer upon layer, the magic flowed at the standing stone. Before long, the web weakened.

Strands pulled taut against the stone and shimmered in the moonlight. They faded and glowed brightly again before vanishing. At first, she was sure it was a trick of the light, but then a few delicate strands dulled and snapped. Before they could reach the ground, the strands disappeared in a puff of smoke.

"It's working," Dayna cried.

Velvet, eyes red-rimmed, implored, "How do you know?"

"We can see their links dissolve."

Velvet couldn't see what they could. Neither had Maize.

As their magic reached out and curled around the strands, she studied the web. They were making inroads, but it was taking too long. The web was fighting back.

"It's not enough."

"I don't think w-we have much more to give," Dayna's strained voice came out in pants.

"We have to try."

When the next strand broke, an incensed scream startled them. The husk of a body lay dead on the altar stone. The general had failed to bring the Legion through to the host in time.

Zahir stormed at them. "You!"

His fists were clenched, and he waved them viciously in the air as he closed the distance. Unlike his army, General Zahir was not physically repelled once he reached their personal protective wall. Instead, he beat his fists against it.

"You will pay for this."

She ignored him and continued drawing as much power from the earth as she was able. Too afraid to look in the coven's direction, she glanced over at her sister instead. The fear reflected in Dayna's expression mimicked her own as the general's voice boomed loud and clear.

"Kill them all!" Zahir ordered.

Not on my watch.

She pushed her palms against the ground with all the force she had left. She fanned her power out and drew deep into the earth. Instead of stopping at the sacred Tree of Life, the Earth Witches' familiar power source, she pushed deeper.

The source resisted. She instinctively pushed farther, not knowing where it would lead her, but certain she was following the right path. The moment she pushed through, her body convulsed at the sudden rush of power that hit her like a tidal wave.

A ripple of shock raced up her spine. This shouldn't be possible. Earth Witches pulled energy from the Tree of Life. The roots of which, in turn, were fed from the Axis Mundi. To connect directly to the Axis was unheard of. And yet, somehow, she had been granted a link to the connection between Heaven and Earth.

Using every ounce of energy, she drew the raw power up through the protective layers of the earth and allowed its magic to consume her. The instant the power entered her body, blinding agony wracked every nerve ending.

She pushed back a scream and struggled to her feet. This was their last stand. If she failed, not only would she suffer the same fate as her mother, but Leviathan would walk through the unlocked gate and reign down hell on earth. She planted her feet firmly on the ground to give her the stability she would need.

"I'll try and buffer you two from the bulk of it, but I suggest you hold on tight."

The pain rose a notch, and she found it difficult to breathe. She couldn't contain the storm much longer.

"What do you think you're doing?" Dayna shrieked.

Without answering, she raised her arms wide, closed her eyes, and dropped her head.

"No!" Dayna begged, her voice full of panic. "Whatever you're doing, stop!"

She opened a wider conduit into the Axis. The resulting rush of pure energy from the Axis almost knocked her off her feet. Some of the current surged through Dayna and Velvet, and they screamed. The next few moments played out in slow motion.

She had accessed something hidden from them for a reason. Their frail bodies couldn't cope with the speed and intensity that now surged through her and controlled every molecule.

She was on fire and frozen at the same time. Shards of lightning emerged from her body. The cracks as it made contact with the earth were deafening. Her body vibrated as pure energy surged through her.

Dayna's voice came from a million miles away. "Velvet, try and channel as much as you can. Don't let her take the entire burden."

The world around her blurred. The vibrations increased in intensity until she thought her teeth would rattle out of her head. The pain and the power reached their peaks.

It was time.

She brought her hands to her body then flung them out again, hurling the energy with as much force as she was able. A magical tsunami erupted from the earth and used her body as its channel to explode into the atmosphere.

Like a shock wave after the detonation of an atomic bomb, a destructive force pulsed and swept out from the circle, knocking everyone in its wake off their feet. Legion, Vampires, Witches, and Naturals. No one was spared.

A measure of the magical bomb used both Dayna and Velvet as a conduit to escape. She tried everything possible to minimize their exposure. From their contorted bodies as it flowed through them, she hadn't managed to buffer them enough.

She only hoped they were not irrevocably damaged. The sound of breaking glass pierced her hearing, and then everything fell silent. The barrier collapsed under the brute force of the magic as it punched through the Legion defenses.

The energy source came to an abrupt halt. Unable to hold herself up any longer, she crumpled to the ground. Her body ached, and the life energy slipped from her, seeping back into the earth. She had nothing left to give.

She had to have faith that Leviathan's access had been cut off. Dayna would know what to do now. It would be Dayna who would prepare the next generation to continue the fight. Her lids, too heavy to remain open, closed.

She would join her mother in an endless sleep. There were still many things she wished to experience in this life, but she had always known fate had other plans for her.

Too tired to fight, she gave herself over to her fate.

The incessant, high-pitched noise ringing in her ears nudged her, and her eyes fluttered open. Was dying supposed to be this loud? She raised her head and looked across at Dayna and Velvet, blood dripping from their ears and noses. They were still standing, confused, but alive. As her vision cleared, her heart skipped a beat. She pulled herself up and grimaced at the effort required to do something as simple as move. So, perhaps not dying then?

Something wet on the side of her face caught her attention, and she brought up her hand to touch her skin. It was hot to the touch, damp, and sticky. She pulled her hand away. Blood? Her fingers were coated in blood. When she looked up again, Dayna was beside her, her lips moving a mile a minute.

Apart from the high-pitched noise in her ears, she couldn't hear a thing. She shook her head to clear her mind. There were so many bodies. The blast radius had flattened everything in its path. Some of the bodies stirred and rose into a sitting position, confused expressions on their faces. Each one reflected the same question. What the hell had just happened?

With agonizing slowness, the Witches and Vampires rose to their feet and stood still as they took stock. A ray of hope washed through her. So far, no Legion had stirred.

Dayna's hands ran over Keira's arms as if searching for damage.

Kiera pushed Dayna away and she attempted to stand but fell straight back down again. A knot developed in her stomach as she took in the damage.

Ryker. She needed to find Ryker. He had to be okay.

She breathed a sigh of relief when Deacon nudged a downed Legion with his foot.

He turned to the others and said something she couldn't make out. From the sudden elation in the crowd, whatever he said was good news. Surely Ryker was safe, or Deacon would be searching for him.

Together, he and other Vampires began methodically checking all the bodies. From his somber expression, Deacon was not ready to celebrate just yet.

The ringing in her ears subsided, and the sounds gradually became less distorted so that she could make them out. Her gaze scanned the clearing for Ryker. Her stomach clenching tighter with each passing moment.

"Where are you," she whispered.

Dayna dropped to the ground and pulled her into a hug. "You did it." Dayna pushed her to arm's length, and tears ran down her face. "I thought we lost you."

Keira pushed her hair away from her face and tucked a strand behind her ear. In the madness, it had come away from the confines of her ponytail. "So did I."

She glanced around the clearing. "Where's Ryker

"Maize!" Zayne stumbled across the clearing and crumpled to the ground, where his wife's body lay.

Velvet's face lost all color, and she stood as still as a statue. How she could stand at all was a miracle. Having that much energy coursing through her body was more stress than anyone could bear. When Velvet's body let go of the shock— the grief and fatigue would consume her. The loss of her mother, so quickly after the loss of her sister, would take its toll on her already-fragile soul.

When she looked back to her sister, Dayna, too, was struggling to understand what had happened.

"Is it really over?" Dayna's voice came out in a whisper.

Keira held back her answer. What if she was wrong? The Vampires were still sifting through the downed bodies. While most of the Witches and Vampires were standing, perhaps the Legion were still alive, merely unconscious.

Unease pricked her.

Ryker? Where was Ryker?

Panic welled from the pit of her stomach. Her gaze darted to the outlying wooded area. Only a few fires had survived the blast. She winced as she stood. Perhaps using her limbs was not such a good idea, but she needed to find Ryker. He had to be okay. She wouldn't accept that he was anything other than alive and well.

"You." She froze when an ominous voice cursed her. "You are responsible for this."

She swung around in time to see General Zahir appear from the pit where the blast had thrown him.

Rage exuded from every pore in his body.

She reached into herself and tried to erect a protective barrier between him and the survivors. She came up empty. Her reserves were depleted.

"I can't summon anything, not even a simple spell," Dayna said shakily, backing away. "What are we going to do?"

She braced as Zahir picked up speed and descended on them. She pushed Dayna behind her. If she drew the brunt of his rage, her sister would have a chance to get away. She raised her arms to ward off the bulk of his initial attack.

From somewhere to her left, a primal snarl cut through the general's tirade. This was quickly followed by something hurtling through the air. Instead of the expected assault, the general was knocked off his feet. The two bodies rolled on the ground and landed in an awkward heap a short distance away. When they separated, she hauled in a breath.

Ryker. He was alive.

The two men were on their feet in an instant. Arms akimbo, they circled each other. Gone was the easy-going and brash Ryker she knew. In his place was a savage creature intent on drawing blood.

The general, a good head and shoulders taller than Ryker, saw his chance and hurled himself at the Vampire. Zahir miscalculated Ryker's agility and floundered when the Vampire deftly evaded his attack.

As Zahir rushed by, Ryker grabbed him by his hair and yanked. The sudden jolt to his head toppled the general. Ryker tossed him like a sack of potatoes, and he flew through the air.

Dayna punched a fist toward the sky. "You show him who's boss, McSexy."

Despite his massive build, General Zahir arched his back and landed on his feet a short distance away.

Once he regained his feet, he turned his attention to Ryker.

Dayna snorted. "Crap!"

Keira let out a cry when Zahir landed a punch to Ryker's midriff. He doubled over, winded. She clenched her fists to summon the fireballs that had been effective against the Legion. But no matter how hard she tried, she didn't have the reserves for magic.

Deacon materialized beside them. "Do not fear. He is fine." He smiled down at her. "If I thought he couldn't handle this, I would intervene." Deacon nodded at Ryker. "Watch."

Sure enough, the moment General Zahir came near, Ryker led with a powerful right hook to the Legion's jaw. A flurry of punches pushed Zahir backward.

From beside her, she heard Dayna's sharp intake of breath.

"Watch out!" Dayna warned. "Amos is alive!"

They had been so focused on the fight, they failed to notice Amos slithering over to the prisoners. When he realized he was being watched, he cocked his arm and launched something at them.

"It's a grenade!" someone shouted.

Ryker swept her into his arms and made a mad dash for the woods. Deacon rushed Dayna and Velvet to safety. In a flurry of dust and swirling breezes, the remaining Vampires carried the rest of the Witches away from the clearing.

Her feet touched the ground at the same time the grenade bounced into the clearing. Her shoulders relaxed when, instead of the expected explosion, an angry hiss burst from the weapon, filling the clearing with smoke.

A second cannister quickly followed and turned the area into a murky gray mass.

When the smoke cleared, both Amos and General Zahir were gone. Ryker moved to follow them, but Deacon blocked his path. "Leave them. We have more pressing needs. Leviathan's not coming through, and they have nothing left to assist her."

One by one, they stepped into the clearing and took stock of the battle toll. Bodies littered the war zone. How would they explain the nearly one hundred dead?

The last of the gas dissolved into the night air, and Zayne's form, protecting his dead wife from harm, was almost too much for her to bear. Her legs threatened to give way. The grief consumed what little reserves she had left.

A light touch caressed her shoulder, and she was pulled into strong arms. Ryker rested her head against his chest and stroked her hair.

"Hey, you can't get all weepy on me now. I have a bone to pick with you, and I can't get on my high horse when you're all puffy-eyed."

She smiled and half-sobbed at the same time.

Ryker tightened his grip. "I told you no heroics, Doc. Poor Trudeau nearly lost an arm when you pulled that stunt."

She pushed him away so she could look at him. "You caught Leon?"

Ryker nodded. "Technically, Mitos did. We were securing him behind that tree when the Brother Superior ..." Ryker faltered, and his voice cracked.

She knew the words he couldn't finish.

Killed Maize. When the Order's Brother Superior took the life of his friend.

She summoned all her reserves to stay upright. "Where is he?"

Not only had the Brother Superior taken Maize's life, as well as other Witches, Leon had killed Marcus and most probably Annie. The knowledge would haunt her the rest of her days.

Ryker wrapped an arm around her shoulders, and she leaned into him. She didn't have the strength to walk far under her own steam. As they approached the small band of prisoners, Mitos booted Leon in the leg. The former deputy cried out in pain.

Mitos' grunted and threw another kick for good measure. "You're lucky I don't aim higher, you fucktard. If it weren't illegal, I'd shoot you in your cahoonas and feed them to the wolves. But I can't force myself to feed the poor animals garbage."

Just as quickly as her anger rose, it subsided. Her body didn't have the strength required to stay upright and hold onto a powerful emotion at the same time. Bright lights swirled in front of her vision as the ringing returned. Her legs wobbled and threatened to give way. She didn't have the energy to demand the justice Marcus and the others deserved. Not yet, not while she could barely stand on her own.

Ryker swept her up before she hit the ground. She rested her head on his shoulder and mumbled, "I'm so tired." Her words came out slurred. Even her tongue was exhausted.

Ryker nuzzled her hair and kissed the top of her head. "I know, Doc, you take a breather. You've just saved the world. Let us handle the rest."

THIRTY-TWO
UNWRITTEN

Ryker's phone rang just as he reached the front door. A quick glance confirmed Deacon was finally returning his call.

"Did it work?" he asked as he tossed his keys on the front table and headed towards his wing of the house to change. "Did they buy Dayna's disguise?"

"Yes. The FBI and the Boston PD believed it was Dr. Keira Wynter delivering the profile. Dayna gave them all the clues they needed, and they should be raiding the building within the next ten minutes. I imagine the news of the recovery of the missing tourists, the arrest of their abductors and the people responsible for the deaths of dozens more will hit the news in less than thirty minutes. With any luck, a huge portion of the media camped out at Mystery Hill will leave en masse to Boston."

Ryker rubbed his temples. Dayna had reluctantly pretended to be Keira so they could provide sufficient information for the Boston PD to locate the building he, Deacon and Bayek had kept Trudeau and the others in while they worked out their next steps.

He only hoped when Trudeau and the other members of the Order were questioned by the FBI, the interviews would go the way they planned.

So much had been riding on the ability of two strangers. Witches and Vampires had played their part in the battle, but it was going to require the abilities of Gifted to ensure the secrecy of it. The body count after the battle at Mystery Hill was too high to explain away without raising too many questions. In addition to the bodies of nearly eighty dead tourists, the battle had taken the lives of five Witches and six Vampires, with a lot more injured.

In the aftermath of the battle, the remaining Vampires, Witches, and lone Human, came to a unanimous decision. There was no way to hide that many bodies. They needed a way to explain the massacre without revealing their involvement, including any evidence of a battle.

Twenty-seven Legion had perished during the fighting. Each with varying degrees of physical injury from third degree burns to broken necks. Fifty-two Legion had dropped dead when Keira unleashed her power. Not one had any visible markings to explain away the death. The Vampires would need to dispose of the twenty-seven before the authorities turned up.

And then there were the members of the Order that didn't get away. The Witches had freed thirteen tourists and captured seven members of the Order, including Trudeau. There was no way of knowing how many had fled.

The tourists not yet turned into Legion were the least of their problems. Heavily sedated, they were pliable and any story the tourist were fed, would be believed once the drug left their systems.

The Order wasn't so easy. After heated discussion on whether to simply kill them, the Witches offered an alternate solution.

The authorities were on a state-wide manhunt to find the people responsible for the deaths at Mystery Hill. While

Deacon wanted justice for the loss of dozens of innocent people, he wasn't prepared to release the Order into the hands of the FBI. Who knew what the FBI would make of Trudeau and the others account of what occurred at Mystery Hill. The risk was too high to the Supernatural community.

A small contingent of the Witches pointed out that the problem could be solved by erasing the Order's memory of the battle. They would need to retain full memory of the atrocities they committed, just not any knowledge of the battle between the Legion and the Supernaturals. That way, justice could be served without the Witches and Vampires having to answer any difficult questions regarding their being present at Mystery Hill.

The Witches proposing the solution declared that to do this, all they needed was at least two Supernaturals with the ability to manipulate memories.

While the plan was sound, the challenge was finding two Gifted with this rare ability. With very little time to spare, the scene at Mystery Hill was cleared of all bodies and evidence, save the fifty-two dead bodies with no visible marks. The tourists still alive, as well as Trudeau and the rest of the Order, were transported to an abandoned warehouse in Boston while a search for their two memory changing Gifted began. In less than four hours they were located. The only problem: one resided in Japan, the other New Zealand.

Ryker reached his room and put his phone on speaker before rummaging for clean clothes. "And what about Nikau and Himari. Where are they now?"

The logistics of getting two Gifted from the far corners of the globe to Boston in the shortest amount of time was more difficult than he ever thought possible. Not to mention making sure they were both fully aware of what memories required manipulation. Everything was hinging on Trudeau and the others taking responsibility for the deaths and forgetting any memory of the battle.

"They're okay. Physically and mentally exhausted, but they both assure me they'll recover fully with some rest. Nita and the rest of the Crossroads Coven will keep them safe and away from prying eyes until they can travel home," Deacon said. He let out an audible exhausted breath. "How did it go with the Medical Examiner?"

Ryker slipped on a clean shirt. "As stellar as you'd expect with the media, families and the governor expecting answers. At least he released Maize and the other Witches bodies. Ananya and Mitos are helping Zayne and the others with funeral arrangements."

Finished changing, he reached for his glasses and cap. God, he felt physically and mentally tired. The past few days were taking its toll. Zayne would be burying his wife less than a week after he'd buried his daughter. No wonder his friend was beside himself with grief.

Three days. It had only been three days since the summer solstice and the battle at Mystery Hill. His chest ached. They had won. But the price had been high. Too high.

"We were lucky the medical examiner released the bodies he did. I don't think the families of the other fifty-two victims are going to be as lucky," Deacon said.

The law required a death certificate. In order for a certificate to be issued, the medical examiner needed the cause, the mechanism and the manner of death. Which the medical examiner was finding it difficult to do. Fifty-two of the victims had no visible marks or obvious cause of death, and the bloodwork showed no known drugs in their system. There didn't appear to be a checkbox for *just dropped dead*.

Ryker headed out the door of his room. There was still so much to do in aftermath of the battle to keep the Vampires and Witches involvement secret. "At the moment I'm putting the unexplained deaths into a problem for tomorrow. We've put a lid on the powder keg for now, but the General and Brother Superior are still out there."

Somehow, what remained of the Order and the Legion had eluded capture. The Vampires had scoured every inch of the state and come up empty. Even the Witches had tried to scry for their whereabouts. It was as if they had vanished off the face of the earth.

"Have faith, justice will be served for what they did. We will find them. It is only a matter of time," Deacon said. "Bayek and his team are more than capable of tracking the General down. Our focus must be on keeping the FBI, media and public from looking too closely at us. The Supernatural community is grieving, we need to give them the space to do so without interference from outside eyes."

Ryker rubbed his jaw. Easier said than done. "That's becoming impossible for some of them. Reporters have set up camp outside Zayne's house. He and Violet can't walk out their door without the press snapping photos and asking inane questions. Jacob was discharged from hospital for his wound's yesterday and the same thing happened to him as he was wheeled out the front door."

"It will die down. These things always do. Dayna's working with the Witches to make sure everyone's stories are aligned … which reminds me," Deacon's voice softened. "How's Keira today? Any change?"

Ryker closed his eyes and held back the flash of terror that swept across him. "No."

Keira had been unconscious for three days and was showing no signs of coming out of it anytime soon. No one could explain how or why, and it was impossible to run tests on her. It pained him to see her lying there like that. What if she never recovered? His stress levels were off the charts and he didn't know which way was up anymore. The crowded emotions that now filled his day confused him more than anything. He neither needed nor wanted them. His life was complicated enough.

"Have faith. She's strong. It's just a matter of time," Deacon said.

Ryker's throat ran dry and he raked a hand through his hair. She had to recover. He wouldn't accept anything else.

"Have you heard from Bayek?" he asked.

Deacon let out a low snort. "Stop changing the subject. You've been unbearable for the past three days. Just admit you've fallen for Keira. It's not a sign of weakness to let someone in every now and then. And besides, she's the only one that doesn't put up with your crap."

Ryker's shoulders stiffened. "I don't know what you are talking about."

The words sounded so hollow they both knew he was lying.

"I'll call you later. There's a vigil up at Mystery Hill for the victims and I'm shorthanded."

He hung up and stared at the spot on the table by his car keys absently. How the hell had Keira gotten so far under his skin? He didn't need this complication in his life.

Just as he was about to turn the door handle, the sound of racing footsteps caught his attention.

Dayna halted on the top step when she spotted him. "She's waking up."

He was up the stairs before she finished the sentence. A moment later he stood just inside the door of her room. Frozen to the spot, he stared at Keira's sleeping form. Her face was pale with dark shadows under her eyes, a stark contrast to her mane of red hair fanned across the pillow.

Ryker's pulse quickened. Their comatose patient was letting out a low moan and Keira's body stiffened into the pillow as if in pain.

Dayna's eyes brimmed with unshed tears as she perched on the side of the bed and held onto Keira's hand. "It's all right. We're here."

Ryker held back, despite all his instincts wanting to reach out and ease her pain.

He let out a deep exhale when Keira relaxed into the pillow and the moaning subsided. She opened her eyelids, or, at least, she tried to. They were halfway open when she snapped them shut. "This has got to be the worst hangover ever."

Her voice came out croaky and dry.

Dayna let out a muffled cry of relief and brushed away her tears with the back of her hand.

Ryker's body let go of the pent-up tension. It took all of his willpower not to pull Keira into his arms and breathe her in to assure himself she was going to be okay.

"I can't remember drinking though," Keira mumbled.

Her eyes flew open. "Maize."

The midday sun's rays streamed into the room and she blinked a few times to adjust to the light. "The gate. We need to stop Leviathan from coming through the gate."

Keira struggled to sit up and let out a small cry as her sore and weakened body failed to comply. She fell back into the soft bedding with a painful groan.

Ryker's stomach lurched. "What's the matter, are you okay?" he asked as he rushed towards the bed, his gaze scanning her body for any visible injury.

Keira brought up an arm to cover her upper face. "Did I get hit by a freight train?"

Dayna giggled as she sat on the bed and reached for Keira's free hand. "Close. You and that magical weapon of mass destruction you conjured were the freight train."

Keira frowned and pulled her arm away from her face. "For Pete's sake, what are you talking about?"

Her muscles clenched and her lips drew into a thin line. She snapped her eyes shut again, hissed through her teeth and hauled in a breath.

Ryker looked helplessly at Dayna. "She's in pain. We have to get her to a hospital." Panic tinge his voice as fear surged through his veins.

"I'm fine, stop fussing." Keira made another attempt to raise herself. "Amos and General Zahir? Did you manage to track them down? And what about the bodies, we need to work out how to deal with the carnage that was left behind." Keira turned to Dayna. "What about the gate? Did you make sure it's secure?"

Dayna pushed on Keira's shoulders and forced her back down. "Relax, sis, it's all sorted."

"How could it be sorted this quickly? It'll take more than a couple of hours to work out what to do next."

He chuckled at her confusion. If she was asking this many questions, she was clearly on the mend. "You've been out for three days."

"Three days? I slept for three days?"

"Calm down, or you'll fall back into that coma," Dayna said. She reached for another pillow and placed it behind Kiera's head to raise her a little. "We had a doctor come in and run some tests. You used up every reserve you had, and the best we can tell, your body shut down to repair itself."

Dayna shook her head. "With all that kerfuffle you pulled when you were out of it, you certainly scared us. In the end, Ryker had to draw your blood. I couldn't look at the needle without wanting to throw up. We were lucky the doctor was Gifted and didn't freak out too much. We did warn him, but you know how it is, typical man, he thinks he knows everything." Dayna grinned and chuckled. "When he was thrown halfway across the room and landed flat on his ass, that showed him he knew diddly-squat."

Keira forehead crinkled. "Stop. Just stop, will you? You're not making any sense."

After glancing at Ryker, Dayna's face morphed into a self-satisfied grin. "Oh, that's right, you have no idea what you did, do you?"

The terror Ryker had lived with for three days evaporated and he sat down on the bed opposite Dayna. His need to touch

Keira outmatched his resolve and he reached out and took her hand. Her pulse, steady and strong provided him a measure of comfort.

He smiled and met her confused gaze. "The moment you fell unconscious, a barrier locked into place and surrounded you like an aura. Only Dayna could see it."

Keira's eyes widened. She turned back to face Dayna. "But I didn't place a protection spell, and I certainly didn't have enough time to transfer the spell to an external object to allow it to stay in place while I was out of it."

"What do you remember?" Ryker asked.

"I remember seeing Trudeau and the others bound and gagged. I remember becoming so tired, I could barely keep my eyes open. It all becomes blank after that."

Dayna giggled. "Well, Hon, you fell, and Ryker caught you just as the weird shit hit the fan."

Weird shit was an understatement. Ryker still struggled with wrapping his head around how what happened was possible.

"I didn't see when things got out of control. Otherwise, I might have been able to stop Vincent from suffering as much as he did." Unable to sit still, Dayna readjusted the pillows. "After Ryker made sure you were still breathing, he needed to help with the spill on aisle three."

"Go on," Keira prompted.

"Ryker wasn't keen to leave you near that weasel, Trudeau, so he asked Vincent to get you and me safely back to the house and wait with us while they sorted things out. The moment Vincent approached, there was an unexpected incident." Dayna picked at a cuticle, and her lips pursed together in a grim line. "I blame myself, really. I was so focused on the chaos that I didn't pay attention until it was too late ..." Dayna trailed off.

"Don't stop there, too late for what?"

Ryker squeezed Keira's hand at the memory. "The moment I tried to transfer you into Vincent's arms, Vincent's body spasmed uncontrollably. Like he was being electrocuted."

"Had I been paying attention, I would have noticed the crimson aura around you earlier. Ryker pulled you back and away from Vincent before he became burnt toast," Dayna said.

Keira inhaled sharply. "Is he okay?"

"He's a Vampire." Ryker shrugged. "What do you think?"

"Anyhow, turns out, the only two people who could get beyond the aura barrier were Ryker and me," Dayna said.

Keira shook her head as if in denial. "Are you sure it was my invocation and not something else? If I was unconscious, I couldn't have cast that sort of spell."

"Well, it certainly wasn't *my* spell that was turning everyone into crispy critters."

Keira groaned. "Who else did I hurt?"

Dayna giggled. "The only person who thought it was a hoot was Mitos. He decided there was a timer on your barrier and that he needed to test the theory. He kept pushing Trudeau in your path. While I have to admit it was a great punishment and Mitos is the strangest person you'll ever meet, it got a bit old very quickly. By the time the doctor bounced off you and electrocuted himself, it wasn't even mildly amusing."

Ryker pulled a stray strand away from Keira's face. "Don't blame yourself. It was a natural self-preservation instinct. Dayna and I delt with it." He gave her a wink. "I even managed to give you a bed bath or two."

Keira's cheeks grew red and her eyes flew wide. "You didn't!"

"Your runes are still safe." Ryker grinned. "For now."

Keira readjusted herself to get more comfortable. "How's Zayne, Velvet, and the others? Did you catch the General and Brother Superior?"

Ryker paused before answering. Not sure just how much he should tell her. "Velvet's fine. She's still a little weak, but she's recovering. The damage is more emotional than physical." He exhaled slowly and his eyes dropped to stare at the fine veins on Keira's wrist. "Zayne's not taking Maize's death very well and I'm worried about his state of mind."

"Everyone is," Dayna said. "But you can't do any more for him than you already are. You're burning the candle at both ends as it is, and I'm sure he appreciates you being there for him each night."

Keira let out a gasp of pain, sank into the pillow and her faced crinkled in agony.

Dayna pointed to the bedside table nearest Ryker. "Quick the meds."

In an instant Ryker's arm slid behind Keira shoulders and pulled her to a half-sitting position against his body. "Here, take this," he said.

Keira reached for the proffered glass of water. He handed her two small white pills.

"Your body still needs time to recover," Dayna said. "If your head's anything like mine was, you'll need these painkillers to sleep it off while your batteries recharge."

Keira downed the meds and handed back the empty glass. "Isn't there a spell to make this all go away?"

Dayna shrugged. "Been there, done that, and it doesn't work. Until a few hours ago, even the simplest of spells eluded me. I suspect that it'll take a few more days before we have access to our full power again. Even then, I don't know if we'll be able to tap into our new powers."

Keira fell back into Ryker's arms and rested her head against his chest. The lines on her face belied the pain she was experiencing. Her heart rate while in her coma had been a steady fifty-five beats per minute. Now it was erratic and faster than he would like. Ryker bent his head down to breathe her in.

Deacon was right. She was going to be fine. "Your body is still weak. You need to rest."

Reluctantly, he slid her back down to the pillow. His desire to protect her battled with his need to continue the search for the General and Amos and seek justice for Annie, Maize and the rest of the Order's victims. "I'll check in on you this evening before I head over to Zayne's." He smoothed her hair while searching her face to satisfy himself she wasn't about to fall back into unconsciousness.

Her eyes fluttered closed and she nestled her face against his hand. "I'm so tired," she whispered.

A moment later she was asleep.

Dayna placed a hand on Ryker's shoulder. "Watching my sister sleep is not going to make her recover any faster. Believe me, I've tried that already."

Ryker stood and reached for his cap and glasses. "If Keira's condition changes, or you need anything—"

Dayna cut him off. "I'll phone you. We've done this dance everyday for the past three days. You've got enough on your plate to worry about. Everything here is fine. She's awake now and just needs to rest. You and she can sort through the funky dance you've both been skirting around once this is all over."

Ryker froze. "I don't know what you're talking about."

Dayna's only reply was a roll of her eyes.

Not wanting to move any further into the conversation, he left the room and headed to his car. There was so much that still needed to be done to sort through the after affects of the Mystery Hill disaster. He had a county to protect and a responsibility to keep secrets hidden away from the outside world.

What he didn't need was a red headed Witch who took up more of his thoughts than he deemed safe.

THIRTY-THREE

GREEN EYED MONSTER

Two more days passed before Keira regained enough strength to physically stand on her own, and another day after that before she had the strength to get downstairs under her own steam. She spent the better part of the day dealing with the constant barrage of messages and emails filling her inbox. The massacre made national news, and everyone wanted inside information. As expected, the university wanted to know when she planned to return. She had already been away far too long for their liking.

The case was now over, and the university officials were applying pressure for her to return to her duties. Though only implied, they wanted to take advantage of the fact she was instrumental in tracking down and apprehending the Mystery Hill killers. Something the university would be milking for months, if not years, to come.

The case and her involvement would mean massive exposure for the university, not to mention the potential cash flow from new sponsors and benefactors. She could never understand how people took advantage of the misfortunes of others in such a callous manner. Money was truly the root of all evil.

Not wanting to deal with the politics of university life just yet, she dressed and headed downstairs. She followed the sound of Dayna's voice and found her in the large family room that opened to the kitchen. She stopped and gasped at the sight of all the flowers, plants, fruit baskets, and plates of food littering the usually immaculate room. Her sister was on the phone, hopping from foot to foot. Something had excited her.

Keira wandered over to the counter and made herself a cup of green tea, just as Dayna finished the call and let out an animated squeal.

"Good news?"

"You could say that." Dayna stuffed the phone into her pocket. "Lovely weather we're having."

Keira narrowed her eyes. Dayna was not known for keeping secrets. This only meant one of two things. A man was involved, or it was something she would disapprove of.

"How did your call with the principal go?" Dayna asked innocently.

Her sister was avoiding the subject. It's a man she wouldn't approve of, Keira decided.

"Department chair."

Dayna would break. It was only a matter of time.

"I haven't spoken to him yet." She pointed to the lack of counter space. "What's all this?"

Dayna smiled. "When the Supernaturals found out what happened, things just started turning up. We've now got everything from free-range eggs to homemade lasagna to knitted beanies. Everyone wanted to show how much they appreciated what we did."

Keira groaned out loud. "And here I was hoping we'd come in under the radar."

Dayna lifted her shoulders. "That was never an option once we decided to let Vampires and Witches in on a history lesson. I even had a little kid come up to me on the street yesterday and hug me. It was the strangest thing you've ever seen. She appeared out of nowhere, threw her arm around me, squeezed, and then ran off." Dayna half-snorted, half-laughed. "All I need now is a string of sexy, half-naked men to do the same, and I'll be in Heaven. Their gifts I won't want to return."

Keira frowned. "I didn't think it would get out so quickly."

"Well, it has. Even Deacon has stopped grumbling about the number of people appearing on his doorstep bearing gifts."

She sat down on the oversized couch. Dayna sat down opposite her and fidgeted.

"I gather no one's back yet?" Keira asked.

"No. Bayek and Makeda are still scouring the area for any clue as to where Zahir and Amos might be. Bayek and Deacon are pretty determined to track that Legion down. From what I can gather, there's some bad blood between them."

Keira was not surprised. The general had given her the impression he recognized many of the Primordial Vampires fighting against his Legion. She took a sip and stared at her cup.

She tried to keep her voice even. "What about Deacon and Ryker?"

She hadn't laid eyes on Ryker since the day she'd come out of her coma. In the fleeting moments when he came home to check on her, she'd been sleeping. She questioned his timing. Was it deliberate? Was he actively avoiding her? Each time she'd awakened to discover she had just missed him. Often, she didn't need to be told he'd been close. His familiar scent lingered in her room well after he departed.

Dayna checked her watch. "Who knows? Could be any moment, could be hours. The backlash over this hasn't been pretty.

Keira's phone beeped, and she scrunched up her nose. Steve, the department chair, was nothing if not persistent. The university had set up a special lecture on cult killers for her the following week, and the message implied it was not optional on her part.

She sat back on the couch as she scanned the room, which was filled to the brim with gifts from strangers. The stark difference between life in LA and the life the Supernaturals led in Salem and the surrounding areas was not lost on her.

Dayna looked up. "Bad news?"

"I've got to get back to Berkeley."

"Can't you stay a little longer? With all that's been going on, we haven't had a chance to catch up."

"I would love to, but I've got students to worry about. I've already been away too long." She tucked her legs under her butt. "Why don't you come with me? You can as easily get a flight back to the UK from LA as you can from Boston. It might be nice to spend some time without the Leviathan drama."

"It was intense, wasn't it?"

"So what about it?"

The way in which Dayna suddenly fell silent had her on high alert.

Dayna avoided eye contact. "Actually, I was thinking about sticking around here for a while. Nothing is tying me to Europe, and the coven needs help …" Dayna trailed off. She cleared her throat. "I've found the perfect house not far from here. It's a bit of a fixer-upper, but it's perfect, and the owners are willing to sell it for a reasonable price."

Keira recalled the conversation she'd interrupted. It took a moment for the information to sink in. Even when it did, she still couldn't believe it.

So that's who she was on the phone to.

"Are you sure that's what you want to do?"

Her sister was impetuous, but to move back to Massachusetts? After all this time?

"I had a few days to think about it, and it feels right. Besides …" Dayna winked. "The place has a lot more to offer than a few hundred years ago."

Keira groaned and facepalmed. "I'm not sure the male population is aware of what's about to hit them."

Dayna giggled and twirled a strand of hair around her finger. "I'm going to enjoy educating them then. Starting with those very hunky specimens at the Salem Fire Department."

"Which one in particular?"

Dayna waved her hand dismissively. "All of them, silly. Maybe not all at the same time … actually …" She grinned, and an impish expression overtook her features.

Keira held up her hand. "Stop right there. I don't need to hear anymore."

Dayna's expression turned serious. "The other reason is that I can't leave the Crossroads coven so exposed. They are still nowhere near where they should be power-wise. The gate's sealed, but with Amos and that general running free, who knows for how long." She fingered the amethyst on her bracelet. "And you heard Bayek, the stones chose us as protectors. I can't walk away from that."

That was something that played on her conscience as well. They had lost coven members, and the ones left were not in a position to defend the entryway between hell and earth. At least with Dayna there, they would have a fighting chance. Something she recognized as guilt pricked at the back of her mind. She sniped at her inner voice. *I've played my part.* With Dayna here, she had no reason to stay.

Are you sure about that? She ignored the bizarre inner conversation and refocused on her sister. "Well, at least we'll be in the same country."

Dayna smiled and tilted her head. "Why don't you stay as well? There's more than one fireman to go around. I'm not that greedy. Or maybe you prefer a different kind of uniform?"

Keira shifted and swung her legs to the floor. She was not having this conversation with her sister or even thinking about it. "You know I must return to work. Some of us don't have the luxury of just up and moving on a whim."

"Suit yourself then. Your loss. If you want to ignore the obvious, who am I to stand in your way?"

Dayna's phone rang. From the way she bolted from the chair, the call had something to do with the house she was interested in. Sure enough, her sister's mile-a-minute bubbly voice coerced someone named Bradley into a showing the next day.

Keira picked up her phone and scanned her messages. Not able to put off the conversation any longer, she made her way up to her room and placed a call to her department head, Steve, before he scheduled any more special lectures and interviews. He'd already lined up enough events that she would have no voice left.

Keira was on edge for the remainder of the day. The conversation with Steve hadn't gone as expected. In fact, she didn't know who had been more surprised, her or Steve, when she gave notice. But now she had done it, there was no turning back. She rearranged the flower bouquets at least three times and managed to get all the food into the fridge. That alone was an achievement, since she'd packed in at least twice the volume the manufacturer deemed safe.

Mother Earth, had she made the right decision? What had possessed her to make such a rash impromptu decision to return to Salem permanently?

She dropped her head into her hands and groaned. How was she going to break it to Dayna?

"Are you well?" Bayek asked.

Keira let out a small squeak at his unexpected arrival. The Vampires really did need to come with bells attached. "All good."

She glanced between Bayek and Makeda. "Any luck finding the General?"

Bayek shook his head. "His whereabouts still eludes us. But it is only a matter of time."

Dayna breezed through the door, a wide smile on her face when she spotted the new arrivals. "I thought I heard a car coming up the driveway."

They gravitated towards the large family room as Bayek gave them a run down of the days events. While Makeda was not much of a talker, Bayek more than made up for it. He spent most of his time flirting with her and Dayna. By the time Deacon returned home, Bayek even managed to relax her frayed nerves.

Deacon walked in and smiled at her. "Welcome back to the land of the living. It's nice to see you up and about this late in the day. For a while, you had us a little concerned."

"Nonsense, my friend," Bayek said as he waved a glass in the air. "She was never in danger. Did you not see the range of her power? Even the Legion were unable to best her."

Deacon gratefully accepted the glass of bourbon Dayna offered him. "That does not mean she and Dayna are invincible. Even they must comply with the laws of physics and nature. There is a limit to what their bodies can endure, and I believe that point was almost reached."

He took up a position near the patio door, looked over at Dayna, and then swung his gaze to her. The strain from the past few days was evident in his haggard expression. Whatever aftermath had erupted was enough to faze the normally stoic Vampire.

His features softened, and a hint of a smile flashed across his face. "I know I haven't had a chance to say it, but your mother would have been proud of both of you."

The back of her throat became parched, and she took another sip of her wine to ease the discomfort. That someone other than Dayna and her remembered their mother and the legacy she left behind was a strange experience.

"So, sleeping beauty finally arises."

Keira's head whipped around to face Ryker.

He pulled off his cap and sunglasses and tossed them onto the nearest chair. He grinned as he made his way toward her. "You know, they lied when they said a kiss would wake the princess. All you did was snore."

She nearly choked on her drink at his jibe. "You didn't. I don't."

He winked at her distress. "If you say so." He nodded in Deacon's direction. "I hear you had words with the governor today."

Thankful the conversation had drifted away from her and onto more serious matters, she studied Ryker's profile. He was standing close enough for her to breathe in his distinct masculine scent. The same one that had been taunting her for the past few days. Images of being safely nestled in his arms, secure in the knowledge he would keep her safe pushed forward. The first one just after the battle and the second when she awoke. Was that why her unconscious state allowed him to pass through her protective aura?

She was not stubborn enough to deny her physical attraction to him. The sexual charge was off the charts. Should she throw caution to the wind and let whatever had been building between them just happen?

A surge of lust rushed up from her core as she recalled the panty-dropping kiss he'd laid on her just before the battle. She wanted to cash in on that kiss's promise and damn the consequences. She was torn, should she have her wicked way with him before or after she let him and Dayna know of her decision? A hot flush brushed across her skin. Had she made the right choice? Impulsive as it was, it felt right two hours ago. Now? Now she wasn't sure.

She had been so engrossed in her inner fantasy, she failed to notice everyone was looking expectantly at her.

"Sorry," she said. "I must be more tired than I thought. Can you repeat that?"

"We were just wondering where you think the Order may head next," Deacon said. "Will they stay close by or try another gate?"

"I think we need to assume both. They were close to getting Leviathan out, and the fact they have Legion on this side gives them options."

Bayek nodded. "I concur. We were considering our options for warning the Vampires guarding the other Crossroads covens. It wouldn't be right to keep this to ourselves."

She'd been having the same thoughts. From Dayna's expression, so had her sister. "I don't think we have the luxury of hiding any longer. The only way forward is to let both the covens and the guardian Vampires know of the danger."

Ryker crossed his arms. "I know this is not going to sit well with either side, but we need to stop the invisible barrier between Vampires and Witches at the gates. If this battle has taught us anything, we're only going to win if we stand together. There can't be any more secrets."

The room fell silent.

Keira took a deep breath. He was right. For too long, they had stood alone. All it did was reduce their numbers and blur the lines between truth and myth.

Dayna quickly came to stand beside her, reached for her hand, and squeezed. "What do you think?"

She locked eyes with her sister. This decision would impact them the most. The lives they'd carved out for themselves would be gone forever. She reached up to cup Dayna's face and smiled. She didn't need her sister to tell her what she believed they should do. It was all over Dayna's expressive face. Her hand dropped away, and she turned back to Ryker, Deacon, and Bayek.

"No more secrets."

Bayek gave her a curt nod. "And so, a new age begins."

"And not without its challenges." Deacon's expression was somber. "How are we going to warn covens if we don't know where they all are?"

Dayna groaned. "There are twelve gates. In addition to Mystery Hill and Stonehenge, we only know of one other location. While we know where some of the gates are, the covens will be difficult to track down."

Keira listened to the conversation for a few minutes before the world started to spin. She sat down before she fell down. She hated to admit it, but she still had a way to go before she was fully recovered.

Ryker perched on the armrest and frowned down on her. "Are you sure you should be up?"

"I feel fine. Stop fussing."

"Don't overdo it."

She rolled her eyes. "Yes, mother."

"Hey, you're the one who had the death wish. Even your sister had granny naps during the day, and she only got a portion of what you did."

"I heard that," Dayna called. "And they're called power naps."

Ryker chuckled and scratched the back of his head. "At your age, they are definitely called granny naps."

Dayna stuck out her tongue at Ryker. "If I still had my nifty new powers, I'd transport your clothes outside, and then we'd see who's all wrinkly and shriveled."

"You wish."

Deacon cleared his throat and interrupted the banter before it got out of hand. "Before I forget, there's going to be a memorial for all the victims early next week. Do you think you'll be up to attending?"

Dayna, who had moved to stand between Deacon and Bayek, tucked her arm under Deacon's and patted him. "Of course, we will. Whatever you need help with, just let us know."

Keira's gaze darted around the room, and she swallowed. This was not the way she had intended to tell them. "Um … I won't be able to attend. Sorry. I'm booked on a flight to LA tomorrow afternoon."

The room fell quiet as if the air had suddenly been sucked from it.

Both Ryker and Dayna shouted in unison. "What?"

If only a hole appeared in the ground and allowed her to disappear into it. She fingered the amulet around her neck. "I have students who depend on me. I've taken too much time out of the term already, and any more will disadvantage them."

Dayna placed her hands on her hips and stamped her foot. "And when the hell were you going to tell me?"

She winced. Her sister sounded more hurt than angry. Guilt ate away at her. She should have told Dayna the moment she made her decision. Not just the fact she needed to return immediately to the university, but her decision to return to Salem for good. "It all happened so quickly. I haven't had a chance to tell you my plans. I was going to talk to you about it later tonight."

Deacon cleared his throat. "Before we get too carried away, I suggest we put things in perspective. Keira's being here was at Ryker's and my request, and originally only for a few days. I can understand the university's reluctance at having a faculty member away for so long." He turned to her. "I am assuming you're not able to take a leave of absence?"

She shook her head. "I've already used up the maximum time allowed for an entire year, just in the past three weeks."

She left out the remainder of the terse conversation with the vice chancellor and her head of department. Hostile wouldn't even cover it.

Deacon skillfully moved the conversation back to safer topics.

Over the next hour Keira attempted to broach the subject with Dayna. She wanted to explain the full story, but her sister refused to speak to her. But the sudden change in Ryker's demeanor shocked her the most. He was normally more rational and asked the right questions.

When she looked up, he was no longer beside her. Instead, he was deep in conversation with Bayek and Makeda. Rather than take on her glaring sister, she moved to where Ryker, Bayek, and Makeda were sitting.

Bayek smiled up at her and indicated a spare seat by them. "I understand that you and Dayna wish to know more about the history behind the stone of Issachar and the Breastplate of Judgement."

She nodded. "Yes. To be honest, we were a little stunned with your revelations about our mother's amulet and what it meant."

Bayek settled back in his chair. "I imagine Annabeth thought she had years ahead of her before she needed to educate you on the final secrets of the gate."

Makeda's throaty laugh distracted her. The sultry Vampire was whispering something in Ryker's ear. Not loud enough that Keira could hear exactly what was being said, but enough to know Makeda was not checking out something behind the couch.

It was not Makeda that had her on edge, it was Ryker's reaction to the woman's advances. He seemed to be encouraging it. When she thought about it, her hackles rose. He hadn't once looked her way.

To top it off, Makeda's overly familiar physical contact with Ryker concerned her. He didn't seem to mind. In fact, the flirting between them was becoming sickening. Her headache returned in full force.

Just before dawn, Keira gave up all pretense of sleep. She had tossed and turned all night. Every time she tried, visions of Ryker and Makeda bombarded her brain. She was ready to scream when she imagined his lips trailing down Makeda's flawless chocolate skin.

Lips that not long ago pressed against hers. How could she have been such a fool to think he actually cared? If he did, he wouldn't flirt so shamelessly in front of her. He wouldn't have left with the stunningly beautiful female Vampire. He wouldn't have left without saying goodbye.

Mother Earth, had she made the right decision? She swung her legs out of bed and reached for her jeans. "It's too late now."

Then why did it hurt so much? She threw some water on her face and tiptoed downstairs, not wanting to wake everyone. She padded into the kitchen and placed a tea kettle of water on the stovetop. When she turned around to reach for a cup, she realized the patio door was open.

A form materialized in the doorway. She clasped her chest and let out a small cry. Before she could let out a full-blown scream, the form blurred, and a hand suddenly reached out and wrapped itself around her mouth.

"Do you really want to wake the house at this ungodly hour?"

Her shoulders relaxed when she recognized the voice, and she reached up to yank away Ryker's hand. "You didn't need to scare me like that."

"Who was scaring who? I was already here, and some woman with hair that looked like a bird's nest stumbles into my kitchen at five a.m. If anyone should be scared here, it's me."

She subconsciously ran a hand down her hair. Being so long, it tended to stick out in all directions with the slightest provocation. "I didn't expect anyone to be up yet."

He leaned against the bench and folded his arms across his chest. "Neither did I."

She became self-conscious as he watched her every movement like a hawk. The awkward silence was killing her. When the kettle whistle blew, she poured a cup of tea. "Would you like one?"

"Not for me, thanks."

Unsure whether to flee to her bedroom with her tea or stand her ground, she eventually decided on the latter and made her way to the dining table.

"You know you threw me with your announcement last night," he said.

"I don't think Dayna will speak to me for a while."

She had tried talking to her sister when they went up to bed. But Dayna cut her off, claiming she was too tired, and they would discuss it in the morning. Something she very much doubted her sister would do. Her eyes flitted toward the door that led to his wing of the house.

"Shouldn't you be getting back before you're missed?" Her voice came out a little more tense and sharp than she expected.

She winced, hoping he didn't pick up on her distress.

"No, after last night, I was too distracted to watch over Zayne, I needed to work out a few things so I stayed home."

Her cup halted midway to her mouth.

"You do know I really didn't need to hear that," she said. She placed her cup on the table and rose. "I know you're pissed at me, but I don't know why you're being so cruel."

She needed to flee before she fell apart. How could she have believed him to be anything other than the player she knew him to be?

Ryker growled. "Have you taken leave of your senses? What are you babbling on about?"

She clenched her fists. "You know exactly what I'm talking about, so don't act dumb."

She turned and marched toward the door.

Before she had taken two steps, he blocked her path. "No, I don't. How about you enlighten me."

"Get out of my way and go back to Makeda."

He stopped short and stared at her. "What does Makeda have to do with this? You think that me and …" He trailed off and laughed. "Is that what this is all about? For such an intelligent person, you're one daft Witch who ever rode a broomstick."

He grabbed her by the shoulder and pulled her toward his room. She struggled the entire way and tried to tear herself away from him.

"Let me go. I don't need to see this."

"Oh yes, I think you do."

He pushed her through the door of his room and turned on the lights.

Shit.

The room was empty, and the bed was perfectly made. No Makeda. She didn't know whether to be relieved or embarrassed.

"You know, for a redhead, green does not suit you."

She gulped. How did she get this so wrong? With as much dignity as she could muster, she raised her chin and turned to face him.

"What did you expect me to think? She was all over you last night. Then you just took off with her without saying anything."

He ran a hand through his hair. "Good grief, you're frustrating. Why would I sleep with her when I'm only interested in you?" He paced the room. "She needed some warm blood. I dropped her off at Deidre's and went over to sit with Zayne. Just like I've done every night. Unfortunately, your bombshell was a bit of a distraction, so I got Vincent to relieve me early."

Guilt over just how much she had misjudged him spread through her. "How is he?"

His shoulders sagged. "I have no idea. I wish he'd scream or yell. Anything but sit there like a statue. I don't know how to get through to him."

"All you can do is be there for him. He needs to come the rest of the way in his own time."

"I know, but it's hard seeing him suffer like this." He glared at her. "Stop changing the subject. We are talking about your irrational state of mind, not Zayne's grieving process."

She wrapped her arms around her chest as if the temperature had suddenly dropped. Right now, she wished for Dayna's teleporting ability more than anything. How was she going to talk her way out of the corner she had backed herself into?

"You know you're killing me," he said in a soft voice.

"Not possible. You're a Vampire."

In a flash, he was standing toe-to-toe with her. He tucked two fingers beneath her chin and tipped her head up until she was looking directly into his vivid blue eyes. He smiled down at her.

"If anyone can, you can." He ran a hand down her locks and tucked a strand behind her ear. "Why am I only now hearing about your decision to return to LA?"

"I was going to tell you what I'd decided, but I didn't want to have the conversation with everyone around us."

A shiver ran up and down her spine as Ryker's hands trailed along her arms. She was quickly becoming a lump of jelly from his magic charm.

"This thing between us." His voice came out low and heavy, sending more tendrils of desire through her. "I don't want to give it up before we have a chance to explore where it's going."

When he pulled the strap off her shoulder and bent down to leave a feathery kiss on her exposed skin, her legs nearly gave way. Her breath became labored as he moved her hair away from her neck and nibbled at the skin along her throbbing vein. Goosebumps erupted on her body as he lightly nipped at the curve of her shoulder.

She threaded her fingers through his hair and threw her head back.

"Don't stop."

Desire ripped through her, and she pulled him closer.

"I don't intend to."

Ryker, with agonizing slowness, continued to torture her neck and shoulders while deftly unbuttoning her top.

"You taste divine," he said with a low, earthy growl.

His kisses removed her ability to think rationally. All she wanted was to feel his body against hers in the most primal way. Skin on skin. Lips on lips. She wanted to explore his body, just as he was exploring hers.

He moved back up her neck, and his breath fanned the shell of her ear. "I was thinking I could move my shifts around and, at least once a month, I could fly out on a Friday night and spend the weekend with you."

She was almost too far gone to take in his words. Almost. She pushed away and stared at him.

He frowned and blinked twice. "What did you expect? I'd let you go back to California and move on? I told you we had unfinished business. If that business means some uncomfortable flights, so be it. Besides, with the way things are going, I could lose my job. Who knows, maybe I can find gainful employment elsewhere. Like … say … the city of Angels and sexy Witches."

This was not how she'd imagined this conversation going. Her sudden panic must have been evident when he let her arms go and took a step back.

"Why do I get the feeling you're not too thrilled about that."

She pulled her unbuttoned top together. "It's not like that."

He narrowed his gaze, and his face grew stormy. "What, am I not good enough to be around your brainiac friends?"

She took a step and reached out to him. "No. You misunderstand me. It's nothing like that."

"No?" He pushed her hand away. "Then, how is it? Everything was fine until I mentioned coming to LA. It's okay for us to have a roll in the hay here, but that's it? That's where it ends?"

She needed to stop this before he got even more worked up. "You're such a pig-headed Vampire. Would you just shut up and let me speak."

She was practically shouting.

He froze, and his expression reflected one of shock. "I see you have your powers back."

"What are you talking about?"

He bobbed his head. She looked down. Two small blue orbs hovered near her palms.

"Shit!"

She shook her hands violently, as if she were shaking water off them. The spheres disappeared as quickly as they'd appeared.

They stood in silence, both breathing heavily, and unsure what to say.

Ryker broke before her. "I believe the floor is yours."

She pushed her hair away from her face and tucked it behind her ear. This was not how she'd imagined this conversation going. To be honest, she'd made her decision so quickly that she hadn't really thought about the ramifications.

"First off, I could never be ashamed to be seen with you. For you to think I could means that you don't really know me very well."

His lips pressed into a white slash. "Then why did you react that way when I suggested visiting you in LA?"

She buttoned her shirt. She needed a barrier to hide behind, even if it was a bit of fabric. "It's because you may not find me in LA."

He frowned. "I don't understand. Why?"

She cleared her throat. This was more difficult than she thought it would be. "I gave notice. I'll be leaving Berkeley at the end of the term."

"But what does that have to do with me com—" He halted mid-sentence. "Where exactly will you be headed when you finish?"

"Some fix-me-up between here and Salem."

He drew in a sharp breath, and she was hauled against his hard body. She groaned at the hunger surging through her. His lips crushed into hers in a searing kiss before she could take a breath. Then again, she didn't think she remembered how to breathe. His potent lips were all-consuming.

His hands wrapped around her waist, and he pulled her against him roughly. At the intimate contact, it was clear just how much he wanted her. He deepened the kiss, and every nerve ending was vibrating with anticipation and desire.

He pulled away. His chest rose and fell, and each breath came out in heavy pants. "You are so damn addictive. I can't think straight."

She reached up and placed her hand on his chest. "Then stop thinking," she whispered.

TOCCATA & FUGUE IN D MINOR

Amos ignored the tug on his jacket and stared up at the majesty of the flock of birds flying above the forest canopy. He sighed and tapped his foot in time with the music.

The third movement built to a crescendo in wave upon wave of notes, and he envisaged himself as a giant, striding the tallest mountain peaks, breaking through the enigmatic fog, and stretching toward the very outskirts of eternity. The timpani drums rolled and ebbed with the tide, and he was now an eagle soaring over the valley.

He steepled his fingers and closed his eyes when the final movement increased in tempo and emotion. Wait for it … This was his favorite part. After its peak, it would conclude with a pulsating melody that cast its light across that landscape and into every dark corner of the world.

The tug at his jacket became more demanding.

He pulled the earbuds from his ears and turned to his companion, hopeful his irritation was not lost on the man. "Yes. What is it this time?"

Zahir pointed to the laptop. "This. I want to see it once more."

He reached over and replayed the video. *Surely, he's memorized it by now?*

The mayor of Salem answered yet another barrage of questions from reporters, and a news anchor repeated the same story that played on every other news channel. He paused the video. He could not take another repeat of that stupid memorial service.

Zahir let out a low growl. "The traitor who now calls himself mayor and the other infidels that follow him will suffer for what they have done. Our Lord Leviathan will smite them all."

"Deacon Hunter and Ryker Kincaid will get what's coming to them, have no fear. But until we have determined another way to bring Leviathan through, we need to lay low. We still have a few Legion, and I have members of the Order hidden in Salem. We will know exactly what they are up to."

Zahir snorted. "We need not your spies. We need power."

"And how exactly do you suggest we get that power? There will not be another conjunction of a full moon with a perfect alignment of more than two planets, and summer solstice for one hundred years."

"We no longer require a celestial event from above when we have the power here on earth."

He frowned. "What are you talking about? What power?"

Zahir pointed to the blonde woman, dressed in a bright yellow dress, standing just behind Mayor Deacon Hunter.

He looked closer. She was one of the Witches who'd destroyed the chance for their lord and savior to return.

"The Witches. They will lead us to the Breastplate of Judgement. With that we can bring down the twelve gates and Leviathan can finally return." Zahir pointed to the small gem that hung off the Witch's bracelet. "Beginning with that stone."

The end … or is it?

ACKNOWLEDGEMENTS

No book is ever written without support. I would like to express my gratitude to the following:

My Whānau

Sebastian and Dominic, you both may be taller than me now, but that does not mean you get to ignore the empty milk bottle rule.

Mum. Thank you for all your unwavering support & love.

Antony. Tag, You're it.

Mark & Matt, this is book number 3, you are going to have to read at least one of them.

To Debbie, Angela, & Heleine. Ladies, you are my rock.

My Iwi

To the RWNZ authors. I am constantly in awe at how much support and advice each of you readily give.

To my editors, Shirley and Sherri. I am eternally grateful for your attention to detail and helping me get through editing hell.

And I am especially thankful for you, the reader who picked up this book and gave an author a chance to let her voice be heard.

About the Author

After failing miserably at world domination and surviving many years of producing technical documentation, project plans and test plans that no one bothered to open, M (pron. M) Greenhill decided to create something that might actually be read.

She enjoys creating paranormal stories that takes the reader on a journey filled with intrigue, excitement and more twists and turns than are bugs in a Microsoft update.

M lives in New Zealand with her two sons, a miniature schnauzer that destroys shoes, and a cat that lets us think we are in charge. Ever the optimist, she hopes that one day she will own a pair of Louboutin's and that, for once, the kids wouldn't leave empty milk bottles in the fridge.

Connect with M Greenhill:

Facebook: https://www.facebook.com/MNJGreenhillAuthor

Twitter: https://twitter.com/MNJGreenhill

Web: http://www.mgreenhill.com